Highland
Rebel

Highland Rebel

Judith James

SOURCEBOOKS CASABLANCA™
AN IMPRINT OF SOURCEBOOKS, INC.®
NAPERVILLE, ILLINOIS

Published by Sourcebooks Casablanca, an imprint of Sourcebooks,
Inc.
P.O. Box 4410, Naperville, Illinois 60567–4410
(630) 961–3900
FAX: (630) 961–2168
www.sourcebooks.com

Printed and bound in the United States of America
QW 10 9 8 7 6 5 4 3 2 1

This book is dedicated to my uncle John, who I think of more as a big brother. You lived your life to the fullest, approached everything with passion, and never stopped pursuing your dreams. Thanks so much for your enthusiasm, interest, and support as I chased after mine. I love you. You will be missed.

One

JAMIE SINCLAIR PUSHED BACK HIS VISOR AND SURVEYED the field. The air was crisp, sharp with the acrid smell of smoke and the bitter taste of winter. A cold sleet was falling, and icy drops of water slithered down his back. His jaw tightened with annoyance as wet strands of hair plastered against his neck. The leaden sky hung low, heavy with cloud, and a tattered curtain of smoke-tinged fog rolled across the valley, obscuring the horizon, parting now and then to reveal a grisly scene. The once bucolic setting of rolling hills, hedge-rows, and square tilled fields was afire with burning buildings, and littered with the sad and twisted corpses of broken horses and men. It was peaceful in a peculiar way. Silent... still... and oddly serene.

The strident cries of bickering carrion birds jerked him from his reverie. He hadn't slept in over two days. Fighting a wave of dizzying fatigue, he shifted in his saddle, trying to ease the strain in his shoulders and trying his best to recall why he was there. He'd shifted allegiance and religion so many times he sometimes forgot which side he was on. What with these mad

Stuart kings—Protestant one day, Catholic the next—a fellow needed to be quick. Fortunately, he was: quick witted, quick with a sword, and more importantly, quick to recognize which way the wind was blowing. Possessed of a cynic's keen perception and willingness to shift with the political tide, he switched masters, mistresses, and religions whenever the need arose. Military prowess and ruthless charm had helped secure him a place in the court of Charles II, and they would do the same in the court of his brother, King James. He was Catholic now, and James II was his master. It mattered little to him so long as it relieved his boredom, served his best interests—and he got paid.

His decided lack of commitment in religious matters was of great concern to Father Francis, the little Spanish priest who traveled with them and imagined himself in charge of Jamie's soul. Never one to miss an opportunity to instruct, he sidled over to Jamie's side and motioned toward the battlefield below. "A great victory, my lord."

Jamie eyed the man with distaste, noting his jeweled rings and blooded mount, wondering why so many of those who made it their profession to decry the accumulation and enjoyment of worldly pleasures seemed to enjoy them so much.

"What? You mean our glorious smiting of yon farmers and sheepherders? Why do you bother me, priest? Shouldn't you be off somewhere tending to the wounded, or saying prayers for the dead?"

"I tend to the living as well. Those men were heretics and traitors. Sinners who turned their back on God's word."

"As opposed to us, Father? Godly men the lot of us. Get away from me. I've work to do."

"Have you no faith then, my lord? Are you hypocrite as well as sinner?"

"I have faith that if there *is* a god, he's a reasonable fellow, and not some bloody-minded fanatic who would approve of this," Jamie said, annoyed with the priest's prattling.

"Your lack of faith is the devil's work, my lord. You must strive to correct it."

"Is it, Father? Some might argue the reverse. Some might say the fervor *you* so admire is a devilish thing, encouraging intolerance and divisiveness and discouraging critical thought. Some might even say it's the root of much evil in the world. What do you think?" he asked with a wicked grin.

The priest blanched, crossed himself, and edged away.

"No? You don't agree?" Jamie called after him. "Run, Father! Run back and minister to Gervaise and his holy butchers and leave me in peace."

He watched with amusement as the priest hurried away, then narrowed his eyes, his gaze caught by a flash of steel and a commotion down the hill toward the river to the south. It appeared Gervaise and his men were all atwitter about something. He sighed and wheeled his mount. He supposed he'd better investigate.

The king, intent on restoring Catholic rule, and lacking the charm, wit, and political acumen of his older brother Charles, relied on intimidation and military might to guard his throne and bully his recalcitrant subjects into obedience. He'd built himself a standing army, a cause of great concern to many so soon after

Cromwell's, and he wasn't above the judicious use of foreign mercenaries. Spanish, Italian, Portuguese, and French, some were highly skilled professionals, but most were murderers and thugs.

Sent to act as nanny over just such a ragtag coalition of butchers, commissioned to hunt down Covenanters, a species of Scots Presbyterian rebel His Majesty particularly abhorred, Jamie was not to interfere with the killing and debauchery—effective tools, after all—for cowing those who would oppose their rightful rulers. His orders were to help where needed, ensure no grievous insult was given to their more important allies, and oversee the distribution of spoils, making sure His Majesty's rights were always respected.

Accountant and minder for a rabble of killers, criminals, and petty thieves. The whole business was distasteful. He'd much preferred Charles and his spaniels to the new king and his pets, but beggars can't be choosers, and he *was* a beggar—his ever-loving sire had seen to that.

He picked his way carefully down the hill toward the riverbank, skirting past squabbling groups of soldiers, camp followers, and ravens fighting over ragged mounds of corpses. The Scots had fought valiantly. There'd been Highlanders in the mix, he was certain of it. They'd stood out, fierce mountain men roaring their battle cries and wielding wicked claymores. Strange, that. They'd appeared from nowhere, rode screaming into battle, fought like demons, and just as suddenly melted away. Why would they come to the aid of Protestant rebels? He shook his head to clear it. It made no sense. If they *had* come to help, why did they leave before the battle was over? They'd stayed long enough to give even Gervaise's hardened mercenaries a fright, and then they'd disappeared like smoke into the misty hills and mountains of the Highlands and the north country, leaving the desperate Covenanters behind.

Gervaise was a butcher and a pig, but an efficient and reliable one. His men had shown the remainder no mercy. Once their savagery was loosed, they'd taken no prisoners. Jamie knew from past experience they'd be regretting it now. Simple brutes, easily entertained and just as easily bored, they'd be missing some hapless victim to torture and torment this eve. He dared to hope he might finally have a solid night's sleep, uninterrupted by the screams and pleadings of Gervaise's unfortunate captives.

Hearing the clash of steel on steel, he urged his horse forward, pushing his way through a gathering crowd. A fight between the men? No… it appeared a good night's sleep was too much to expect. They'd found a victim. A young lad, by the look of it. Surrounded, the youth wheeled his horse in a tight circle, sword drawn, fighting to keep the jeering mob at bay. Jamie remembered him from the battle—one of the Highlanders, if he wasn't mistaken. They'd engaged in a quick skirmish before the melee had torn them apart. He'd been surprised by his opponent's agility and slight stature.

He felt a twinge of pity. The lad could hardly be more than a boy. They were playing with him like a cat with a mouse. When they tired of it, they'd strip him of his armor, strip him of his dignity, and then, very slowly, strip him of his skin. It was a harsh world, and youth and courage wouldn't save him. There was nothing Jamie could do to help. He spat and looked away. His orders were clear. He was not to interfere. His Majesty couldn't trust all who swore him allegiance, but he trusted those he was paying good coin. He needed these men.

He nudged his horse and moved away, noting with approval that Gervaise had already set the men to work making camp, though they seemed to have abandoned their duties for the moment. Placed next to the river, the camp had been well fortified, surrounded by trenches, artillery, and sentries to guard the perimeter. These men were savages, yes, vicious and venal, but they knew their business.

He could see his man Sullivan on the far bank, setting up a square-walled tent. He was an island of sanity in a sea of chaos, mud, and blood. Jamie had laughed out loud when he'd first set eyes on him. With hunched shoulders, head too big for his slight body, and a long neck that thrust forward when he walked, he'd reminded Jamie of a turkey, until he'd seen the sad, sweet face and felt ashamed to be comparing him to such an ungainly beast. A perverse impulse born of boredom, curiosity, and something he'd refused to examine had prompted him to pluck the man and his mother from a pitiful stream of Irish prisoners headed for transportation or hanging. It had proven a sound investment. Though his mother had never aspired to be anything more than an opinionated bully and an indifferent cook, Kieran O'Sullivan had become squire, butler, and friend.

Jamie closed his eyes a moment, fighting to stay awake. The sooner he was quit of this place the better. He'd return to London soon and make his report, and the last six months of fighting, filth, and blood would all be worthwhile. The king would reward him as he'd promised, binding him close, helping him find a Catholic wife, helping him find an heiress. God knew his late father hadn't, and without one, without funds, he would always be the cur of one man or another.

He urged his horse into the river and started across, looking forward to Sullivan's cooking, a pint of ale, and blessed sleep, but the sound of the crowd behind him was growing steadily louder, and halfway across he pulled up his mount and wheeled around. A large group of men were hooting and yelling, taunting the boy amidst howls of laughter, their voices shrill with excitement and something else. Wondering what was so fascinating they'd left off stripping and looting the dead, Jamie ignored his horse's impatient fretting and stayed to watch.

Their hapless captive was bound by his wrists, with another rope pulled taut around his neck. They were dragging him to the river—intent, it seemed, on drowning or strangling him. The boy was struggling for his life, but his movements only drew the thick hemp tighter, choking off his breath. He couldn't know it was a kinder fate than many that might await him. His struggles knocked his helmet from his head, and Jamie watched, stunned, as chestnut hair tumbled loose to flow past his shoulders. There was more hooting as they pulled off his breastplate. Good Christ! It was a woman! What in God's name?

Taunting and leering, they pulled her into the fast-moving river and started dragging her across.

"Have a care, boys!" Gervaise shouted from the far bank. "I promise you it's a better ride if they're still alive. The fun won't start until we've tidied up here, though, so those that's got jobs to do best get to them. The rest can escort the... lady... into camp."

A group of men detached themselves, grumbling under their breath, while the rest hauled the girl across the river, pulling her up by the rope around her neck when she stumbled and fell, and manhandling her gleefully in the direction of the mess tent. Jamie followed, with Sullivan, who'd rushed from the tent at his master's approach, close behind.

Coughing and retching, raging with thirst and wheezing for breath, the girl tried to swallow some water as they pulled her across the river, but the rope was too tight, and all she managed were a few drops. She'd been relieved of her weapon and armor, and as they climbed the bank and approached the center of camp, the men spun her about, pushing her from one to the other and tearing at her clothes. Dizzy and wet, she dropped to the ground and scrambled to an overturned wagon, pressing her back into it and hugging her knees, teeth chattering, lips blue with cold.

She struggled to gather her wits and catch her breath. The battle had exhausted her. She was bruised, battered, and very afraid. She prayed her uncle's men had escaped. She prayed for strength and tried to conserve what little she had left. She knew what happened to women in war. She had no illusions. What she did have was her father's dagger, thrust in her boot. When they tired of playing with her, when they moved in to take the spoils, she'd have one chance. If they wanted her they'd have to kill her, and she'd take one or more of them with her.

Jamie beckoned Sullivan, dismounted, and handed him the reins. He'd played many roles in his ill-spent youth: adventurer, gambler, courtier, and spy. Now he played the arrogant, cold-blooded aristocrat. There was nothing like disdain and a hint of menace to put a certain kind of man in his place, the kind a fellow needed to keep at his feet, lest they leap for his throat. He'd yet to assert his authority with this lot, choosing to mind his own business and let Gervaise and his men mind theirs, but he flexed it now.

She watched his approach, turning to look to her right, though she'd barely enough strength to lift her head. Fine-featured and graceful, he was tall and lean. His dark hair was tied in a queue, and he was dressed as a cavalier. He looked as if he'd just stepped from a drawing room or a dance floor, not a battlefield. As he approached, he shook out the lace from his wrists, motioning the men back with a curt wave of his fingers. Despite his languid manner, his eyes were sharp, his face was harsh, and other men moved aside when he passed. He stopped a few feet away from her, planting his sword tip in the ground, resting his hands on the pommel as if it were a walking stick. Looking down his aristocratic nose, he regarded her coldly.

She blinked, perplexed. Who was he? A dark angel? One of Lucifer's minions come to collect the dead? He was as incongruous as a flower on a dunghill. He should have looked ridiculous, but he didn't. He looked dangerous and cruel.

Amused by her incredulous perusal, Jamie suppressed a grin, cocked his head, and examined her carefully in turn. She was wet and bedraggled, there were rope burns on her neck and wrists, and her face was battered and covered with blood. She was shivering, whether from fear or cold he couldn't tell. Despite years of hard work to suppress them, his quixotic tendencies had the rude habit of surfacing at the oddest and most inconvenient times. There was no denying the wench was a damsel in distress. He felt a twinge of annoyance. Damned foolish chit! The last thing he needed right now was complications.

The men were crowding in, grumbling and sullen, fearing he meant to rob them of their toy. He hefted his sword, testing its weight, and turned to face them, silencing their protests with a dismissive gesture. One of them left on the run, looking for Gervaise, no doubt.

Returning his attention to the woman, Jamie took off his coat and draped it over her shoulders. "Sullivan!"

"Sir!"

"Fetch food, a blanket, and water."

"Right away, sir."

He got down on one knee and reached out to brush away a mat of tangled hair, trying to get a closer look. She shuddered and flinched, and he felt a stir of pity.

"Easy, lass," he said softly in French. "I'm not going to harm you." Taking her by the chin with gloved fingers, he turned her face sideways, noting the livid bruise across her jaw. "Tsk, tsk." He turned her jaw the other way and a tired sigh escaped him. "What a pity. These brutes have only one way of dealing with a woman, I'm afraid. What's your name, child?"

She stared at him, blank-faced, then pulled her head away. He felt a moment's disappointment. He'd been hoping she spoke French. It would have been a sign of education, quality and breeding, something to assist him with the plan fast forming in his mind. She was likely some luckless camp follower, who'd stolen horse and sword in a desperate bid to escape.

Well, heiress or whore, it hadn't done her any good, and she was in far more trouble than she knew. Wondering if she was in shock, he tried speaking in English. "What's your name, girl?" He gave her head a shake. "Your name!"

"Catherine… Drummond," she said through gritted teeth, then spat full in his face.

The watching men broke into gales of laughter, hooting and jeering. "That's a gentleman right there! See how smooth he is with the ladies?"

"She fancies you, she does, my lord!"

Damned ungrateful chit! He should leave her to her own devices. Casually, he pulled out a handkerchief and wiped the spittle away, then grabbed her by the hair and pulled her close. He looked quizzically into fierce, cat-like eyes, then leaned over to whisper in her ear, "Catherine… Cat… hellcat… that wasn't wise. Here you're nothing but a wet and shivering little mouse, and little mice should stay very quiet, and keep very still."

He rose to his feet, gripping her by the front of her tattered shirt and hauling her up with him. She blinked and tried to focus as the leering men, the camp, and the dark lord who held her began to spin in dizzy circles around her, and then she slumped unconscious in his arms.

"There! You see, Sullivan? I've made another conquest. They swoon in my arms," he said to his man, who'd returned with a blanket and canteen.

"Indeed, milord. I've often marked upon it. I take it I'm to tidy up?"

"Just so. You may deliver her to Father Francis." He grunted as he passed his burden over to his servant, then straightened his sleeves. "And have a care. She's somewhat hefty for such a delicate flower."

The disgruntled mumblings and protests of the men grew heated as Sullivan made to leave with his bundle, rising to a crescendo with the arrival of Captain Gervaise.

"Here now!" the captain shouted, shoving through the crowd to plant himself in front of Jamie. "It's not your place to be giving orders, Sinclair. Put the wench back!" A belligerent man at the best of times, he had a pugnacious face, with lips that twisted in a perpetual sneer and a chin that thrust forward, always ready for argument or battle. He reminded Jamie of nothing so much as an ugly bulldog.

"I represent your employer, Gervaise. The sovereign lord of these lands. Show a little respect!" he snapped.

Gervaise took a step back and spat on the ground.

"Even so, Sinclair. What's his is his, and what's ours is ours. We've a right to any spoils we find on the field and well you know it! You'll not expect me to believe *our* employer has any interest in a rebel whore. He's busy enough with the ones at court. The men have fought hard and well and deserve their entertainment." He turned to his men and waved his hand toward the bundle Sullivan held in his arms. "Shall we dice for her, boys?"

The men responded with a raucous cheer, their eyes lit with excitement.

"Quiet! Listen to me carefully, Gervaise. She's a noblewoman, not some camp follower. She may be useful as a hostage, she's certainly worth a ransom, and she's not for the likes of you and your men."

"And how do you know all that?"

"Open your eyes, you fool! You saw her weapon, and look at the horse she was riding. No common strumpet would ride a beast like that."

"Unless she stole it and was trying to escape. I say no well-bred slut would be traipsing about a battlefield waving a sword! Give her back, Sinclair!"

"Look at her. She's nigh frozen and half drowned! You said yourself she's of more use alive than dead. Let the priest tend to her. She's not going anywhere." Jamie looked over his shoulder and barked an order. "Sullivan! Stop lolling about and do as I told you!"

"At once, milord." Sullivan started forward again, but at a nod from Gervaise, two men stepped out, swords drawn, blocking his path.

"Think it through carefully, Gervaise," Jamie said dangerously, drawing his own. "Do you really want to make me your enemy?" *Jesus Christ!* He was making a mess of it! He'd always minded his own business and let Gervaise and his men mind theirs, but now he'd backed the man into a corner in front of his men. Gervaise might be a cur, but he was a useful one. The king would have Jamie's hide if the man grew disgruntled and sold his services elsewhere. *Curse the wench!*

Having taken authority and bravado as far as they'd go, Jamie decided it was time to try charm and guile. "Oh, do sit down with her, Sullivan. I swear you look as taxed and sullen as an overburdened donkey!"

There were a few guffaws and the tension started to ease.

"Put away your swords, fools!" Gervaise snapped, somewhat mollified. He turned back to Jamie. "Now it's best *you* listen, Sinclair. It would be very sad if you were to suffer an accident so near the end of your commission. Ponder that before you seek to pit yourself and your... man... against me and mine."

"I seek only to protect His Majesty's interests, Gervaise. The girl's name is Catherine Drummond. I know this name," he lied. "The family's an important one, and it's for the king to decide her fate."

"I don't care if she's the Virgin Mary, Sinclair! We both know you're claiming her for yourself!"

"And what if I am? I've fought alongside you these past six months. You'd have been dead a week past if not for me. I've taken no spoils, made no claims... well, now I do."

"Fair enough. You're a devil on the field and you've been a reasonable man until now. I'm a reasonable man too, but we both know she's a rebel whore and meant for hanging. You can have her first, but when you're finished, you'll pass her along. I'll see my men have some use of her before it's done."

"Don't be an idiot, man! She's worth money, I tell you."

"If there's a ransom, her people will pay it, whether we touch her or not. If there's not," Gervaise shrugged, "then we'd best enjoy her before the hangman does his work. I'll tell the lads to be extra careful not to kill her before we know if her blood be red or blue."

Struck by a sudden inspiration, Jamie returned Gervaise's smirk with a cold smile of his own. He turned to his man. "Sullivan!"

"Sir?"

"Drop the girl and fetch the priest."

Used to his master's sudden whims, Sullivan lowered his bundle carefully to the ground, and ran off to find Father Francis.

Sensing victory, the crowd pressed forward. "Fetch the dice!" someone shouted. "She'll be ours now."

They were stopped by a blur of blue steel.

"Back off, gentlemen, if you please, and give the future Lady Sinclair room to breath."

"Here now! What nonsense is this?" the captain demanded.

"I say her blood is blue, Gervaise," Jamie said dangerously. "I say she's no rebel. I say she's an heiress, who's fallen, quite literally, in my lap. Why should I settle for ransom when I can have her money and her lands? I say… she's going to be my wife."

He laughed at the looks of stunned surprise all around him, feeling that curious rush of excitement and elation that gripped him before any risky endeavor, whether at court, at the card tables, or in the field. What would his acquaintances say if they knew he was about to marry a camp follower? They'd be horrified. Well… his mother had been a whore, his father a vicious drunk, and he sold his services to the highest bidder. The chit would be in good company; but he wagered there was none who'd dare molest—much less hang—his wife, and he should be able to come up with a plan to extricate himself once the danger was past.

Gervaise cocked his head to one side and regarded him carefully, wondering if he might be telling the truth. "A Scottish heiress, is she? And you'd steal her then? Right out from under your master's nose? You've a set of balls on you, Sinclair, I'll give you that."

"*Carpe diem,* Gervaise. My father called me bastard and cut me from the teat. If I want a wife and lands, I must see to them myself. You'll not credit it, gentlemen," he said, raising his voice and playing to the crowd, "but handsome fellow that I am, none of the wenches will have me back home."

The men broke into genuine laughter, without the dangerous edge that had greeted his earlier sally.

"I've nothing against a fellow trying to improve his lot, Sinclair, but lord or no, no man plays me for a fool. You *will* marry her. This very day, with all here to bear witness, or we'll be taking her back to use as we please and you'd best not interfere."

Father Francis joined them, huffing to catch his breath, mopping his brow, and sweating profusely despite the damp chill. He looked with annoyance at the woman lying unconscious on the ground, lifting his robe to step carefully around her before nodding to Gervaise and bowing before Jamie. "You wished to see me, my lord?"

"Yes, Father. I wish you to watch over my fiancé until we're joined in wedded bliss."

Father Francis blinked, confused. "I'm sorry, my lord. I'm afraid I don't understand."

"Sinclair has found his true love at last, priest. Today. On the battlefield. Imagine that! You will marry them tonight," Gervaise said acidly.

"Yes, Father. I'm quite overcome," Jamie called over his shoulder as the men, intent on entertainment, pulled him away for an impromptu celebration. "Put her away somewhere until she's needed, and let Sullivan tend to her, if you please!"

"Are you mad, man?" the priest shouted after him. "You can't marry a camp follower! You'll shame your family and bring ruin to your name!"

"I try my best, Father," he shouted back to roars of laughter.

Several hours and few stiff drinks later, Jamie stumbled to his tent. It had been a near thing. Gervaise and he had been circling each other like wary wolves for months now, and one wrong move could have tipped the balance. He could have killed Gervaise and more than a few of his men and they both knew it, but then the rest would have torn him and Sullivan apart, and they both knew that, too.

He rubbed his temples and grimaced, bleary from exhaustion and alcohol. He might also have left her to her fate. What imp of nature had impelled him to risk everything—his and Sullivan's life, the king's favor, the heiress who waited back in England with the land and money to restore his fortune and his name—all for an ungrateful, mud-spattered, spitting doxy? Boredom, he decided with a weary sigh. Ah well. Those that do in haste repent at leisure, as Granny O'Sullivan was wont to say.

Sullivan was outside the tent, his customary look of censure etched upon his face.

"Step aside, man. I've a mind to steal a few moments' sleep."

"There's no time for that I'm afraid, milord," Sullivan said through pursed lips. "The priest wishes to see you—"

"Damn the priest!"

"Is this wedding to be a farce then, milord? They've taken the girl from him and are holding her in the center of camp. They've been drinking," he added, eyeing Jamie up and down. "Shall I wake you from your nap once they've decided what to do with her? Or would you prefer I wait for morning?"

"You are insolent and impertinent, Sullivan!"

"Yes, milord."

"Very well," Jamie said with a sigh. "Where's the priest?"

"I believe that's him coming now, milord."

"Good. Well… I'm off to fetch her then. Do what you can to tidy up. Find a bit of food—she's bound to be hungry—and make damn sure you leave me something to drink!"

"Of course, milord," Sullivan said with a bow and a click of his heels.

"Ah! Father Francis! Where's the girl? Misplaced her, have you? Let's go find her then, shall we?" Jamie gripped the priest by the shoulder and turned him around, pushing him toward the fire burning brightly in the center of camp.

"You can't be serious, my lord! Surely, you don't mean to go ahead with it now you've had time to think. She's a Protestant whore, my son! Only think about what you're doing. It's not too late to change your mind. It's my duty to remind you that—"

"Where's your charity, Father? I'm going to marry the wench and save her soul! I'll turn her into a good Catholic whore. That should please you. Now hurry along, if you please. We don't want the festivities starting without us."

Two

CATHERINE PEERED INTO THE DARK THROUGH HALF-closed eyes. Her vision was blurred, her head was aching, and her throat and wrists were burnt and raw. After losing consciousness, she'd awoken to find herself slumped in a pile with sacks of grain and powder, watched over by a sour-faced priest. Another man, a sad-faced fellow with kind eyes, had given her water and removed her bindings. She'd been left in peace after that, until moments ago. She'd done her best to conserve her strength. She didn't know why she'd been given a respite, but she had a fair idea of what was coming next.

When they came for her, dragging her to her feet and into the center of camp, she strove to master herself. She was a Drummond, and a Drummond didn't cower before dogs. She thrust out her jaw and stood straight and proud, looking them in the eyes and daring them to come. She was no stranger to warfare or the ways of armed men. She knew where battle and bloodlust led. She wondered if they intended to kill her when they were done.

She forced herself to remain composed, keeping her breath calm and even, straining to see in the dark, counting their numbers, and trying to orient herself as her head began to clear. The camp was by the river, guarded by pickets. Several rough-looking men sat around a table piled high with spoils from local farms, feasting and drinking, leering faces and piggish eyes lit with lust and the hellish glow from the bonfire. Others circled her in the flickering dark, approaching then backing away like wary curs, their shadows cavorting in a macabre and drunken dance around her. They argued, snarling and snapping amongst themselves, watching avidly with predatory eyes, grinning and growling, hungry two-legged wolves shouting comments and making obscene gestures. They spoke a polyglot of Spanish and several other languages, and she understood but a fraction of what they said.

Steeling herself not to flinch when they darted towards her, she watched it all, her face expressionless. They'd yet to touch her, and she wondered what they were waiting for. The dagger in her boot burned like ice against her calf. She'd have time to take down one, maybe two of them. They wouldn't be expecting it. The thought gave her a flicker of satisfaction and her lips curved in a slight smile. They wouldn't find her easy prey.

Prodding the reluctant priest forward, Jamie stepped into the circle cast by the bonfire, eager to claim the girl and make a quick retreat before anything went wrong. He'd had a bit too much to drink while cementing the camaraderie between himself and his new friends. That, combined with fatigue from a day on the battlefield and two nights without sleep, had left him a little unsteady on his feet. His bride commanded the center of camp, silhouetted by a wall of towering flames. All things considered, it didn't seem a good omen. He couldn't stop the quirk of amusement that twisted his lips.

"Make way for the groom, gentlemen," he shouted, stepping forward to collect her. She stood mute and rebellious, with tangled hair and tattered clothes. Her cheek and jaw were bruised, and her lip was torn and bleeding, but otherwise she seemed unharmed. He was almost moved to pity, but he'd caught the glint of savagery in her eyes. Lady or strumpet, the girl was going to be a handful! He stopped in his tracks, grinning in appreciation, feeling the first stirrings of anticipation since he'd committed himself to this folly. "Christ, Gervaise! You might have cleaned her up a bit. She looks like a dockside harpy."

Catherine tensed, readying herself. The tall, dark-haired one with the cruel face staggered towards her, reeking of alcohol and shouting out some jest that sent the others into gales of drunken laughter. *So... they've been waiting for him.* She recognized him from before. He'd spoken to her in French, though she'd pretended not to understand. She'd spat on him and he'd given her his coat. She'd thought him their leader at first, but it appeared she'd been mistaken. It was the little man with the angry face who barked orders others scrambled to obey. The tall one was important though. He appeared to be a gentleman. They listened when he spoke, stepped aside when he passed, and no one barked orders at him. It seemed he was to have her first. Then he'd be the first to die.

He stepped forward suddenly, taking her by surprise, grasping her by the waist and pulling her so tight against his side she could hardly breathe. The drunken company surged forward and he pulled out his sword with his free hand, laughing and waving them back. She struggled against him, but no more than he might expect. The dagger in her boot was her only hope. She needed to keep a cool head and wait for the right moment.

Despite his drunkenness, she could feel the tension in his body as his arm encircled her. She could feel his strength. She stumbled and his hand gripped her shoulder, steadying her. It was somehow reassuring, giving the illusion of comfort and safety, and for a brief moment, she wanted to surrender to it and sink back against him. Then he made some remark that sent them into howls of laughter, and she could hear the hunger fueling their glee.

Her captor lifted her off her feet, cutting off what little air she had, and began to walk backwards, sword outstretched, maneuvering toward a large tent on the outskirts of camp. He stopped a few steps away from it and dropped her to the ground with an exaggerated grunt, much to the amusement of the crowd. He barked an order to the little fellow who stood outside, the one who'd brought her water, then sheathed his sword with a grin, trading it for a mug of ale he downed in one swallow, to a round of cheers. Tossing the mug aside, he motioned for the sour-faced priest, who approached with a look of grim disapproval. The priest produced a bible and began to read from it, droning in what seemed to be a mix of Spanish and church Latin.

Catherine was bewildered. Was this her executioner? Were they going to spare her their attentions and give her directly to the hangman? She looked about wildly for noose or gibbet. The priest cleared his throat impatiently. He seemed to be waiting for some kind of response. Confused, dazed from hunger, fear, and lack of air, she gazed at him without comprehension. Her captor shook her, then grasped her hair, pulling her cheek next to his. He spoke in her ear, startling her, saying coolly and clearly in perfect English.

"Give us a nod or go to the devil, girl. I've other things to do, and you've caused more than enough trouble for one day."

Without thinking, she did. He rewarded her by squeezing her breast with his free hand, prompting whistles and catcalls from the vicious pack gathered around to enjoy the show. She snapped, turning and slapping him with a crack across his face that silenced them all. They waited, breath bated, eager to see her punished for her defiance. His jaw tightened and his eyes glittered dangerously, and then, without a word, he heaved her over his shoulder and hauled her, kicking and cursing, into the tent amidst the raucous cheers of the crowd.

Twisting and writhing, struggling to break free, she bit him, sinking her teeth into the tender pad of his thumb, tearing the skin, tasting copper and blood.

"Lord thundering Christ, woman!" he swore, seizing her by the hair with his free hand and pulling until her eyes watered. "Let... go... now!" He threw her onto the bed and retreated to a stool, nursing his hand and a bottle of whiskey, cursing her roundly. "Damned savage bitch! I should have left you to Gervaise's tender mercies."

Catherine scuttled to the far corner of the bed and turned to face him, crouched and ready to attack. She knew she'd made a stupid mistake. He was big, he was in his cups, and now he was angry. His drunkenness alarmed her, but it also gave her hope. Men were often vicious in that state, but when he was done with her, when at last he slept, he'd sleep soundly. She reached for her boot and retrieved the knife, palming it in her hand. Let him drink, the oafish brute. Eventually he'd sleep, and when he did, she'd use the dagger to cut his throat.

Several moments passed and he made no move. He seemed in no hurry to deal with her. His eyes were half closed and he looked as if he might drift off. The waiting unnerved her. "Why didn't you?" she asked finally, breaking the silence.

He looked at her incredulously, still clutching his hand. He was dark and light in the shadows of the lamplight, cruel mouth, ferocious smile, dark hair, and fire-lit eyes. There was blood on his lip, and his face was red and swollen from her blow.

"Why didn't I what? Leave you to Gervaise? Are you mad, woman? Have you no idea what he'd have done to you? No care for your person? You were on the menu tonight, hell-spawned vixen. He would have taken you on the table in front of his men, and when he was done, the rest would have diced for you, then taken you one by one."

"So… you're to have me first… What then?"

"Why then, my love, you'll be so grateful and repentant, you'll love, honor, and obey me, till death do us part. I've claimed you as my wife."

"You've what?" she gasped, horrified.

He shrugged. "I'm no more pleased by it than you, my sweet, believe me, but there was no other way. I'm here on sufferance as it is. I've a mission to complete. I can't damage this alliance by stealing you—you're a prime piece of booty after all—and though I might stake a claim for your… er… services… along with the rest, the only way to safely remove you was to marry you."

Her mouth opened and closed several times. Stunned, she could find no words.

"I know. I know," he said, taking another swig from his bottle. "I'm sure you're grateful, love. There's no need to thank me, though it *is* the custom in many parts of the world after one has been rescued." He turned his head and regarded her quizzically. "Are you quite alright, my pet? You're very quiet all of a sudden."

"But… but… but it isn't legal! It can't be! I never agreed to it," she sputtered. "I never said the words!" He grinned and stretched, leaning back against the cross pole and crossing his ankles, and a part of her brain noted coolly he had a pleasing countenance and an athletic form.

"My dear child! Your input was hardly required, but the priest *is* one of God's shepherds, and you did nod your agreement, in front of witnesses, as I recall."

"But I don't *wish* to be your wife!"

"Well, there we are then! I don't wish to be your husband. It seems we're in perfect accord! Perhaps we shall suit after all." He motioned towards the door. "I can throw you back to the wolves if you insist. See if you can make a go of it on your own. I doubt they'll allow you armor or a weapon, though."

Hating him for her predicament, hating him for his smug smile, she fingered her dagger and said nothing.

"Well then," he held out his hand, examining the wound in the lamplight, "we'll discuss it no further. You're a vicious hellcat, I'll grant you that. You'd surely have been more than our friend Gervaise bargained for. It might have been entertaining to watch you geld him, but I don't think you'd have enjoyed the aftermath."

He rose unsteadily, still clutching the bottle, and approached the bed. She eyed him warily. He'd removed his coat, and his linen shirt hung loose and half opened, a victim of their earlier struggle. He hadn't shaved, and the hard-planed features of his face looked harsh in the shadows. He perched on the edge of the bed and offered her the bottle, shrugging when she shook her head no. He placed it on the floor, then reached out a finger and touched it lightly to her knee. When she made no move to protest, he reached for the front of her shirt, gathered it in his fist, and pulled her closer.

She erupted suddenly, clawing and cursing and slashing with her knife, but he was fast—much faster than she was. He straddled her in one fluid movement, imprisoning her wrists, the ferocity of his grip numbing her hands and fingers, forcing her to drop the weapon. He shifted hard against her stomach, winding her, and hauled her hands above her head, holding her there with one hand as the other traced the soft contours of her body.

"What's this then? No gratitude, wife? No welcome for your husband?" he mocked, as she lay mute beneath him.

Catherine blinked back tears of anger, humiliation, and despair. She'd had only one chance and she'd failed.

He shifted, allowing her to breathe, and cupped a breast through the thin fabric of her ragged shirt, grinning as he brushed a thumb across its pebbled tip. "You've sharp and pointy teeth, mouse, but the rest of you is soft and warm." His hand traveled her length, his fingers lingering over her curves before stopping to pluck the dagger from where she'd dropped it on the bed. Still holding her, he twirled it through his fingers.

"Shall I give this back?" He waved it in front of her, teasing, pretending to consider it, and then shook his head. "No… I think not. Not until you've learned to control that temper." He drove the dagger forcefully into the headboard, burying it halfway to the hilt.

"Let go of me!" she snarled, infuriated by his arrogance and smug smile. Twisting and bucking, she wrenched her hands free and struck him full across the face, cracking his nose and making him see stars.

"Unnnngh! Damn it, woman! Cease and desist!" he roared, reasserting his hold and shaking her hard. "The deed must be done or they'll not acquit us man and wife. I'll try to help you as I may, but not to the extent of jeopardizing my mission or my life. You need to choose, princess. Go back to Gervaise and his crew, or make your bed with me."

The truth hit her, sudden and hard. He was much stronger than she was, and she'd wasted her best opportunity, lost her only weapon. She was cold, she was hungry, and she was tired. There was no way she could win this battle, but she didn't know how to stop fighting. "Just get it over with then," she snapped.

Jamie winced, tenderly feeling his nose, and ran his eyes up and down her length. She wasn't like any of the women he'd known and pleasured in London. She had the same soft curves in all the right places, but she was strong, strapping, her body toned and sculpted, a warrior woman. It pleased and excited him, but she lay there stiff and rigid, like some virgin sacrifice. A sullen, hostile, angry, virgin sacrifice. His lips twitched in a smile. He reached out a hand to touch her, thought again, and carefully withdrew it. Reaching down, he hooked the whiskey, taking a sip as he contemplated the situation.

He knew she was afraid. He could see it in her eyes, though she hid it well. She'd have to be mad or a fool not to be. Nevertheless, she hadn't panicked. She was unusually brave for a wench. No submissive wee mouse, this one. His hand and his face were throbbing. Best not forget she was a dangerous opponent. It wasn't unexpected given where he'd found her, in the middle of a battlefield wielding a sword and screaming her defiance. She eyed him now, watchful and wary, calculating, waiting to make her next move. It was amusing, endearing, and most unexpected. It was… interesting.

He grinned in appreciation and wondered what she'd look like clean and cared for. He wondered what she'd look like naked. He'd find out soon enough. However he'd never been partial to rape—had hoped to find the girl at least somewhat accommodating, perhaps even grateful. As it was, he wished he hadn't drunk quite so much. If he took her now, considering both their states, it was certain to be a disaster. Still, it would be worse for them both if Gervaise and his men suspected he'd left her untouched. Pondering the dilemma through a haze of alcohol, fatigue, and lust, he grinned as he hit upon a solution. *In vino veritas!*

Jumping up, he grabbed the coverlet and yanked it from the bed. Safety first! The violence of his sudden insight sent her tumbling to the floor with a shriek of anger. Good! The bloodthirsty wench deserved it! He strode around the bed and picked her up, managing to avoid some of her wilder kicks, wincing as she pulled sharply on his hair, almost tearing it from his scalp. Grunting as a well-placed foot just missed the tender parts of his anatomy, he threw her back onto the bed, dropping heavily on top of her, pinning her down and pulling off her boots. There were no more hidden weapons. He countered her struggles with mild amusement and no small degree of lust. It really was too bad the wench was unwilling, she was proving to be a spicy little armful of fire and venom.

"Temper, temper, love! I know you're eager," he soothed. "Give me but a moment and I'll make a woman of you, I promise." He held her like that, his grip unbreakable, until she tired. When her struggles ceased, he rewarded her by loosening his hold. "You're quite the armful, my love. I'd no idea you were so enthusiastic."

"Bastard!" she hissed, struggling anew.

"And so very astute," he said through gritted teeth, gripping her tighter and giving her a shake. "Listen to me! I'm not going to harm you. Now... hold... still... don't... move."

She could feel it then, his arousal pressed hard against her, prodding against her belly. She looked into emerald eyes, amused, drowsy with drink, and quickening with interest, and her movements stilled.

Grimacing, he grasped her shoulders and pushed himself upright. "That's much better, mouse. Now stay there like a good girl, and be still. No more hopping in and out or tossing to and fro." He nodded in satisfaction, patting her clumsily on the shoulder, and rose from the bed.

Catherine sputtered in indignation. Hopping in and out! Tossing to and fro! *He'd* thrown her onto the bed. *He'd* tossed her onto the floor. She watched him through narrowed eyes, saying nothing as he removed his boots, then his breeches. His abdomen was hard and flat, ridged with muscle. Broad shouldered and tall, his body was lithe and graceful, his buttocks firm and... blinking, blushing, horrified, her eyes followed him as he turned around, returning to the bed, an erection of massive proportions jutting proudly at attention.

Her muscles tensed and her stomach clenched with fear as she prepared for battle once more. She'd tried to stab him. She'd scratched him, hit him, and bit him, drawing blood. She might have broken his nose. She hoped so. Now it was his turn, but she knew he still underestimated her. Arrogant cur, he'd mocked her by leaving the dagger within her reach, stuck in the bedpost. Sooner or later she'd find a chance to use it. One less enemy and the sweet taste of revenge.

The bed sank under his weight and she closed her eyes, steeling herself. After several moments, she opened them again. He sat cross-legged and naked, sucking on the mangled pad of his thumb. She watched with a detached fascination as he took the knife and worked the tip into the jagged wound her teeth had left, grunting in satisfaction when it reopened, and blood began to flow. He smeared it against the sheets, then straddled her in a sudden move. Holding her wrists with one hand, he hooked her breeches with the other, forcing them off as they wrestled silently, she grim and desperate, he almost negligent, chuckling, and grinding against her as she struggled.

Her shirt had torn open, a victim of their earlier skirmish, and he grinned in appreciation, admiring her naked form. She was everything he'd imagined and more. She had the body of an Amazonian huntress! Healthy and strong, long and sleekly muscled, with full, firm, rose-tipped breasts and beautiful, shapely legs that a man might—

She jerked hard against him and he recollected himself, releasing her wrists and letting her go.

"There!" he said proudly, gesturing at the smear of crimson on the sheets and nursing his wound. "'Tis my blood on the sheets, as you're too mean to offer your own. It should do well enough to convince our friends Gervaise and Father Francis that you are in truth a lady and we are truly wed." He eyed the scene carefully. "Hmmm… it's not quite right, though. Just one more thing."

Pinning her shoulders, he stole her breath in a demanding, whiskey-soaked kiss, rubbing his bristled jaw against her tender flesh and leaving her lips swollen and her tender skin abraded. Catherine knew she should fight him, but his grip was firm rather than cruel, and though his lips claimed and insisted, they didn't brutalize. She was losing the edge of fear that had fueled her earlier struggles, and weariness clawed in its wake. He didn't seem to want to hurt her. He'd said as much. She was exhausted and chilled, and his heat enfolded her like a blanket, making something inside her unclench, loosening stiffened limbs and bow-tight nerves, and melting her resistance. She felt as if she were underwater, every movement a struggle against a current that pulled her down, promising peace and rest if she'd only stop struggling and let herself float. For a moment she did. It wasn't surrender, but something like acceptance, tinged with a distant curiosity.

He responded by gentling his kiss to one of invitation, his breath tantalizing and teasing, hot against her skin. His hands released her shoulders, and his fingers traced the delicate curve of her collarbone. Her shiver had nothing to do with cold or fear. He smelled of wood-smoke and leather, he tasted of whiskey and rain, and his body pressed against hers, solid and warm. Somewhere between waking and sleep, hesitation and desire, she sighed.

He broke the spell suddenly, letting her go abruptly, sitting up to survey the scene with a pleased grin. "There now, mouse! All the world's a stage. They'll think me a veritable bull, and you properly chastened." He mussed her hair and chucked her under the chin, then playfully offered her the knife again, tossing and catching it when she grasped for it.

"Oh no, my dear. You'd like that far too much. You're a naughty wee mouse, with very sharp teeth, and you've already bitten me once. I swear you've used me ill on this our wedding night. I had so hoped you would be gentle. I may never recover." He drove the knife back into the bedpost, ready for quick use if needed, then placed his sword on the ground beside the bed. Leaning overtop of her, he reached over and filched the coverlet from the floor, dragging it across them both before sinking with a groan into the mattress. He was stiff, sore, and bone tired.

"Well, mouse? How does it feel? Your first experience was memorable, I trust? If you *were* a virgin, you are one no longer, at least not in the eyes of the world, but you'll still be enough of one in the eyes of the church to win us both an easy annulment. Brilliant, don't you think?"

When she failed to respond, he grunted and stretched, pushing her to the edge of the bed and grabbing most of the coverlet for himself, remarking as he turned over, "Here I am in my marriage bed, and I'm the one with torn flesh and blood spilled upon the sheets. Be damned if I can't get the simplest things straight!" So saying, he rolled over and went to sleep.

Catherine lay in the dark, heart pounding, confused, uncertain as to what had just transpired. Part of her was unaccountably disappointed, and part of her was still prepared for a battle that had never come. The camp had quieted, though she could still hear low voices and the occasional burst of laughter. A steady rain was falling, beating a tattoo against the canvas roof. Underneath it she could hear the river rumbling over rock and gravel just thirty yards away. He lay on his back, one arm flung above his head, throat exposed, his breathing deep and even. She eyed her dagger, still jutting from the post behind him. Easing from the bed, she pulled her shirt tight, retrieved her breeches and boots, and crept around the other side. She edged toward the post, her fingers extended, gingerly reaching for the haft of the knife.

She froze, heart in mouth, as the bed creaked and he shifted position, muttering something in his sleep. When he subsided, she continued, working the haft up and down, back and forth, slowly prying it loose, grinning in triumph when she'd finally worked it free. Alone, surrounded by enemies, a female at the mercy of men who didn't pretend to any civilized code of conduct, it had taken all her nerve not to succumb to hopelessness and fear. It was the weapon hidden in her boot, a last gift from her father, which had kept her from panic and allowed her to imagine that she had a plan, as feeble as it was. When the Englishman had taken the dagger from her, plucking it from her grasp with wink and a grin as if it were a toy, she'd felt the first stirrings of despair.

Gripping it in one hand, she ran her fingers along the blade, testing its edge. It was razor sharp, deadly, and she didn't feel helpless anymore. The thought of using it against an armed camp was laughable, but it would be lethal against one man. She edged closer, examining his sleeping form, watching the steady rise and fall of his chest. The visage she'd earlier thought harsh and cruel had softened in his sleep. A faint trace of stubble defined angular cheekbones and framed full, sensuous lips, curled now in an innocent smile. Dark bruises were beginning to form on his cheek and under his eyes, a sign of her earlier struggle. He looked surprisingly boyish and vulnerable, and for a split second, as she stood there shivering in the dark, she imagined herself crawling back under the blanket with him to share his warmth. What kind of woman would think of such things even as she plotted her husband's death?

The strands of dark hair tangled around his neck looked like blood in the lamplight. It would only take one thrust, quick and clean. He'd have no time to call for help. She raised her arm, poised to strike, but she couldn't stomach the though of cutting his throat as he lay there defenseless. Despite his drunkenness and her provocation, he'd done her no real harm. He'd given her his coat to shield her from the cold, and his protection, however unwelcome, to shield her from Gervaise and his men. She licked her lips, tasting his kiss. He was a brute, an arrogant and handsome brute, but not, apparently, the kind of brute that would rape a helpless woman, even in his cups when it was legally his right.

Legally his right! She stumbled over the thought. Oh, my God! He *was* her husband! She was his wife! What a tangle! She lowered the knife to her side. She had to escape. It had to be now. There was little time left before dawn.

An explosion rent the air, shaking the ground and shattering the stillness, and the camp broke into bedlam. He was on his feet, sword in hand, between one breath and the next. Shaken, she realized he hadn't been sleeping, nor had he drunk as much as she'd assumed. He'd been playing with her. Waiting to see how far she'd go. The hiss of arrows was followed by a brilliant flash of light, and a moment later the night erupted. Whistling ordnance hurtled through the air, followed by the bark of musket fire, the clanging of metal against metal, and shouts of rage. Catherine stumbled as the ground shuddered and he caught her, righting her, glancing at the knife but making no move to take it away. He pulled on boots and breeches and belted his sword, all traces of the amiable drunk dispatched.

"Stay here, mouse. Get under the cot. Don't leave and don't move until I come for you." Brushing aside the tent flap, he stepped out into the chaos.

Catherine knew it had to be Jerrod and his men. They were here for her, but they wouldn't know where to find her. Lifting the flap to take a look, she found her way blocked by her captor's determined retainer. He clutched a sword nearly as tall as he was, and wore an overlarge helmet perched on his head. They were obviously his master's castoffs, but he wore them proudly, and his voice was earnest and reassuring.

"Please stay in your quarters, madam. You'll be safe there. Rest assured I'll let no man enter save my master."

She realized she didn't know his name. Heavens, she didn't even know her new husband's name! Her eyes darted from left to right, catching a flash of movement on the riverbank. Nodding gravely to her new protector, she dropped the flap and withdrew inside, then, moving to the back of the tent, she used the dagger to slit open the canvas, and stole silently into the night.

Three

CATHERINE COVERED HER HANDS AND FACE WITH mud and hugged the shadows, crouching low and melding into the dark. *Little mice should stay very quiet and keep very still.* She grinned, wondering if the Englishman would be pleased to know she was heeding his advice. She crept forward, silent amidst the uproar of running feet and the cursing and shouting of angry men. Darting from tent to tent, slipping and sliding through muck-filled trenches, she edged her way toward the river.

Ten feet from the water she stood upright, putting fingers to lips and giving a low whistle before scrambling down the gravel bank, dislodging stones and pebbles and plunging into the swift flowing current. Icy water rose hip-deep, stealing her breath. She clutched at a hitch in her side, gasping for air, running as best and as fast as she could, ignoring the frigid stabs of pain biting at her limbs. She could hear the sound of horses splashing through the water but she refused to look, grimly determined to reach the other side. Struggling forward, feet and legs heavy and numb with cold, she took a misstep and almost fell, but someone hooked her elbow and grabbed her sodden shirt, almost hauling her off her feet. Slashing the air with her dagger, she fought to break free.

"Ease off, Cat. Leave be! It's me, Rory."

"Rory?" she croaked. She made no further protest as her burly redheaded cousin pulled her up behind him. She clutched him tight, teeth chattering, shivering with cold. She was free! Rory gave a shout. It was answered by low whistles and the sound of hoofbeats clattering into the night. From behind them, the sound of shouting and gunfire continued a few minutes more, then stopped as abruptly as it had begun.

Jamie walked the outer perimeter of the camp, perplexed. It was cold enough to see his breath. He could hear Gervaise and his men calling out, their voices sharp and clear in the chill night air, cursing as they searched with lit brands and torches, but there was no one to be found. As far as he could tell, their invisible enemies had made no serious attempt to breach the camp. After using arrows to light the powder stores, they'd contented themselves with shooting from the shadows and then melted into the night. It made no sense. He could have sworn that with this day's battle, the area had been pacified and subdued, and any viable fighting forces crushed into submission or forced into retreat. So who were they... and why had they suddenly broken off their attack? His eyes were caught by a jumble of fresh hoofprints and he knelt to examine them in the glow of his torch. Heavy horses... carrying well-armed men, but what were they—

"God curse it!" He leapt to his feet and stalked through the camp, ignoring all questions and pushing men aside. "Sullivan!" he bellowed.

"Yes, milord, what's wrong?"

"Where's the girl?"

"Why, she's in the tent, milord, where you left her. I—"

Jamie brushed past him and flung open the flap. The bed was a sodden mess. A pool of muddy water covered most of the floor, rippled by gusts of wind and the driving rain pouring in through a gaping hole in the canvas. His lips twisted in a sour smile and he gave a bitter snort of laughter. He had four cardinal rules, compass points by which he led his life. He always acted in his own best interest, he trusted no one and depended only on himself, when he gave his word he kept it, and when he accepted a commission, he made sure to see it through. He'd already broken the first one to help the hellcat, and now he was paying for it. It looked like he'd have to break a couple more in order to help himself.

He'd suspected she was no camp follower when he'd fondled her breast and she'd hit him, though he knew even a tart could have a temper. Whoever she was, it seemed someone wanted her back. Well, she had a husband now, and he wanted her too. A missing wife was a useless wife... worse, she was a dangerous one. He'd been counting on the smug and eager help of Father Francis to arrange a quick annulment once he'd shown himself repentant. That was going to prove damned difficult without the cooperation of the bride. If he couldn't accept the heiress the king had chosen for him, His Majesty would be deeply offended, and it wasn't wise to offend the king. He'd no choice but to retrieve her.

He heard a sound behind him. Sullivan stood white-faced and shaken at the entrance.

"I beg your forgiveness, milord. I've failed you."

"No, it's me who's failed. I should have known better. I've brought this on myself." He smiled and clapped Sullivan's shoulder. "Pull yourself together, man, and never admit a woman's laid you low. I'll wager better men than you and I have been cozened by my trickster wife. It seems the little mouse would have me chase her. I'll have to go and fetch her or it won't bode well. Tell Gervaise I had business to attend to. Tell him nothing else, and stay out of his way until I get back. I'll return as soon as I'm able."

He spoke with a confidence he was far from feeling, but there was no point making Sullivan feel worse than he already did. He couldn't have expected the girl to leave the safety of the tent, and he couldn't have known it was a disaster that she had. He needed to move quickly. He had to retrieve her before Gervaise struck camp or risk being accused of abandoning his mission, but he'd wager she knew this country a damned sight better than he did, and he knew every step she took away from him saw his hopes for the future slip further from his grasp.

A good three hours to the north, Catherine clung to Rory's back, struggling to keep her grip as they climbed steadily higher. The air grew colder as they rose, and her stiff hands were refusing to obey.

"Are you alright, lass? Have those bastards harmed you, Catherine?"

"No. I'm tired and sore, Rory, and I've a thirst that could drown a river, but I'm not harmed."

"You're frozen through though, Cat. You're shaking so bad you're rattling *my* bones." Rory pulled up his horse and wheeled around, waiting for the rest of the men to catch up. There were murmurs of excitement and some good-natured teasing as they surrounded Catherine, ruffling her hair, slapping her on the shoulder, and punching her arm.

"Ouch! Damn it! Willie, that hurt!"

"Not as much as falling off your horse did though, eh lass?" Willie said to guffaws all around.

"Enough!" Rory barked. "There's no time for sport. Who can spare me a breacan?"

"It's a bitter night, Rory. Did you not bring one of your own?"

"It's not for me, you blasted fool! It's for the lass!"

One of the McCormick boys handed over his great kilt, and Rory wrapped it around her and tied it at his waist, securing her tight against him. "Alright, lads. We're off."

They rode like that for several hours, bundled close together. Catherine relaxed, snug in the warm breacan, the warmth of Rory's body drying her clothes and driving away the chill. The rocking motion of the horse made her tired, and she leaned into his heat and yawned.

"Go to sleep, Cat. You've had a rough day."

She sank against him, closing her eyes, and just for a moment, she imagined a devilish grin, flashing eyes, and the mocking voice of her husband.

The rain had changed to snow and a bleak dawn was inching up the mountain when they finally reached their camp. Her Uncle Jerrod, far more demonstrative than his phlegmatic eldest son, held out his arms and caught her as she slid from the saddle. Tall, bald-headed, and built like an ox, his hooked Roman nose and steely gaze reminded her of an eagle. He reminded her of her father.

"Uncle, please! Put me down" she gasped. "I can barely breathe."

"God bless you, lass! I feared we might never see you again!" he said, releasing her. "Once we'd secured your fool of a brother and bundled him away, we made for the hills, and with the bloody fog wrapped tight around us it was a good two hours before anyone noticed you were gone. If those mongrels have touched you, I'll—"

"You needn't worry, Uncle. Other than being squeezed and shaken and tossed about, I assure you I'm quite unharmed."

"How's that possible, lass? We've both seen their handiwork. They're butchers! Savages! I'd not have expected a woman to survive inta—Well... ah... no doubt they mistook you for a lad."

"Yes, Uncle, they did," she said with a tired sigh. "And once they saw I was a woman, they couldn't decide what to do with me—kill me, ravish me, or hold me for ransom. I believe they were trying to find a way to do all three." She didn't tell him about her marriage or her husband. She didn't know what to make of it. She didn't know what to say.

"Aye, lass, but here you are, safe and sound and back like a bad penny."

"Aye, Dad," Rory broke in. He resembled his father, with proud beak and flinty gaze, but he towered over him by a good six inches and had a great deal more hair. "She made it easy for us too. We'd scarce arrived to the rescue and she was already free and halfway across the river! You did the Drummonds proud, Cat!"

"Aye, that you did, lass," Jerrod said. "Now come with me. We'll share a wee dram of whiskey and then be on our way."

Catherine followed her uncle to a place by the fire, and dropped to the ground, slumping against a wizened log. "Tell me then, Uncle. What of my brother… and who did we lose?"

"Drink your whiskey, lass. It's not a pretty story. We lost Robbie McIntyre, one-eyed Perry, and Matthew Robertson. Your brother Alistair… was not appreciative of our efforts. It seems he had his heart set on being a martyr, the silly git. You'll not see him here. He kept shouting for help, wanting rescue from his saviors, and frankly, I could stomach him no more. I had him clubbed and bound and sent home straightaway, and now we've got you, we'll all be on our way."

"Perhaps I should have left him to his fate as Donald wanted, but I couldn't. He's only a boy. Still… three good men dead because of him, and on my orders. Rory's wrong. There's naught to be proud of this day."

"What nonsense is this? Are you daft, girl? Three good men gone, aye. But that's no more than you might expect from a good cattle raid or a hard night's reiving. Your fool of brother might fancy himself a pious rebel, Catherine, but he's a Drummond, and your father's son. It's bad enough all the Highlands know he's a Presbyterian and a Covenanter. We'd have never lived it down if we'd allowed some prancing foreigners and a British lordling to hang him! You did the right thing, girl. Anything else would have made us appear weak to our neighbors. You've a good head on your shoulders, Cat. Better than Donald *or* your brother, but if you hope to lead this clan as your father wanted, you'll have to grow a thicker skin."

"I'll bear that in mind, Uncle," she said, tossing back her whiskey and rising to her feet, "but the point is moot. That's not what my father wanted, and Cousin Donald leads us now. That's what our people have chosen. Let's go home."

"You'll not challenge him then? Each of us here would support you," Jerrod said, walking alongside her.

"That makes thirty men. I'll not challenge him, Uncle. These are dangerous times and there's enough feuding between the clans—we don't need any within it. My father would not have wanted that."

"You know what that means, girl. He'll give you to the O'Connor. He wants the alliance and he wants to be rid of you. He'll marry you off as quick as he can."

Aye, Cormac O'Connor wanted her. His eyes lit with greed whenever he saw her—counting cattle, whiskey barrels, and all of her gold—but she was under no illusion he wanted her as a woman. Her uncle assumed she'd been mistaken for a man, and she'd heard the O'Connor, talking in his cups, tell his friends any man who took her risked cutting himself on her bones, her tongue, *and* her sword. Even her arrogant English husband had been surprisingly easy to dissuade.

Struck by a sudden thought, she turned to her uncle with a brilliant smile, her eyes lit with mischief. "So you think he'll marry me off then, do you, Uncle Jerrod? I'll certainly be interested in seeing him try."

Four

It was several days arduous journey to the Moray Firth and Catherine's family castle northeast of Inverness. They took a circuitous route, making it difficult for any pursuers and avoiding any hostile clans. The weather cleared after the third day, and they increased their pace, all of them eager for home. A lifetime spent in the Highlands hadn't inured her to the breathtaking beauty around her, but she passed spectacular mountain scenery, rugged glens, raging cataracts, and dramatic seascapes, without taking any notice at all.

Jerrod's words still troubled her. What had her father wanted? There was a time she'd thought she knew and had done everything in her power to give it to him, but he'd become a stranger to her over the years. She felt his presence always, a bitter blend of sorrow, anger, and regret, but there'd been good times… wonderful times… in the early years.

Her father, Ian Drummond, laird and chieftain of clan Drummond, Earl of Moray and peer of France, had been a vigorous and powerful man. The Highlands had ruled his heart and Catherine's mother had owned his soul. When she'd died giving birth to Catherine, it had broken his heart. He'd wept for days, consumed with grief, inconsolable until Catherine's nurse Martha had thought to place the bawling infant in his arms. She had her mother's eyes, he'd said, and from that day on, he'd kept her close, spoiled and coddled, her father's first and favorite child.

As she grew, she'd followed him about the castle, toddling after him on stubby legs. He'd scoop her up, chuckling, and tuck her in the crook of his arm, carrying her with him wherever he went. Once she was old enough to ride her own pony, she accompanied him with the men and boys when they went hunting and fishing, and in the council chamber, she sat at his right hand.

Her life had been carefree and full of adventure until she'd turned nine and her female relatives had begun hounding him. In his grief he'd neglected to remarry, they told him, depriving her of a mother's care and influence. In his grief, he'd kept her close, raising her as a son. She would start to look like a woman soon, and she must be taught to act like one. If she didn't learn her role and accept her place she'd never be accepted by men, or by women as one of their own.

Only her old nurse Martha had disagreed. "The girl is fine as she is. A rare jewel shouldnae be set in a common mold."

Not long after, he brought home her new Mama, Liselle. She was French, she was beautiful, and given how much she hated her new Highland home, she was kind. Between bouts of frenzied tears, lamentations that bordered on hysteria, and a never-ending litany of complaints, she saw to acquiring for Catherine a wardrobe fit for a young lady, and instructed her in the rudiments of genteel conversation, deportment, and dance. Catherine was inclined to like her, but it was difficult to warm to someone who detested her father and the home she loved.

She hadn't known until years later that her new mother, alone and friendless and given no choice, imagined herself in love with another man, but when she thickened with child and begged to return to France, her father had readily agreed. He'd accompanied her to his Barony in the Loire Valley and stayed for the birth and christening of Alistair, their son, and then returned home to teach his daughter the arts of governance, trade, and war.

She was an apt pupil, but she wasn't a male, and throughout her youth she had to fight to be included, and fight to be herself. Most of her father's men grew to accept her as a comrade, though some regarded her with suspicion and others disapproved. Her uncle Frazer was one, as was his son, her cousin Donald. Donald had come to live with them when Frazer was killed on a cattle raid. He was a strapping, unsmiling, redheaded boy, full of bravado and overly proud, but she knew he missed his father and was eager to show her father his worth. He was always quick to protect her and she knew he loved her in his way, but he was jealous of her abilities, resentful of the attention her father paid her, and amazed a girl should be allowed such liberties, chieftain's daughter or no.

Alistair came home when he was six. She'd tried to befriend him, but he was another who objected to her behavior, and he pushed her resolutely away. Even as a child, he was ascetic and disapproving, bookish and severe. Jerrod had taken to calling him the little Presbyterian. Little had they known. Slight of stature and far from robust, he was as strong-willed and brave as any Drummond, but he was prone to fits of temper and seldom stopped to think before he acted. Within a year of his coming, her father had pulled her aside.

"A man can't live forever, Cat, though I intend to do my best. But it's my duty to think of who's to succeed me as chieftain."

Her heart had quickened and swelled with pride. She'd struggled all her life to make him proud, to live up to his name and her heritage.

"Alistair's my only son, by rights it should be him, but the clan regard him as a foreigner, he does nae seem suited in body or mind, and between you and I, I'm far from certain his blood is mine. He's young yet. He may grow stronger and wiser with time, but I fear he shares his mother's unsettled nature. Donald wants it badly. He's a fine warrior, well liked, too, but he's rash, hotheaded, and stubborn. It's you who's shown the most promise, girl. It breaks my heart you're a woman."

She'd blinked, stricken, and an empty chill had seized her that was with her to this day. It had only gotten worse.

"Our people love you, Catherine, as I do. They trust and respect you, but they won't take their orders from a woman. Not so long as there's any other choice. But if we find you the right husband, someone with the wit to recognize your skills and abilities, rely on your experience and counsel…"

He'd continued on like that for some time, but she was frozen inside, and she'd barely heard a word. He sent her to France shortly after, to stay with Liselle and be schooled as a lady. She went to Paris and Versailles, polished her dancing and her manners, and was presented at the court of Louis XIV. She was courted, feted, and pronounced a great success, but the whole time she felt like an imposter—awkward, indelicate, and overlarge. She'd returned home two years later with a new hairstyle, a new wardrobe, and a fashionable new cynicism, and watched while her beloved father tried to sell her… for the good of the clan.

Her suitors pricked with interest when they saw her. She didn't account herself a great beauty, but she knew she was comely enough when you added her inheritance and the prospect of becoming chieftain of a powerful and prosperous clan. She'd turned them down, one by one. It took but a moment to see in their eyes: this one would rule her, this one ignore her, and this one was naught but a peevish child. She'd struggled against it for nearly four years, joining the men on hunting trips and raids, then returning to her solar to be coiffed, dressed, and marched out on sullen display.

In the end, her father lost patience, telling her to choose or he'd choose for her. She'd felt hurt and betrayed, and at Michaelmas a year past, she'd told him she hated him. She'd seen the hurt in his eyes and felt a stab of remorse, but she'd refused to take it back. Ten days later, he'd keeled over across the dinner table, sending overturned goblets and red wine running the length of the cloth, clutching at his arm ashen-faced, wheezing for breath and struggling to speak before crashing to the ground. She'd watched, horrified, as his hand slowly opened, releasing his goblet, and red wine pooled like blood on the floor.

Catherine jerked upright in the saddle, looking around her and wiping her eyes with her sleeve. The wild, snow-peaked Cairngorm Mountains were behind them, and before them the landscape dropped to low hills, crisscrossed with cattle and whiskey trails. Far in the distance, the sun glinted bright off steel-blue water and crests of white foam, and she could see and smell the smoke that drifted from the fishing villages dotting the coast. They were nearly home.

Her father's death had changed things irrevocably, laying open rivalries and fault lines that had lain dormant under his skillful rule. Rory, her uncle Jerrod, their men, and several others, stepped forward immediately offering their allegiance, but more had looked to Alistair and Donald. Sick with grief, she understood it was this her father had hoped to avoid. Donald stepped forward, Alistair stepped back, and she'd stepped aside, leaving it to the council to decide.

They'd chosen Donald, but her father had left the bulk of his lands and fortune in Scotland to her. It hadn't taken long for Donald and Alistair to try and control her, Alistair as her guardian and Donald as her chief. She snorted in disgust, startling her mount. Donald resented that she was invited to council, resented that she spoke her mind, and resented that when he spoke, they looked to her to see her reaction. He considered her a rival and he wanted her gone. It galled her to listen to his impassioned ranting and her brother's pretentious and uninformed opinions, and it worried her to listen to their dangerous and ill-conceived plans. She knew her father would expect her to speak up, but each time she did, they became more determined to set her on the path of proper womanhood and put her in her place.

They'd made it a priority to find her a husband, and in the end, despite her objections, they'd affianced her to Cormac O'Connor, a friend and boon companion from Donald's youth. They offered an alliance and a sizable dowry, and all he had to do for it was take her away. Large and rough, a brash and arrogant man who was quick to anger and slow to forgive, Cormac would seek to rule her. She knew the type. He was a simple man with an overabundance of pride, not unlike many of her father's warriors. She'd learned how to manage them long ago. She'd be able to manage Cormac. It rankled though… to be usurped, to be cast from the land and people she'd been trained to fight for, care for, and protect. It hurt like hell. Nevertheless, when Alistair journeyed to Edinburgh and landed in trouble with the Covenanters, she had organized the raid to retrieve him.

He'd stumbled onto a meeting and quickly found himself enamored. It didn't surprise her. Presbyterianism as practiced by the lowland Scots was a hard, unyielding faith. It abhorred graven images, didn't recognize Easter, and looked on Christmas with suspicion and distaste. The Covenanter's refused to accept the royal decree that the king was head of the church and signed a covenant stating only Jesus Christ could command that position. They might as well have signed their own death warrants. The combination of severity and courageous defiance, romanticized into a struggle for faith and independence against a tyrannical and too-English king, must have appealed immensely to Alistair's rigid nature and his youthful need to rebel. Still, Covenanters were no friends to the Drummonds, and Alistair's misguided folly teetered perilously close to a betrayal of his clan.

When word came that he'd joined an assembly on the River Clyde near Hamilton, and a paid company of king's men was descending upon them, she'd argued for his rescue, reminding them that others would notice if they failed to protect their own. Donald argued that Alistair's foolishness should not be allowed to endanger the clan. The council had looked back and forth between them, and in the end, it was decided a small force would go.

She'd taken ship with a group of handpicked men. From Edinburgh they'd moved overland, intending a quick surgical strike, but by the time they got there, the battle was already joined. They'd watched the slaughter from the hills, silent and grim, straining to spot Alistair in the melee below. A fog had moved in, rolling over the hills and along the river, making it difficult to see. When it lifted for a moment, she'd caught a glimpse of the crimson Drummond plaid down by the bank. She'd given a whistle and waved her sword, pointing in his direction. She wasn't supposed to have taken the field, but the flash of her weapon drew unwanted attention, and within minutes, she'd been surrounded by a bloodthirsty mob.

She'd tried to retreat, struggling to turn her horse around, but in the melee, she was forced down the hill and back toward the water. At one point a giant swordsman banged into her, stunning her and almost knocking her from her mount. He took a lazy pass at her with his sword and she threw herself sideways, reaching back and almost catching his thigh. He'd seemed disinclined to pursue her, breaking off his attack and allowing her to retreat. She'd pressed on toward Alistair's position, only to find she was cut off and he was already gone. She knew now who the giant had been. She'd realized it in his tent. Even without a helmet, she'd recognized his height and his sword.

She stretched and twisted, cracking her neck, and looked back at her men. They were the best of the Highland Scots. She'd fought with them as was her duty, and she never wanted to do it again. It was nothing like the lightning-quick skirmishes and rousing night raids she'd been on with her father. One took some livestock, one laughed with one's companions, and on occasion, some heroic fool took things a step too far and got himself killed. This had been a hacking, slashing massacre. It could have been worse, though. The Englishman had spared her on the battlefield and protected her in the camp. She owed him a great deal. She owed him her life. She grinned. Too bad she was never going to see him again to pay him back.

Five

THEY DESCENDED PAST TUMBLING ROCKS, PEAT bogs, and rolling wooded hills into a valley that come summer would ripen with barley. When malted and combined with the peaty water from the burns that flowed down from the surrounding mountains and hills, it would capture the unique flavor and aroma of her beloved home, becoming *uisge beatha,* the potent whiskey that served as medicine, comfort, and the currency upon which her family's fortune had been made. Crossing the River Spey, she felt a bitter-sweet ache, remembering sunny afternoons fishing for salmon with her father. There'd been no talk of marriage, succession, or duty… only golden days, swift moving waters, and her father's rumbling laugh.

The castle village was a fishing harbor, nestled against a heather-covered hillside along the sandy shores of the North Sea. They were greeted with excitement, then tears, as Jerrod informed Robbie McIntyre's wife he wasn't coming home. Catherine took note to see her well cared for, Perry and William's families, too.

The castle was perched on the summit, giving it a commanding view. It backed on a forest of oak and beech and looked across the sea to Norway. She looked up as she climbed the steep path, pretending she was seeing it for the first time, and wondering if it might be her last. Standing six stories high, with soaring turrets, steep gables, and tall chimneystacks, it had always reminded her of something from a fairy tale. When she was a child, she used to pretend she was a warrior princess, sworn to defend it. Well… that dream had fallen flat.

Right now, it hummed with a palpable air of excitement. The courtyard was bustling with activity, the servants were scurrying to and fro, and both her brother and Donald were waiting, frowning their disapproval. She glanced back at Jerrod, fairly certain the welcome wasn't for them. He shrugged his shoulders. Turning back, she caught Alistair's glare as he motioned rudely for her to join them. It seemed her prodigal brother and the cousin who'd counseled leaving him to die were already reconciled. Over her, no doubt. This farce was rapidly losing its appeal, and she was rapidly losing her patience.

Weary, grimy, stiff, and sore, she slid from her horse and passed the groomsman the reins, pausing to look at the family motto etched in stone above the entrance. *Virtutem coronat honos*. Honor crowns virtue. She'd spent years puzzling over what it meant. When she'd asked her father, he'd only laughed and ruffled her hair, saying "Cat, my girl, that's for you to decide." She knew how her brother would interpret it. She ambled over to him now, curious to know what the fuss was about, and smiling with approval at the lump still visible on his forehead.

"Brother… cousin," she said, looking at them both in turn, "what's all this fuss?"

"You look disgraceful, Catherine!" Donald snapped. "Go to your rooms and get cleaned up at once."

"But of course, cousin," she said in a pleasant tone, "just as soon as I've seen to my horse, seen to my men, and seen to my stomach."

"See to your manners first, woman, and do as your chieftain tells you!" Alistair barked.

"Are you speaking to me, pup?" she asked, rounding on him as her men snickered in the courtyard. "Because I don't think you can be. Because I know if you were, you'd be saying thank you to me and my men for risking our lives to save you from your folly. I know you'd be telling us how sorry you are that Robbie and Matthew and Perry lie cold and dead, their wives weeping in the village, while you strut and preen and play the little lord! I know you aren't talking to me, but I *am* talking to you. You deserve a sound thrashing, little brother, and if you ever… dare… to raise your voice to me that way again, I'll take a whip to you myself!"

Alistair stumbled back, white-faced with shock and anger.

"That's enough, Catherine! The boy's been through an ordeal."

"He needs to be told, Donald! If you cared about him you'd do so yourself. He's sixteen years old! He needs discipline and good counsel. You're his chieftain, you're his elder, and you're his family. You should act as his father, as my father did for you."

Alistair clenched his fists and stalked away, calling over his shoulder, "Tell her, Donald!"

"Had your father raised you properly, Catherine, you'd not be standing in this courtyard screeching like a scold! Your brother is too young to correct you, but Cormac O'Connor is not. He arrived here yesterday, and you'll be married to him tomorrow. You'll not shame us by going to your husband dressed like that. Go and get ready… Now!"

Her lips quirked. Husband? She already had one. The dark-haired English Lucifer with the twisted sense of humor. He hadn't appeared to mind the way she dressed, and it seemed he wasn't done aiding her yet. In fact, he was proving to be very helpful, indeed.

"Well, cousin," she said softy, "there's a slight problem with that, you see. Unless the laws have changed, and I'm allowed to have two."

"Don't play with me, woman. Two what?"

"Why, two husbands, cousin."

"Are you mad, girl?

"I don't believe so, Donald… but I *am* married."

"Damnation! How? When? I've made arrangements. You had no right!" Enraged, he gripped her by the arm and shook her, stopping suddenly when he felt cold steel pressed against his throat.

"Now that's no way to be handling the old chief's daughter, Donny boy," Rory said softly in his ear, as Jerrod moved to stand beside her.

"There's no need for that, Rory." Catherine shrugged loose from Donald's grasp and stepped away. "Donald is merely surprised and a little overwrought.

He'll settle down in a moment. Won't you, Donald." It was a statement, not a question.

"Well, I'm bloody well surprised and overwrought, too!" Jerrod said, almost shouting. "Just when did this happen, Cat?"

"Perhaps you should explain it to the council," Donald said. "Let them see you for the shameless hoyden you really are."

"Enough ya rank bastard! I'll not have you—"

"No, Rory. It's a good idea. Let's speak to the council, shall we?"

It felt strange to be in the great hall and watch Donald take her father's place. *Power ill becomes him.* It was an instrument he hadn't the skill to use, so he used it like a bludgeon.

"Well? What are you waiting for, girl? Tell us about this so-called marriage, or will you name the father only when you're thick with child?"

"I am the daughter of Ian Drummond, who was Earl of Moray, Baron Vichy, laird of this castle, and chieftain of this clan for over forty years. You're my kin, Donald, so I'll not require you to use my titles when you address me, but you *will* speak with respect!"

There was a drumming of hands on the table and a chorus of "aye" and "well said." Donald turned a bright red but said nothing more, motioning her to continue.

"Very well, as most of you know by now, in our attempt to rescue my brother, three men were lost and I was captured. One of their number, an English officer, heard the cry of Drummond and decided to snatch a bride. He assumed I was one of the lowland Drummonds and hoped to acquire some lands, I suppose," she added nonchalantly.

"Cat! You said no one had touched you!"

"No, Uncle, I said I was unharmed."

"Then… ?"

"I'm bedded and wedded, and by a priest, no less. I am married in the eyes of God." She wasn't lying. He *had* bedded her, though not in the way they assumed. Her words were met by shocked faces, shouts of anger, and murmurs of horror and dismay.

Donald jumped to his feet. "It will be undone! You're to marry Cormac O'Connor, not some… Sassenach! I've given my oath!"

"Well, I've given mine too, Donald, and to a higher power than you have! What would you have me do? Would you have me live in sin, married to two men?"

"And just who is he, this new husband?" Jerrod asked. "What's his name? How is he known?"

"I don't know, Uncle."

"You don't know? How can you not know?"

"Surely to God there's one or two of you who've stolen a bride before! My own father did. Did you stop and make polite introductions first? They were speaking Spanish most of the time, and frankly, Uncle, I wasn't really paying attention. I had other things on my mind and I was rescued before I could ask."

"Well then," Rory said. "It seems simple enough. We find out who he is, track him down, and make you a widow, Cat. You've no objections to that, I take it?"

"Other than the fact that he's in the center of an armed encampment amongst a host three times our size, the snow will be upon us soon, and we've already lost three good men? No, gentlemen, I have none, but might I suggest we use common sense. The poor weather's with us already, and it's not a good time for campaigning. Let's tend to our business, make some enquiries, and deal with it come spring."

Donald regarded her coldly. "Why didn't you tell your men when they might have done something?"

"*Because* they might have done something, Donald. It would have been suicidal. Now I beg you gentlemen, give me leave to rest. I'm feeling poorly and I've been through a great ordeal!"

She made to rise and stumbled, clutching at the table. They hurried to help her to her feet, filled with solicitude and concern—all but Donald, who regarded her with anger, and Jerrod, who watched perplexed. She hurried to her solar, gleeful and giddy and filled with relief, barely able to contain her smile. She'd always disdained feminine tricks such as fainting and weeping, but she may have been wrong. They appeared to work remarkably well. She supposed she owed him a great deal, this sharp-tongued, sarcastic Englishman. He'd saved her from Gervaise's men and an unhappy fate, and now he'd saved her from an unwanted marriage and set her free!

Six

UNAWARE HIS WAYWARD MOUSE WAS CONSIDERED a very great prize in the Highlands, Jamie set out in search of his errant bride within hours of finding her gone. A sullen dawn found him skirting the edge of camp, searching for her trail. Picking it up in the sodden earth with little difficulty, he followed it to the forest fringe, and soon found himself climbing, winding ever upward through lower slopes of pine, spruce, and larch, to a summit ridge with a fine view of the surrounding area. Farmland, lush forest, and rolling hills stretched in front of him for miles, kissed here and there by thick bands of Scotch mist, still heavy and dark with rain. He could see the rugged Highlands in the distance, their snowcapped peaks obscured by angry clouds, but there was no sign of his quarry.

He'd hoped to catch them quickly, before they'd cleared the glen and melted into the high country to the north, but it soon became apparent the adventure was going to be measured in days rather than hours. He looked back over his shoulder at the encampment below. Tiny figures bustled about and wisps of smoke from scattered cooking fires drifted through the camp and up the hill. The smell of field bread, cooked meat, and porridge wafted to him on the morning breeze.

He debated turning back, eating a hearty breakfast, and finally getting some sleep, but it was much too late for that. It was curious how a man could strive mightily for years, determined to change his life in some small degree, and meet naught but failure. Then suddenly, with his goal in reach, some small, unexamined act could change it irrevocably in ways he'd never imagined, endangering everything he'd labored to build or keep, sending it careening helter-skelter beyond his control. He knew such a moment had come for him and there was no turning back.

Ah well… there was nothing for it but to soldier on and hope for the best. Sullivan should be able to make his way home with Gervaise, and if he wasn't too far behind them with his bride in tow, he might salvage the thing yet. Turning his back on breakfast and his bed, he shrugged his shoulders and resigned himself to the north. He'd yet to decide exactly what he'd do when he found the mouse and her rescuers, but he felt certain he'd come up with a plan when the time was right. He only hoped he'd find them soon.

Luck and nature conspired against him. The steady rain that had saturated the ground, leaving muddy prints a child could follow, turned into snow as he wended his way into the Highlands, making the steep paths slick and treacherous and covering any trail. By the end of the first week, he was deep in the mountains. Several times he had to stop, taking shelter under the lee of giant boulders or making a hole in the snow as the wind howled around him. On such occasions he tended to his mount, did his best to make some tea from Sullivan's supplies, roasted a plump ptarmigan or two, and cursed the only woman who'd ever run away from him. Well… not counting his mother, of course.

At first, occupied with staying on the path, staying alive, and keeping track of his quarry, he paid scant attention to the beauty surrounding him, but as the weather lifted and he became accustomed to the rugged terrain, he marveled at the wonders before him even as he cursed the meandering route. When he climbed almost three thousand feet to a grizzled summit of shattered cliffs and bare boulders only to be met by four pathways heading off in different directions, he found himself cursing her again. Deciding it best to wait for morning, he immersed himself in the splendor of his surroundings, sitting on a cliff edge with his feet dangling over the side.

Looking out over a forest of towering pinnacles and jagged rocks to the rolling hills and forested glen below, he imagined he was sitting on top of the world. The sun was setting in glorious hues of purple, fire red, and gold, and an eagle soared in the distance, its great wings spread wide as it caught an updraft, wheeling and spinning above the earth. He watched in childlike wonder until it was too dark to see, then crawled under his blankets and into his heather bed, amusing himself for a time observing the glittering sky and trying to recall his constellations. They seemed so close he might have been among them. When he tired of that, he closed his eyes and entertained himself imagining what form of revenge he'd take on his ungrateful wife, once he'd managed to reclaim her.

It took him two more days to descend from the mountains, and he was soon a day behind her, then two, then three. He might have been in an alien world and the spectacle never ceased to amaze him. He made his way through a pinewood forest that opened into rolling hills dotted with standing stones and ancient Pictish carvings, and a superstitious chill crawled up his spine. He looked back over his shoulder several times in dread and delight, remembering childhood tales of giants and trolls told by servants late at night. Further north, descending still, he crossed a narrow bridge over a gorge carved by raging torrents of cascading water, and entered a land of cliffs, strange rock formations, and cheerful burns that fed into a giant peat bog. He laughed out loud, amazed and delighted to find a series of natural stepping-stones that took him most of the way across.

The civilized English countryside was tamed and domesticated, fenced and hemmed into pleasant farmlands, or shaped and styled into elegant, manicured woods and gardens, reflecting the English love of order and penchant to master the natural world. This land was a glorious wilderness, wildly beautiful, oddly whimsical, untamed and free. An admirer of the philosopher John Locke, the only heaven Jamie believed in was the one he experienced through his senses, but as he traveled through the Highlands he found himself wanting to believe in magic and fairies and almost believing in God.

"If you're anywhere, you're here," he mused out loud. He envied them, these Highlanders. How could a man—or a woman, he thought with a grin—be anything less than proud, independent, and free, raised in these lands. Well… the mouse might be proud and independent, but she was married now and no longer free.

Each day he fell more in love with the Highlands, and further behind his prey, but somehow, through divine providence or blind luck, he never lost the trail. "My true love guides me. The little mouse leaves crumbs for me to follow," he told his indifferent mount, a surefooted, dependable creature he'd found wandering the field after the battle. He'd left his own blooded stallion with Sullivan. It was a high-strung beast, ill-suited to climbing mountains, and far too valuable to risk.

He finally came to the edge of a great valley dotted with lochs, rivers, and barley fields stretching as far as the eye could see. It had to be the Great Glen, and as he urged his stolid mount along the steep trail skirting its rim, he knew he was approaching Inverness and civilization. He could smell the ocean now and see it from the higher elevations. Wary and alert for trouble, he encountered no one on the trail, but when he came to a network of castle paths and a bustling market town, he knew it was time for a plan.

Jamie had a talent for mimicry and languages he'd discovered as a child and honed in service to King Charles on clandestine missions in France, Spain, Holland, and His Majesty's own court. As a boy, he'd made the happy discovery that the high and mighty took little notice of the poor and meek. Those who were lowly and useful, those who served, were invisible, everywhere given entry, and everywhere ignored. By changing his manner, clothing, and speech, he could disappear among them, hiding in plain sight, a privileged observer who switched back and forth between one world and another as circumstances dictated or his mood and curiosity allowed. In London, he'd often stood unnoticed, a mean and humble servant, bowing and scraping and tugging his cap as courtiers he'd played cards with the night before played at sedition, oblivious to his presence just feet away.

He decided on a tinker. The making and mending of domestic metalware was a common occupation, and a tinker had skills that made him welcome in any residence or keep. Selling useful items like pins, needles, hooks, and scissors, and fripperies such as perfume, ribbons, and combs, would put him in the presence of any women of a household. The masquerade had served him well in the past, and he'd gone so far as to acquire a basic level of competence as a coppersmith and some rudimentary skills as a gun and locksmith. To effect a convincing disguise, however, he'd need suitable clothing and supplies.

He found a small cottage on the outskirts of the settlement and filched some ragged, loose-fitting clothes from a line, leaving his saddle and bridle behind. There was a slight risk the inhabitants might report this strange event in the village, but he was willing to wager they'd keep it to themselves, preferring to keep what was clearly an expensive saddle, rather than risk having it claimed by someone in town.

He applied a little mud and grease to face and hair, attached his handkerchief jauntily around his neck, and became a gypsy. He knew he should bury his sword, hide it, or trade it for something less valuable. It was far too fine a weapon for the role he played, but he'd grown attached to it over the years and couldn't bring himself to leave it behind. Using his blanket as a cloak to hide it, he wandered into town, hunched over to disguise his height, leading his horse by the halter, with his own fashionable coat, boots, and clothes slung across its withers. After some spirited haggling he was able to trade the lot for a sturdy pony, suitable clothing, all the supplies a successful tinker might need, and supper and a bed.

A couple of rounds of whiskey and some convivial conversation at the local inn led to the happy discovery that a party of horsemen from clan Drummond had passed through just three days past, headed for their stronghold some twenty miles to the east.

Despite his humble disguise and modest clothes, Jamie still managed to attract a fair bit of attention from the local ladies, no doubt due to his easy manner, charming grin, and enticing sack of goods. A raven-haired doxy, whose breasts kept escaping her bodice despite its heroic attempt to contain them, came over to sit beside him.

"Well now, you're a fine looking laddie, aren't ya? What's your Ma been feeding you?" she asked, pawing drunkenly at his coat and tugging at his trousers.

"I'm almost in my dotage, sweetheart. It's clean living and a pure heart that's kept me looking so young." He took his would-be inamorata's hand from the bulge in his breeches and raised it to his lips.

"How about I sample your wares, tinker, and you sample mine?"

Jamie shifted and grinned. He'd wager she hadn't bathed in several months, and her whiskers were nearly as long as Granny O'Sullivan's. "I'd love to, my darling, but I'm off to rescue my own true love. Kidnapped she was, by wooly-headed giants who carried her off in the dead of night."

"Is that so? And you're just stopping to do a little business along the way?"

"A man has to feed himself, sweetheart." He motioned the innkeeper over for a round of drinks. Three other women had joined them, pressing against his back and shoulders and watching with a delighted chorus of ooohs and ahhhs as he spread a collection of gaudy rings, colorful ribbons, and perfumes and mirrors across the table. "Some of these be magic, my darlings," he said, raising a mirror for them all to admire. "I look in this whenever I lose my sweetheart's trail, and wherever she is, I can see what she's doing as clear as day."

"Wouldn't want my old man getting hold of one of those!" a stout goodwife shouted to gales of laughter.

"What does this one do, dearie?" an older woman asked, holding up a ring.

"Why this one protects the bearer's heart, my love. It's both a blessing and a curse. Whilst she wears it no man can steal her heart, and no man can wound it." A crowd had gathered at the table by now and he leaned in closer, almost whispering, "But neither can she give her heart away."

"I'll buy it!" a blowsy blonde declared, reaching for it eagerly. "I've no use for the bastards anyway—excepting yourself," she added with a cheeky grin.

The table was soon surrounded by women, young and old, respectable and not, and Jamie charmed and entertained them with flashing eyes and teasing grin, spinning tall tales and stories that turned the garish and mundane into something enchanted and unique. Within an hour, his store of magical ladies' fripperies was completely depleted. He was enjoying himself immensely, but when the busty blonde plopped herself in his lap and flung her arms around his neck, causing the more respectable ladies to snort and purse their lips, ruffled and annoyed, he realized he was attracting too much attention and it was past time to go. He squeezed his well-rounded companion appreciatively, enjoying her plump curves, and rose to his feet with her tight in his arms, kissing her lustily before placing her on her feet and pointing to the slight bump and bruising near his nose.

"Alas, my beauties, you're as lovely and tempting a group of ladies as any I've encountered, but my mistress is fearsome, jealous, and cruel. In truth, it's not the wooly-headed giants I fear, but the wrath of my coldhearted witch of a wife. If I stray she beats me unmercifully!" There were guffaws and laughter from all around, and in the general merriment Jamie managed to slip the clutches of his admirer and retire to his room.

He set out for the stronghold of clan Drummond early the next morning, still pure of heart, stopping at the market to replenish his supplies. He'd made good money at the inn, and he grinned as he entertained the notion of chucking king, country, and ambition, and making a life in the magnificent Highlands, traveling the road, roaming hill and dale, seducing the ladies into sampling his wares.

It was a complete mystery to him what these remote Highland Scots had been doing on the banks of the River Clyde, who the little mouse was, and what she'd been doing there with them. He'd heard stories that the Scots army that marched on Newcastle during the Civil War had included female soldiers, but frankly, he'd never believed it. He wondered now if it might be true. Running his forefinger along the bridge of his nose, he chuckled at the thought. She might prove useful yet. She was certainly more adept than Sullivan was when it came to using her fists and wielding a weapon. In any case, he supposed he'd have some answers soon.

The busy little town flanking Drummond Castle rose in a series of terraced streets above a snug harbor full of fishing boats and merchant ships, and as he climbed the hill, pulling his pony and his wares behind him, he could see a long spit of golden sand stretching far to the north and south. He was making slow progress, pausing every few minutes to trade with the locals, selling needles and combs and kitchen utensils with a wink and a grin and a convincing Scot's brogue. Halfway to the top, he heard a commotion and looked up to see a large, colorfully dressed fellow in a saffron shirt barreling toward him with an excited crowd chasing behind.

"Hold up, Cormac!" a red-haired, full-bearded Highlander was shouting. "You don't have to leave, man! What about our alliance? I promise you we can come to some kind of arrangement."

A big man himself, but not today, Jamie pressed against a stone wall, trying to be unobtrusive and get out of their way, but the street was crowded and the florid-faced giant was the kind of fellow who claimed a lot of space.

"You can take your bloody alliance, Donald Drummond, and shove it up your arse! I was promised land and whiskey! I was promised coin! I was promised the girl!" the giant bellowed, shoving people rudely aside and bashing into Jamie, knocking him sideways and almost to the ground. Keeping his temper, Jamie bowed his head and mumbled apologies, but the man was looking for a fight, or at least someone on whom to vent his anger.

"Watch your step, you poxy bastard, or I'll give you a good thrashing!" he snarled, grabbing Jamie by his tattered cloak and shoving him hard against the wall.

There was a moment of dead silence, followed by a swell of excited shouting as a gleaming silver sword glinted in the sun.

"What manner of tinker is this?" Donald roared. "Who are you, ya bastard, to be sneaking about my town hiding a weapon? You're not one of mine and you're not the O'Connor's!"

Cursing, Jamie pulled out his sword and looked to the left and the right, calculating his odds and assessing his chances for escape. He should never have kept the weapon. By far the most crucial element of disguise was absolute commitment, and neglecting it might well have cost him his life. The harbor seemed the best chance. He might be able to hide in the warren of fishing boats and dockside shacks; he might even manage a dinghy. He grinned, giving friends Donald and Cormac a rude gesture before leaping onto the lower wall and vaulting to the street below. Landing on his hands and the balls of his feet, he was startled to find himself looking at long legs and a shapely derriere encased in leather breeches. Rising in an instant, he found himself staring straight into a pair of very surprised, amber, cat-like eyes.

Well, I'll be damned! he thought, a second before a club caught him from behind and sent him crumpling to the ground.

Seven

HE CAME TO, COUGHING AND SPITTING AS A BUCKET of icy water hit him in the face. He appeared to be in a courtyard adjoining the stables. He was lying on a scaffold, soaking wet, stripped of everything but his breeches. Several men held him down as his hands were tied together and pulled over his head by a rope they passed through a ring. He was yanked to his feet and hauled up until he dangled in the air, his toes barely touching the ground. The courtyard was crowded. There were women, children, and even old ladies. It seemed he was to be the day's entertainment. These Drummonds were a bloodthirsty lot—though to be fair, public torture and execution drew a festive crowd in London as well. *Damn the wench!* She was ill-fated! She brought bad luck and it seemed she was going to be the death of him.

He was still a little groggy from the blow to the head and was just getting oriented when someone punched him in the face, sending him spinning. He went with it, accepting rather than fighting, and managed to keep a rising tide of nausea at bay. He could see the harbor through the stable gate. It was a crisp, cold, late-November day. He was punched and spun again, and watched detached as people flowed by like a river—tall ones, short ones, fat ones, skinny ones—against a background of stonework, sea, and sky. He could see fishing boats… a man with a whip… and a flaming brazier. That didn't bode well… not well at all. Someone kicked him and he spun again. *What an interesting lady!* She floated by in shades of cream, copper, and azure blue. Be damned if it wasn't his wife! She was wearing a dress. It was most becoming. It seemed she'd dressed up to come and watch him bleed.

A bald-headed man, built like a bull, yanked on the rope, almost wrenching Jamie's arms from their sockets, sending a thrill of agony coursing through his body, nearly making him scream. "Let me introduce myself," the man said pleasantly. "I'm called Jerrod, and I'd be captain here. Everyone knows me in these parts, and I know them, too… so I know that you… well… you're not from around here. And you're not a damned tinker! Not with those pretty hands and that pretty sword." He grabbed Jamie by the hair and yanked his head back. "Now there's no need for this to be any more unpleasant than it already is. All you have to do is answer my questions, laddie, and we'll get along just fine. Who are you, man? Who sent you and why are you here?"

Jamie grinned and spat, knowing how it worked, knowing once they had the information they wanted from him, his life would be measured in moments rather than hours, and wondering what, if anything, his still-silent wife would have to say about it.

"I asked you your name!" Jerrod barked, hitting him with a mailed fist, knocking his head back and bloodying his lip.

His response was half a chuckle, half a moan. His vision cleared and the chit caught his eye, shaking her head, no. Ah… so… nothing to hope for from that quarter. Apparently, she wasn't inclined to come to his rescue, claiming him as her own true love and offering him the same protection of family and duty he had offered her. Oh well. He never revealed a lady's secrets. He spat blood and managed a pained wink in her general direction. Abandoned by his lady love, trussed like a chicken, his life measured by hours, if not minutes, there was little left to do but maintain a graceful exit, hopefully one that would be remembered for its courage and pathos and… well… flare. He hoped they wouldn't make it too difficult. He hoped they weren't as inventive in their tortures as Gervaise and his men were with theirs.

The one name Jerrod smacked a fist in his face again, and he bit back a groan. If the mouse hadn't broken his nose, this fellow surely had. He coughed and laughed, spitting blood as the bull went to hit him again.

"Careful, Jerrod!" the one called Donald warned. "I want answers, not a corpse. Moderate your questioning accordingly. Offer our guest a taste of the whip. He smells like a Murray to me. I want to know what he's doing here. Let's see how well he takes a flogging."

Jerrod clutched Jamie's matted hair and pulled him close. "Are you a Murray, man? Got lost in the mountains and just trotted down for a stroll? I'm about to take the skin off your back, laddie. Best you take a moment to think." He shoved him away and watched him swing a moment before picking up the whip. "Last chance, man. Are you certain you've nothing to say for yourself?"

Jamie nodded his head, motioning the bull closer. "Yes, I've something to say" he managed through gritted teeth. "Best be careful, Bucephalus. My easygoing nature is getting sorely fucking tested. I'm going to remember you."

The bull roared with laughter. "You're a brazen bastard, I'll give you that! It's a shame you're not a Drummond."

He took the flogging well. He'd learnt how at his Puritan father's hands, and he'd survived worse as a child. He didn't know how long it went on. The worst thing was the cold. Every time he passed out, they'd wake him with a pail of freezing water. He would freeze to death before too long. At least it was numbing his body and helping him ride the pain. He'd managed to keep his dignity this long, just a short while longer and at least he'd have a glorious death. He'd die with a curse and a laugh, not whimpers and screams.

As he spun and grimaced through the last few hours of his life, he watched his wife whenever he could see her with a certain detached admiration. *She's beautiful,* he thought, *and vicious, too.* Any question as to whether or not she was a lady had long been answered. She watched his torture with coldhearted indifference. She'd have fit comfortably with any of the flint-eyed, back-stabbing bitches in either Stuart court.

It had been hours now, and his world was one of agony. His arms screamed in their sockets, his wrists and back were raw and bloody, and his nerve endings shrieked with jagged-edged pain. Why not tell them? a voice whispered. Why not tell them who you are and make it stop? To protect the girl? Because she'd asked him not to? Would they harm her if they knew she'd married an Englishman to save her life? She was a stranger to him, someone he'd passed on a battlefield, someone he'd helped on a whim, as a joke. He owed her nothing. Nothing at all. Still… he was a dead man now, one way or another. Whatever wasn't raw and bleeding was frozen stiff, and soon, very soon, he'd slip into the dark and a bucket of water wouldn't bring him back.

The idea frightened him. He didn't believe in hell any more than he believed in heaven, unless it was an infinite emptiness lacking any kind of amusement, experience, or sensation; but now that he was on the brink, with time to think about it, he found the idea of an eternity of nothingness, an eternity of boredom, so chilling and abhorrent he almost panicked and begged them for his life. It was stubbornness more than anything else that made him bite his lip, stifle another scream, and refuse to tell them what they wanted to know.

His head was jerked back and he was forced to look as one of them approached, a hot iron in his hand, and his heart began to thump louder in his half-frozen body. He shifted his head with difficulty, to glance at his lovely wife. He was far away from home, and though they were strangers, she was the only person here he knew, the closest thing he had to friend or family. It was good to know he wouldn't die completely alone. She watched stone-faced. It heartened him a little that she didn't show the same excitement as the others, though one could hardly blame them given the dearth of novelty or entertainment in a backwater like this. Still… one was not inclined to be charitable when—his thoughts were interrupted by searing pain across his chest, and the sound of someone screaming. Mercifully, he passed out before he realized who it was.

He could hear her screaming, begging and pleading, and the dull repeated smacking of flesh upon flesh. He wanted to help her. He wanted to kill him! But he was only little, and he was scared. He huddled under the stairs, arms wrapped around his knees, crying.

"Whore!" his father shouted, "Shameless adulteress! Is that hell-spawned brat even mine? Whose bastard is he, woman?"

He heard the sounds of breaking furniture, shattering glass, and a slamming door, followed by his father's footsteps, monstrous and heavy on the stairs. He hugged himself tighter, wanting to disappear, and watched with amazement as a small, furry, bright-eyed creature poked its head from around the corner, watching with intent and curious eyes. It approached him cautiously, looking from side to side. "You're just a little thing," he whispered. "Little and brave." He scooped it into his pocket, feeling braver now himself. He had a job to do, and something to protect. He crept down the hall, looking for his mother. He found her huddled in a corner, sobbing. Her dress was ripped and ugly bruises marred

*her neck and face. He wasn't sure what to do. He looked
around for a servant, but they'd all fled. He approached her
uncertainly, wanting to comfort her, but not sure how. He
reached out a tentative hand and touched her shoulder...*

*"Get out!" she screamed. "You've caused enough trouble.
Get out! Get out! I hate you! I never want to see you again!
Get away from me! Get away from me!"*

Jamie opened his eyes and looked dazedly around. He
was suspended in the air. A cold rain mixed with sleet
was falling, and his body was racked by shudders. As
his mind began to clear, his body screamed with pain
and he gasped aloud. *Oh, good Christ! Why can't I just
die?* He seemed to be having no luck at all. It was full
dark and his tormentors appeared to have left... all but
one. Someone was tugging at his leg, and far off in the
distance he could hear a voice.

"Can you hear me, English? We have to get out of
here. We have to get away from here. English! We
have to go! Now!"

"Why hello, mouse," he croaked, blinking and
doing his best to manage a jaunty grin. "Did you come
to fetch me after all?"

"Yes. Can you move your legs? Can you stand? I'm
going to cut you down."

"Of course I can stand, child!" he scoffed, before
slumping unconscious into her arms.

Grunting, Catherine dragged him to the edge of the
scaffold where she'd left her horse. With a great deal
of effort she managed to pull him across the saddle in
front of her, slapping at his hands in exasperation as

even unconscious, frozen, and half-dead, he somehow managed to grope her breast. "Get your hands off me, you oaf!" she muttered, before covering him with wool blankets and several sacks. She headed for the castle gatehouse, draping her cloak over him as best she could, waving to Alan Johnson as she passed.

"It's a foul night, Cat. Where are you off to? Shouldn't you be warm and snug in bed?"

"I've some clothes and goods for Robbie's widow. She's been having a rough go. She's not been sleeping since he passed. I'll be sharing a jug of whiskey with her, Alan, so don't expect me back tonight."

"You've a good heart, lass. I'm glad we won't be losing you to the O'Connor. Give Mary my love, will you?"

"Aye, so I will, Alan, though maybe come spring you should do so yourself."

She stopped at Mary's first. Leaving her horse tethered outside, she gave the younger woman several bundles and a warm hug before joining her for one quick tot, followed by another and then another. "So… I'll sleep here with you tonight, Mary, shall I?" she asked, just before the other woman nodded off to sleep. Then she crept outside, mounted her horse, and started down the beach, carrying her English husband, knowing the tide would wipe away any trace of her passing.

Eight

CATHERINE RODE ALONG THE BEACH FOR ABOUT three miles before turning inland to follow a path that skirted a large limestone outcrop. The sky had cleared for the moment, and the moon hung low and full. She followed the steep track up and then down, to a narrow inlet where seawater met river at the mouth of a limestone cave. The entrance was wide enough for her to ride right in, and at high tide, a boat could enter. She splashed through a pool of water and went inside, taking a moment to get her bearings in the dark. She'd come here often as a child, looking for her mother. Her nurse had said her mother was a selkie who'd strayed from the ocean for love of her father, leaving Catherine as comfort when she'd had to return to her watery home. She'd kept coming long after she'd outgrown such childish notions. No one else bothered to stray this far from the castle, and she'd claimed it as her own.

She slid from the saddle and searched for the oil lamp she kept hooked on the wall, lighting it and raising it to pierce the gloom. The flickering lamplight cast an eerie glow over the strange Pictish script and many drawings on the west wall, including the figure of a dancing woman, an old Viking ship, and a leaping salmon. The cave went back a good thirty feet before it narrowed and dropped to an underground river. Halfway back was a ledge spread with several sealskins and a heather bed. She noted the stack of wood and coal, and the buckets, kettles, blankets, and sacks of food piled neatly by the fire pit, and nodded with satisfaction. The cave was as comfortable as it could be. Martha had done well.

Grunting, she pulled the inert body of the Englishman… her husband… off the long-suffering mare, stumbling and nearly dropping him. Staggering under his weight, she managed to heave him onto the heather bed face down, before dropping to the floor to rest and catch her breath. Her exertions had opened the wounds on his back, and her shirt was stained with blood.

He'd stopped shivering, which wasn't a good sign, and his body was bluish and pale. She hurried to build a fire, stoking it high and placing a kettle over it to boil. She tethered the horse near the entrance where its heat could help warm the cave, and rifled through the supplies, looking for rags and whiskey and Martha's poultice. A daughter of clan Macbeth, an ancient family of bards and healers hailing from Ireland, Martha had also been her nurse, and her father's before her. Her loyalty was absolute. She was the closest thing Catherine had to a mother, and she was the only one who knew what she'd done. She hadn't asked any questions when Catherine had asked for her help, just winked and grinned and given her instructions on what to do.

She followed them now, sitting on the ledge beside him with hot water, a rag, and a jug of whiskey. The fiery liquid was well known as a medicinal drink that could prolong life and relieve palsy, colic, and smallpox, but Martha insisted it could also prevent infection and fever when applied to a wound. Catherine dutifully applied liberal amounts of hot water and whiskey to her patient, cleaning his wounds and rubbing him briskly, trying to bring some warmth to his body, although with little apparent success.

She couldn't help but admire him, as she applied Martha's salve to his back. The poor man had come here looking for her—he must have! But despite hours of torment, he hadn't said a word. What could he possibly want? He'd known nothing of her fortune. They weren't even... they hadn't even... he hadn't wanted her, in any case. He'd talked of an annulment and he'd all but told her it was an inconvenient chivalry that had prompted him to come to her aid. She'd honestly thought he'd be glad to be rid of her. Now here he was—a big nuisance, a very big nuisance indeed! He was a brave man, though. To walk into her lands, bold as you please, straight to her door. He'd shamed them all with his courage. He'd taken a vicious beating and whipping with nary a scream or a whimper. Even among the Highlanders, there were few who could claim as much.

Her heart had jumped and her pulse had been racing when he'd landed in front of her, appearing from thin air, and it wasn't all from shock and surprise. There'd been a thrill of excitement and a start of pleasure, too. She wasn't sure why, but it had pleased her to see him again. She continued working the salve carefully into his wounds, noting that his back, though badly lacerated, was taut and well muscled, and he had a strong neck, broad shoulders, and sinewy arms. She moved higher, worked vigorously on his shoulders and arms, massaging and kneading, hoping to ease muscles that had been tormented, stretched, and torn.

She blushed in the lamplight when she realized she'd been rubbing salve on them as well, and returned to tending to his back. Despite her efforts, his skin was still clammy and cold. She looked with concern at his soaked breeches. They would need to come off. She reached gingerly around his waist and released them, then tugged and cursed, struggling to remove them, tripping and landing on her behind in the process. When she was done, she washed his lower body... well, his backside at least. She felt a slight twinge of shame as she rubbed down his long, muscular legs and taut buttocks. He groaned and shifted and she stopped, her hand in the air, blushing bright red. Good heavens, what was wrong with her? He was her patient, her husband! She was acting as if she'd never nursed a man before. Well... she'd never nursed a man who looked like this.

When she'd finished washing him, she replaced his wet bed with dry heather and rolled him back upon it, applied the poultice, bandaged his wrists, and covered him with strips of linen, a soft wool blanket, and a couple of sealskins. She lifted the whiskey to her lips and took a healthy swig as she admired her handiwork.

"Well, English... how does it feel to be helpless and completely under my control?"

"I don't know. I'll let you know if it ever happens. Have you anything to drink, love? I'm parched," he rasped.

She gasped and jumped up in surprise. "What? I thought you were... how long have—"

"In and out, love. In and out. Christ, girl! Have mercy. I'm freezing and I'm dying of thirst."

She filled a hipflask with whiskey, honey, and hot water, and hurried over to him, holding it to his lips.

"Bless you, lass," he mumbled, and was gone again.

She sat watching him, lost in thought, contemplating her new situation and trying to figure out what to do next. The sound of the waves on the shore was muffled and distant, the river outside sounded barely a trickle, and all was silent but for her horse's occasional snorts of impatience and the steady drip of the water falling from the limestone roof. He was a handsome man, striking, even—and he was bloody inconvenient! She'd finally had the upper hand with Donald and her brother, and he was going to ruin all her plans.

If she'd left him hanging on the scaffold he'd be dead by now, and her life would be that much simpler. That was unthinkable, of course. He'd saved her life, whatever his reasons, and when he'd had her in his power he'd been careful not to harm her. She'd been too frightened to realize it at the time, but she'd thought about it since. She'd bitten him, smashed his nose, bloodied his lip, and taken her dagger to him. He'd been remarkably tolerant of it all. Nonetheless, she wasn't going to let him complicate things any more than he already had. She would help him, as he'd helped her, but that was all. She'd see to it he recovered, and as soon as he was well enough, she'd see him on his way.

Hearing a sound outside, she leapt to her feet, but it was only Martha.

"Well? I've come to see what all the fuss is about. Where is he? I haven't got all night."

"Over there, Martha. I did everything you told me. I've tended him as best I can."

"Oh, my! He's a braw one isn't he, Cat? Who is he, child?"

"He's my husband, Martha."

"Is he now? The Englishman who stole you from the O'Connor? And he came all this way to find you? A hungry man smells meat far, my Ma would say. You've done the right thing, girl. 'Tis your duty to protect him. This one will give you fine, strapping sons."

"I've no intention of having fine strapping sons with him, Martha. He's... he's English... and I don't even know his name! As soon as he's strong enough I want him gone."

"Well, don't be in a hurry, lass. English, Irish, Scots, or Welsh... under their trousers they're all the same. No need to throw a perfectly good one away. He may grow on you yet. Let's take a closer look, shall we?"

Catherine watched as Martha bustled around, humming to herself as she peeked under bandages, heaved Jamie over onto his back, felt his forehead, and poked and prodded him all over.

"Happy is the maid that's married to a mitherless son."

"What's that, Martha?"

"Eh? What?"

"What did you just say?"

"Oh heavens, child! You know me. I'm always blathering on about something, and half the time I dinna know what it is."

But it always ends up meaning something, Catherine thought. "Will he be alright?"

"Hard to tell, girl. You've done a good job here, but you're going to have to find some way to warm him or he's like to die of shock and cold before the morning," the older woman said, giving her a meaningful look. "We need to keep his wounds clean and hope there's no infection, but he's a strong lad, as tough as any Highlander I've ever seen. I would never have guessed he was aught else from the brave show he gave in the courtyard. You must be very proud. If you can get him warm and keep away the fever, he'll soon be right as rain. He's a bonny fellow isn't he, lass? Not as broad as the O'Connor, but quicker I'd wager, and taller, too." She passed her fingers over his face, feeling the swelling and bones. "Nose is broken. Twice in a short span, I'd say. He's a belligerent lad, or a clumsy one, but I can set it straight. It won't spoil his looks, Cat. I promise you."

Catherine turned away, hiding a guilty flush. There was a slight cracking sound and she cringed in sympathy. She was glad he was unconscious. He'd suffered more than enough for one day.

"There… that should do it! We'll shift him over on his side now. He'll breathe easier and it'll be better for his poor bloody back."

As Catherine moved to help her, Martha flipped back his blanket and grinned. "Will you look at that, lass! Faith, but I was wrong! They're not all the same under their trousers. I'll wager he outdoes the O'Connor there, too!"

"Martha! Leave the poor man alone!" Catherine cried, scandalized.

"Oh hush, child! Every man has one. Why, I used to wash your father's when he was a bair—"

"Martha, please! I don't want to hear it. That's quite enough!"

Martha grinned. "Well lass... I'll be off now and leave you to it. Take good care of your man, lucky girl! You *must* keep him warm. I'll be back to check on him in the morning."

Catherine gave her a hug and walked her to the entrance, then returned to her charge. Long lashes and tangled strands of hair framed sculpted cheekbones marred with livid black and purple bruises. His face was drained of color and his full lips were tinged blue. He looked defenseless and forlorn, and her heart stirred with pity. She reached out her fingers and brushed back his hair. He *looked* like a motherless child. His skin was icy to her touch, and she remembered Martha's words, 'You're going to have to find some way to warm him or he's like to die of shock and cold.'

The blazing fire and several layers of furs and blankets had failed to warm him, and she hadn't brought him here to watch him die. Removing her clothing, she slid in beside him, gasping as she did. He was freezing! She piled on more furs and blankets and wrapped her arms around him, hugging him tight, trying to share her heat, but he felt like a block of ice and soon she was shivering and her teeth were chattering, too. Desperate to warm him and herself, she began vigorously chafing his arms and legs, continuing for almost an hour, not stopping until she felt life returning to his body. Exhausted, she rested her head against his shoulder and her hand on his hip. Moaning and mumbling something incoherent, he reached for it, grasping it and pulling it down, cupping it over a huge erection. She tried to pull it back, but his grip was determined and strong.

"Aye, Molly, my love. That's it! Right there. You do wonders with those fingers, sweetheart."

She narrowed her eyes, wondering who Molly was, and indulged herself for a moment, letting her hand close round him. She'd never had a sweetheart. No man but Cormac had been tempted to cut himself on her tongue, sword, and bones. But she'd grown up with the frank talk of the village and castle women; and, accepted as one of their fellows, she'd been privy to the unguarded talk of the men. She'd long been curious—he *was* her husband, and there was no one to know.

He was hot and heavy in her hand, and he jumped to her touch. Feeling just a little guilty, she caressed him gingerly, amazed he could feel so hard and solid, yet silky smooth. She'd grown up around men wearing kilts and seen a kit or two in her day, but she'd never touched one. Martha was right! He was certainly—

He began to grind against her. Mortified, she yanked her hand away, placing it firmly against his chest. He groped for it and found it, gripping it tight, but this time he was content to leave it there. He quieted against her, clutching her hand to his breast, and she relaxed and closed her eyes, listening to the sounds of distant water, her restless horse, and her husband's even breathing close against her cheek. He smelled of camphor, herbs, and whiskey, and it lulled her to sleep.

She woke several hours later. Years of traveling and adventuring with her father's men had taught her to sleep anywhere and wake when she needed, completely alert. It was still full dark, but dawn was coming soon. Somehow, in the night, they'd shifted positions and now he was holding her, one hand in her hair, the other clasping her breast. Curse the man, he never stopped, not even unconscious or in his sleep! She batted his hand away, removed his arm from around her waist, and slipped from the bed, shivering and hugging herself in the chill air. He'd warmed up considerably overnight and his color had returned. She dressed quickly, added coals to the fire, checked his bandages, and adjusted his covers, and then hurried back to town, crawling into bed with Mary as the village started to wake.

She stood by the river with her father, just past the footbridge, watching closely as he used light green silk to wrap a jay's and a peacock's feather around a body of deep green mohair. "There, Cat, like this," he whispered, handing her the fly, a delicate work of art and beauty. "Only the finest will do for the bravest of fish." The sun was high overhead, dappling the water and warming her face despite the cold spray from the salmon leap just yards away. The fish surged through the booming water, powerful, glorious, iridescent in the light, and her father took her shoulder and passed her the rod.

She jerked awake, startled from her sleep by a booming at the door. A moment later, it cracked open on its hinges, as Mary shrieked in alarm.

"Good Christ, you fools! What are you doing? What is wrong with you?" Catherine shouted, leaping from the bed.

"We've been looking for you, lass," Jerrod said. "The prisoner's missing and we feared he'd taken you with him."

"Who's going to mend my door, Jerrod Drummond? I've lost my man and now you're pulling my house down about my ears!" Mary cried.

"Hush now, Mary. We were that worried about the lass. I'll have a couple of the boys set it straight, right away."

"What do you mean, he's missing? And didn't Alan tell you where I was?"

"We didn't think to ask him until just now, Cat. No one knew you were gone until Donald sent for you and you didn't appear. We thought he might have come to steal you. He wouldn't have known you were already married, and you'd make a bloody fine prize."

"Aye, like a prize heifer or mare, only with lands and money attached."

"No need to get your dander up, lass. It is what it is."

"So while I was visiting with Mary, you lot were busy boasting and drinking and breaking down poor widow's doors, while a man who was strung in the air, whipped bloody, and nigh froze, detached himself and went for a stroll?"

Jerrod blushed red and grunted, shifting uncomfortably. "There's no call to be cruel, lass. He escaped... one way or another, likely with help. We're thinking he might have had others with him. A raiding party. Donald wants you back at the castle. Now."

"Pah! What nonsense! He was in no shape to be stealing a bride after the harsh treatment you gave him, Jerrod, but if he was, than mayhap I want to meet him and leave you lot behind. He could be the man of my dreams. You all want to sell me to the O'Connor and ship me to Ireland anyway."

"You know I didn't approve it, Cat. And you've seen to it for now in any case."

"Aye, until one of you can find my husband and make me a widow, then marry me off with blood on my hands. The man kept me safe. He did me no harm, Jerrod."

"You've too soft a heart, lass. Cruel times call for cruel measures. Like yesterday."

"I never saw my father do that to a man."

"No, lass, you didn't. Your father had men to do it for him," Jerrod said with a hard look. "So you're not coming, then? What shall I tell Donald?"

"Tell him I'm a married woman, and as he's not my husband, I'm free to do as I please."

"He's your chieftain, Cat."

"Aye, but these lands were left to me. I'm laird here. Not Donald, and not my brother."

"You're a woman. Have a care not to push things too far."

She returned to her solar in her own good time,

indulged herself in a warm bath, changed into some warm and comfortable clothes, and lay down to rest. Martha would be watching over their patient in the daytime, and she would do the honors at night.

Donald himself came to find her later, barging in without knocking.

"Have you no manners then, Donald?"

"I'll show you mine if you show me yours, Cat."

She grinned, remembering the early years when she used to like him, and motioned gracefully for him to sit down. "How can I help you?"

He barely managed a stiff smile. They'd been rivals and adversaries too long. "I'll ask you to listen, Catherine… and think carefully on what I'm about to say. I'm well aware you've no liking for the O'Connor, but he would have treated you fairly and it would have been a good match. One your father would have approved of. Your wild behavior in chasing across the country after Alistair has put an end to that. No one outside the clan knows about your English husband and no one can. We'll find him and make you a widow soon enough.

"O'Connor was told you wouldn't accept him. He's left in a great fury and he'd not have you now if we begged him, but you're going to have to marry, girl, as soon as your Englishman is dead. You're the greatest prize in the Highlands right now and that bastard yesterday was only the first of many. The man who claims you, claims this castle, Catherine. And he has to be someone your clan approves.

"You think the man you captured was here to steal a bride?"

"I'm certain of it. We'll head out today, to catch

and kill him and whomever he's with, as a warning to others with the same idea, but they'll keep coming until someone succeeds or you're safely married. It would go ill for you, girl, if some backwoods North Country savage carried you off. Now, I'm willing to admit I've made some mistakes. I should never have considered sending you from your home. So what say we make a fair deal, lass? You'll not stray from the castle until the matter of your marriage is settled, and I'll not force a man on you that you don't want. I'll choose three, and then you choose the best of the lot."

"So… I'm to stay in the castle, forgo this and any future raids, and once you've murdered my husband, I'm to choose one of three men you will provide for me."

"Aye, the one you like the best."

"Change the boundary from the castle to the river, give me five men from which to choose instead of three, and swear if I marry again I'll remain here, and we'll have a deal, Donald."

Surprised at how easily she'd agreed, Donald fought to suppress a look of triumph, and held out his hand, clasping hers.

"Deal!" they said in unison.

"Thank you, cousin," Donald said. "I will dare to hope this signals warmer relations between the two of us." He gave her a formal bow and left.

Catherine couldn't believe her luck. They'd be gone for days on a wild goose chase without wondering why she hadn't offered to go with them, leaving her free to deal with the Englishman without fear of discovery. She was always heading off alone to go fishing or for a walk, and no one would question her comings and goings. It was perfect, and with any luck she'd have her inconvenient husband well on his way before they returned.

Nine

DESPITE CATHERINE AND MARTHA'S BEST EFFORTS, their patient developed a fever, and for three days and nights they didn't know if he'd survive. One of them was with him at all times, changing his dressings, giving him liquids, cooling him down, and making him as comfortable as they could. He was often delirious, and when he wasn't shouting, laughing, or joking, or muttering sweet nothings to Mary, Molly, or Bess, he was pawing at Catherine's bosom or trying to kiss her, but by the fourth day, the fever was receding and the worst had past. His back was healing nicely and the swelling around his nose and face was almost gone.

Catherine sat beside him and brushed back his hair. There was something boyish and appealing about some men when they slept. Martha had been by earlier and shaved him and washed his hair. She seemed to be enjoying Catherine's husband just a bit too much. There was much to appreciate, though, from a physical standpoint. He was a strikingly handsome man with a beautiful body, as Martha delighted in pointing out. Catherine had admired the statue of David while in

Europe, but she liked her husband's body more. She spread her fingers, absently caressing his shoulder, and squealed when he caught her arm, pulling her down against him.

"I've caught you, minx," he growled "and now you'll pay the forfeit or I'll send you back to your husband."

His hands were everywhere, reaching under her shirt and tugging at her clothes. She tried to push him away but he rolled on top of her, trapping her with his chest and leg. He took her lips in a searing kiss, almost devouring her, and his hands wandered to her breast, tweaking its peak through her clothing, between thumb and forefinger. She squealed and struggled to push him off, but as the kiss deepened, she started to respond. She stopped her struggles and relaxed against him, wrapping her arms around his neck, remembering another kiss that had tasted of whiskey and rain, what seemed a lifetime ago. He *was* her husband. He'd soon be gone, and she might never have a better opportunity to enjoy a man's kisses. She closed her eyes and felt his lips as they nibbled and caressed hers, and she tried to respond in kind. She groaned when his tongue plunged into her mouth, causing sensations that tingled throughout her body. His fingers still played at her peak and she arched her back like a wanton, inviting more.

"You love that, don't you, Molly girl," he whispered.

Molly again! "Damn it, get off of me, you oaf!" She shoved him away and sat up straight, clutching at her shirt, red-faced and humiliated. She should have known. He was delirious and he was adulterous! Making love to another woman while he was in bed

with his wife! "Bastard!" She shoved his shoulder hard
and tried to climb from the bed.

"If you touch her again I'll kill you. I'll cut off
your balls and shove them down your throat. I should
have killed you years ago. Hit *me* if you want to hit
something, you pious fucking hypocrite. But I promise
you I'll hit you ba—"

"Stop it, English! You're talking to yourself. You
have a fever. There's no one here but you and me.
You're scaring me!" she said, shaking him by the arm.

"Eh? Is that you, mouse? Come to sit with me in
the dark? Come to play?" He pulled her down into
his arms, and tucked her underneath him. "You're a
brave wee mouse. You came to fetch me and now I've
caught you."

He threaded his hands through her hair, cupping
her head and seeking her lips again before trailing hot
kisses down her throat. She knew he was still delirious
and rambling, but at least now, he was kissing the right
person. She tried to edge away, but he was sprawled
on top of her, pawing at her clothes. She wiggled and
squirmed and he pulled and tugged and somehow she
was naked. A thrill of anticipation and fear coursed
through her, mixed with curiosity and something
else. *He's my husband. It's allowed. This might be my
only chance.* She ceased her struggles and lay very still,
holding her breath.

He pulled her close and held her tight against him
as one hand roamed her body, squeezing, kneading,
and petting. It was damp and cold in the cave, and
his body was hot on top of hers. She arched into him,
drawn to his heat. He muttered something incoherent.

His lips brushed her throat, her collarbone, and then trailed wet kisses along the outer curve of her breast and fastened on her nipple. A new sort of thrill, an exquisite aching pulse, traveled from the tip of her breast to the tip of her toes. His hot mouth closed around her and he tasted her with his tongue. She gasped for breath and whimpered. Her thighs were slick from her own moisture and an exquisite heavy throbbing was building between her legs. His tongue swirled lazy patterns across her breasts and she pushed against him, uncertain how to relieve it but yearning for something more. He pressed against her and she held him tight, her back pressed against the wall of the cave, and then she felt it. She peered in the dark to look at her hand, and knew it was sticky with blood.

"Enough, English. You're tearing your bandages. You'll hurt yourself," she said, trying to wriggle free, but he didn't seem to hear her. He was rocking against her now and she could feel his shaft, rubbing and prodding, seeking entry to her core. Part of her wanted him to stop—one good shove and he'd tumble to the floor—but she didn't want to hurt him, and though the spell was broken, she still wanted to know. She'd be sending him on his way soon. She had no intention of marrying anyone else, and she might never know a man if not this one. No one would blame her if she ended up with child; they suspected she might be already.

Uncertain of exactly what she wanted, she wrapped her arms around his neck and opened herself to him, pressing against his length as he whispered endearments, caressing her with nimble fingers and claiming her lips in a wild kiss, plunging his tongue deep into her mouth. When he pushed hard against her, she allowed it, spreading her legs to accommodate him. He entered her in one brusque move.

He was too large! She felt invaded. He filled her and stretched her and all she felt was panic and stinging pain. She gasped in shock and pounded his shoulder, pushing him frantically away. "Get off! Get off! Get Off!"

"Mmmm." Still feverish, he mumbled something unintelligible and rolled over onto his back, one hand flung over his head.

If he called her Molly now, she swore she'd kill him! She snorted in disgust. The burning pain between her legs was cooling to an unpleasant ache. She supposed she was a woman now. It had all seemed quite pleasant, right up to the act itself, but she failed to see what was so wonderful that married women sighed for it, grown men killed for it, and poets and storytellers told tales about it. Well... she'd oft been called an unnatural woman. No doubt, somehow, she'd got it wrong. She didn't suppose it helped when one's partner was delirious and didn't even really know or care that one was there.

Unaccountably, she wanted to cry. Thunder rumbled in the distance, and a moment later rain fell hissing outside. Wiping away a tear, she settled along his length, pulled up the blankets, and slept until it passed.

Two days later, Jamie woke from a dream. It had been a jumbled, incoherent mess. He remembered bits and pieces… his father shouting… his mother's screams. He could see her with her back against a wall in the arms of a man who wasn't his father, staring at him with hatred, hissing at him to get away. He turned his head and opened his eyes. He was in a world of blackness, though slowly, moment by moment, it was taking on form. He wondered if he'd been mistaken after all. Perhaps there was an afterlife. If so, this must be hell. Still… he wasn't cold anymore, and his pain had greatly eased.

He tried to collect his thoughts. The last thing he remembered was hanging by his arms, wet and cold and dying. He caught a movement in a far corner, a thin sliver of light, and he heard someone humming. He tried to sit up, and fell back down immediately. Curse it, he was as weak as a kitten! The humming stopped and he felt a cool hand on his brow, and then a cup was placed to his lips. He drank something sweet and potent, and lay back against his pillow, exhausted. Pillow? There was a snap, a spark of light, and the smell of sulfur, then the lantern was lit. He winced, his eyes sore from the light.

He recognized her scent before he saw her, a heady musk of heather and pine. She sat beside him on a blanket in breeches and boots, her hair flowing loose, the same fetching gamine that had stirred his blood at the River Clyde. *Good God, but life's uncertain! One moment a fellow's dying, and the next he's falling in love.*

"Mouse?"

"Yes, English?"

"Why do I smell like a tavern?"

"You don't remember falling down drunk on our wedding night? I had to hunt you down in the tavern and drag you home."

He felt a moment's bewilderment, and then he chuckled. "I think not. But you *have* managed to bind me with silken cords and drag me to your lair."

"Yes, I have. The tables have turned, English. You're *my* prisoner now. It's about time you woke up." She studied him carefully, looking for any trace, any memory of the other night, but it was clear she'd left no impression. She was both relieved and disappointed, but she wasn't really surprised.

"How did I get here?"

"Like a sack of potatoes, English. I threw you over my mare and brought you. You were in a bad way. You've been here over a week now."

"And you've been taking care of me?"

"Sometimes me, sometimes my nurse, Martha. She's quite taken with you."

"Why?"

"She thinks you're bonny and braw and will breed fine sons."

"No, mouse. Why are you helping me?"

"Did you expect me to leave you to die?"

"Well… yes. I rather thought that was your intention when you failed to fling yourself in my arms and claim me as your man."

"I was betrothed, and you are a great impediment to a useful marriage. Had I claimed you, you'd have lost your head in a heartbeat."

"As opposed to taking their time and pleasure over it."

"I'm sorry for it, English, but there was naught else I could do."

"My name is Jamie, love. Do you know, my dear, for complete strangers we share a great deal in common. We both find ourselves saddled with inconvenient spouses."

He accepted the cup of tea she passed him, enjoying himself as she plumped a pillow and helped ease him into a sitting position. "Now tell me, sweetheart, if I'm so great an impediment, why *did* you save me? Wouldn't it have suited you better to see me dead?"

"*I* didn't want the betrothal, so for me, it's very useful to be married to you. It wouldn't be at all convenient if you were dead." Although it would have been… so long as they'd never realized who he really was.

"Ah! I see."

He seemed genuinely disappointed and she relented a little. "Well, there was that… and I also felt I owed you something. Despite your boorishness and ill manners, you did come to my aid at the River Clyde."

"How awkward it must have been for you, indebted to such a lout."

"Indeed. We're even now though, English. Or we will be once you're on your way."

"My dear child! I'm shocked and hurt. Why so eager to be rid of me? It's most unseemly in a wife. I'm usually accredited an interesting fellow by the ladies. I'm sure I'll grow on you over time. There are few amongst the fairer set that can long resist my charms." He gave her an appealing grin.

She almost answered with a grin of her own, and then she remembered Molly. "Is that so? You'll permit me to say I'm surprised. I've found you to be highhanded, smug, and... conceited. You flail about and cry out in your sleep, and every time I've seen you, you've smelled like a distillery. I can't say I find that appealing."

"That's hardly fair! I'm a British peer. I can't help but be highhanded, conceited, and smug. As to the rest, I'm an invalid. I assure you, on most occasions, it's the ladies who flail about and cry out in my bed."

She snorted and rose to her feet, turning her head to hide the crimson flush staining her cheeks.

"Why is it again? That I smell like a tavern?"

"It's the whiskey. We've been using it for medicinal purposes. Why did you come, English? What do you want from me?"

"My name is Jamie. James Sinclair. I came to find you. You're my wife now, my responsibility."

"In name only. That's no reason to travel for days in hostile territory risking accident, capture, and death."

"Would you believe me if I said I was smitten the moment I first beheld you, and I couldn't eat, drink, or sleep soundly again until I held you in my arms?"

"No," she said flatly.

"I thought not. You don't strike me as the romantic sort. Well... has it occurred to you this business might be terribly inconvenient for me as well? I'm badly in need of funds, my dear. I have a lovely cow-eyed heifer... er... heiress... waiting for me back home. One that doesn't bite or beat me, and whose family don't wish me dead. I can hardly marry her if I can't be rid of you."

Ah, yes, of course! She should have known. Now it was she who was stung. "*You don't strike me as the romantic sort.*" Well… no point in holding that against him, she didn't strike anyone else that way, either. When they looked at her, they saw barrels of whiskey and stacks of gold. "I've explained to you, an annulment would inconvenience me right now. Besides, I'm needed here. I can't go with you."

"I'm sorry, mouse, but I really must insist."

"You're in no position to insist on anything, English."

"It's Jamie."

"My family calls me Cat. Why do you insist on calling me mouse… *English?*"

"Because you're such a shy and timid little thing, my love, and when I first saw you, I wanted to scoop you up and put you in my pocket."

She looked at him carefully, and then threw him a wineskin. "I've brought you a treat. If you're going to smell like it, you might as well enjoy it. There's water over there, and I've brought you biscuits and cheese. Martha will come and check on you tonight. Save your strength. You'll be needing it. You'll have to leave here soon, before my cousin returns, or you'll be trapped here all winter."

"Well, that hardly seems an evil fate, what with one's loving wife close by to keep one warm." He winced as a wrapped bundle landed on his chest with a heavy thud. "Good lord, girl! Are these your biscuits? Remind me not to dismiss my cook."

She turned to go, ignoring him.

"Wait a moment! Hellcat… Mouse!"

She stopped at the entrance and sighed, then turned to face him. "What?"

"Thank you… for saving my life."

Catherine regarded him steadily, and then nodded. "Thank you… *Jamie*… for saving mine." She slipped out the entrance a moment later and was gone.

Jamie smiled and stretched, groaning as his tortured muscles and tender back complained. His fair maiden had a heart, albeit a flinty one. She'd not abandoned him to torture and death, and she'd nursed him back to health. That was a novelty. No one had ever nursed him before that he could recall. There were unexpected advantages to having a wife, even a bad-tempered, inconvenient one. He grinned. If she thought to use him to keep another at bay, she was badly mistaken. He would bring her to London, and then, at his leisure, he'd decide if he wanted to keep her, or get an annulment and send her back home. She had a streak of honor, his little hellcat. Too bad for her he didn't. As soon as he was well enough, he'd take her with him, bound and gagged and slung over his saddle if need be. A vision of her fetching behind, laid across his lap and bouncing in front of him as he made his way home, brought a wicked smile to his lips as he drifted off to sleep.

It came as a great surprise two days later when old Martha came with her three strapping sons. They knocked him on the head, bound and gagged him, and put him in a dinghy, rowing him out to toss him aboard a waiting clipper with orders he not be let loose until he was over the border and well on his way to London.

Ten

JAMIE RESTED ON HIS BACK, HIS LONG FRAME BRACKETED by two plump redheads, a pretty pair who looked so much alike they might have been twins. He yawned, stretched, and spread his arms wide, bringing his hands to rest on full, firm breasts. He laid there, eyes closed, a smile on his lips, as he captured nipples to his left, and his right. The girl on his left—Lucy, if he recalled—rewarded him by finding his shaft with her stubby little fingers, stroking and squeezing him back. He moaned and turned his head to kiss her partner. Daisy… Dolly? Whoever she was, she was an angel, and her intrepid little fingers joined Lucy's, playing expertly with his scrotum and chasing all his cares away. He released plump breasts and chuckled, ruffling both their hair, pulling one and then the other to his mouth for a hot, slow kiss before guiding them down his chest and abdomen to the thrusting erection that strained and twitched for their attention. "Sweet, sweet angels," he murmured, before losing himself in a haze of warm flesh, clever fingers, and hot seeking mouths.

Some time later, sated and already a little bored, he leaned across Dolly… or Daisy, patting her on the rump as he pulled the bell cord. "Up you get, my darlings," he said, planting a kiss on the back of Dolly's neck before trapping Lucy's foot and planting one there as well.

She shrieked and kicked, laughing and giggling, "That tickles, my lord!"

He grinned and released her. They were sweet, accommodating lasses. Their tender ministrations had eased his night, letting him sleep, banishing, if only for a short while, all his troubles, but the light of day was cracking through the thickly draped window, and it must be nearly noon. His creditors would be at the doorstep soon if not already, and it was time for the girls to leave.

"Ah, Sullivan! Good day to you. Ladies, this is my man Sullivan. There's no finer fellow in all of London. Sullivan, would you be so kind as to have Cook send us some chocolate? Oh, and bring me my purse if you please."

Lucy squealed and clapped her hands with excitement. "Chocolate, my lord? They say it's wondrous good!"

"Aye, bloody marvelous is what I've heard," Dolly chimed in. "Never tried it, though. It's only the quality can afford that."

"Well, my dears, it's criminal ladies as wondrous fair as your sweet selves have never tried it. Have no fear, we shall soon set all to rights," Jamie said, rising from the bed.

"Milord, if you please! Put some clothing on! I've no mind to watch your private bits dangling about.

The ladies may not object, but I most certainly do," Sullivan huffed as he returned with the purse.

Jamie leaned into Dolly's shoulder. "He's Irish, my dear, up from the country and a prude. Pay him no mind. Hand me my breeches, will you, love?"

Giggling, Dolly handed him his breeches and he hopped over to the fauteuil, pulling them on as the ladies searched for their discarded dresses and hose. They hurried over to join him by the fire, squealing with excitement when a footman arrived with an ornate chocolate pot and elegant porcelain cups. It was an unheard-of luxury to them, and they crowded around Jamie, leaning over his shoulders in awe and delight as they watched him prepare it and pour.

"Ladies?" he said, offering a delicate cup to one and then the other. "This is a magical beverage brewed for a mighty God of fertility on the far side of the world. Only the richest and most favored there may drink it. Savor it, my loves. Sip it like so, and enjoy its aroma as well as its flavor." He showed them how, and they gravely followed suit, gasping in astonished pleasure.

"Oh, my lord, 'tis better than anything! It's even better than fucking!"

"For shame, girls! It might be better than coupling with the dour Mr. Sullivan, but surely not with me," he said, pretending to be affronted and sending them into gales of laughter. "Sullivan? Would you care to join us?"

"Er… no thank you, milord," Sullivan said, eyeing Jamie's bounteous half-clad companions and backing away.

Jamie took his time with his chocolate, teasing his companions and enjoying their obvious pleasure and excitement as they savored the unexpected treat. When they were finished, he tossed them the purse and they scrambled for it, wrestling and giggling.

"Thank you, ladies, for your gracious company. I do apologize for cutting our visit short, but I've a great deal to attend to, I'm afraid. Mr. Sullivan? Would you kindly take the young ladies to the kitchen for a meal? I can attest to their appetite."

"Of course, milord."

"Thank you, and when they've finished please arrange a carriage to take them home. Ladies?" he said, bowing and taking their hands one by one for a lingering kiss. "*Adieu.*"

Starry-eyed and blushing, they followed Mr. Sullivan from the room.

Jamie watched them leave, then closed his eyes and sighed. He felt bored, restless, and tired, all at the same time. He should have let them stay to wile away the afternoon. They'd not have minded. They would have been glad for it. But he was in a foul mood and he hadn't the patience to be kind, nor the inclination to be cruel. He finished dressing, went to the mantel, stirred the fire, and poured himself a drink. Sitting down, he crossed booted feet against the windowsill and tossed the brandy back.

"Rather early for that isn't it, sir?"

"A pox on you, Sullivan. Mind your own business."

"You *are* my business, sir. The… ladies… have left."

"Yes? So? What of it? You have something to say? Spit it out, man."

"Very well. How is it you can afford to be so generous to these young women when you cannot settle the household accounts?"

"What? Have I forgotten to pay the staff again? Have no fear. I'll be in funds again this evening."

"That's not the point, milord."

"Then what exactly is the point? I'm losing patience."

"A carriage? Chocolate, breakfast, and a purse? These are luxuries we can ill afford, milord. Yet you bestow them on strumpets, treating them as if they were the finest ladies of the court."

"Good Christ, man! Since when do I need to justify myself to you or anyone else? Do you begrudge them the chocolate? You saw how pleased they were. They're good-hearted lasses, their life is hard, and it's likely the first and only time they'll enjoy such a treat."

"It's the purse I begrudge, milord! It's not you who'll be turning creditors from the door all day. It's not you who has to go to the market or tell the servants they must wait for their pay. You gave then two guineas, milord!"

"Ah… did I? Well, you're right then, Sullivan. It was far too much. Why didn't you say something sooner? You might have warned me. Isn't that your job?"

"If you will excuse me, milord."

"Don't scamper off in a snit. You're worse than a wife with her courses! I shall be in funds tonight. Enough to settle the household accounts at least, and pay you and the staff."

"You'll play cards then, milord," Sullivan said with marked disapproval.

"Yes, I will, and then I'll play with the lovely Lady Beaton."

"And what if you lose, milord? There was never a bad situation that couldn't be made worse."

"Damn it, man, I won't lose!" Jamie growled, finally losing his patience. "And if I wanted Granny O'Sullivan's advice I'd have kept her here in London. What do you suggest I do? My ever-loving sire left me properties without the funds to manage them, and my king has turned his back on me, stripped me of my commission, and forbidden me the court. Would you have me join Gervaise and his men and traipse about Europe killing and maiming? Because I promise you, the thought grows more appealing by the day!"

"You might beg an audience with the king, milord. If you present yourself humbly and explain the circumstances he—"

"Enough, Sullivan! You go too far! I'll not be lectured on humility by a stiff-necked Irish rebel who'd have hanged with his poor old mother rather than bend the knee! You've no talent for it yourself, so don't be thinking to teach it to others, and try to remember you're my servant, not my schoolmaster!"

"I most humbly beg your pardon, milord," Sullivan replied with a sniff and an exaggerated bow. "It's still a great pity you're not free to marry the heiress he chose."

"As opposed to my Scottish wife, Kieran? She was a waspish little ragamuffin, wasn't she? But I confess I found myself somewhat taken with her."

"I've never known you not to be taken with a young lady, and as I recall she was not a little thing but rather more of an Amazon."

"Oh, well, perhaps you're right. At least she would have seemed so to you. In any case, it was deuced uncivil of her to have me bashed on the head and trundled away like some press-ganged sot."

"Indeed, milord, a proper lady would have waited meekly for you to abduct her."

"One doesn't abduct one's own wife, one retrieves her. She *is* in effect my property now, mine to command."

"It might have been useful, milord, had you found fit to share that with her. Better half hanged than ill married, as they say back home."

"As always, Sullivan, I'm deeply indebted to you for your wise and pithy comments, but I don't need you to remind me. Shall I hire an army and go to collect her? Hire a witch to curse her to death and make myself a widower? Perhaps send her a gift of poisoned gloves or sweets? What would you have me do? If you've no practical suggestions, might I suggest you find some suitable task with which to occupy yourself so I'm reminded just why it is I'm supposed to pay you?"

Waving Sullivan away, Jamie slouched down comfortably, threw back his drink, and tossed the glass in the fireplace. Something else for Sullivan to wring his hands over as he tried to prevent his errant charge from going to hell. He was too late though. If any place was hell it had to be the endless succession of dreary days in the choked air, filth, and tedium that was London. Jamie had been to heaven once or twice, though, for a fleeting second, in the warm and willing embrace of one of his whores. A pox on Sullivan and his miser's ways! They deserved their chocolate if only for that.

He'd always had a soft spot for serving maids and strumpets. They'd been his only source of comfort and affection as a child. It was the cook who'd told him stories, the washerwoman who bandaged his knee, and the maidservants who hugged him when he'd felt frightened and alone. As he grew, some offered comfort in other ways. At fourteen, when he'd been caught in the stables with a maid who warmed his father's bed, he'd suffered a vicious whipping without flinching or making a sound. He'd stared straight ahead, his eyes black with hatred and contempt, but when his father turned the whip upon the girl, he'd torn it from his hands, thrashing him until he begged for mercy on the ground. The man had never raised a whip or fist to him again. It was years in the past, but the memories remained as clear as if they'd happened yesterday.

He'd been sent to school immediately after that. It was nearly as savage as his home, but he'd grown up tough and resilient and he'd thrived. Unlike most of his friends who devoted themselves to the pleasures of drink and fucking, he'd been captivated by his studies and the world of ideas. Enthralled with the philosophy of John Locke, he joined in impassioned discussions in taverns and in coffee houses, excitedly arguing that a man should use evidence and his own reason to search for truth, rather than accept the pronouncements of family, church, and state. It bordered on sedition, smacked of heresy, and was heady stuff to a cynical, angry youth who had to defy his father's judgment or accept himself as something misbegotten and of little worth. His friends mouthed the words, but he'd lived them and used them to cut himself free.

Hated by his sire and abandoned by his dam, he'd left to try his fortunes in the court of the restored King Charles II, where men like Sedly, Buckingham, Rochester, and Charles himself, set a glorious example of sin and dissipation no callow youth could ever hope to match. He'd done his best, though, trying to make a mark in a court and an age where treachery and adultery were the fashion, and cynicism, cruelty, and barbed wit were the qualities most admired. He played at intrigue, cards, and mistresses, and when his father disowned him, he made himself useful to both the king and his younger brother, the Duke of York, playing at soldier, diplomat, and spy.

He acquitted himself well, made a name for himself in mercenary engagements, and showed he could be trusted with delicate matters concerning England's dealings with the Netherlands, France, and Spain. He'd proven himself useful in matters of internal security as well, and five years ago, after a plot to assassinate the royal brothers on their way home from the races ended before it began, Charles named him Earl of Carrick and rewarded him with an Irish estate that had once belonged to Sullivan.

Though the principal conspirators were minor figures, Charles used the incident to dispose of several of his enemies in the Whig party, including its leaders, Lord Russell and Algernon Sidney. Even John Locke, with his questionable views, was dragged into the net, though he heeded a friendly warning and escaped to Holland. Of those arrested, only Charles's bastard son, Monmouth, the congenital conspirer, had been allowed to wriggle free.

The whole business had left a foul taste in Jamie's mouth and led to a growing disenchantment with Charles, the Stuarts, and kings and politics in general, but it hadn't stopped him from accepting the reward. Charles was tight-fisted with everyone but his family and his mistresses, and it was the only tangible reward from him Jamie was likely to get. It didn't help that Kieran O'Sullivan was one of the few truly principled men he'd met. He'd made him his steward, leaving him to manage and care for the people and property that had once been his.

When Jamie's older half-brother died suddenly, followed by his father less than a year later, he'd become Earl of Carlyle, too. He couldn't help but smile at the thought that his father's worst nightmare had come to pass. The demon seed, the bastard son his wife had foisted upon him as she cuckolded him over and over, had inherited it all.

He'd thought he didn't need the Irish properties anymore, and he'd entered into an arrangement with Sullivan, keeping half the income and leasing him and his future heirs the lands in perpetuity for one pound. He'd slept a far sight better at night, and when he'd learned his vindictive father had left him mortgaged properties, crushing debts, and no funds, he hadn't worried overmuch. He was young and strong and the future looked bright. He began a small breeding operation with Sullivan's Irish mares and a champion stud he'd acquired from Charles, and when the man died almost two years ago, he'd continued to serve the Stuart cause.

He'd taken pains to maintain good relations with both Charles's Catholic brother and his Protestant bastard son, but he knew the Duke of Monmouth was rash and ambitious, and he'd stood well to the side when, three months after his uncle James ascended the throne, Monmouth raised an army and declared himself king. James wasn't the sentimental sort. Nephew or no, the duke's handsome head had rolled, coming to a stop as a decoration atop Tower Bridge. Though it took several swings of the axe to accomplish the task, the duke was more fortunate than his followers, many of whom had their guts ripped out and their bodies quartered before their heads joined him there.

Jamie had chosen correctly. A quick conversion to Catholicism and his star was on the rise again. He'd made himself as useful to the new king as he'd been to his brother. He served and charmed and maintained a presence at court, and the king, anxious to build and strengthen his Catholic support, had sponsored a match that would provide him with the funds he needed to secure his position and his lands. He'd been so close.

And then the mouse had come along and he'd made a terrible mistake. By marrying the girl, he'd ruined himself. After his bride had disposed of him so precipitously, he'd returned to London to find Father Francis and Gervaise had been stirring up trouble with the king. Father Francis had trumpeted to all and sundry that he'd mocked the king's gift of an heiress by marrying a battlefield whore as a drunken prank, in a ceremony that had been witnessed, consummated, and was valid in the eyes of the church. Gervaise had accused him of abandoning his post to chase after her.

He'd defended himself strenuously, arguing that the girl was well bred one of His Majesties loyal subjects whose family was useful to the king. He maintained he'd been protecting her the only way he could, but his protest had fallen on deaf ears, and without her presence to show them, his cause was lost. Despite his best efforts, hard work, and years of loyal service to the Stuart cause, his erstwhile patron was inclined to believe the worst. The king turned his back, withdrew his favor, and Jamie was no longer welcome at court. He was suspect now—at best a disreputable lout who'd behaved irresponsibly, failing in his commission and insulting his king, at worst a rebel sympathizer, and either way, a fool.

He might have groveled and begged, pleading his case and reminding the king of his past service. He knew it was expected, and given his usefulness he might have been forgiven, but he was far too proud. And so he sat, abandoned and disgraced, exiled from the glittering court that had been his livelihood and promised him a future. There'd be no quick and easy annulment, no rich heiress, and no further commissions or postings from His Majesty James II.

Well, that was almost a year ago. With a useless wife and an unforgiving monarch, rich mistresses and cards were among the few sources of reliable income he had left, unless he wished to return to selling his sword on the continent, a thought that grew more appealing by the day. He still had hopes for his stable, though. His old drinking partner, Buckingham, had sent two of his mares to be covered, and where Buckingham went, others would follow. He allowed his mistresses to give him gifts and settle some of his debts, a time-honored tradition amongst the young gallants of London, and he invested every penny he could in his horses.

Jamie shifted in his seat and looked out the window. The afternoon was almost gone. The dark would be descending on him soon. He rose and poured himself another drink. The fire had gone out and a dank chill permeated the room. He considered calling Sullivan, but decided against it, not wanting another lecture about chocolate and whores and the price of coal. Besides, he was rather enjoying feeling sorry for himself while sitting in the dark. The last time he'd done so was in that blasted cave in the north of Scotland, with his prickly ragamuffin wife.

He ran his fingers lightly over his nose, tracing the bridge and feeling the slight indent with a wry chuckle. *Better half hanged than an ill wife.* It was she who'd brought him to this pass. Catherine... Cat... hellcat... She'd been a ferocious armful, his little mouse, with her feline eyes, her knife and sword, and her sharp little teeth. He dreamt of her sometimes. Dreamt she was tight beside him, silky smooth and as sweet and delicious as the hot whiskey and honey drink she'd fed him. It was hard to remain annoyed with her when he had dreams like that.

He grinned and tossed back his drink. The jade had been quicker than he was, he'd give her that. Clever girl, she'd beaten him fair and square, tossing him out on his arse before he could plan her abduction... before he could even stand! He lifted his glass in a silent toast. *Long life and good health to you wherever you are, Cat Drummond. There's never been a man or a woman to cozen Jamie Sinclair as neat and as thorough as you did*. Ah, well. She'd proved entertaining and his admiration was genuine. It was too damned bad that the things that afforded him amusement were always so bad for his health.

Eleven

JAMIE HAD AN ASSIGNATION WITH THE LOVELY LADY Beaton at her theatre box before going to play cards. A good comedy should cheer him up, and Lady Beaton was his favorite type of woman: mature, no nonsense, sure of herself and what she wanted. She was a lady who'd survived a difficult marriage and was intent on enjoying the fruits of her widowhood. She had no interest in remarrying and looked only for congenial company and physical satisfaction. Pleasingly plump, of cheerful temperament, with a bawdy sense of humor and a genuine talent for friendship, she was the closest thing to a friend Jamie had besides Sullivan. Unfortunately, her box was empty, though her footman was waiting with a letter. Her elderly mother, it seemed, had taken ill, and she had rushed to her countryseat to be with her.

He looked about the theatre. The pit was full. Lords and ladies, orange girls and apprentices, shopkeepers and laborers, crowded elbow to elbow to see Dryden's latest *oeuvre*. He was debating enjoying the box and staying to watch the play—it wouldn't hurt to be seen there, still of interest and still in London—when a rustle of skirts and a possessive hand on his arm caused him to turn his head.

"Jamie dear, you've been abandoned! How very sad! Has the widow found herself a new toy and left you standing all alone?"

His lips twisted in annoyance. It wouldn't have mattered to him if she had. Their relationship was not exclusive. They both enjoyed other lovers. The thing that set Mary Beaton apart was that they were also good friends. "Good evening, Caro. Are you out taking your husband for a walk?"

Lady Caroline Ware had been a merchant's wife before catching the eye of Lord Ware. He'd made her a widow and then made her his wife, and soon after, she'd made him a cuckold. They had a brood of six children, though it was widely rumored none of them were his. Lord Ware doted on his commanding wife, and if she wished to accessorize with lovers, he chose to indulge her. It kept her happy and was cheaper than keeping her in jewels, and he consoled himself with numerous diversions of his own.

Temperamental and controlling, she was the kind of woman Jamie tried to avoid, but he'd made the mistake of sharing a brief sexual encounter with her and she'd been determined to bring him to heel ever since. Certain of her charms, ruthless in her pursuits, and vicious when crossed, Jamie's lack of interest was a challenge and an affront, and having trapped and cornered him, she was determined not to let him go. She clung to his arm, whispering comments he couldn't hear above the catcalls, whistles, and running commentary from the unruly crowd. After the theatre, she followed as he joined a crowd of well-heeled rogues and reprobates heading to a gathering hosted by the Duke of Buckingham.

Best friend and cousin of kings, a congenital devotee of the game of thrones, Buckingham—or Bucks, as his friends called him—may well have been mad, or at least so highly bred one was hard-pressed to tell the difference. His father had been a favorite of Charles I, and some said much of the family's influence came from the intimate services his jaded and calculating sire had provided for the smitten James I. An accomplished musician and singer, a sparkling wit and unsurpassed mimic, he was a natural entertainer who could be counted on to charm or provoke.

When his illicit connection with the Countess of Shrewsbury led to a duel in which her husband, the earl, was fatally wounded, Bucks had outraged the court by installing the widow in his house alongside his wife. Even so, rumor had it that living with both wife and mistress hadn't stopped him from enjoying a dalliance with one of the foremost male actors of the day. Whatever his faults—and they were many—he was good-humored, good-natured, and far too powerful for any king to arbitrarily spite or smite. He did what he would and favored whom he pleased. Jamie amused him—his discernment in matters of horseflesh and women impressed him, and he'd taken him into his circle years ago. It was one of the reasons Jamie was still accepted on the fringes of the court and not banished to the country or the continent.

When the party retired to the rooftop banquet room to indulge in music, wit, and wine, Jamie settled in the salon for a night of playing cards. Pouting, Lady Caroline followed him. Coming to stand behind him, she rested her hands on his shoulders and bent over to whisper in his ear.

"Surely there are other games you'd rather play tonight, my lord?" she teased, trailing her fingers along the nape of his neck and rumpling his hair.

He pulled away in annoyance. "Enough, Caro! Can't you see I'm occupied? Go find yourself a pretty boy somewhere and leave me in peace."

"I don't want a pretty boy. I want a big, bad man."

Her tongue flicked and darted in his ear and he stifled the urge to swat her as if she were a bothersome fly. She took the seat next to him and he sighed and picked up his cards. The cloying smell of countless burning candles, unwashed bodies, and sweet perfume was almost overpowering. He closed his eyes. The hum of muted conversation whirled around him, punctuated by the sound of clinking glasses, harsh laughter, and the roll and rattle of dice. He didn't feel comfortable in the room or in his skin.

He imagined for a moment the wild fragrance of the highlands and the faraway shriek of the eagle he'd watched from his perch on the mountain and wished himself far away, but the feel of Caroline's foot rubbing his crotch brought him back to the room. Reaching under the table, he gripped her ankle and shoved it away. The woman was vulgar and obvious and wouldn't take no for an answer. Despite her ample bosom and obvious

charms he had no interest in her at all. She had claws.
She wanted acolytes. She bored him.

"You can't always have what you want, Caro. I'm
not a boy, and I'm not in the mood to play with you.
I'd rather play at cards."

"Come now, Jamie," she purred, leaning into him.
"My husband is called away to Holland for several
months at least. I'm to be left all alone!"

"How fortunate for you both," he drawled,
returning his attention to his hand.

She narrowed her eyes and glared, snapping her
fan shut and shaking it like a furious little bee before
taking a breath and calming herself. "Jamie, you're
incorrigible!… Jamie!" She tapped his shoulder with
her fan, forcing him to attend her.

He sighed and pushed his cards away. "What,
Caroline? Have I not made myself clear?"

"*Lady* Caroline, and your pretended lack of interest
doesn't fool me at all. I've seen you watching and you
must know I watch you. They say you find yourself
without adequate funds." Her fingers brushed against
his shoulder, feathering the hair beneath his ear.

"What else do they say?" he asked dryly.

"They say you're more than adequate in other
ways, a fact I can attest to. We both have needs, and
happily, they seem to coincide. Why don't we offer
one another comfort, my dear? I sense we might
be very good friends. You might visit me while my
husband is away. You might even send your creditors
my way should we become… close friends."

"Am I to be your whore now, Caroline? How
much am I worth?" he asked pleasantly.

"My husband gives me a generous allowance. You need friends, Jamie. I can be a very good friend… or a very bad enemy."

He knew it to be true. It was said she'd made arrangements to have her servants slit the nose of a pretty young actress who'd dared to mock her in a recent play, and her latest lover had been set upon by thugs and nearly beaten to death just hours after leaving the theatre with a new conquest in tow. "I've seen you with your lovers, Caro. You require them to worship at your feet. That's never been my inclination," he said mildly.

"That's why you find yourself in your current circumstances, Jamie, forced to gamble and cheat to earn your bread." She drew her fingers across his cheek and reached under the table, squeezing him firmly through his breeches.

He caught her hand in a vice-like grip. "I prefer to choose my whores, Caro, not have them choose me. And I do not cheat. If you were a man, I'd have to call you out for that."

"Bastard!" She slapped him hard, the sharp crack causing heads to rise and necks to crane.

"You are making a spectacle of us, Caroline," Jamie said tiredly.

"Let them watch, you ingrate! You're nothing here. Nothing and no one! People talk about you. They pity you. They say the king is done with you and you've nothing of your own. I could help you return to favor and to court, and I can also complete your ruin!"

"Have at it, madam," he said with a shrug. "Though I daresay it's easy enough done that it should hardly be crowed about as an accomplishment. Now if you'll excuse me, this night has grown unbearably tedious. I believe I'll impose upon my lord Buckingham's hospitality and retire." He shoved his cards away and rose from the table.

Unaccustomed to defeat, Lady Ware rose with him, changing her tactics with the speed and assurance of a top-notch general. "Jamie, don't be like that," she pleaded, her voice husky and contrite.

"Return to your husband, madam. He's watching us from across the room. Perhaps he can find some use for you. I assure you I have none." His voice was loud and clear and carried to all corners of the room.

Lady Caroline gasped, outraged. "You dare to refuse me?" she hissed. "You think yourself better than me? You, who were scorned by your own father and now by the king? You're nothing but a penniless rogue. I'll arrange it so you'll not be received anywhere! You won't even be able to play cards. And when you've lost what little you have left and come prettily begging my forgiveness, I will spit in your face!"

"Pray wait until then and avoid doing so now, madam," Jamie said with a grimace of distaste as he wiped her spittle from his cheek.

"Careful man, watch your back and guard your vitals. 'Hell hath no fury,'" a drunken Buckingham chortled, enjoying the entertainment and looking around for a servant. "Where is the wine? Bring us more wine!"

Caro was a vindictive bitch. It was a mistake to have made her an enemy, but one it was too late and too onerous to rectify. His luck having deserted him,

Jamie retreated to one of Buckingham's numerous guest chambers, throwing himself down and falling instantly asleep.

He woke to the sound of a piercing scream.

"Assault! Assault! I've been assaulted!"

Lady Caroline was lying in bed beside him, her nightgown torn, her hair a mess, one breast artfully exposed. She took a moment and took a breath and eyed him with a malicious sneer, before wailing again.

"Oh good Christ!" Jamie swore.

The door burst open as Lady Caroline's porcine husband, jowls quivering in fury, rushed to the rescue surrounded by a bemused Buckingham and a motley assortment of lords and ladies.

"Rogue! Beast! Swine! How dare you assault my wife! I demand satisfaction, sir!"

"From me, sir? That's never been one of my vices. Surely you should ask it of your wife, or perhaps my lord Buckingham might assist you."

"Here now, Sinclair! I'll manage my own assignations if you please," Buckingham protested with a grin.

"How dare you, Sirrah!" Lord Ware blustered, shaking with what might have been anger or fear. "I've issued you a challenge! Are you a coward as well as a rapist?"

Jamie was sorely tempted to kill the man, if not for gross stupidity, then to put him out of his misery. It was pathetic. He was more afraid of losing face and being laughed at than certain death. Jamie had often reflected that Charles's and James's edicts against dueling had no effect for precisely that reason. If the British nobility were frightened of death, they wouldn't duel. What terrified them was being humiliated. Rather than threaten the tower, exile, or execution for dueling, the king would do better to threaten a day in the stocks. The indignity of being put on such shameful display would deal a deathblow to the practice of dueling overnight.

In any case, he had little taste for murder. He leaned on his elbow and turned to Lady Ware, who trembled and sobbed beside him. "Madam, you aren't worth dueling over, let alone killing a man. I beg you be gone. I'm fatigued and your wailing is disturbing my rest."

There were gasps and titters from the crowd gathered at the door.

"You're a coward, sir. A base, ignoble worm." Unable to believe his luck, Lord Ware was not averse to milking it for all it was worth. "You'll go down on your knees and apologize, and then I'll have you horsewhipped, and only then will we call the matter quit."

"You're testing my patience. I *will* kill you should you insist upon it. Leave my room now. Before I change my mind." Jamie leapt from the bed stark naked, causing a shriek from Lady Ware and a moan and several worried steps backward from her husband. Jamie grabbed a now truly frightened Lady Caroline by her shift and hauled her to her feet, then pushed her to the door. "Get… out!" He slammed the door in their faces, barred it with a chair, and climbed back into bed, wondering how he'd made such a mess of things. Desertion, disloyalty, now cowardice and rape—in the past year he'd been publicly accused of everything but cheating at cards.

Over the next several days, the story spread through London of Lord Carlyle's brazen attack upon a sleeping Lady Ware, and his cowardly retreat when challenged by her husband. It was met for the most part by amused disbelief. Tales of the lady's voracious appetite and her avid pursuit of the handsome but impoverished earl cast doubt on the first accusation, while Jamie's notoriety as a duelist and Lord Ware's reputation for bluster over action put the lie to the second, particularly as my lord Buckingham continued to welcome the earl into his home. But the lady was angry and vindictive, and the whispers wouldn't stop.

"I don't understand you at all, milord," a worried Sullivan pressed Jamie. "You have such skill with women. Why would you choose to make an enemy of this one? She can only make trouble you surely don't need. Why not go to her with presents and honeyed words? Apologize. Do you wish her to ruin what's left of your reputation? It might not be too late to salvage the thing."

"Will you act as my pimp, then? Shall I send you to her to beg her forgiveness and arrange an assignation?"

Sullivan blinked and blushed scarlet. "I… Is that what she wants, milord? Are you certain?"

"I forget you're an innocent lamb far from home. I'm quite certain—though now she'll expect me to grovel as well. You'll forgive me, I pray, if I chose disgrace and genteel poverty over Lady Ware's jeweled leash."

"Of course, milord. No! I meant to say, I'm sure things will improve."

But they didn't, they only got worse. Charges of cowardice and assault leveled by a woman known for accommodating everyone from the linkboy to the royal brothers, while highly titillating gossip, was not enough to bar a fellow from the homes of those unsavory sorts who enjoyed gaming, drinking, and other forms of vice, so Lady Ware spread the rumor that Jamie Sinclair, Lord Carlyle and Earl of Carrick, cheated at cards.

The stories circulated slowly, rumor and innuendo piled upon truth and half-truth. "*Did you hear? His father disowned him and left him no funds. He's desperate for money, and in disgrace with the king… he's a cheat… a cheat.*" There were many who attested that he won far more often than an honest man should, and some who claimed Lady Ware had caught him at it herself. It was why he'd attacked her, coming to her room to threaten and intimidate. It was simply too much to ignore.

It didn't take long. Within a week he was refused entry almost everywhere. Those who'd made arrangements to breed with his stud sent word they'd changed their minds. He was no longer welcome at the card tables of even the meanest homes or establishments. Unable to play, except with those who were as skilled and ruthless as he was, he sold paintings and furniture, draperies, tapestries, and silverware, trying to stave off selling his broodmares and stallion. Only those who circled the fringes—the disgraced, the unscrupulous, the untrustworthy, and, of course, Buckingham and his coterie of malcontents and rascals—had any welcome for him at all.

Jamie eyed Buckingham now. Aging, ill, and waning in influence, he was still charismatic, sitting at the table telling another ribald story. He'd brought a handsome new pet Jamie didn't recognize, as well as Sidney, Lauderdale, Sir Albert Scopes, and Musgrave, who'd been in perpetual disgrace since reputedly seducing James's second daughter Anne. Several buxom actresses and an orange girl from the king's theatre, all in various states of disarray, had joined them as well. Jamie had one ensconced on his lap, eating grapes and rubbing against him like a cat. Booted feet upon the table, he tried to peer over her mountainous breasts to see his cards, assessing his opponents at the same time.

Pragmatic men whose main loyalties were to themselves and increasing their estates, they'd backed the wrong play, and like Jamie, were in disgrace and generally considered dangerous to know. When King James had come to the throne, they'd scrambled to retain their influence. Hoping to prevent a Catholic renaissance that would have threatened their power and resulted in the kind of absolute monarchy the English had come to abhor, they'd backed Monmouth. Not to the extent of being caught naked with their arses and tarses waving in the wind when the stripling would-be king had been tried and executed as a rebel, but enough to be tainted and tarnished, and pushed, at least for now, to the farthest edges of society and the court.

Suspect himself, Jamie knew it did him little good to associate with them, but damned if he wasn't already tarred with that brush, and a fellow had to have *someone* to play cards with. He found it deliciously ironic that men he'd spied upon for Charles were now his only friends. He put down his cards and reached for some grapes, inadvertently dropping one down his half-naked thespian's wide-open bodice. "Your pardon, my dear," he whispered in her ear. "Shall I fetch it for you?"

She giggled and nodded, purring as his deft fingers began tugging at her ribbons and loosing her stays.

"Why have *you* yet to desert me, George?" he asked Buckingham curiously as he went about his task. "Such touching constancy is most unlike you."

"Birds of a feather, my dear. I'm a cheat too, don't you know, and you're one of the few amusements I have left." His sally was greeted by a roar of laughter. "Besides, there's no better time to play cards with a man than when his luck has deserted him. You need to marry, Jamie. A rich country bride. A little money will sort you out. I have a distant cousin of some sort. Not terribly well bred, a bit of the merchant in her, but beggars can't be choosers. She's bad tempered, pox-marked, and ugly as sin, but she's rich as Croesus and she'd consider herself lucky to have you."

"I thank you, George, but as I've told you several times, I'm already shackled."

"So you jumped the broomstick with some ignorant Scots savage. You're not the first randy fellow to be trapped in such a coil. Damned foolish of you not to have taken care of it straightaway, though. Still, it's not too late. Pay her off, make her disappear, arrange an accident, get on with it. If she can't be found, who's to say she's not dead? Bribe a witness or two and declare yourself a widower. There are ways around these things, my boy, and I promise you, my sweet but ugly cousin and her noisome kin will be glad enough to call her countess they'll not be asking any questions."

"The priest who married me might."

"Bah! He might also eat a piece of bad fish and die. Outside of the palace, being a Catholic's not good for one's health. It's not left you in the pink, now has it? Come and visit me at my country estate. At least take a look at the girl."

"You truly are a cold-blooded creature, aren't you, George?"

"As I said, Sinclair, birds of a feather."

Jamie shrugged, disinterestedly retrieving the grape, sliding it slowly up the girl's midriff and popping it into her mouth, looking up quizzically as Sullivan stepped determinedly into the room.

"Yes, Sullivan? What is it? Spit it out." The man was clearly agitated about something.

"It seems… ah… er… there's a lady… here to see you, milord."

"Eh? What lady? Blast it, man! Tell her to decamp! Tell her I'm not at home. Better yet, tell her I'm busy with liquor, strumpets, and cards, and have no wish to be disturbed."

"Odds fish, Sinclair! Surely you're not so badly burnt you've forgotten a pretty bird can be entertaining. You there, fellow! Bring her in."

Sullivan regarded Buckingham with distaste and turned to Jamie.

"Don't turn your back on me, man! Your servants are impertinent, Sinclair!"

"Aye George, I've often remarked on it, but I don't pay them well enough to object. You heard me, Sullivan. Send the jade on her way."

"I do not feel that would be appropriate, milord, as the lady appears to be your—"

The door swung open and a tall, handsome, tawny-haired Amazon, richly gowned and jeweled, stepped into the room.

"Good evening, English."

"Good Lord! Speak of the devil! I seem to have conjured the girl herself! Good evening, Catherine. Gentlemen… please… allow me to introduce my wife."

Twelve

COMING TO LONDON WAS NOT A DECISION CATHERINE had taken lightly. She'd enjoyed her status as a married woman without the encumbrance of a husband underfoot. For the first time in her life, she'd been truly free, with no one to answer to but herself. Unfortunately, it seemed she'd ridden her phantom husband as far as she could, for when spring and then summer passed without any word of him, the talk had begun. *Why steal a wealthy bride and not lay claim to her? It's a strange kind of marriage, with no witness, no bairn on the way, and no sign of a groom. No husband at all is what she wanted, and no husband at all is what she got.* The talk kept growing, and it wasn't only Donald and the old women. Even Jerrod and Rory, her most dependable allies, began to look at her askance, and when Jerrod came to confront her, she knew her time had run out.

"It's unnatural, Cat, for a marriage to be thus, where the bride disnae know the groom's name, his whereabouts, or if he be dead or alive," he told her. "You're nae with child, girl. We should apply to Rome for an annulment. You've more than sufficient cause to end this marriage. Under the circumstances, and with sufficient gold, we should be able to get you free of it."

"And why should I want to do that, Uncle Jerrod?" she'd replied. "So you lot can arrange another one? I don't *want* to be free of it. I *like* the one I've got. Things suit me fine as they are and he's all the husband I need."

"You're not some village lass, Cat. You can bring advantage to your clan. Land, allies, men, gold— things that will make us stronger and our position more secure."

"You're beginning to sound like Donald."

"Well, he has a point, doesn't he? If you were a lad you'd be expected to make a useful marriage as well. Tell me true, lass. They're beginning to talk. They're saying there never was an Englishman, and there never was a marriage."

"Do you think I was lying about it, Uncle?"

"I don't know, girl. I do think you're putting your own interests over your duty to your clan."

"And what about their duty to me?" she'd demanded, her voice quivering with resentment. "My father's will named *me* laird here, not Donald or Alistair. He expected my husband to be chief, but they tried to steal my inheritance and send me from my lands and home to marry a brutish boor, and for what? Gold? A few more men? A better trade route and a little less trouble on the Irish Sea? Or perhaps to fuel war with our neighbors? Back to feuding with the Murrays, is it? Am I to allow myself to be sacrificed to fund adventures my father would not have approved?"

"Your father wanted—"

"My father wanted me to stay here, keep the peace he fought so hard to maintain, and raise his grandsons."

He'd had the grace to blush and look away. "Things change lass. Your day has come and gone. Donald rules now, and he'll have his way. I know he promised you could stay, but it's a promise he can ill afford to keep. It's not good having one of you laird of the castle and the other chief of the clan. I'm warning you, Cat. You haven't got much time. You'll name your husband if you have one, and you'll free yourself to make a useful marriage, or Donald will have you placed in a convent and none will object. Folk have grown accustomed to his rule."

"He wouldn't dare!"

"He would. Then he'll be laird, no questions asked, and his sons will rule here after him. Find your husband. Produce him. Annulled or dead, you need to lose him or admit you made him up. You'll be forgiven. And then make haste to marry or you'll lose it all."

It had been a devastating blow and had left her questioning notions of family, clan, and loyalty that had been her life's blood since birth. Despite the constant maneuvering, bickering, jealousies, and quarrels that were a part of her clan and, she assumed, most others, she'd always trusted she could depend on their loyalty just as they could depend on hers. She realized now that nothing was as she'd thought it, and she was truly on her own.

Jerrod had accused her of putting her own needs before the good of the clan. Well, the more fool him if he thought Donald would make better use of her lands and fortune than she would. These were dangerous times, Protestant against Catholic, Whig against Tory, and Scot against Scot. The last thing they needed was war on their borders. She'd done her best to prevent Donald from breaking the fragile peace her father had cobbled over the years, but given the chance, his pride and avarice would destroy it and the clan would blindly follow: quarrelsome, lusty men, eager for glory, gold, and blood. Eager for war, the fools!

Well, she'd not be a part of it, and neither would her gold. She was no sheep to follow meekly where she was led. She was her father's daughter, part wolf and part fox, and she would take care of herself. It was time to find her husband.

She was cool and calm when she spoke before the council. This new king, James, was a Catholic, was he not? His reign had just begun and his throne was far from secure. He needed friends. Though he quarreled with the Covenanters to the south, he had no quarrel with them. Wouldn't he be grateful to be reminded of Catholic allies in the North? Perhaps he'd support a lucrative trade agreement for their whiskey in return. Why not best their rivals on the field of commerce instead of the field of war? It was said he had a weakness for women, much as his brother before him. Who better to go than she? While she was at it, perhaps she could track down her English husband.

They'd agreed to it immediately, and a message was sent on behalf of clan Drummond, begging an audience between his Catholic Majesty, James II, King of Scotland, Ireland, and England, and Lady Catherine

Drummond, Countess of Moray. She had set out with footmen, armed guards, and a lady's maid in tow, but no cousins, brothers, uncles, or aunties, because she'd no intention of going back. She was going to settle things with her husband, and then she'd be free. Her investigations had revealed he was in need of funds, and though she felt some trepidation given how they'd parted, she was certain he needed her help.

She'd had to admit the idea of seeing him again had provoked other feelings as well. There'd been something almost playful about him she'd found instantly appealing, and there'd been moments when she'd felt a sense of camaraderie and acceptance she'd never felt with anyone else. It was nonsense, of course. A result of shared secrets and dangers and her own sense of isolation. They had, in fact, been intimate, in the truest sense of the word, and he hadn't even noticed or remembered. She did, though—hot kisses that curled her toes and rough caresses that left her body thirsty and aching for more. She was grateful he'd never know what an awkward mess she'd made of it all.

Well now here she was, standing in his dining room, trying her best to appear sophisticated and cool, heart pounding, breath ragged, filled with anticipation and dread. He was sitting with what appeared to be a group of drunken cronies, all of them holding on to half-naked women and tankards of beer. Cards and bottles cluttered a magnificent table, and a couple of large dogs, one with a torn ear and missing eye, lolled in a corner. The room was otherwise spartan and bare. Awkward seconds ticked by as his guests digested his words.

Buckingham, who was far more accustomed to shocking than being shocked, finally broke the silence. "Good Lord, man! Is this is your rebel whore?"

"Careful, George. Mind your manners," Jamie said in a pleasant tone as he fastened the orange girl's bodice and eased her off his lap. "Sullivan, please escort the ladies out and see to it they find their way home. Then you can see to the gentlemen." He rose and bowed. "Welcome to my humble abode, Catherine. What a great pleasure to see you. And in a dress, no less! How charming! It's been what, just over a year?"

She'd been expecting anger, surprise—not quiet mockery and an amused grin. "Just under, I believe," she replied uncomfortably.

"And might I enquire as to what's brought you to London after so much time? I was under the distinct impression you were less than anxious for my company."

"It seems you improve with time and distance, Eng—husband," she replied, recovering her wits.

He choked back a startled laugh. "James," he said gravely, recovering his own.

"It's been a long journey, *James*. Might I sit down?"

"Yes, of course! I do beg your pardon! I've quite forgotten my manners." He gestured to the seat directly across from him. "Get out, Sidney. You're sitting in her chair."

Sidney stumbled and nearly fell as he scrambled from his seat, mouth agape, offering awkward apologies as he swiftly calculated how many suppers, country visits, and other handsome invitations this night's gossip would bring him.

Catherine nodded to Sullivan as he pulled back her chair, and then to her husband's guests. "Gentlemen."

"I'd be delighted to make formal introductions, my dear, if only I knew how," Jamie said, offering her some wine.

"It's Catherine Drummond, as you already know, my lord, laird of Drummond Castle and Countess of Moray in my own right, as you may not. I suppose I'm also countess of…?

"Carrick and Carlyle," he said with a slight bow.

Thomas Sidney, busily composing scurrilous verses to honor the occasion, watched avidly from where he'd been relegated at the end of the table. Jamie's phantom wife had been the subject of much delighted gossip since he'd first returned from Scotland almost a year ago. It was generally held she was a camp follower he'd married as a drunken jest. No one had credited that his story might be true, but it appeared she really was an heiress, and a rich and titled one at that! Gossip was currency, and gossip this delicious couldn't wait to be told. Anxious to hear more, but more anxious to be the first to impart this astonishing news, he jumped to his feet, made a hurried apology, and scurried from the room.

"How odd!" Catherine remarked, sipping her wine.

"Yes, he is. How was your journey, my dear?"

"Tolerable." Which was more than she could say for the conversation. They were talking like polite strangers, trying to outdo one another with displays of amused boredom when there was so much to say, so much to discuss, so much at stake! She wanted to reach out and slap or shake him, anything to provoke an honest reaction. No sooner did she think it than she noticed a slight crookedness to his once-perfect nose. She couldn't help a shamefaced flush. The poor man! He'd only been trying to help her. Still, Martha was right. It hadn't spoiled his looks. Somehow it made him look both rakish and endearing.

"Is there something wrong, mouse?"

She blinked and flushed brighter, a deep crimson now. "Yes, English, there is. There are important matters I should like to discuss with you, in private, if you please."

A bemused Buckingham stirred himself at last. "Here now, Lady Carlyle," he said, with a languid wave of his handkerchief. "The night is young and you are both this evening's entertainment. I'll wager the Sinclairs' touching reunion is all anyone will be talking about tomorrow and for weeks if not months to come. Won't you indulge an aging roué and let us watch the play unfold?"

"I regret, sir, that—"

"Leave her be, George," Jamie said sharply.

A sodden Sir Albert waved his arm and wagged his finger at her, knocking over his wine as he rose to his feet. "I say, Sinclair. The wench is ordering us out!"

"Then *get out,* sir!" he snapped. He winced in disgust, imagining what she must be thinking. After a year, she'd decided to make a visit and this was how she found him, surrounded by whores, fools, drunkards, and Buckingham. He felt distinctly uncomfortable. Apparently, he wasn't as shameless as he'd imagined.

Her sudden arrival had unsettled him and he wanted to be rid of them and find out what she wanted.

"Sullivan, fetch a footman, would you? Have him put Sir Albert in a carriage and send him on his way, then see to the rest. My lady wife and I will be in the library. Have someone send a meal for her there."

"Very good, sir," Sullivan said, bowing smartly in approval.

Grumbling and complaining, his guests were herded from the room by Sullivan and a brawny footman, except for Buckingham, who sauntered out with a wink and a wicked grin.

"I believe you've made a conquest, my dear."

"I believe I made a spectacle of myself."

"Well, that was your intention, wasn't it? It was a grand entrance, combining high drama and the element of surprise."

"Yes, I suppose it was," she admitted with a sigh. "I was afraid if I sent word you might refuse to see me."

"Why would I do that?"

"I thought you might be annoyed, after I—"

"Abandoned me? Bashed me on the head and had me thrown in a cargo hold? Come, I'll show you the library. We'll be more comfortable there and you can tell me why you're here."

Thirteen

JAMIE PUSHED OPEN THE DOOR AND USHERED HER
inside. Unlike the dining room, the library had the warmth
and character of a place that was lived in and valued as
somebody's home. It was a sizable room, paneled in oak,
with elegant mahogany bookcases lining the walls from
floor to ceiling in numbered order. A great fireplace,
well situated to ward off an evening's chill or provide a
soft light for reading, was surrounded by a sturdy settee
and several comfortable chairs. It was a comfortable and
welcoming room, and clearly, a great deal of thought
and care had gone into it. He might be scrimping
and saving in other parts of his house, but not here.

"This is a surprise, Sinclair."

"I'm full of surprises, mouse. It's part of my charm."
Pleased with her reaction, Jamie escorted her to a small
table by the fire where a simple supper had been laid.
She ate like a soldier. He chuckled as she tore into the
cold mutton and bread, whatever she'd been about to
say forgotten.

He lounged on the settee, watching her. The shock
of seeing her so unexpectedly had rapidly turned to

acute embarrassment, but now that they were alone he felt curiously lighthearted. "I was annoyed with you when I first came home," he ventured, "but it didn't last long. I'm seldom bested at games of strategy or chance, yet you did so twice. A fellow can't help but admire that. You needn't feel bad about it. I had every intention of binding you hand and foot, slinging you over my saddle, and carrying you home. You simply beat me off the mark—which begs the question, why *are* you here?"

"Perhaps I've come to give you your annulment."

"Have you indeed? Well, that's damn noble of you, I dare say. A little late though. Since you cruelly cast me out, my life has been ripped asunder, and what little reputation I had left, damaged beyond repair. I've been styled deserter, coward, both Papist *and* Protestant sympathizer, and an ungrateful and disloyal bastard. The ladies decry me as a rogue, jilt, and despoiler of women, and worst of all, I'm everywhere accounted a pauper and a cheat at cards. No one will have me now. If I let you go, I'll live out my days worthless and alone."

"Based on my own experience you're certainly no coward, and though you can be an arrogant oaf, you're no despoiler of women, nor do I believe you cheat at cards. Who accuses you? Perhaps I can help." She glanced at him curiously, as she plucked the last mouthful of mutton from her plate and finished with a sip of wine.

Jamie watched her delicate fingers, wrapped firmly around the fluted stem of the glass, and raised his gaze to her lips as she spoke. They were full and inviting, shaped in a natural pout that seemed to invite a man to kiss them. Best be careful. A man might easily founder on that shore.

"Sinclair?"

"What? Ah! Yes, my accusers. One was my fiancée, of course. I mentioned her to you, if you recall. Her family was prepared to sacrifice her on the altar of my lust in return for a title. She'd overlook my bad behavior, and I her evil disposition. A most convenient marriage, if you will. She thought I'd thrown her over for a Scottish strumpet. So did the rest of the court. Needless to say she was deeply embarrassed, as were her family and the king."

His hand tightened around his own glass. He didn't like to think about it. The girl had borne the brunt of months of gleefully malicious gossip, becoming a favorite topic for the vicious lampoons and satires of the court wits. She was the only innocent in the whole affair and he'd never meant to hurt her, though he doubted that was any consolation.

"My would-be mistress was an altogether different tale. Suffice it to say, when she discovered that my disinclination to worship anything included her, she was mightily annoyed. She matters little and is no fault of yours."

"How is any of it my fault?" Catherine asked defensively.

"Because you, my pet, denied me an annulment when I needed it, though now it seems you wish to grant me one when I don't. I mean you no disrespect, but you've been a most inconvenient, dare I say a most *useless* bride. I've not even had the pleasure of fuck—er, making love to you."

Catherine rose from her seat so quickly she almost jumped.

He regarded her flushed face quizzically. "Is something wrong?"

She walked slowly along the shelves of books, pretending to examine the titles, as she regained her composure, banishing heated images of their coupling in the cave. "No. I'm just tired of sitting still after days spent in a carriage." She turned to face him. "I can see why your friends were so fascinated. We're quite the couple, are we not? A lowbred Scottish camp follower and a well-bred penniless lout."

"Who sells his loyalty, ravishes young women, and lies and cheats at cards. What with Buckingham's tattling, Sir Percy's complaining, and Sidney's execrable verse, we shall be gloriously notorious within days."

"And this pleases you?"

"Gambling, drinking, and recreational bed-hopping are among the favored indoor sports of the leisured classes, my love. Most of the sins ascribed to me are easily pardoned in this enlightened age, but being penniless and cheating at cards are decidedly not. Gossip is currency, boredom feared more than the plague, and being interesting buys one indulgence from a multitude of sins, even those."

"I'm aware of that, Sinclair. I spent two years at the French court. Does it mean so much to you, to be accepted by those you speak of with so little respect?"

He looked at her as if she had two heads. "I have but two ways of making a living, Catherine, on the battlefield or at the gaming tables, and both are seriously curtailed by my current circumstances. I need to be accepted in society and at court if I wish to pay my servants, feed my horses, maintain my properties, and clear my debts. Unless, of course, you're here to offer an alternative? An annulment, is it? Too late for me to marry a fortune, but just in time to confirm the rumors? I can hear it now," he said, mimicking the clipped phrases, lengthened vowels, and malicious drawl of court gossip. "'Even his savage Scottish bride lives in fear of him! Ravaged her too, poor thing, then tried to steal her land, but the chit escaped him and the Pope himself intervened to grant an annulment.' Frankly, my dear, I fail to appreciate how that will be of any benefit to me."

"I believe there's another avenue open to you that you've neglected."

"And what's that, my dear?"

"Why, the stage, sir."

"You're a perceptive child, but I assure you pretty compliments won't turn my head. I've been far too accommodating already, much against my better judgment, and I'm still paying the price. It's not a mistake I intend to repeat. Whatever it is you're wanting, there'd best be a substantial benefit to me."

Catherine was having difficulty finding the man underneath the performance. She'd thought herself perceptive, but the Englishman was nothing like her blunt, straightforward Scottish brethren, and she found him impossible to read. She suspected that if she succeeded at stripping one layer away she'd only find another, and then another, peeling until he was gone like smoke, and there was nothing left to find.

She found herself following his lead more often than not, forced into communicating through glib repartee and barbed wit when she wanted to shake him and ask, *Are you as confused and anxious as I am? Are you glad to see me? What are you thinking? What do you feel?* Instead, she pointed to the settee. "Do you mind if I sit by the fire?"

"No, of course not. This is your home, after all. Would you care for a whiskey?" A tray with a whiskey decanter and two crystal glasses sat on a low table in front of the fire. He picked up both glasses and sat down next to her, crowding her into the corner of the settee. Leaning forward companionably, he put one arm around her shoulder and handed her the drink. "Now then, little wife, suppose we have a talk, you and I? You spoke of an annulment. Has that hard heart of yours finally softened? Do you now long for your beefy Irish lover? You wish to join him in connubial bliss?"

"No," she said shortly, shifting so that her elbow lodged firmly against his ribs, and giving a hard shove. "It's my family that longs for him, not I. Have a care, Sinclair. You'll make me spill my drink."

"Then it must be me you long for," he said huskily, ignoring the sharp point of her elbow and pulling her into his lap.

"Damn it, Sinclair, attend me if you please!" She slapped at his hands, struggling to free herself, spilling her drink in the process. "I appreciate you're angry with me, despite your words to the contrary. I wish you'd just come out and say so instead of playing these games."

"You've never seen me angry, love. It's not something you'd soon forget. I was merely ascertaining that you're solid and real and not some figment of my inebriation. I remember what a hefty armful you were," he added, giving her a slight squeeze.

His warmth surrounded her, and she could feel his arousal pressed firm against her bottom. His mouth, just inches from hers, smelled of whiskey, and she wondered if it would taste like it, too. He'd kissed her three times, once on her wedding night and twice in his delirium. Each time she'd felt a mix of guilt and pleasure and a giddy sense of expectation. She wondered what it would be like to kiss him as a lover, as a wife kissed a husband. She relaxed against him for a moment, and then elbowed him sharply when his fingers began tracing her décolletage.

He grunted and let her go. "What? No kiss? After more than a year of cruel separation this is your greeting once we're alone? I'm very disappointed, Catherine. This is hardly the reunion I've been dreaming of."

She rose abruptly, tired of sparring with him. "You *are* angry with me, whether you admit it or not. I can see there's little point in trying to discuss anything with you right now. When you've done amusing yourself, my lord, do you think you might direct me to a bedchamber?"

He wasn't angry, though. At least he didn't think he was. Shocked and surprised to see her, yes. Confused and wary, certainly. Curious, intrigued, and decidedly unsettled. She'd seemed so cool and collected, walking back into his life out of nowhere with God knew what on her mind. She'd been nothing but trouble so far.

And now here she was, back as if they'd parted only yesterday, an aristocratic stranger as cool and sparkling as one of her blasted highland burns. It was a relief to provoke a reaction and find the hellcat dwelled there still. Now that she'd shown herself, he wasn't ready to let her go.

"You're a cruel and merciless overlord, madam. You beat and bit me, left me bruised and bloody on my wedding night, tied me hand and foot and tossed me to the mercy of the sea, and now that you've ruined my reputation, you are seeking to abandon me. Surely it is I who am the aggrieved party here. Pray sit down and tell me what I've done to deserve your ire."

She sighed, exasperated. "I'm actually quite wealthy, you know. You didn't strike such a bad bargain. Moreover, my family and I are on friendly terms with the king. Indeed, I'm invited to court to discuss matters of trade. It's part of the reason I'm here."

"Tell me more, my dear," he said, patting the place beside him.

"Will you behave yourself?" she asked suspiciously.

"I'll put the angels to shame, my love. I give you my word."

She eyed him warily, motioning with her hand for him to move farther to the right. He did so, then poured them both another glass of whiskey, handing one to her and putting his booted feet on the table as she settled down beside him.

"A toast, my dear? To new beginnings?"

"To new beginnings." Catherine watched him toss back the fiery liquid, and not to be outdone, she did the same.

"You drink like a soldier, little wife." He reached for her glass and refilled it.

"I drink like a Scotsman, English."

He held out his glass to her again. "To old acquaintance renewed. I thought we'd agreed you'd call me Jamie?"

"To old acquaintance renewed," she said, clinking her glass with his and downing her drink in two swallows. "I'll try and do so, Sinclair, if you speak to me as yourself and not some prancing courtier."

"But I am a prancing courtier, love."

"No, you're not." She pulled up the edge of her skirt and rested her own boots on the table. "I've seen you on the battlefield. I've seen you on the scaffold. I've seen you as a mercenary and a tinker. I've seen your scars and I've seen you fight. I don't know what you are, but I *do* know what you're not. I suppose you have your reasons for the games you play, but if you want me to call you by your own name, then don't play them with me." She held out her glass for another refill, and though he raised an eyebrow, he complied.

He tilted his head on an angle, his lips quirked in amusement as he watched her curiously, enjoying the view of petticoat and leather clad ankle. "So we're to be honest with one another, are we? It's a novel idea, my dear, but I fear overall a dangerous practice. Why don't you start? I'll observe from a distance and see if it's safe."

She couldn't stop a quick smile in reply.

He tapped his boot against hers and gave her a gentle nudge. "Did you worry about me at all, mouse? Did you think of me when the nights were cold and long and the wind rattled at your door?" His voice was soft, insistent. "Did you miss me, Cat? I missed you. I dreamt of you. I dreamt I held you in my arms, wrapped in furs, as the sea pounded at my door."

Her heart stuttered and she blushed in the dark, wondering how much he remembered. The silence was relieved only by the popping and hissing of the logs on the fire, and she watched the flames dancing and pulsing in the crystal goblets, strangely beautiful in the hushed room. His thigh rested warm and solid against her own, sending a shiver coursing through her veins that had nothing to do with the cold. She'd miscalculated the state of her nerves, and the strength of the whiskey. It had gone to her head, and she waited, in fear and anticipation, for him to press his advantage. As the minutes ticked by and he didn't, she began to relax against him.

"No answer, love? Or has my honesty put you to sleep?"

The spell broken, she rallied instantly. "I do apologize, English—"

"Jamie... Please."

"Jamie... I *have* had a rather long day and I'm feeling just a bit unwell. I'd prefer to leave our discussion to tomorrow, if you don't mind."

She rose unsteadily to her feet, waving him away when he moved to aid her. "I'm quite capable of standing, walking, and other mundane tasks without the help of a husband, thank you." The sudden movement unsettled her balance and she tottered precariously to her left. When he scooped her into his arms, she clutched his neck to keep from falling. She was unusually tall for a woman, but he held her easily, making her feel dainty and ladylike, much to her amusement. When he stumbled and cursed, catching his toe on the corner of a bookcase, she gave a snort of laughter.

"It amuses you to have me trip and fall like an underfed slave boy?"

"I was merely reflecting that I'm more of an armful than you imagined," she replied primly.

"You've always been an armful, mouse." He shifted her in his arms and used his foot to nudge open the door.

"You'd do well to consider that before you decide to keep me. I'm a brawny hoyden, sharp tongued and opinionated, better with a sword than a needle, and not the least bit biddable. I'd make a terrible wife."

"You're a lovely Amazon, my dear, long muscled and sleek, yet smooth and rounded in all the right places. You must trust me in this. I'm a connoisseur of such things. Ah, here's Sullivan. Sullivan, have we a room ready for my wife?"

"Indeed, sir, this way."

Jamie followed Sullivan down the hall, enjoying the feel of her in his arms. He felt it when she slipped into sleep. He laid her on the bed, waving Sullivan and the servants, including some squawking Scottish lass, from the room. He pulled off her boots, his hands lingering over supple calves and circling slim ankles, and then he covered her with a soft lamb's wool blanket. He took a step back and looked at her warily. He'd never expected to see her again. What did she want from him? What trouble would she cause next?

He touched the bridge of his nose and a slow smile spread across his face. He was going to have to be careful. The sight of her had set his heart to racing and momentarily stilled his breath. She brought out the worst in him, his lovely Highland lass. She made him reckless and impulsive and set him to craving, so he forgot all his best-laid plans, but he'd no intention of letting that happen again.

Fourteen

CATHERINE OPENED HER EYES AND CLOSED THEM again, as the room spun in dizzying circles. The blood was pounding in her temples, and the clatter of silverware and china set her teeth on edge. Harsh sunlight beat against her eyelids in a painful white- and red-tinged haze. She moaned and covered them with the back of her hand. She was used to traveling long distances on horseback, but it seemed the endless rolling of the coach hadn't agreed with her. She rolled over and buried her head under the covers, and memories of the last evening came flooding in. She'd seriously misjudged the strength of the whiskey, though not its lack of refinement. It clearly lacked the subtlety and smoothness that characterized her own. She supposed she'd also underestimated the extent of her own anxiety, else she'd never have drunk so much.

She vaguely recollected her English husband carrying her to bed. It seemed she was still wearing her traveling clothes, so it was safe to assume nothing untoward had happened. Had he tried to kiss her? She seemed to remember something of the sort. The clattering was getting louder and a moment later her nostrils flared, catching the dark and delicious aroma of fresh-brewed coffee. Peering through her fingers she saw one of her maids, Maire McKenna, setting out a cup and saucer on a nearby table. She was a pretty girl who bustled rather than walked, hummed rather than chattered, and despite her constant motion, had a presence about her that put one at ease.

"Ah, thank you, Maire! How did you know?"

"Mr. Sullivan sent it, ma'am. He said his lordship is looking forward to meeting you in the breakfast room."

"Is he? I'd not have taken him for a man who rises before midday." But she knew it wasn't true. She knew better than to underestimate him. Whatever game Jamie Sinclair was playing, he wasn't a spoiled and pampered aristocrat, but a wily and seasoned opponent who'd traversed the Highlands and entered enemy territory on his own. She didn't care how clever he was, though. There wasn't an Englishman born who could beat a canny Scot when it came to hard bargaining.

Maire led her to a sunny breakfast room. The coffee had revived her, though her nerves were still a little tender, and the smell of fresh-baked bread made her mouth water. Her English husband was drinking chocolate and reading a newspaper. Still a little unsteady on her feet, she returned his cheerful greeting with a careful nod as she edged around the table and gingerly sat down.

He winced in sympathy. "The room isn't moving, my dear. You needn't grip the table so. Shall I have Cook make you a posset?"

He bellowed for Sullivan and she gripped her head between he palms. "Beast!"

"I'm right here, sir. There's no need to shout."

"Thank you, Sullivan. Fetch my lady something for her head, would you?" He turned his attention back to Catherine, rising to pour her some chocolate. "Try this. It helps." Sitting down beside her, he patted her hand solicitously. "Now tell me true, my love. Will I spend my married life dragging you home piss drunk from taverns?"

She gave him a glacial look. "I do *not*… get… piss… drunk. I drink for medicinal purposes, and at other times I… tipple."

"Well you tippled enough last night to put a bishop under the table, but if that's how a Scotsman holds his drink, I'd have to say they drink like… girls." He grinned and dodged her elbow.

"I was tired from a very long journey and anxious about my reception, and the whiskey was… well, I'm a guest, and unlike you, I'm polite and I'll say no more," she replied hotly, stung by the insult.

"You needn't feel anxious of your welcome, my love. We're family now, after all."

"I'm not your love, English. I'm your unwanted and inconvenient wife."

"You promised to use my name."

"And you promised not to play games."

"Very well, but it's you who've come to see me. You spoke of an annulment last night. What precisely did you have in mind?"

"I thought we might help one another. Perhaps come to some kind of arrangement that would be mutually beneficial. You're in needs of funds. I want my freedom and control of my fortune so I can keep it from the hands of my family.

"Ah, not so loving kin, internecine warfare, Cain and Abel?"

"Nothing quite so biblical. They would not use it wisely."

"One suspects they might say the same of you."

"Indeed they might. Particularly if they thought I intended to share it with a womanizing Sassenach rogue and gambler."

"And is that your intention?"

"It might be."

"No offense, my dear, but we *are* in fact married. As unfair as it might seem to you, what's yours is now mine. Why should I consider any other arrangement?"

"*Pax*, Sinclair… Jamie. We won't get far if you seek to rule me."

"I don't seek to rule you. Some say I'm barely able to rule myself."

"We both know that's false."

"Do we?"

"Yes, so why this pretense?" she asked, genuinely curious. "The scapegrace courtier, the dissipated rogue?"

He shrugged. "Some men have many faces, mouse. Who's to say which one is real? Why do you avoid my question?"

"Because you'll not like the answer, I'm not sure how best to explain, and my head still hurts. Can we declare a truce? I'd like to discuss it with you, not argue. I'd like to take a walk to clear my head and then sit down somewhere comfortable and see if we can't come to some kind of arrangement."

"Taking a walk through the noxious streets of

London is hardly likely to clear your head. Might I suggest we go for a ride in the park?"

"You wish to accompany me?"

His face lit with mischief. "I do indeed. And after, I'll have Sullivan make the rounds and place wagers on the identity of the mysterious beauty who accompanied me."

"You do cheat!"

"Heavens no! I merely improve the odds wherever I can."

"Will you promise to leave our discussion until later?"

"I will be your vassal, your dedicated guide. I'll hold your pretty ankle and boost you into your saddle, carry your parcels, and menace any ruffians who dare to look your way."

She eyed him suspiciously, but when he set out to charm he was impossible to resist. He took her back to the mews and introduced her to Charlie Turner, a tiny, wizened man who was groom and sometimes jockey. For a man in dire financial straits, his stable housed some of the finest hacks she'd ever seen: long-limbed, high-stepping beauties that combined the intelligent eyes and fiery carriage of a desert mount with the height and strength of an English hunter.

"Jamie, these beasts are magnificent! Wherever did you get them?"

"Mmmm," he shrugged with apparent indifference, but she could see the pride shining in his eyes. "I've had a mind to try my hand at breeding since back in Charles's day. He was kind enough to pay off a gambling debt by allowing me to breed a Barbary mare to his stud, Old Rawley."

"The champion race horse?"

"You know of him?" he asked with a pleased smile.

"But of course I do! He's a racing legend!"

Jamie nodded, and lifted her easily onto the back of a fine black gelding. "So he is. As it happens, I've had a bit of luck with it all since then. The mare produced a colt that won the cup at Newcastle twice. I've bred him with several of Sullivan's mares and he's sired some fine racehorses and hunters. Those that aren't suitable for racing or hunting I use as hacks and pleasure mounts. I was beginning to make a bit of a name for myself as a breeder before this unfortunate business with Caroline. Only Buckingham gives me his business now."

They continued into the park, talking amiably about horse racing and breeding, neither of them paying any attention to the stir they were creating. Catherine enjoyed herself for the first time since Jerrod had come to warn her to cooperate or be imprisoned. It was strange how easy she felt around this man, as if she'd always known him, and strange that when she found herself threatened it was him she turned to and trusted, rather than her own flesh and blood. They chattered and laughed, amusing each other with observations about the colorfully dressed fops and sparks strutting by like peacocks and the vulgar calls of the orange girls passing by on their way to the theatre.

Returning to the house, they settled comfortably in the library, just as the sun began to set, bathing the room in shades of pink and indigo blue. Jamie poured two glasses of brandy and came to sit beside her. "So... rash and reckless little mouse. You've managed to avoid my questions thus far, but here we are. What has brought you quick and curious to my lair? What is it you propose... and why should I accept?" They sat companionably, sharing the well-upholstered settee in front of a cheerful fire, feet propped on a low table.

"I'm the creature you've always dreamed of, Sinclair," she said, sipping her brandy. "A rich and titled heiress, ripe for the plucking. My father hoped I'd marry someone who could help me lead our clan, but I failed in that duty and my cousin Donald became chieftain after my father's death. Donald feels, and my family concurs, that a woman with a husband no one else has ever seen must be a lunatic who imagined him in the first place, or desperate to divorce him so she might marry again. I'm to procure an annulment or lead you to slaughter, so I can marry as my loving family wishes. If I don't, my cousin will have me immured in a convent until I return to my right mind."

"Aah! And then your fortune goes to him."

"That part which is held in trust for the clan would certainly come under his control, yes. I suspect that, should I wish to be released, I would have to sign over the rest as well." She lifted her glass in a mock salute. "To false friends and not-so-loving families."

"No point in bitterness, love. It's the way of the world." He clanked his glass against hers. "You've already passed on the opportunity to see me slaughtered, though. I take it you have other plans?"

"I do," she said, shifting to face him. "I found out what I could about you before I came here, through my agents in London."

He blinked in surprise. "You have agents in London?"

"Yes, of course! In Ireland, France, Edinburgh, and the Netherlands as well. My father used to say one good piece of information is worth a thousand armed men."

"He discussed such things with you?"

"I was raised at his side. He'd intended... well... none of that matters now. I doubt he'd have approved of this marriage. I do think he would have liked you, though."

"And what did your agents tell you about me, love?"

"They said you were out of favor with the king, and you'd been left properties and a title, but your father had otherwise disowned you and left you in desperate need of funds." She didn't feel it polite to mention the rest.

"He *tried* to disown me. He was convinced I wasn't his. He wrote me out of his will and left me saddled with mortgages and debt, but he couldn't stop me inheriting. He must have found it galling in the extreme."

"I'm sorry."

"To not-so-loving families," he said with a crooked smile, raising his glass in another toast.

"Jamie, I wouldn't want you to think... that is to say, my father wasn't... my father was a good man."

"I'm glad to hear it. Mine wasn't. Pray continue with your tale. You escaped the clutches of your greedy cousin and flew to the arms of your beggared, ne're-do-well husband... why?"

"As I've said, I came seeking an annulment or divorce. You'd said you wanted one and I assumed, overall, you'd be pleased. I thought I might settle a generous sum upon you, once I was beyond my cousin's reach. My father left me ships and I've long wanted to travel. I could go to France, perhaps from there to Italy, the Americas, or even the Far East. None of my family other than my father and Uncle Jerrod have traveled much beyond the Highlands. They're an insular lot, somewhat ignorant of the rest of the world, and I doubt they'd follow me, particularly if I renounced any claim to Drummond lands."

"Uncle Jerrod? Isn't he the fellow—"

"Yes, he is. He's not a bad sort really. At least he gave me some warning."

"Forgive me if I'm not inclined to think warmly of a man who tortured and meant to kill me."

"He was quite impressed with you, you know. He called you a 'cold-blooded bastard with balls of steel.'"

"High praise indeed!"

"Well, if it's any consolation, your escape and his failure to recapture you made him look a fool. It damaged his reputation and standing in the clan, and he lost his place as captain. He never suspected my part in it. He never suspected a thing. I felt bad for it. Everything changed after that, and he's Donald's man now."

"Save your pity for those who deserve it, mouse, not those who turn their backs on you." The room was growing chilled and he rose and went to the fire, hunkering down to poke and prod until it blazed high again. He looked back at her over his shoulder. She lounged against the arm of the settee. Her head rested against her curled fist, one leg was drawn up beneath her, and she appeared lost in thought. He couldn't help but smile. She might be a countess who'd been schooled in the French court, but she moved like a lad, fought like a man, and ate and drank like a soldier. She looked very fine indeed in emerald silk, though, with her copper-hued hair tumbling about her shoulders, catching the flame from the fire. He'd never met anyone like her. *She's as fresh and lovely as the first day of spring.*

"Sinclair? Is something wrong?"

"Nothing at all, my dear. I was simply wondering what you consider to be a generous sum." He rose to his feet and went to sit beside her. *Best be careful. She'll singe you hotter than those flames, char you from the inside out,* he told himself, but it didn't stop him from moving closer. "Don't be coy, sweetheart. You hope to buy my cooperation? You must have a sum in mind."

"The sum I had in mind was twenty thousand pounds."

"Twenty thousand pounds!" Jamie nearly choked on his drink. "What exactly are you worth, Catherine?"

"Well... much of what my father left me is Drummond land, held in trust for the good of the clan. It will be fought over by my brother and my cousins once I abandon my claim. It's of no use to you. You could never claim or hold it."

"I might surprise you."

"I was named laird over my little brother because he was too young and too French. The clan would *never* accept an Englishman. You'd be murdered at the first opportunity. The only way you could hold those lands is with a sizable army, and even with my funds, you couldn't afford to keep one. I do have other properties and income left me by my parents, though, as well as my father's share of the distillery, and shortly after his death, I converted the assets he left me in horses and cattle to gold. Not counting the income from my properties, I'm worth a little over sixty thousand pounds.

He stared at her in amazement. "Good Christ, woman! That would make you one of the richest heiresses in England!"

"Perhaps. I don't know. It makes me one of the richest women in the Highlands at any rate. I'd intended to cede my properties in Scotland to my family and, in return for your cooperation, settle twenty thousand pounds on you. I confess I never considered how it might affect you. I knew you needed money and I thought that would be enough. You implied last night that an annulment at this time would do further damage to your reputation, and it's not my desire that you be worse off for having helped me. If you prefer, I'd consider making some pretense of a happy marriage for a while. You've been good for me, Sinclair. If you continue to be, and if you allow it, I'll repay you."

"How?"

"You claimed I was a Catholic heiress to the king. As it happens, I am. I'm expected at court to discuss matters of trade and my family's whiskey and offer military support if and when required. The king will be surprised and pleased to discover such a useful woman is tied in marriage to a loyal member of his court, will he not? I'll rehabilitate your reputation, Sinclair, as a husband, a good Catholic, a loyal subject, and a wealthy man. Later we'll arrange an amicable divorce and we'll both be free."

"I'm intrigued, love, but I seemed to have missed something. Why would I agree to any of this? You *are* my wife, after all. Why should I settle for a third when I can have it all?"

"Under *your* laws perhaps, English. I come from the Highlands, where a chieftain who can hold his lands is a law unto himself. My father chose me as his heir, though my clan chose my cousin as chieftain. This is the part you're not going to like."

"Dear me!"

"My father had close to a dozen lawyers. My inheritance is left to me under my sole control. It's now in the hands of a Scots banker who owes his life and his fortune to my father, and his loyalty is to me. He'll release funds to my bankers when and as I ask, but he'll not release a penny to my husband, cousin, brother, or anyone else, without my consent. Without my cooperation, you'll never see any revenues from any of my properties, and my bankers won't let you touch a farthing."

"A pity, that. Sheathe your claws, hellcat. I simply asked a question. What if I took you to court?"

"You might try, I suppose," she said with a smile. "But between my bankers and lawyers, your great-grandchildren would be grey-haired old men before they saw any of it."

He smiled back. "So what is it you propose? Will you pay me to remain as your loving spouse or to be gone from your life altogether?"

"Which would you prefer?"

"I'm partial to the one where you stoop to take my hand, raising me up beside you whilst restoring my reputation to its former pristine glory, and me to the bosom of my king."

"You're being pettish now, English."

"Am I? I must be hungry. What makes you think we can get our marriage dissolved, once it's been publicly acknowledged? It will be much harder than it might have been a year ago."

"Actually, I've given it a great deal of thought."

"Have you indeed?" He watched with a bemused smile as she sat cross-legged, tugging at her skirts to adjust and smooth them, before eagerly launching into the pros and cons of the many ways they might end their marriage. *What an odd conversation to be having with one's wife!*

Catherine had done her research. "There are, in fact, several remedies to an unwanted marriage, each varying in the length of time, degree of difficulty, and the expense involved. Fortunately, I have access to competent and reliable lawyers, the expense is not a problem, and if we undertake it as a cooperative venture rather than a combative one, things should be that much easier. My lawyers feel they can make the appropriate submissions and arrangements within a year or two at most."

"Do go on, it all sounds fascinating," he drawled, pouring himself another drink.

"Very well," she said primly. "In Scotland, one can obtain a divorce through the Commissary Court of Edinburgh on the grounds of adultery, desertion, and cruelty, though cruelty is difficult to prove. We were married in Scotland, and that might be an option, but I'm uncertain as to how it would hold up in an English court. In England, one's choices are somewhat limited. One can apply to Parliament for a private Act to dissolve a marriage, but it requires a great deal of expense and no doubt a certain amount of influence, something you're sadly lacking at present. If we can rehabilitate you, however, and return you to favor, this might prove a feasible route."

"Lucky me."

She chose to ignore him. "We might also pursue a *divortium a mensa et thoro*—that means divorce from bed and board—through the ecclesiastical courts."

"There's no need to condescend. I know what it means, Catherine. If you can speak Latin, why didn't you do so the night of our wedding, when it might have helped us both? Surely you understood the priest?"

"I did not! He was barely intelligible. He had a heavy Spanish accent and his pronunciation was atrocious. I thought you were going to rape then hang me. I thought he was reading a prayer for the condemned! Do you want me to continue or not?"

"I'm sorry if you were frightened."

"I'm a Drummond! I was not frightened!"

He held up his hands in a gesture of surrender. "Of course not. You were ferocious. I still bear the scars."

She relaxed against the arm of the settee, somewhat mollified. "Yes... well, the most obvious solution, of course, is to secure a degree of nullity, establishing that the marriage was void *ab inito*, from the beg... never mind. The most obvious grounds are pre-contract, nonconsummation, and… ah… impotence." She cleared her throat, feeling the blood rush to her face, and shifted uncomfortably. "I… ah… I feel there's a good deal of fertile ground for us to explore there."

"Is that so?"

"Yes indeed," she continued, missing the dangerous tone in his voice as hers grew more animated. "If we could establish there was a contract between you and your heiress—"

"Or you and your beefy beau."

"I… yes, quite. Well, it's an avenue we might explore, at any rate. Failing that, as we have no children, we could proceed on the basis of… ah… nonconsummation or impotence. There does appear to be some latitude there. The Countess of Summerset was able to secure a divorce on the grounds that her husband, though not impotent to women in general, was impotent to her, and Lady Desmond was successful on the grounds that her husband had an insufficiency to please a reasonable woman."

"I can assure you, my love, no one will believe either of *me*. *If* we should decide to go that route, our best chance for success would be on the basis of your frigid, cruel, and unaccommodating nature, and your unwillingness or inability to provide me with an heir."

"Oh," she said, blinking in surprise.

She reminded him of a ruffled owl and he had to bite his lip to stifle his laughter.

"I… I suppose we could if you thought it best. It doesn't seem terribly chivalrous."

He choked on his brandy, covering with a cough as he rose and placed his glass on the table.

"Are you laughing at me, Sinclair?"

"Not at all, my love," he said, sitting down again and patting her knee. "Not at all. You've done excellent research. As you say… fertile ground… or infertile if you will."

"Beast!"

He grabbed her wrist before she could punch his shoulder. "Pull in your claws, hellcat."

"Then stop mocking me!" The struggle to free her arm drew him closer, and his laughter cut off abruptly as their eyes caught and held.

She was intensely aware of his parted lips, the feel of his fingers wrapped tight against her skin, and the rise and fall of his chest, just inches from hers. She watched, mesmerized, as he lowered his head towards her, holding her breath as he nuzzled the curve of her shoulder and neck. The house was silent but for the snapping of logs on the fire and the pounding of her heart. He released her arm and she rested it on his shoulder, drawing him closer still. His breath was warm against her ear, sending shivers through her body, and she turned into him, seeking his mouth.

"Will you be dining this evening, milord?"

Catherine let out a little yelp of surprise as Jamie jumped to his feet.

"Bloody hell, Sullivan! Are you *trying* to drive me mad?"

"No, milord," Sullivan said, wrapping himself in wounded dignity. "I was *trying* to perform my duties. You've not eaten since breakfast and it is now after nine. I assumed you and milady would be hungry, and I thought you might like a light supper before Cook retires for the evening. I apologize if I was overzealous."

"Yes, quite," Jamie said, running a hand through his hair and favoring Catherine with a rueful look. "It seems I've forgotten my manners, and the hour. My apologies to you both. Are you hungry, Catherine?"

"Ravenous, actually."

"Well, there you have it, Sullivan. You're right as always. Please bring us a tray of whatever Cook has left from supper. In future though, if a door is closed, I would ask that you knock."

Once Sullivan had left, Jamie returned to the settee, lounging beside her and favoring her with a knowing smile. "Well… I think we both know where that was heading. How are we to prevent our natural inclinations from tearing your schemes asunder? I shall try my best to contain myself, love, but can you?"

"I don't know what you mean."

He leaned into her, his shoulder snug against hers. "Yes you do." His voice was warm and seductive, his mouth just inches from her ear. His fingers trailed along her jaw, brushing her ear and caressing her skin before cupping her face and turning her into his kiss. Lowering his mouth to hers, he coaxed her to open, dragging softly back and forth across her parted lips and probing gently with his tongue. She sighed and turned into him, melting against him and winding her arms around his neck. He groaned and reached for her waist, pulling her tight so her body pressed warm and eager against his.

Catherine arched against him, heart racing, her skin pricking with excitement and her body pulsing with delicious new thrills. She opened her mouth wider, inviting him deeper, but he broke off the kiss suddenly, bending his head to nuzzle her throat. He flicked her with his tongue and bit her gently, then kissed her cheek and brought his forehead to rest against her own.

"*That's* what I meant, love," he said, his voice hoarse. He took a deep breath and took her by the shoulders, guiding her back upright. "What if our passions overwhelm us, destroying all your well-laid plans?"

She pushed him away and sat up straight, struggling to regain her composure. "Don't flatter yourself, Sinclair! There's no danger of that!"

"Excellent! I shall rely upon you, then. I shall rest easy knowing at least one of us can be strong. If ever I forget myself, you need only growl or hiss and spit to put me in my place. I still tremble to recall how you trounced me."

"Oh, do be quiet!" *Damn him!* What kind of cold-hearted creature was he to entice and bewitch her, teasing her with a glimpse of something that promised to be magical, and then abruptly closing the door? It was all a game to him, and that was something she'd do well to remember.

"You must admit it could be a problem though, love, and despite your careful planning, I'd wager it's one you never considered."

"Yes, well... now you've pointed it out I'm sure we'll both be careful—Sinclair!" His fingers were playing absently with a ribbon that trailed from the lace gathered at her elbow, and she slapped them away. "You said you'd try and contain yourself."

"Did I? I'm so full of good intentions, they're difficult to recall." He laughed and pulled away.

They were interrupted by a loud insistent banging at the door.

"Do come in, Sullivan. You've made your point."

The Irishman entered, bearing a tray of bread, cheese, cold capon, and venison.

"Thank you. Just leave it on the table and bring us some sack, would you?"

They fell to the meal with gusto, tearing at the capon and washing it down with the cold dry wine, their conversation temporarily halted. Jamie finished first, and watched with undisguised admiration as Catherine devoured the remnants of the bird, daintily licking her fingers when she was done.

She caught him watching and paused, the tip of her finger still in her mouth. Her cheeks burned crimson as she reached for a napkin. "What? I was hungry."

"I can see you're a woman of strong appetite. I'm waiting to hear you belch."

"Can't you be serious, Jamie? I've offered you a proposition that can help us both. I want to be free. I've no wish to be any man's chattel. I don't want to submit to the dictates of someone else, be it brother or cousin *or* husband. I want to choose my own path. I think you want the same. I can give you enough money to do whatever you wish."

"Ah yes… the money. How would that work?"

"We'll agree upon a sum, sign a contract, and I'll transfer you the funds once the marriage is terminated."

"So… nothing will change between times. Your fortune remains your own, and though we're wed, you don't want me to fu—bed you. Or do you?" he asked, a curious gleam in his eye.

She blushed and turned away.

"It amazes me that a woman who's been to the French court and roamed the wilderness with a horde of wild barbarians, sword and pistol by her side, should blush as often as you do."

"It amuses you to provoke me, Sinclair. I hope it's some consolation that although I'm not all you desire, I'm at least a ready source of entertainment."

"It's a great consolation, love. You're very good company. I've been bored since we parted."

She looked up in surprise, astonished he'd think such a thing, let alone say it. "I'll not be altogether useless, you know. I'll pay off your creditors and settle any reasonable debts. I'll provide for your household and pay your expenses, and I'll sing your praises to the king and anyone else who may inquire. You need only play your part."

"And what would that be?"

"That of a reasonably attentive and indulgent husband. One who, if not faithful, is at least respectful and discreet. Can you play such a role?"

"A reasonably attentive husband? No. That's too boring. It would be far more amusing to play a besotted one."

They spent the rest of the evening ensconced in the library, hammering out an agreement. Jamie put up a token resistance when Catherine insisted they put it all in writing, to be witnessed and signed by their respective solicitors, but despite his arguments and protests, he recognized she was being remarkably generous, and he knew the advantage was hers. He was puzzled, uncomfortable, and grateful. He'd never expected much from others. His rescue of the chit had been a wild, quixotic impulse, one that had later embarrassed him and he'd blamed for most of his troubles, but it seemed that his battlefield wife was going to prove useful after all. He knew she had ulterior motives for helping him, she'd been clear about that, but she also offered friendship and alliance at a time he badly needed them.

In the end, a bargain was struck. They shook hands and agreed to formalize it in the morning. The next day Jamie's solicitor and one of Catherine's London lawyers reviewed it. It was signed, with Sullivan as a witness, two days later. Shortly thereafter, James and Catherine Sinclair, Lord and Lady Carrick, Earl and Countess of Carlyle, made their debut.

Fifteen

THE SINCLAIRS' SURPRISING REUNION HAD BEEN THE
focal point of gossip among London's cynical elite
since Sidney had scampered from their table five days
earlier. Between him, Buckingham, whose delight
in wild speculation was exceeded only by his joy in
creating mischief, and the curious spectators who'd
caught a glimpse of Catherine riding in Hyde Park,
the entire court—including the king—was buzzing
with curiosity. The few days Catherine and Jamie
had gone to ground to work out the details and
finalize their contract had only whetted the appetite
of bored and jaded courtiers who were constantly
on the lookout for any new diversion. Everyone was
talking, everyone wanted to see for themselves, and
within days of her arrival, Catherine, along with her
husband James Sinclair, Earl of Carrick and Carlyle,
were summoned to Whitehall.

Catherine was received in the banqueting hall.
The light and airy two-story room, with its crown
glass windows and glorious ceiling panels by Rubens,
reflected a refined Italianate style. It was a great honor,

signaling James's interest in cementing relations with one of the more powerful Highland clans, and his appreciation of Catherine's gift of thirty-six barrels of Speyside whiskey, which, with its unique fruity flavor overlaid with a taste of honey, was far superior to anything London had to offer.

Dour and serious, the new king disapproved of drunkenness, dueling, and the relaxed manners and frivolity that had characterized his brother's court, but he was far from immune to the attractions of the opposite sex. His warm reception gave Catherine hope that a charter to supply whiskey to His Majesty's court would soon follow.

A curious throng crowded the room—absent Lady Ware, who'd left for the country in a fury, deeply affronted that Jamie was recalled to court. They stood to either side, murmuring excitedly, heads bent in avid curiosity as Catherine advanced through the room. Jamie stood back and the room quieted as the king motioned her forward. Conscious of her status as a creature of gossip and innuendo, and mindful of the king's taste, she'd dressed in a magnificent outfit of sapphire Chinese silk, cut in the mannish style popular among the queen and her ladies. Performing a deep curtsey to both king and queen, she met James's smile of interest with a demure one of her own.

He welcomed her graciously to London and his court and motioned Jamie to join them. "Where have you been hiding, Sinclair? You've been absent from court for far too long. It's Carrick now, isn't it?"

"Yes, Your Majesty, a gift from your brother, if you recall."

"Yes, quite," the king snapped, suspecting the remark was meant to chide him for his own refusal to reward the man and his banishment from court. The effrontery! One didn't reward arrogance and failure. Nevertheless, the Drummond girl might prove useful, and she was a handsome chit indeed. More than his interest stirred as he watched her. "There's no doubt you served my brother well, despite your recent negligence to me. You're a rascal and a rogue, sir, but it pleases me that you've given up your rakish ways to settle into marriage. Where have you been hiding this pretty jewel? Why didn't you tell us who she was? Were you afraid someone might steal her?"

"My husband is not the sort to be jealous, Your Majesty," Catherine said with a winsome smile, wishing she might smack her arrogant husband on the back of his over-proud head.

"Nonetheless he hid you from us, madam. I'm hard-pressed to forgive him."

"It's not he, but I, you must forgive, Your Majesty. If he seemed negligent in his duty it was because of my foolishness. He rescued my life and honor, and offered me marriage when he found me trapped on a battlefield, but I thought he played me false and so I ran away."

"Led him a merry chase then, did you girl? The vixen flees the hound?"

Catherine looked down modestly. "Indeed, sir. I thought he'd follow me all the way home, but it seems he lost heart, so *I* had to come and fetch him." She looked up again with a mischievous grin.

James II, known for his serious demeanor, burst into delighted laughter. "God's blood, Sinclair! The minx appears a handful! Are you sure you can manage her?"

"I shall endeavor to do my best, Your Majesty."

"Good! Don't lose her again. Keep a watchful eye on her and be sure to bring her with you whenever you come to court. The Queen has arranged a play tomorrow evening. We shall expect to see you there, and you may join us at banquet tonight."

The audience was over. Jamie bowed low, collected his wife, and together they walked from the hall. "Be careful, mouse," he said, close in her ear, guiding her through the throng of courtiers and well-wishers pressing forward to greet them. "He thinks himself a lion and he'd love to have a taste of you."

"I'm hardly a sufficient morsel for one so grand, but let him try my whiskey and he'll be my slave," she said with a happy grin, leaning into him so he could hear her.

Putting his arm around her waist, Jamie tugged her sideways into a short passage, then another and another, passing through a warren of small corridors and hidden stairways, until they were in a long gallery that led to treed garden set with rose bushes and rows of statues.

"You certainly know your way around, Sinclair."

"Please, my love. Try Jamie, or husband, if that doesn't suit."

"Very well, Jamie. And you might try calling me Cat. That went rather well, don't you think? Although you certainly didn't help matters by baiting him. How is it we escaped that mob so handily?"

"I know every secret passage in this place, love."

"Oh? And how did you learn that?"

"Hiding from suspicious husbands, how else?"

"Ah! I thought perhaps you'd been a spy."

He gave her a sharp look. "Think you so?"

"Well, one wonders how and why an aristocratic Englishman acquired the skill to pass himself off as a tinker and a Highlander," she said with a shrug, following him to a bench and sitting down.

"Amateur theatrics, my dear."

"If you say so. Damnation but I hate these dresses! My corset's so tight I can scarcely breathe. No wonder all the ladies totter about on the arm of some man or another. A stiff breeze would knock them flat."

"You'll be missing your boots and breeches, I suppose."

"Perhaps I'll take to wearing them and shock your wicked friends."

"I have no friends."

"You have Sullivan and me."

"You're both family. I hate to disappoint, my love, but it's been done before. Hortense Mancini was wearing just such garb when she arrived to take London and Charles by storm, and James's wife Mary has had her portrait done dressed much the same. It's been the fashion on and off among some ladies of the court, a thing both Charles and James were partial to, though those women were mere poseurs, while you my dear, are an original. Wear them and you'll melt James's heart if you haven't done so already. I've had the pleasure of seeing you in trousers and boots, my dear, and can assure you that while your dress accentuates the perfection of one set of curves, your breeches do the same for another."

His finger traced a path along her décolletage as he spoke. Her breath caught in her throat. She closed her eyes and shivered, knowing she should slap his hand away, but his husky voice and light caress entranced her, and as her breasts swelled and hardened, she leaned into his touch. He spread the fingers of one hand through her hair, drawing her to him, while the other roamed the smooth silk of her dress, caressing her waist and gently squeezing. His lips touched hers in a feather-light kiss, then nibbled at her jaw and earlobe. Alive with sensation, she pressed close against him, threading her fingers through his hair, unable to stop a moan of excitement as he deepened his kiss. She gasped when his fingers brushed the pebbled peaks that thrust against the thin silk of her bodice, wanting to feel the heat of his skin on hers, eager for his touch.

"Easy, love," he murmured. "Not here, not now. Good Christ, but you're a bounteous handful for any man!"

Mortified, she slapped at him, pushing his hands away, her struggle growing more heated when he clamped his hand over her mouth.

"Well, that's deuced strange! Where have they got to, do you think, Carlyle and his Scottish hoyden?"

Catherine stopped struggling and he let her loose, holding a finger to his lips in a gesture for silence.

"Damned if I know. Has the devil's own luck though, doesn't he? Seems the camp follower's turned into a countess, and just when Caroline Ware thought she'd got her revenge."

"Ha! A rich countess with gold and whiskey and the ear of the king. How'd a faithless rogue like that ascend to such heights?"

"By being a faithless rogue."

"I was speaking of the girl. How did he find her? She's freakish tall."

"Aye, fitting prey for Dismal Jimmy. Do you reckon he brought her on purpose, to dangle in front of the king?"

"He wouldn't be the first to pimp a wife or daughter to a Stuart. Many a fortune's been made that way. The father an earl and the offspring duke and duchess!"

As the sounds of their laughter drifted away, Jamie returned his attention to Catherine. "Sorry, love, old habits die hard."

"To which do you refer? Your penchant for lewd behavior or your penchant for spying?"

"Why, to both, dear child. You mustn't let them bother you. This court depends on gossip and malice as its life's blood. You're not a success until they loathe and envy you."

"Why hasn't it worked for you?"

He gave a startled laugh. "You've a clever wit, Catherine. If Charles had met you, you'd have five or six royal bastards and be a duchess by now."

"You judge me by your own lax standards, Sinclair. I'm no one's mistress but my own."

"There's no need to hiss and spit, hellcat. I meant it well. You take things too seriously at times. I'm baffled how a woman can have so much wit and so little sense of humor."

"You're trying to provoke me again, Sinclair. I'm baffled that a man surrounded by enemies, who claims he has no friends, insists on taking everything as a joke."

Catherine was still annoyed with Jamie a few hours later when they joined the king and his guests at banquet. How dare he assume she'd been so eager for him that she had to be restrained? *"Easy, love. Not here, not now."* Arrogant, conceited oaf! And to think he mocked her sense of humor! Her sense of humor was as good as anyone's! She simply had a Scottish sensibility, one more attuned to subtlety and irony, not the Sassenach penchant for ribaldry and broad farce. Perhaps he'd like to see her get drunk and juggle, then fall on her behind.

"Still angry, my love?"

"To be angry I'd have to value your opinion. Why do they call him Dismal Jimmy?"

"It's a sobriquet given him by Nellie Gwyn, because he's so dour and humorless."

"Ah! Just like me."

"No, mouse, never," he said with a laugh. "You've a sparkling wit. One that delights and entertains. No one's ever said that of our Jimmy."

Mollified, she allowed him to guide her to her seat, pointedly ignoring the curious looks and spiteful comments sent her way. If they'd hoped to find entertainment at her expense they were quickly disappointed. She was richly dressed, her clothes reflected the latest Paris fashions, she was better educated than most of her peers in the English court, and her manners had been polished at Versailles. It didn't stop them whispering, though. It was a commonly held prejudice amongst the English and lowland Scots that Highlanders were barbarians. They called them the wild Irish and imagined them unsophisticated, savage, ungovernable brutes that delighted in warfare, pillage, rapine, and murder. *"I may enjoy pillage and murder, but I defy anyone to say I'm nae a sophisticated man,"* her father had once protested in mock indignation, but even he had been wary of the isolated clans that lived deep in the mountains farther to the north.

Her father had taught her well, and she was far more interested in observing than being observed. If she were to live among these people, she'd do well to understand them, and as they milled about or took to the dance floor, she watched them as avidly as they watched her. The men strutted about in their red, high-heeled shoes, many sporting matching ribbons and red bows under their long cravats. With their full wigs, and feathered, wide-brim hats, they towered over their ladies, though none besides her husband rivaled the king in height, who at six-foot tall was still three inches shorter than his brother Charles.

She looked at her husband and smiled. His own dark hair hung loose about his shoulders and he wore his cavalry boots, complaining "men's heels have grown so ridiculous a fellow can neither fight, nor run, nor sneak about in the damn things." He was wearing an elegant suit of dark silk with matching coat and breeches, a silver-trimmed waistcoat, and a ribbonless cravat. *He has no need to accentuate or conceal. He's strikingly handsome, quite beautiful, in fact.* He caught her look, returning it with a dazzling smile, and her heart beat faster. *Careful girl. He's likely had half the women in this room. It's all a game and you're but one among many.* No wonder several of them regarded her with daggers in their eyes.

As Catherine learned the ways of the English court, Jamie returned to the obligatory rounds of social functions, dancing, cards, and light flirtation, with his Highland wife in tow. He found himself enjoying her company more and more, though her frankness and honesty were somewhat disconcerting. It wasn't the way of a courtier, it wasn't the way of the women he knew, and he wasn't sure he liked it. It seemed to demand the same in return, and that was something he wasn't comfortable with. Still, it was novel at least, even refreshing, and he supposed if employed judiciously it would do no harm. Bit by bit, he lowered his guard.

Although he was free to pursue other women, provided he was discrete, he found he'd little interest in it anymore. He'd also lost interest in gambling and carousing and many other pastimes that had filled his days and nights before Catherine came. It was far more entertaining to bait her and tease her and show her the city. As he accompanied her to the theatre and dinner parties, fetes and balls, concerts and fireworks on the Thames, things he'd once found dull and boring now excited him, provided she was there.

Catherine was as bemused as Jamie was. She hadn't expected him to be so congenial and amusing. She hadn't expected to find him so accepting and attentive.

She hadn't expected to find him so damned attractive! She wondered why he bothered. The contract had been signed. He'd have his freedom and his money soon and there was nothing to be gained by charming her, but he insisted on playing the besotted husband. In the process, he was always touching her, placing a hand on her elbow or the small of her back, or an arm around her waist or shoulders. When they sat side-by-side, talking in the library, gossiping at the theatre, or taking a private moment in company, he always sprawled beside her, his big body solid and warm against her own.

She knew that at court, romantic love between husband and wife was considered unseemly and ridiculous. She knew they were mocked in satires and scurrilous verse. She knew his former lovers were shocked and hated her, and she knew, despite their snide remarks and comments, that they envied her, too. She also knew it provided her husband two of the pleasures he enjoyed most: theatrics and thumbing his nose at the court. He obviously found it immensely entertaining, and she decided she might as well relax and enjoy it, too.

He filled her with excitement and he made her laugh, but though he petted, squeezed, and fondled, he hadn't kissed her again since her first day at court. He thought her untouched and had taken pains to keep her so, and she knew it was why he restrained himself even now. How could she tell him she wasn't the innocent he assumed? At first, in the cave, she hadn't told him because she felt it was none of his business. She was nothing to him but a problem to be dealt with and a fragment of a dream. When she'd first arrived in London, she'd feared his mockery, and now she feared his anger and mistrust.

She should have told him before they signed a contract, but it had happened so fast, the threshold between it being none of his business, to her being a lying jade, had passed in the blink of an eye. She'd been trying to find a way to tell him ever since, but she could never seem to find the right time. How did one *start* such a conversation? When the time came to seek an annulment he'd have to know. She resolved to tell him when the opportunity presented and not to worry until then. He'd be angry and hate her or he wouldn't, but she'd enjoy him now, while he was in a good mood, because Jamie Sinclair in a good mood was something magical, a joy no woman would ever forget, and once this adventure was over, she'd never have as much fun again.

Mid-February they were invited to see a play at the Royal Cockpit theatre in Whitehall, by the well-respected female playwright, Aphra Behn. During the scene changes, Jamie took Catherine to tour the boxes and dressing rooms, pointing out persons of interest as they went. He stood behind her, his hands resting on her shoulders, his long fingers stroking the sensitive hollow between shoulder and neck, and his breath caressed her ear as he spoke. "Over there, with the magnificent breasts, is Lady Wyndham. Her beauty is only exceeded by her lack of wit. She was one of Charles's minor mistresses and is dresser to the queen dowager now. The one in the corner is Katherine Sedly. She's James's favorite mistress and was maid of honor to the queen. Mary wants her gone and James has pledged to lead a life of virtue, but as you can see, she's still here. She's said to be as mad as her mother and as vicious as her father, but even Charles recognized her as a wit. She was to be married to Churchill, the tall gentleman over there."

As if hearing him, Churchill raised his head and nodded, and Jamie nodded back. "Very handsome looking gentleman, wouldn't you say?"

"Yes, I suppose," she said, only half attending, distracted by the shivers running up and down her spine.

"He's Earl of Marlborough now, but when he was a young ensign, he was Lady Castlemaine's kept man."

"I thought she was King Charles's mistress."

"Yes. She was the favorite for several years, but Charles was never faithful and he didn't begrudge her her fun. He told Churchill he forgave him as he only did it for his bread. She paid him five thousand pounds for clothes and he invested it in an annuity from whence comes the great fortune he has today. He's always been good with money, him. It was a great surprise when he refused Sedly and married Sarah Jennings. She was practically penniless. His family was in shock."

"You mean he married her for love?"

"Apparently so, or some other such foolishness."

"Well, you married me thinking I was likely a camp follower and a traitor to your king. What does that make you?"

"A lucky man," he said with a grin. He nuzzled her ear and bit it gently, making her squeak.

"Jamie!"

"What?" he murmured, hot against the back of her neck as his hands caressed her throat.

"What are you doing?"

"I'm just playing my part," he said innocently, removing his hands from her neck and sliding them down to her waist, brushing the sensitive outer curve of her breasts on the way.

She gasped and her nipples tightened, clearly visible through the sheer silk of her dress. "You're enjoying this!" she hissed. He pulled her tight against him and she could feel his erection prodding her from behind.

"Of course I am. Are you?" He laughed and tugged her hair. "Now hush, love. Here comes Buckingham." Buckingham sauntered toward them, mischievous and resplendent, and Jamie hugged Catherine against him, crossing an arm across her chest.

"Ah, dear boy! We've missed you at court, some of us more than others. Lady Beaton wonders where you've been and if you're well."

Catherine twisted her head, but Jamie ignored her sharp look.

"Good evening, George. You remember my wife?"

"I do indeed! The glorious Amazon who rode forth from her snowy fortress to bring you succor and relief. Good evening, madam," he said with a courtly bow. "Everyone's talking about how thoroughly you've fixed the lad's attention. We've never seen the like before, at least not between husband and wife!"

"Yes, well, like all good courtiers we strive to entertain," Jamie broke in. "Forgive me for saying, but you don't look well. Is there ought amiss?"

"Ech! Well… been plagued by colic and gripe, dear

boy, brought on by a taste for the finer things in life, no doubt. Such a pity the things we most enjoy are inevitably bad for us."

"I quite agree," Jamie said, his gaze shifting to Catherine.

"In any case I'll be off to my estate for some fishing in a fortnight. Simple food and good clean air will soon set all to rights. Jimmy and I have never been particularly fond of one another, and the air in London at the moment is bad for my health. Speaking of which, might I have a brief word with you in private?" He gave Catherine an apologetic look.

Reaching behind him, Jamie filched a scarf from its perch on the back of a nearby chair and draped it over Catherine's shoulders, then kissed the back of her neck.

Red-faced, she pulled it tight across her chest.

"Forgive me, love, this won't take but a moment."

Buckingham, waiting expectantly, barked with laughter. "Good lord, man! You *are* pleased to see me."

Jamie looked back at her, shrugged and grinned, and followed Buckingham into a small alcove. Her face burning, Catherine turned to face the stage.

"A word to the wise, Sinclair. A certain lady's returned to court and heartily wishes you ill, whilst our beloved monarch grows more obdurate, suspicious, and vindictive by the day. He won't listen to reason. You know as well as I he's embarked on a course that can only lead to trouble. It's always good to keep a foot in both camps, but be careful whom you play with. If the Ware bitch can take you down she will, and Jimmy boy is not a forgiving man."

Jamie smiled and pulled away, squeezing Buckingham's shoulder. "I've not been away from court *that* long, George. You know I'm always the soul of discretion. Take care of yourself, my lord, and trust that I shall do the same."

"Heh, that's what I've always liked about you, Sinclair. One can always trust a man who looks after his own best interest, so long as one knows what that is."

"And you can never trust one that loves to meddle," Jamie replied with a smile.

He returned to Catherine, taking her possessively by the waist, and Buckingham took his leave.

"I swear you delight in causing gossip, James Sinclair."

"I do. Particularly this way," he murmured, giving her a squeeze.

She leaned back into him. "What was that all about?"

"Intrigue, mischief, and a woman scorned. Is it ever anything else?"

They were greeted by several others after Buckingham had left. Courtiers who'd been among the first to cut Jamie cold when he'd fallen in disfavor were eager to renew their acquaintance now that his star was on the rise. "Have you ever seen a more grasping group of hypocrites and whores?" he whispered in her ear. "If you've seen enough of the royal menagerie, I suggest we return to our seats."

Catherine had found the play delightful so far, and the idea of a female playwright fascinated her. She was eager to see the rest, but when she returned to her seat, she found a particularly scurrilous pamphlet waiting for her. It mocked her height, lampooning her in a series of drawings depicting her in unnatural sexual positions with Sir Richard Danby, one of the tiniest men at court.

"What's the matter, mouse? Is it the play that afflicts you or the company?"

"The company. It appears I'm already a great success." She tossed him the pamphlet. She felt a sudden wave of homesickness. For the most part the Highlanders were blunt and forthright. If they had a thing to say, they said it. If they had a quarrel, they declared it in the open and then they fought. A man knew who his enemies were and could trust in his friends.

"It's envy and resentment, Cat. Nothing more. You're a rich and powerful woman. One who doesn't cringe or back down and gives as good as she gets. You're also a Catholic, someone they regard as a foreigner, almost French, and you have the favor of the king. They consider you fair game."

"Fair game? I don't know how you stand it, Jamie. Is this all there is? Intrigue and conspiracy, an endless scramble to be noticed, night after night of vicious gossip and ceaseless rounds of cards? Does no one do anything useful? No wonder all these people do is drink and fuck!"

"Catherine! I'm shocked!"

"No, you're not."

"Well I would be if it weren't so diverting. You need to take it all with a grain of salt. Intrigue and gossip are parlor games for the rich and disaffected, a way to pass the time for those who have no purpose. They must make themselves important in some way. A motley collection of aging roués, pox-ridden gallants, and overdressed whores see you as a threat and want to hurt you. Laugh in their faces and pay them no mind. They'll soon move on to easier sport."

"I know. I know. You're right. I just... sometimes I just miss my home." A fierce wave of homesickness gripped her heart and she blinked back tears.

He placed a warm hand on her shoulder and gave a firm squeeze. "Sometimes I miss it too, mouse. I spent but a short time in your wild Highlands but they worked their magic and claimed a piece of my soul. I can only imagine how it must be for you, who grew up there. Still, I recognized you for what you were the moment I saw you."

She looked at him, startled. Even she didn't know who she was. She was still trying to figure it out. Wary, she waited for the jest.

"You and I are much alike in some ways, love. We can't accept the world as others serve it to us. We want to choose our own dinner. Always asking questions, always asking why, always wanting to see for ourselves. You love your home and you love your people, but they're a hidebound, stubborn race. It's hard to belong when to do so means losing yourself. You've the soul of a traveler, Cat, and the heart of an adventurer, and if you learn to accept it, you'll always be at home."

His answer took her aback. Was he right? What about family and duty? It was easy for him to say. What did he know of responsibility? He'd as much as admitted he switched his allegiance as easily as he changed his clothes. Drat the man! She'd been expecting a jest. Why couldn't he be predictable?

"That's easy for you to say, Sinclair. You're a man.

All your life you've been free to go where you want and do as you please. I'd like to see you try it dressed in skirts, with every dog and cock either sniffing at your heels or painting you a freak."

"You've grown mean and bitter, Catherine."

"And you've grown girlish and sentimental!"

His bark of laughter caused heads to turn and earned them glowering looks and a chorus of shushes.

"No one's as free as you think, love."

"But some are freer than others."

Jamie leaned closer. "Would you like to be freer than others? I can show you how."

His breath tickled her ear and she shrugged her shoulders to dislodge him. "I thought we'd decided against that."

"No, love, that's not what I meant, though I daresay it would do you good." She stiffened and he chuckled and hugged her tighter. "I can take you adventuring right here in London. I can show you a man's world, show you things and places no lady's ever seen... if you're game for it."

The last was spoken as a challenge, and since the early days of childhood, Cat Drummond could not resist a dare.

Sixteen

"WHY ARE YOU DRESSED SO ELEGANTLY WHILE I LOOK like one of those prancing fops we saw in Tunbridge Wells?" Catherine asked with displeasure, turning about in a circle, feathers, lace, and ribbons flapping in the breeze. "I swear this suit boasts more adornments than any dress I've ever worn."

"Because you *are* a prancing fop," Jamie explained patiently, "an untutored young pup, trying to make his mark as daring and original. As such, you must look like all the other fops. You *must* stay in character, my love. What does a young lad new to London want? What does he fear? How experienced is he? You have to ask yourself these questions. Anyone can don an outfit and play make-believe, but it takes study and practice to *become*. You must look like all the other rustics trying to impress."

"I should rather be a gallant young spark," she sniffed.

"Excellent! That's the spirit! So would all the other fops. You can go in costume if you like without practicing the rest. I can keep you safe, but they'll spot you quick enough for what you are, a lamb in wolf's clothing, a curiosity and diversion, and you'll soon become the center of attention, the one observed. But if you mark me well and do just as I show you, you'll disappear among them, an insignificant pup beneath anyone's notice, yet privy to their secrets, an invisible traveler in the world of men. It's up to you, Catherine. Would you rather be the watcher or the watched?

"The watcher," she said, springing to her feet and swaggering across the room. "There! You see? I can walk like a man."

"You walk like a country bumpkin."

"I beg your pardon?"

"Well, you do, love," he said with a smile. "That's how an apprentice boy would walk, not a young lordling. Now attend me, please, and try to walk like so."

"Is this really necessary, Sinclair?"

"Yes it is, my love. The walk is essential. All the courtiers do it. I would best describe it as an elegant swagger, a graceful strut. Observe if you will." He stood, head held high, one hand on his hip, one leg leading away from his body, with his right hand extended as if holding a *mouchoir* or cane, and then began to walk in a gliding, rolling stride, swinging his leg out and back round in a circular motion, exposing the inside of his thigh with each step. The sauntering swagger and fluttering handkerchief reminded her of the first moment she'd seen him on the banks of the River Clyde, and she smiled to think what a strange thing was fate.

He stopped in front of her. "Now you try."

"You can't be serious!"

"But I am, my dear. You must practice and perfect it if you hope to pass. If you lurch about like a Highland laddie, you'll be seen as a rustic boor no matter how fine your clothes. A courtier will appear a courtier even dressed in rags, so long as he has the walk and can do like so." He waved the handkerchief in an affected manner, bringing it to his nose. "I should have thought you'd have learned as much at the French court."

"I observed it and thought it affected and ridiculous. I never strove to emulate it."

"Of course not! You were a young lady, but now you're a gallant young spark."

"Is that all there is to it?"

"Well, it would help to affect an air of tremendous ennui," he said with an exaggerated sigh, fluttering the handkerchief again. "You are to be my cousin after all, a step above the average fop."

"Ah, is that what you are?"

He blinked, taken aback, then burst into laughter. "Why no, my dear! *I* am a practiced rake and libertine. You've a sharp tongue on you, Cat Drummond, and a sharper wit. I predict young Reginald Sinclair will be a great success."

"I detest the name Reginald."

"Very well, I christen thee William. Now watch again."

Catherine burst out laughing. "You look like a peacock!"

"Precisely!" he said, nodding solemnly, "and so must you."

They continued like that for the next hour, laughing and playing like children. Catherine couldn't remember ever having such fun, but there was nothing childish about the thrill that ran through her whenever he smiled, or the way her skin pricked and her heart hammered whenever she felt his touch. *Why must he be so charming?* She found herself making deliberate mistakes, hoping he'd correct her with a hand to shoulder, elbow, or wrist, but bit by bit her disguise became more natural and her manner more assured. She was somewhat annoyed he didn't seem to notice.

"Sinclair, why are you standing there with your head cocked to one side? Am I still doing it wrong?"

"Good heavens no, my love! You're a remarkably quick study. You nailed the thing a half hour ago. I was merely admiring your splendid arse!"

She blushed and made a face at him. "Well, pray don't when we're out in company, else no one will take me for a boy."

He choked on his drink and put it down, sputtering and laughing. "Good Christ, my love, but you're a God-awful innocent!"

"What do you mean? Why do you say that?"

"Never mind, it's not important." He reached for a handsomely plumed wide-brimmed hat and handed another to her. "Come along, little cous, the night has yet to begin, and London and adventure await. Remember to speak as little as possible, and keep your voice pitched low. Don't worry if you squeak a bit. It will only add to the effect."

He took her first to The Puritan coffee house on Aldergate Street, a respectable establishment known for political discourse. Coffee was looked upon as a great stimulant for the mind, and The Puritan had become a popular social gathering place for intellectuals and literati, a place where men could relax in good company, exchange opinions, and hear the latest news.

"You're about to enter *the* most sacred bastion of the London male, Cat," he told her as they stood outside. "Any man can enter, provided he's reasonably dressed and can pay his penny, but no females are allowed. By bringing you I mark myself a traitor to my sex." He favored her with a wink. "This is a Londoner's true home, where every man is equal, and every man a king. If you ever need to find a fellow, don't ask what street he lives on, ask where he drinks his coffee."

Catherine peeked over his shoulder, anxious and eager to look inside. She was grateful for the tight waistcoat and coat that bound and hid her full breasts. It was a tight squeeze, but not nearly as bad as wearing a corset. She resisted the urge to clutch Jamie's arm and remembered his words from earlier in the afternoon. *"What does a young lad want? What does he fear?"* Will Sinclair was an inexperienced youth who feared making a fool of himself, she decided. He wanted to impress his cousin and wanted to be a seen as a man. *It seems we share a lot in common,* she thought with a grin. Young Will would be awestruck and cocksure by turns. In fact… he'd be feeling the same anxiety and excitement as she was right now. She took a deep breath, tilted her hat at a rakish angle much as she'd seen Jamie do, threw back her shoulders, and with a hint of a swagger, paid her penny and followed him inside.

She blinked and coughed and Jamie patted her back solicitously. The place reeked of tobacco and the rich, dark smell of coffee. Conversation swirled around them, roaring and receding like waves on a beach. Men sat in corners or at long tables, scribbling and reading, drinking coffee and smoking, engaged in heated discussions and quiet discourse. Newspapers and pamphlets were strewn about, free with the price of admission, and bulletins and announcements of auctions, sales, and shipping news covered the walls.

A handsome gentleman came over to greet Jamie, nodding politely her way in passing. She recognized him—Churchill, the Earl of Marlborough—and was relieved he didn't recognize her. He and Jamie were soon deep in conversation, and she wandered over to the back wall, wondering in passing what it was that made them both so intent. A sheet was posted on the wall, entitled "Rules and Orders of the Coffee House." She perused it, fascinated. It stated that all men were equal in a coffee house, and none need give up his seat to a finer man. Anyone who swore must pay a fine of twelve pence, and the man who started a fight must buy every man a meal to atone. Maudlin lovers were not to mope in corners, sacred things must be excluded from conversation and—

"William!"

It took her a moment to realize he was speaking to her.

"William! I've secured us a table, come and sit, you chuckle-headed dolt. You've been staring off into space like a moonstruck calf."

She lifted her chin and strolled over to join him, giving him a frosty look on behalf of an indignant Will, before sitting down.

"Here, have some coffee, lad. Maybe that will wake you up."

Several other men had joined them at the table, none of whom she knew, but they all seemed well acquainted with Jamie. No one gave her more than a cursory glance, and though she was accustomed to discussing and arguing politics at council and at table, she hung back, choosing to listen rather than speak, melting into the background, a watcher like Jamie had said.

There were men from all walks of life, carpenters and bankers, soldiers, sea captains, apprentices, and statesmen, and not a few of London's elite, but they sat shoulder to shoulder, and any man's view was as good as the next if he could explain and defend it. She delighted in the conversation, surprised at its breadth and depth and the liberty of ideas, and impressed with Jamie's encyclopedic grasp of the issues of the day.

Here was the London she'd heard so much about, a vibrant crucible of thought and innovation years ahead of anywhere else in Europe. This was where it had been hiding. It wasn't born and nurtured in the halls of power by a glittering elite, but in the streets and theatres and coffee houses of the city, where doers and thinkers from all walks of life could meet and share their views. *What a pity no women are allowed! What might we contribute, what might we accomplish, if not excluded from this feast?*

A sudden commotion drew everyone's attention as a breathless youth burst through the door and went to the counter to collect a cup of coffee and speak to the proprietor. "The boy is a messenger," Jamie explained, turning to her. "They send them around the coffeehouses whenever there's some news."

A moment later, it was announced that a clipper ship en route to Jamaica had been lost in a storm, provoking white faces and gasps from some—investors, she assumed. The news that followed provoked an angry grumbling and heated conversation. It seemed His Majesty had chosen an ardent Catholic supporter, Richard Talbot, as Lord Deputy and his chief governor in Ireland.

"Good Christ, that's all we need! There's no helping the witless fool," Jamie muttered under his breath. "Come along, Will, there's more to see and do. Time we be off."

They stepped out into a grey and dreary late winter afternoon.

"We're not done yet, are we? There's so much more I'd like to see."

"Perhaps another time, love. Something's come up that I must attend to."

"Can't I come with you?" she pleaded. "You promised me a night to remember and it's only been two hours. I can be discreet." She touched his arm and gave him an imploring look. She knew it was shameless, but she wasn't ready for the adventure to end. Ever since the swoon in her council chamber had brought men who'd opposed her running to assist, she'd been convinced that in a world that gave every advantage to men, a woman must use whatever tools she had.

He looked at her uncomfortably, his whole body aware of her hand on his arm. An erection stirred, straining against his breeches, and he was vaguely aware that this wasn't the way to be looking at his cousin Will. *Blast the wench!* Whenever he was with her, he couldn't seem to think straight. She'd always been fetching in breeches, though. There were few women who had such long and shapely legs, or such a pleasing derr—

"Well?"

"Well what?" He blinked and focused. He had no use for innocent misses in general, but this one was his wife. They'd come to an agreement. He'd promised not to bed her and let her go within a year, but he still owed her his protection and he considered her a friend. He needed to stop imagining her naked. He needed to find a whore and relieve himself of whatever it was that plagued him as soon as he was able.

"Can I come?"

"I'm sorry, Catherine. I've several stops to make, some in places a lady, or even cousin Will, should never go. It could be dangerous, and I'll be gone most of the night."

"I'm not a lady tonight, and I'm not your cousin Will. I'm not delicate, Jamie. I wasn't in a parlor doing my stitching when you found me. I've been on cattle raids. I've proven myself in battle. I know how to fight."

There was something in her eyes, an earnest plea for recognition. Something moved deep inside him, and he couldn't tell her no. He sighed and removed his hat, running one hand through his hair. "There won't be any fighting. You'll stay close beside me at all times, unless I tell you otherwise. No wandering off to explore like you did in there," he nodded in the direction of The Puritan. "You won't speak to anyone unless spoken to, and if you have to speak, you'll keep it short. You'll do exactly as I tell you at all times, and if we become separated, you'll wave down the nearest carriage and go directly home. Is that clear?"

"Absolutely!" she said, beaming.

"If you fail to do as I tell you, I'll never take you adventuring this way again," he warned, but her excitement was contagious and he put away his doubts, returning her grin with a smile and a wink, motioning for her to follow. "You never told me how you came to be on a battlefield," he remarked as they walked along.

"Didn't I? I'd come to rescue my little brother. He got himself mixed up with some Covenanters in Edinburgh and I didn't want you to kill him."

"Ah, black sheep of the family, was he?"

"No, apparently that was me."

"Something else we share in common."

"Why did you call the king a witless fool?"

"Because he's hanging to his throne by his fingers, and every day he makes matters worse. He's autocratic, stubborn, and vindictive, and he's rapidly losing friends. Charles was wise enough to recognize the English have a deep distrust of Catholic rule. They fear it would mean far less power for Parliament, and far more for the church and king. It's a feud that's been responsible for years of trouble and grief. I believe he was Catholic in his heart, and I'm told he returned to the fold on his deathbed, but he never let it interfere with governing the country.

"James insists on flaunting his faith, and despite all warnings, on forcing it on the country. One by one, he replaces his advisors. He's taken a Catholic wife who any day now may become pregnant with a Catholic heir to supplant his Protestant one, Mary. He keeps a standing army at the ready, and now he's taken steps to bind the Irish to his cause.

"Dick Talbot's first task will be to create an Irish Catholic army that James can use to coerce his English subjects. Sullivan may be happy, as my Irish properties used to be his. He'll be hoping for his ancestral lands back, as will most of the Catholics in Ireland, but the Protestants Cromwell settled in their place are bound to object. It's going to upset a great many powerful men. It's going to start the engines of civil war and rebellion all over again. You'd best not get too close to it, nor put too much faith in English treaties, trade arrangements, or alliances. It's something to warn your family about when you return to your snowy home." The thought caused an uncomfortable pang and he turned away.

"I'm not sure what I'm going to do, but I don't expect to ever go home. Why were you given Sullivan's land if you are Catholic too?"

"I was Protestant then, which illustrates precisely why one should always be flexible in matters of dogma and religion. You ask too many questions, love. Now look you to the left." They were turning onto Deveraux Street, and Catherine craned her neck to see. "That's the Graecian. Most coffee houses cater to specific groups and interests. Men of money and business frequent those on the Exchange. The Graecian's famous for its scholars and philosophers. Sir Isaac Newton calls this one home. When you hear men refer to coffee houses as penny universities, it's places like this they mean."

They found seats in a far corner and ordered steaming bowls of chocolate. Sir Isaac wasn't there, but Catherine listened with delight as an impromptu debate arose among several members of the Royal Society as they attempted to arrange the events of *The Iliad* in chronological order. She had to bite her lips several times to keep from joining in.

She was all but bouncing up and down when they set out on their way again. "Did you get your business done there, Jamie? It was certainly stimulating, but it hardly seemed dangerous to me."

"How many coffees have you had, love?"

"Three... four I think. And two chocolates. It does indeed have healthful properties as I've heard many people say. I've seldom felt more energetic."

"I can see that," he said dryly, "and no, my business isn't done. I had no business there. I just thought you'd like to see it."

"I loved it! I'm so happy you're showing me all this. I'd never have known it existed otherwise." She stopped and removed her hat, holding it gracefully in one hand as she performed a courtly bow. "To think I believed your debauched and rackety court was the best London had to offer. I freely and most humbly admit my ignorant mistake and tender you my most sincere and heartfelt apologies."

He plucked her hat from her hand and plopped it back on her head. "No more coffee for you, love."

"Jamie!"

Where The Puritan and Graecian had been stimulating for weighty debate as well as their coffee, their next stop on Russell Street was an entirely different affair. They stepped into Will's amidst a roar of laughter, followed by thumping on tables, cheers, and shouts, and then laughter all over again. Jamie was greeted with handshakes and much backslapping and pulled immediately into a merry throng. Reaching back, he grabbed Catherine by the shoulder of her coat and tugged her down into the seat beside him.

Putting an arm around her shoulder he leaned into her and shouted to be heard above the din. "Look over there, Will. Do you see the gentleman surrounded in the corner?"

Catherine looked over and saw a long-nosed, sloe-eyed older gentleman keeping court, and nodded.

"That's Dryden, the playwright. People come here to talk literature and be entertained. We'll be staying a while. Stay close, enjoy yourself, and watch your purse. There are sharpers, rogues, highwayman, and thieves in these places, too."

She nodded and he returned to the conversation he'd been having with a fellow who looked to be just the sort of man he'd described. They stayed well over an hour, and she clapped, hooted, and shouted with the crowd at each comedic turn, as wits, critics, and satirists took their turns at lampoon, inspired mimicry, and clever libel. One verse in particular was making the rounds from table to table, though she just caught the end of it.

Dare was an auld prophesy found in a bog,
Lilliburlero Bullen a la!
That Ireland would be ruled by an ass and a dog.
Lilliburlero Bullen a la!
And now the auld prophesy has come to pass,
For Talbot's a dog and James is an ass.
Lilliburlero Bullen a la!

Jamie's head was bent in earnest conversation with one man, then another, and though she'd strained to hear, it was impossible to tell what was said over the noise of the crowd. He turned to her now with a grin, clamping a hand on her shoulder and pulling her close to shout in her ear. "That ditty is the work of Wharton and Dorset, I'd wager," before returning to his companions.

"They say at court that half the fellows in these places are traitors and spies," she ventured, after they'd clambered into a hackney carriage and were on their way again.

"Mmm… yes. Charles used to call them seminaries of sedition. He'd have closed them down if he could. Tried once, but it lasted all of ten days before he had to open them again for fear of causing an insurrection."

"So… which are you?"

"They're flip sides of the same coin," he said with a sharp look. "I'm your husband, mouse. That's all you need to know. It's an impertinent question as well as a dangerous one. Why would you ask it?"

"Because everywhere we go some furtive fellow or another is always trying to engage you in private conversation."

"Not furtive enough, apparently. You said you could be discreet."

"And I am, very."

"Then I'll tell you this. Much like yourself, I like
to be well informed. Access to the halls of power can't
get a man as close to the heart of a matter as the talk at
his local coffee house can. Now no more talk of spies
and treason, although I grant you our next two stops
are known for it. Filled with radicals and republicans,
revolutionaries and *agent provocateurs*. The sort who
appeal to all the ladies. I'm sure you'll quite enjoy it."

They stopped first at Jonathan's in Exchange Alley
and then The Cromwell. Catherine had perfected
her courtier's swagger, and a low-pitched, slightly
bored drawl, an unconscious but effective imitation
of Jamie's. Comfortable in her role now, she'd
forgotten Jamie's strictures and joined in with the
throng. Confident in her abilities, common sense,
and discretion, Jamie let her go. He watched with
fond amusement as she went to fetch her umpteenth
cup of coffee, every inch the eager stripling on his
first big night in town. No mean wit herself, she
traded jests and sallies as she jostled through the
crowd. *Her performance would bring a theatre roaring to its
feet,* he thought with possessiveness and pride. *What
madness though, to bring her.*

Why had he? The same reason, he supposed, he
liked to taunt and tease her and to make her laugh.
He loved to see the excitement shining in her
eyes. When he was in her company, things seemed
fresh and new. The world throbbed with color and
everything pulsed with life. In three short months,
she'd become so much a part of his life it seemed
she'd always been there, and it was almost impossible

to imagine her gone. He watched as she returned, bearing gifts of chocolate, eyes bright with exhilaration, and felt a stab of sadness that he'd never been that young.

A hand on his elbow pulled his attention away from Catherine. "Buckingham? What are you doing here? I thought you'd left for the country. Good God man! You look like you're at death's door."

"I'm doing well enough, Sinclair. I leave the day after tomorrow. Now look you there, and heading our way. That's the tonic I need," he said with a leer.

"No, it's not."

"You're a timid sort of rake, Jamie. A man can make do with a comely lad for want of a comely lass."

"The lad is my cousin," Jamie said, a note of warning in his voice. "Keep your hands to yourself and mind your manners, Bucks, the boy doesn't share your vices."

"Pity," Buckingham replied with a mischievous grin.

Jamie made the appropriate introductions and Catherine removed her hat and made a gracious bow.

"No need for that, lad. We're not at court here." Buckingham's eyes flicked over her with interest. "The lad's a green one, Sinclair."

"Green as springtime, George. Leave him be. Is there ought you wanted to discuss?"

"Yes, actually… " His gaze shifted back to Catherine and sharpened. "Here now, boy! Have we met somewhere before?"

"I'm not a boy, Your Grace."

"Drink your chocolate and mind your manners, Will. My lord Buckingham and I have a matter to discuss and then we'll be leaving."

While Jamie occupied himself with Buckingham and others, Catherine joined a game of basset. Sprawling in her chair, she slouched, elbow on the table, a fashionable young buck who watched the play just like a sharper. After an hour, she had a tidy pile of winnings. She was about to take her turn as banker when a hand clamped on her shoulder.

"Now then, William. What would your dear father say to see you occupied this way?"

"'Twas he who taught me, cousin. Would you care to join us?" she asked with a jaunty grin.

"Aye, Sinclair, you've been scarce around the tables these days. Come join us. Perhaps the lad can teach you a thing or two," a rotund and sweaty gentleman invited, to snorts of laughter.

"Well… perhaps a round or two. Then we must be on our way."

Catherine flashed him a grateful look and he returned it with a wink and a grin. She'd been hearing since childhood that she was too outspoken, too independent, and too proud, a tomboy and a hoyden who was too muscled and too tall. Jamie's easy acceptance was the first she'd known in her adult life. She looked at him now as he raked in his winnings, flashing her a brilliant smile. Her heart squeezed painfully and she had to catch her breath.

"How could he not recognize me?" she asked him as they left.

"Who, Buckingham? People tend to see what they expect. Particularly people like him."

"What do you mean, people like him?"

"The rich and privileged. They live inside their own little world. People rush to give them what they want and need, so they grow accustomed to their expectations being met. Be careful of him. He's a predator, and you're just the sort of prey he loves."

"What's that supposed to mean?"

"Daring, witty, a challenge… a beauty who can pass as a boy."

She flushed, pleased with his offhand compliment. "But I'm your wife. You're his friend."

"You're no longer in your Highlands, love. Honor's worth spit here. Each man for himself and damn the rest. Buckingham never lets such flimsy contrivances as friendship or loyalty stand between him and what he wants."

"I am forewarned."

"You've done well tonight, Catherine. I know no other woman I could trust on such an adventure, but for this last stop, you must stay close. The element where we're going is far from refined."

"Try living in the field with a band of hairy Highlanders."

"I'd rather not. There'll be men of the sort I warned you against."

"Rascals and rogues? The type women swoon over? I shall try to restrain myself. In any case, I already have one of my own. Do they have food? I'm famished."

"They serve fine food on silver dishes, coffee in china cups, and wine in crystal glasses. They also serve… er… other things. You'll see women there, but no ladies.

Her eyes lit with interest. "You're taking me to a whorehouse? A brothel?"

"No… it's technically a coffee house… but… "

"You needn't worry, Sinclair. I promise you I won't have fits or faint, unless it be from hunger. Set me at a table with a meal and go about your business. I'll be fine. Oh dear! I just realized how that sounded. You'll not be about that kind of business though, I'm sure. I shouldn't like that very much."

"Of course not. I hadn't planned visiting here when I said you might come, but something came up at The Cromwell I must see to tonight. Would you prefer I have a carriage take you home?"

"No! I'd expire from hunger on the way, and I'm curious. It's something I'd never otherwise get to see."

"I should hope not! Very well. I'll be in and out as quick as I can. Be warned, though. You're likely to see far more than you bargained for."

Seventeen

THEIR DESTINATION WAS IN SOUTHWARK, A COFFEE house called Peg's. It was grander on the inside than she'd expected. The parlor promised comfort and relaxation, with its heavy ornate furnishings and silk and velvet covered chairs. Gilt-framed portraits and landscapes dotted wainscoted walls, giving the impression one had entered a substantial private home. It had the same rich smells of coffee, chocolate, and tobacco, the same excited bustle and hum of conversation, as the other places she'd visited that day, but the sounds were interspersed with feminine shrieks and giggles, and the smell was overlaid by perfume and the succulent flavor of slowly roasting beef.

Gripped by a sudden pang of hunger, Catherine's mouth watered and her nostrils flared. She looked about her, trying to trace the scent. It was only then she noted a large round table in a second parlor across the hall. It was full of men and women playing cards, all of them, it seemed, in various states of undress. One fellow was holding his cards with one hand while the other squeezed the naked breast of a woman who was straddling him, her skirt hiked above her hips. She was bouncing up and down, breasts bobbing energetically, the one that was unhindered brushing her lover's face as she rose and fell.

Catherine watched wide-eyed as he dropped his cards and grabbed his rider with both hands, jerking the chair itself up and down before collapsing against her with a groan. Next to them another fellow lounged, elbow on the table, legs stretched out, his head resting back against the ample midriff of a woman wearing only her chemise. She stood behind him, leaning over his shoulders, one hand caressing him under his shirt and another clearly playing about inside his breeches! The man's eyes were closed and he moaned as if in pain as his hips thrust up and down, but he didn't put down his drink.

Catherine took a step backward and gave an involuntary squeak as she bumped into something hard. A hand clamped her shoulder to steady her.

"It's rude to stare, Will. I thought I told you to stay close?"

"Sorry," she mumbled, her face burning.

"Well, come along, lad. You said you were hungry. Peg has a meal for us in the dining room."

She followed Jamie up the stairs and down a hall to the second-floor dining room. Despite her attempts to look straight ahead, a flash of movement through an open door to her left caught her eye and she craned her neck to see. A well-dressed gentleman stood by a fireplace, his breeches about his ankles, as a redheaded woman stroked and kissed his—

She was jerked by her collar, sideways and back, a moment before smacking into a doorjamb. "Careful Will, don't gawk."

"Is this the lad's first time?" Peg inquired, giving Catherine a motherly smile.

"Indeed, Peg, he's as innocent as an untried maid, but at the moment he's rather more starved for food than affection."

"Don't you worry, young man," Peg said, taking her by the arm and leading her into the dining room. "English Peg can take care of *all* your needs."

The dining room housed a massive table piled high with meat on silver dishes, and was crowded with men, serving girls, and a couple of well-dressed women. "I thought you said there were no ladies here?" she whispered to Jamie.

"Those are courtesans, my dear," he whispered back. "High-end trade for the gentry."

Catherine settled into a chair, somewhat overwhelmed. She found this place unsettling. The garish display of naked lust devoid of commitment or affection seemed a strange and hollow thing to her. She wondered why men sought it, yet she was fascinated also; for didn't lovers do those very things to one another, too? She glanced at Jamie, who was deep in conversation with another furtive-looking man. *What's he up to?* A serving maid approached him, balancing on his shoulders as she leaned across the table with a platter full of meat, her pendulous breasts shoved tight against his arm. He rewarded her attentions with a charming grin. *Why must he seek to charm every woman he meets?*

It seemed they knew him well. She narrowed her eyes and watched him closely. Not for Jamie wigs or powder. His hair fell in tangled strands, loose about his shoulders. Her gaze moved to his full, sensual lips, and she wondered if he'd ever kissed the serving girl. She wondered how many times he'd sat at tables or at cards with a woman in his lap or kneeling before him. Had he done those things with the maid? With Peg? With other girls? How many? He'd been sitting with his hand down a woman's dress when she'd arrived in London, after all. No doubt he couldn't help himself. *Men are pigs!* It was none of her business, of course, provided he was discreet.

He caught her watching him and gave her a sympathetic look. She glared back at him in return.

Picking up his wine glass, he came to sit beside her. "Feeling better now you've a full belly, Will? I'm almost finished. One more coffee and then for home?"

She gave him a sullen nod.

"Is there something amiss?"

Before she could answer, a pleasant-faced, ginger-headed sea captain, dressed in uniform and sporting an engaging grin, came over to join them.

"Sinclair! Or Carlyle, or whatever they call you these days. Finally laid the vicious old bastard to rest, I hear. And you inherited after all. Congratulations!"

"I thank you for your condolences."

"Not at all, man. Not at all. It's damned good to see you!"

"And you, Harry. I thought you were in Holland."

"Was there... here now... You heard the news, I suppose, so I expect I'll be heading back. Who's the lad?"

"My cousin, William Sinclair."

"He's a pretty boy."

"I know. I'm trying to keep him from being buggered, and I'm showing him the ropes. I've had to warn off Buckingham already."

"Is he still alive?"

"Aye, but he won't last long at the rate he's going."

Annoyed at being spoken of as if she wasn't present, Catherine folded her arms across her chest and leaned back, making no attempt to join the conversation. Closing her eyes, she pretended to sleep, and settled in to listen.

"Look there, Sinclair. You've an admirer."

Catherine opened her eyes and sat up straight, looking to where Captain Carrot Top was pointing. It was one of the courtesans, a voluptuous, dark-haired beauty in red silk, sporting glittering jewels and a heart-shaped beauty patch near her mouth. *Why would anyone use them? They look ridiculous!* she thought. She rolled her eyes and grunted, settling down again. *She looks like she forgot to use her napkin after dinner.*

"She's a beauty, don't you think? And only just arrived from the continent. An actress in need of a protector, and she's had her eye on you ever since you arrived."

Jamie gave him a sideways look. "Apparently you have, too."

"Would you like an introduction?"

"I couldn't afford her. Haven't you heard? My wife is up from the country. It's a sad business, really, but she controls the purse strings."

"What? Have you become a Tom Otter? I can't believe it from you, of all men!"

"You've been away from London too long, Harry. Between Old Rawley and Dismal Jimmy, it's become the fashion now."

"True enough, Sinclair," the captain said with a laugh. "Leave it to the Stuart boys, but they were hen-pecked by their mistresses, not their wives. What's the worst she can do?"

"She'll bite me and make me bleed."

"Ah! She sounds a veritable Gorgon. Well then, if you're not here for pleasure, let's get to business. Some place a little more private, perhaps?"

"Aye, if you make it quick. Come along, Will, you lazy lump. You're the only lad I know who'd fall asleep in a whorehouse."

"I thought you said it was a coffee house," she grumbled under her breath.

"Either or, it's a singular accomplishment. Wait for me here. I'll not be long." He deposited her in the front hallway by the parlor where they'd first come in, and retreated to an alcove with the captain, looking up every few minutes to be sure she was still there.

Catherine returned his glances with a little wave, and tapped her feet impatiently. The night had been a grand adventure, but she was tired now, and bored. Her imagination had been captured every other place they went, but there was nothing for her here. She had a sudden image of the woman upstairs, cupping the man's ballocks and kissing his... well, she'd never realized women kissed a man *there*. It certainly seemed they liked it. He'd been moaning and trembling and—

"All by yourself, young sir? That won't do. Old Peg promised she'd take care of you, didn't she?"

Catherine reddened as the bawd reached for the front of her breeches and struggled to shrug her off, looking around desperately for Jamie.

"Here now, Peg! Leave the lad alone. He's already spent his allowance." Jamie spoke from right behind her.

"What's wrong with the boy, milord? Shy, is he?"

"Aye, Peg," he replied with a wicked grin. "I promise you it would be Willie's first time with a woman. He's inexperienced yet. It's enough for him to ogle."

"But I have girls that specialize in making a lad's first adventure a memorable success," she said, motioning to a virginal looking blonde in white lace petticoats.

Jamie examined her, as if considering. "Well… "

Catherine shot him a murderous look. "I thank you and the young lady for your kindness, madam," she managed, with a barely perceptible squeak, "but I fear I've eaten something that doesn't agree. I'm in need of air." She backed out of the hall, bowing and flourishing her hat, then bolted into the street.

"Well!" Peg sniffed, mortally offended by the slur on her food.

Jamie shrugged and bowed apologetically, then hurried out the door to retrieve his wife. Still laughing when he caught up with her, he put an arm about her shoulders and pulled her close. "It seems your education in the manly arts is sadly lacking in some respects, love."

She elbowed him hard in the rib cage, but he didn't let her go.

"I'm glad I provide you so much entertainment, Sinclair."

"As am I, mouse. As am I." He looked up and down the narrow street. "Our driver seems to have abandoned us. It's not safe to wander about at this hour. We'd best find another carriage or a chair. You there! Boy!"

A scruffy young linkboy with a hungry look came trotting over, waving his torch, and Jamie tossed him a farthing. "Two more when you find us a carriage."

The boy's face sharpened with interest; it was triple his usual fee. "It's been right busy here tonight, sirs, but there be a couple looking for business just down the way. Follow me, milords."

"Look over there." Catherine tugged at Jamie's elbow. "Across the street under that sign. I think those men are watching us."

"Of course they are. We're a handsome pair," he said, glancing over his shoulder.

The boy led them through an alley to the next street over and then turned toward a well-lit building further down the road. They'd only gone a few yards when a mocking voice called from the alley.

"Tsk tsk! Are ya afraid of the dark then, gentlemen? Two such likely lads as yerselves? Ya needn't run away. We just want to talk. Pass on a message, as it were."

The linkboy dropped his torch and scampered off down the street. Jamie caught it and raised it high. Two men stood behind them, bulky figures in ragged clothes. The stench of alcohol, tobacco, and unwashed bodies wafted from them, noticeable even on the streets of London. The speaker stepped forward into the light, tossing and catching a wicked looking club. He was huge, with a broken nose, a broken face, and the remnants of an ear that looked to have been bitten off. *A boxer,* Jamie decided. They were somebody's bullyboys, but whose?

There was a metallic whine, as the smaller of the two, waiting in the background, pulled out a sword and took a step forward.

"It seems I've been asking too many questions," Jamie said to Catherine, putting her behind him and unsheathing his own weapon. "And who's this message from, gentlemen?"

"You've angered a very fine lady, pretty sir."

"Ah! You've no quarrel with the lad, then. Let him pass. He'll just be in the way."

"If he steps back and minds his own affairs, we'll leave him be. He can go once we're finished with you. Can't have him running for help now, can we?"

"There's two more," Catherine said calmly, "coming from the other direction."

Jamie looked down the street where the boy had disappeared. Two hulking forms had detached from the shadows and were heading purposely their way. He cursed under his breath. He'd had no right to bring her with him, no matter how prettily she'd begged. Pray God they never realized she wasn't a man. "Step away, Cat, and run," he whispered. "They won't chase you, it's me they want."

"I'm a Drummond, Sinclair. I've never run from a battle and I'm not ready to be a widow just yet," she said under her breath. Drawing her own sword, she faced away from him, so they were standing back to back. She stood, body balanced, elbows bent and close to her body, feet spread shoulder-width apart, with her sword held in a middle position that covered her from her torso to the top of her head.

"You promised to obey me, Will," Jamie said evenly.

"Well, it's a bit too late for that, Sinclair," she retorted, and then she put him out of her mind, concentrating instead on her opponents' advance. Jamie had fixed the torch in a wall bracket behind them, and she strained to make them out as they approached the pool of light. They moved without caution, sure of their bulk and numbers, and Catherine reflected that they'd never seen her husband fight. She focused on a tall, rat-faced man with greasy hair. He held his sword straight out in front of him, arms extended like a novice, his gaping grin revealing blackened, broken teeth. The other had a skinning knife.

Her sword was light and nimble, quick and made for stabbing, and she held it at the ready, pointed toward the tall man's throat. She saw the flicker of hesitation as he checked his advance and the glint of brute determination when he decided to charge. His reach exceeded hers, but he was clearly no trained swordsman, and he left his legs exposed. She took a step to the left and pushed his weapon off to the right, grunting with the effort, then used the opening to attack, stabbing at his groin and catching him deep in his thigh. He stepped back cursing and dropped his sword. It clattered on the ground as he grabbed his leg with both hands, trying to staunch the flow of blood.

"Damn it, Catherine, are you alright?" Jamie shouted, forgetting her disguise as he cut through his opponent's defenses, leaving a foot-long gash from shoulder to elbow and another across his chest.

"Yes, I'm fine," she gasped, as the one with the knife moved in. "Oh God, Jamie! I can see three more."

His opponent was tiring rapidly from loss of blood, and as Jamie ducked the other man's swinging club, he thrust forward, catching the swordsman through the throat. The man looked startled, then afraid, and then with a gurgle he slid to the ground. Jamie reached for Catherine and slammed her back against the wall of the building so they stood side by side instead of back to back, and looked down the street. Three more men were indeed headed their way, all of them with swords drawn.

"Take the fellow with the knife and I'll do for the one with the club. We need them finished before the others arrive. Keep your back to the wall and mind you don't slip in the blood. We can do this."

"I know."

"Good girl! That was nicely done, by the way," he added, nodding at the rat-faced man who was now unconscious on the ground.

"Thank you." Catherine took a deep breath and readied her sword, but their remaining two opponents had learned caution and wouldn't comply, staying just out of reach as they waited for reinforcements to arrive. She should have been frightened. It was foolish to think they could best five armed men, three of them fresh to the battle, but she was gripped by a wild exhilaration. She'd felt it on occasion in the past, but this was different, just she and Jamie, balanced on a knife's edge, forced to work together and trust each other to survive. They were comrades in that fierce and singular way known only to those who have fought together side by side. She turned to him with a wide grin, her eyes sparking with excitement, and he grabbed the front of her coat, pulled her close, and kissed her. It was fierce and violent and he let her go right away, but it left her heart hammering in her chest in a way the forthcoming battle had not.

"Just in case, hellcat. I've been wanting to do that all night."

"Here now, the lad's a lass!"

"And worth more in a battle than the two of you," Jamie taunted, but they still wouldn't come.

As the other men drew near, Jamie reached for her hand and squeezed it. "Ready?"

"Aye, I'm—

The loud clatter of iron-shod hooves on cobblestone made them all look up, startled as a heavy coach and four came careening around the corner and barreled down the street, heading straight for them.

"Bloody hell!" one of the newcomers shouted. Jamie pressed Catherine into a recessed doorway in the wall and the men who'd been menacing them dove out of the way, then scrambled to their feet and hared off down the alley. The vehicle screeched to a halt amidst the jingle of harness and an alarmed snorting and stamping of feet.

"Evening, governor," the driver called back to them, doffing his cap with a spit and a grin. He had a handsome face, despite a few missing teeth and a pockmark here and there. "Name's Johnnie Mercer. The boy here said you were in a spot of trouble and

you'd be wanting a ride. Said you'd pay well, too."
He tipped his head towards the linkboy, who clung,
white-faced, on the seat beside him.

"And what's your name, lad?" Jamie asked the boy.

"Tim, sir."

"Mr. Mercer, young Tim," Jamie said with a deep
bow. "I am indebted to you both."

"Aye, that'd be two farthings worth to me, milord,
just like you promised."

Jamie tossed the boy a guinea. It was nearly as much
money as he made in a year and more than he'd ever
held in his life.

"Thank you, sir!"

"You and Mr. Mercer might well have saved our
hides. You earned it, lad. If either of you ever need
employment, go to the home of Lord Carlyle, south
of St. James Park, and ask for Mr. Sullivan." He threw
another guinea to the coachman. "Mr. Mercer, will
you take us home?"

"Be glad to, governor! For a guinea I'd carry you
there on my back and treat you to dinner at me poor
old mothers on the way."

The coach was a good deal more luxurious than the
hackney they'd taken earlier, and Jamie leaned back
against the cushions and relaxed. He'd never been so
frightened in his life. The men had been nothing more
than hired ruffians, no doubt in the pay of Caroline
Ware. They were untrained, brutish, and cowardly,
and attacked in packs like dogs. He'd had a reasonable
chance of holding his own against the four of them,
but he'd feared Catherine might be harmed. Seven
was a stretch, even for him. He chuckled under his

breath. *Damn the chit!* She'd defied him and refused to flee, but she knew her way around the business end of a sword and she'd held his back as well as any man. Damn Caro anyway! She'd pay for endangering his wife, the vindictive bitch.

"You make a fine companion, Catherine. A fellow could do worse than have you at his side."

She wanted to say something brave and witty, but her teeth wouldn't stop chattering long enough to let her reply.

Jamie tapped on the roof and the carriage rolled to a stop. A moment later Johnny Mercer poked his head inside.

"What can I help you with, governor?"

"Have you anything to ward off an evening's chill, Mr. Mercer?"

"That I do, sir," Mr. Mercer replied with a grin. After a few seconds of rummaging, he returned with a worn silver flask. "My compliments, gentlemen. You'll not find anything finer to warm your bellies this side of hell. Enjoy!"

Jamie passed Catherine the flask and she took a long swallow before giving it back. The fiery liquid left a blaze of heat in her throat and belly, but it was *his* warmth she craved.

He pulled off his coat and wrapped it around her, and then hauled her into his lap, enfolding her tight in his arms. She made a token struggle and he shushed her. "You're shivering, love. Let me warm you."

A monotonous drizzle had started almost the moment they climbed into the carriage, and the steady clopping of hooves was gradually changing to a loud splashing as rain pattered against the roof. It was intimate and cozy inside the cab, and she melted against him, burrowing her head into his shoulder and holding him tight.

He kissed her temple and hugged her, clutching her as if afraid to let her go. "Try and sleep now, mouse. You've had a full night."

She could hear his heart, beating slow and steady against her cheek, and she wished he'd kiss her again, but other than his blistering kiss in the alley, he made no attempt on her virtue at all. The rational part of her brain reminded her he thought her a virgin, and a stab of fear more violent than any she felt in the alley made her catch her breath. How would he react when she finally told him she wasn't what he thought? She gave a worried moan and his fingers brushed her hair to soothe her. Damn it, why did he have to be so nice? *And why can't I keep him?*

Eighteen

CATHERINE WAS IN A RATHER PECULIAR MOOD
when the coachman finally dropped them at the front
door. The judicious use of Mr. Mercer's fine medicinal brandy had calmed her fears and banished any
unpleasant thoughts. She was feeling proud and cocky
about her performance, both in passing as a man and
as a worthy companion in a tight spot. The combined
effects of copious amounts of coffee, the excitement
of forbidden adventures, and an unexpected brush
with death percolated through her veins, warring
with physical exhaustion. She felt exquisitely alive and
completely relaxed at the same time. All in all, it was
a very pleasant feeling. She entered the house, eyes
bright and shining, and skipped through the foyer,
only to collapse in a parlor chair.

Sullivan appeared instantly, followed by Catherine's
little Scottish maid, who looked decidedly flushed.
Jamie looked from one to the other with curiosity,
and then waved them both away. "Thank you for
waiting up, but it really wasn't necessary. You can
both seek your beds. I'll see to my wife." He returned

his attention to Catherine "I'm sorry things turned out as they did, mouse. I should never have brought you with me. It was stupid of me and I—"

"What nonsense, Jamie! I don't know how to thank you. It was the most exciting, the most astonishing, the most magical night of my life!" Jumping up she threw her arms around his neck and hugged him, giving him a brandy-soaked kiss on the cheek before plopping down again.

"God's blood, girl! You must be the only wife in the world who'd thank her husband for taking her to a gambling hell, a whorehouse, and a brawl in the streets."

"And you're the only husband in the world who'd take me," she agreed with a happy sigh. "Nothing has ever made me feel more alive, not even my first time in the rigging or my first cattle raid."

"Good heavens, child! You've had an eventful youth! You must tell me all about it sometime." He watched her as she pulled at her boot, swearing as she struggled to get it off. She certainly had a colorful store of curses. He debated going to her aid, but she presented such an enchanting picture, coat unbuttoned, hat askew, that he refrained.

"There!" she cried in triumph as her boot tumbled to the floor. "Someday, Jamie," she grunted as she worked at her other boot, "you must tell me all about your family."

His mood fell flat. "Mine's not interesting in the least. There's really nothing to tell."

"I rather doubt that. You're full of secrets, Jamie Sinclair," she said, waving an unsteady finger at him, "and you're always pretending to be something you're not. I find that very interesting. I… on the other hand, am *exactly* what I seem, something that's caused me no end of trouble over the years."

The wench is far too perceptive. She took another swig of brandy and he stepped forward and relieved her of the flask. "Perhaps you've had enough of Mr. Mercer's elixir, my love. You've had an eventful evening. It's time to go to bed."

"Shouldn't you cosset and kiss me first? I hope you're not so cavalier with all your women."

"Catherine… " there was a note of warning to his voice.

She held out her hand, raising her eyebrows in expectation, and he bent and kissed it, then grasped it and pulled her up.

She swayed, unsteady on her feet. *How very peculiar!* She wasn't the least bit tired. Striving to maintain her balance, she leaned against his chest. It was a nice chest. Broad and manly and… hard. Warm, too. She sighed and rested her cheek against it, listening for his heartbeat as she had in the carriage. It beat a slow and steady rhythm, a cadence of blood and life. He was alive, though men had tried to kill him. She was alive, through her own determination and skill. But what if Tim had abandoned them and Mr. Mercer had never come? An image flashed of Jamie sprawled on the cobblestones as his life bled away amongst the puddles and filth of a London roadway. She hugged him fiercely and made no objection as he scooped her in his arms.

"Jamie?"

"Yes, love?" he asked as he climbed the stairs.

"Do you think I killed him?"

"No, little hellcat," he lied. "You gave him a nasty scratch to be sure. No doubt he'll have a wicked scar to remember you by, but so long as his comrades took the trouble to find him a physician he should survive."

"You killed one."

"That I did."

"Does it bother you?"

"Not nearly so much as the thought of one of them killing you or me."

"How many men *have* you killed?"

"Too many to count. I've been a soldier and a mercenary for much of my life, love. It's what one does."

"Does it ever bother you?"

"Not often. I seldom lose sleep over it, but… "

"But?"

He kicked open the door to her room and sat down with her on the bed. "But whether it's a duel or a battle or a brawl in the streets, I've never killed an unarmed man." He had a vivid image of farm-boy soldiers armed with pitchforks and bent swords, and he grimaced. "Lately I've lost my taste for war."

Catherine flopped back on the bed, arms behind her head and legs dangling over the side as she kicked them back and forth. "So have I."

"Really?" he said with a slight laugh. "I didn't know you had one."

"I did. It lasted all of ten minutes. Just long enough to make the crest of the hill at the River Clyde. Then there was just mud and blood and bits of people, and everyone cursing and screaming. Nothing bloody glorious about that."

"No, love. Nothing glorious at all." He reached out and smoothed her hair, gazing at her fondly. Dressed in sumptuous gowns she glittered like a fine gem, rivaling the greatest ladies of James's court, but here with him, as she'd been this evening, as she was now, she was a far rarer jewel. Unthinking, he cupped her jaw and bent his head, brushing his lips feather-light against hers.

"Mmmm, that's nice," she murmured, moving her hands to his shoulders and trying to pull him closer.

He chuckled and gripped her wrists, pushing them back against the pillows. "Sleep now, mouse."

"I don't think I can. Every time I close my eyes, I'm back in that street. I want you to kiss me. Properly."

"I did just kiss you properly."

"Not *that* kind of proper, Jamie."

"Ah… the other kind," he said, letting go of her hands.

"Yes. You hardly ever do it. You don't even try," she said with a sniff.

"I was under the impression you wished me to forbear."

"Well, I've changed my mind. I'm curious. You're my husband. It's your duty to… to show me and teach me such things." She had a sudden image of a smiling Jamie, sprawled in an armchair like some eastern potentate in his harem, surrounded by Peg's girls with their soft bodies and busy hands. "Unless I'm not the type of woman you prefer."

"You're definitely not."

She knew it, but it hurt to hear it stated so baldly. "What? Too intelligent? Independent? Opinionated?"

"No, love, though you're certainly all those things. The truth is I generally prefer someone *else's* wife. Things are much less complicated that way."

He patted her on the shoulder and made to get up, but she stopped him with a hand on his sleeve. Her head was clearing, and although she didn't know what it was she wanted, she knew she didn't want him to go. She'd never felt so close to anyone as she'd felt to him this night. He'd treated her like a younger brother, but for the kiss in the alley, yet he'd lowered a wall and shown her a glimpse of the man behind it. She'd liked what she'd seen tremendously, and she feared if she let him go now he'd put back his slightly bored, slightly jaded courtier's persona, and she wouldn't see her Jamie again.

"Please don't go! I feel safe when you're beside me. Can't you stay until I fall asleep?" She tugged at his sleeve and he subsided, lying on his back beside her with a sigh.

"You aren't making this easy, love."

She knew she wasn't. It was true she felt safe beside him, but she was also playing on his guilt and exaggerating her fear. Jamie Sinclair had formidable defenses and she needed to use every advantage if she was to breech them. "You said you'd lost your taste for war, Jamie. What will you do with yourself now?"

"Ah! Well…" he folded his hands under his head and looked up at the ceiling. "I've plans for a grand racing stable, my love. As fine as any in England. Charles had a fine eye for horseflesh, you know. He was a remarkable horseman and a damn fine jockey, too, which was extraordinary for someone over six feet tall. Old Rawley, his stud, won several important races and I have one of his sons, as you recall. With your money, once you choose to give it to me," he added with a grin, "I hope to launch a breeding operation in earnest. I'll keep the best and race them, and sell the rest. I'm interested in breeding English stock to more hot-blooded mounts from the desert. I might even travel there to see for myself. One hears wondrous tales of the speed, endurance, and beauty of the Bedouin mares."

Catherine closed her eyes. He sounded eager, almost boyish. She listened contentedly to the low rumble of his voice, soothed by the feel of his length beside her.

"Am I putting you to sleep?"

"No… not to sleep." She rolled onto her side, facing him, and reached out to touch his sleeve, admitting to herself that she wanted him. It was no surprise. He was a charming, vibrant, handsome man, and she'd felt an attraction to him from the moment they'd met. What harm in a kiss? Her fingers moved tentatively along his forearm to his bicep. She could feel it, iron hard beneath the smooth fabric of his coat.

"Catherine… what are you about?"

"I'm trying to seduce you, but apparently I lack the requisite skill," she said sourly, snatching back her hand and folding her arms across her chest.

"I'm sure you could be very skilled with a bit of practice," he said, patting her shoulder.

"Don't condescend!" She shrugged him off and turned her head away.

He laughed and ruffled her hair. "You're not yourself, love. You've had a scare and it's ruling you now, along with alcohol and coffee. You've heard of battle lust, haven't you? It's more than just excitement.

When it seizes a man, he knows no fear, feels no pain, and loses all inhibition. While it lasts, it's the most wonderful drug in the world. A man never feels more alive than when he dances along the precipice between life and death. Once the danger's past, he craves it still. A rush of pleasure, a warm body, soft breath, and the pulse of blood, all these things make him know he's still alive and make him rejoice in it."

"You feel it too?"

"Yes… I feel it too."

"Why won't you kiss me, then? You did in the alley. It's alright, Jamie. I want you to."

"It's not alright. If I kiss you now it won't be as you imagine. It won't stop there. I'll want other things, and then where will we be? Our bargain ruined, your plans in tatters. In the morning you'd be most dreadfully annoyed."

She sat up, held out her hand imperiously, and snapped her fingers. "Give me back my brandy! You're back to being amused and I'm already annoyed. You've no comfort to give and I need something to help me sleep." She grabbed the bottle and took a healthy swig, her stomach roiling. It was intolerable going on like this. She didn't know which was worse, being quiet and letting him think her some delicate virgin, or telling him the truth and having him think her a liar. She took another swig to rally her courage, protesting when he reached to take it away.

"You won't think *that* was a good idea in the morning, either."

"Who would have expected that behind his mask, Jamie Sinclair was a prudish country parson? If you're so afraid a single kiss will leave you trembling and unable to control your lust—"

"I assure you I can leave you purring and pleased, hellcat, and still *virgo intacto*," he said with a glint in his eye, relieving her of her flask.

"Well…" she took a deep breath, and let it out in a pronounced and elongated sigh. "I've been meaning to tell you… I fear there's a bit of a problem with that in any case."

"How so, love?" he asked, easing her back onto the pillows and holding her there, his fingers brushing her shoulder in a soft caress.

"I…" she hesitated, and then plunged ahead. "I'm afraid I'm no longer *virgo intacto*, Sinclair… you see."

His fingers stilled, and then withdrew. He was sharply disappointed, though he could find no reason for it. "No?" he asked idly. "Your Irish fiancé? Some wild and brawny two-legged Highland bull?"

"No! A vexing, degenerate, British ne're-do-well and wastrel."

"Do you mean me?" he asked, blinking in surprise.

"Hah! At least you know yourself."

"I hate to disagree with a woman I'm in bed with, but I must adamantly deny my guilt. I'm certain I would remember such a… well… such a *sensitive* moment. I feel certain the earth would have shaken, the angels would have wept with joy. I feel certain I would have remembered."

Stung by his mockery, she hit him with a pillow, but he clutched it and pulled it from her, propping it behind his back.

"I... you'd been fed whiskey and poppy juice and you were delirious, out of your mind. It was after I'd set your shoulder."

"In the cave? Damn it, woman, I thought I'd dreamt that!"

"You remember?"

"Bits and pieces. Christ, Catherine, I'm sorry! Did I harm you?"

"No, no!" she hastened to assure him. "You were gentle and weak as a kitten. It was just... well... you were so insistent, you see. You wouldn't stop and I couldn't make you settle down. I would have had to hurt you and after all that work setting your shoulder... I..." her voice trailed off and her face burned bright scarlet. "I... well, in any case, it was my fault not yours, and I take full responsibility for it."

"Are you saying you ravaged me, hellcat, while I was helpless as a kitten?"

"No! It wasn't that way at all," she protested hotly. "I... you... damn you, Sinclair! Stop laughing. It *isn't* funny! I've been so worried. At first I was afraid I'd be with child and we'd be stuck with each other forever, and then I thought you'd be angry I hadn't told you, and then I realized... I... well... how will we ever manage a divorce now?"

Could the man take nothing seriously? Not even this? She'd been propositioned by a madam, set upon by thugs, and now she'd revealed one of her darkest secrets. One that had been preying on her mind for weeks. Tears of frustration were threatening to spill over and she wiped at her eyes. "Damnation Sinclair! Won't you stop? I've been so worried. This is all a game to you!"

"No game, love," he said. He brushed a stray tear from her cheek with his finger, and gave her hair a gentle tug.

She flung back her arm and pushed him away. "Well, you don't seem terribly upset!"

"Why should I be? It changes very little. You're making a great to-do about nothing. These things can be smoothed over if the right witnesses are bought. It's nothing a fistful of gold won't cure and you've plenty of that. Failing that… well… you can accuse me of unbearable cruelty and unnatural practices and surely the church will release you."

"Given your reputation, it would be easily believed," she agreed.

"Well… yes… but—"

"Thank you. You've taken a great weight off my mind." *A great to-do about nothing! Insufferable, selfish boor! I just told him he took my virginity and it means nothing to him at all!* "Do you know, I'm so relieved I believe I shall be able to sleep after all. In fact, I can barely keep my eyes open. You must be exhausted as well. I've been terribly selfish. You needn't stay any longer. I'll be fine. Thank you for a lovely evening." She rolled over, turning her back to him, and gave an exaggerated yawn.

"Catherine?" When she didn't answer, he prodded her shoulder. "Catherine? Cat?" Damn the chit! She'd gone to sleep on him!

Jamie retreated to his room, fuming. The girl grew more unsettling by the day. In one breath she'd tearfully told him he'd deflowered her, in the next she'd gleefully agreed to paint him a monster so she could escape his clutches, and then she'd thanked him, dismissed him, and sent him on his way.

Bloody hell! A man with his experience, fumbling his woman's initiation. Her first time ought to have been memorable, something she couldn't wait to repeat. At least she didn't seem averse to trying it again. *My woman.* He played with the words, enjoying them. They left him with a satisfied proprietary glow. Somewhere along the way, he'd come to think of her as his, and now it turned out she was. Wherever she went in the future, whatever she did, whomever she was with, he'd been the first, and he'd always have a claim on her.

And she on me. He brushed the thought aside.

Surely, he was no longer bound by their prior agreement. Perhaps it was time to create some memories both of them could share. The next time she begged for his kisses, he'd give them to her, and a good deal more besides. He'd make damn sure that when she remembered him her toes would curl. He grinned in anticipation and closed his eyes, imagining her hot and eager, squirming beneath him. Groaning, he used his hand to relieve himself. Christ! He'd really been too long without a woman.

Lying back spent and at least temporarily relieved, it didn't take long for him to have second thoughts. A man warmed to a woman after he bedded her, and she'd caught him at a time when he was down on his luck and badly in need of a friend. There was no doubt he'd grown fond of her. She'd blurred the boundaries of friend, comrade, and partner, and she'd already burrowed too deep under his skin. He needed to place her somewhere she might stay and keep her there, not allow her this undefined space. It was far too big, far too *central* a place to allow anyone inside him. Besides, even if they were careful, to be lovers was to risk having a child. She was a business associate and should be treated as such, with courtesy, respect, and an eye to the profits. No more kissing, no more nights on the town, and no more late-night conversations lying beside her in her bed.

Just across the hall, Catherine lay sleepless, playing their conversation over in her head. She'd just shared her darkest secret, one that had been troubling her for months. She'd told him he'd taken her virginity, one of the greatest gifts a woman could give, a gift she only gave but once, and he'd laughed at her! He was cold-hearted and cruel, incapable of any real emotion, an unfeeling lout! She'd wanted him to hold her in his arms and kiss her. She'd wanted him to care. She'd practically thrown herself at him, and he'd patted her on the head like a faithful hound. The tears she'd been keeping at bay threatened to overwhelm her. *Damn! Damn! Damn!* Thank God, he'd left the room. She'd feared he'd never go.

She sniffed a few times and took several hiccupping breaths, getting herself under control. James Sinclair might have ice water in his veins, but she was a Drummond, a countess, and a woman of affairs, and she didn't need any man. She'd done fine without for all these years and she certainly didn't need *him*. She took a cloth from the basin by her bed and washed her face, the cool water a welcome balm against her flushed skin. No doubt the Englishman was right. She'd had far too much coffee and their adventure in the alley had affected her more than she'd realized. In the morning, she'd act as if she didn't remember, and he'd never see her make a fool of herself like that again.

They began the next day with remarkably similar intentions, aware that something had changed between them, and intent on putting things back the way they'd been.

Jamie had gone to bed firm in his decision. She might wheedle, nag, challenge, or plead, but there'd be no more clandestine adventures, no more breathless late-night talks, and definitely no more talk of kissing. It was time to find himself a new mistress or renew his acquaintance with an old one. His failure to keep one was already causing unwanted talk and speculation. Lady Beaton came to mind. She knew what she liked, knew what he liked, and was always a charming companion.

Nevertheless, when Catherine joined him for a breakfast of bread and chocolate, he couldn't help but notice how her green silk nightgown set off her tousled curls and amber eyes to perfection. It was really quite stunning. And the way the jeweled clasps fastened her gown as if they were fingers, holding it tight around a thin chemise whose delicate lace trim seem to be almost... caressing... her décolletage. It was artfully done! She also looked fetching in breeches, of course.

He wasn't sure which he preferred. Those long legs incased in thigh-high boots would make any man weep, and that arse!

"Sinclair!"

"Eh? What?"

"I *said* I'll be going to the exchange with Maire today. Is there anything I can get you?"

"Oh! No. Thank you. There's nothing I need. Nothing at all. I've matters of a private nature to take care of today, Catherine. In fact, I expect to be rather busy for the next several days. I've instructed Sullivan to have the coach kept ready for your convenience. Now you've toured the city and are familiar with the court, I expect you'll be able to muddle through without me constantly underfoot."

"I shall endeavor to do my best," was her frosty reply.

"Excellent! A woman who can navigate the Highlands should have no trouble in the wilds of London. I'll be off then. I wish you a pleasant day."

He gave her a sweeping bow, punctuated with a flourish of his plumed hat, and left without saying a word about the last night's adventures. She'd steeled herself to present an indifferent front, but he'd never given her the opportunity. He'd completely refrained from baiting or teasing, and he'd been accommodating, formal, and polite. She told herself firmly his unexpected discretion was a tremendous relief.

And so it continued. As winter turned to spring, they lived separate lives, nodding as they passed each other in the halls, and meeting occasionally at court functions and parties. When Buckingham, a man she'd thought was Jamie's friend, died at his country home in April, it wasn't he that told her. She learned of it at court. If they'd shared some special bond it seemed to have ended as quickly as it had begun, and if the sight of Jamie dancing, flirting, and being pursued by other women was a bitter torture, no one knew it but her. They were a handsome pair, witty and urbane, unfailingly courteous to one another, with just the right air of amused tolerance, and they were considered a model couple in James's court.

Catherine had her pursuers, too, though she paid them little heed. It surprised her at first. She'd never considered a man might pursue her for anything other than her fortune, but it seemed that they found her attractive, and many enjoyed her wit. The more she employed it to keep admirers at bay, the more insistent they became. Amusing at first, and a salve to her pride, it soon become a burden. King James had bowed to his pretty wife's pressure, sending his mistress, Katherine Sedly, to the wilds of Ireland. Now he was looking for new game and his eye settled increasingly on her. The trade arrangement for her family's whiskey had been concluded on the most favorable terms, and a rumor was floating about that she'd soon be offered a position as maid of honor to the Queen.

She did her best to discourage without causing affront, as so many things hung in the balance: her family's fortunes, Jamie's future, and her own divorce. For now, at least, the royal satyr was enjoying the chase and in no great hurry to conclude it. She'd never enjoyed the social games that powered most European courts, and her heart ached for the Highlands. She missed Rory and Jerrod and crusty old Martha; she'd even be glad to see Donald. She'd never been so surrounded by people, or felt so alone.

Nineteen

LONELY, BORED, AND INCREASINGLY UNHAPPY, Catherine decided there was no more need to suit her behavior to the dictates of others here than there had been at home. She found the life of an English courtier shallow, dull, and wearying, a mind-numbing, soul-destroying round of gambling, drinking, and gossip. If she was to survive it, she needed some kind of relief. Sinclair had given her the keys to another city, a vibrant, bustling, thriving world spilling over with ideas and adventure. He'd shown her the way, and given her the tools to continue her explorations with confidence. As he'd said himself, anyone who could navigate the Highlands should have no trouble in the wilds of London.

Pulling on her breeches, she felt a thrill of anticipation, and stepping into her boots she felt free. Sinclair had told her disguise could be liberating, but she wondered if he had any idea what that really meant, having never lived life as a woman. She began by visiting coffee houses, exploring as many as she could find, and as she did, her familiarity with the city grew.

She was soon frequenting Will's and the Graecian. Jamie had called them penny universities, and both places filled a thirst that had nothing to do with coffee. She'd had an excellent education and the best tutors her father could find, but it had been a solitary business, she and her books and various dry old men. She'd never had the opportunity to argue and persuade, or to join in boisterous debate, and she loved it.

Another favorite haunt was Lloyd's, by the Tower Bridge, with its clientele of ships' captains, merchants, and businessmen. Her father had left her ships, and shares in his business ventures, including the distillery, and what the conversation lacked in excitement it more than made up for in valuable information. She also loved its location on the bank of the Thames, and she spent many a spring afternoon sitting on the embankment, watching the crowded river, thick with ships waiting to unload.

This day she'd had the good fortune to arrive just as a battered-looking sea captain was launching into the tale of his harrowing escape from Algerian pirates. She'd forced a place at the table and was sitting shoulder to shoulder with the rest of his enthralled audience, shouting in astonishment and cheering him on. She turned around in annoyance when a heavy hand gripped her shoulder.

"Cousin Will? Can it really be you? I'd no idea you'd returned to London. Good heavens! Why didn't you tell me?"

"Good afternoon, my lord," she answered coolly, introducing him to her friends. "I'd no wish to trouble you, cousin. One knows how busy you are now you've risen in the world. I would hardly expect so important a man to condescend to entertain me."

The saucy chit! Jamie pulled up a chair and made a place beside her, heedless of the grumbles and protests from the men he was shoving out of the way. He threw an arm companionably about her shoulders and gave a tight squeeze. "But we're family after all, eh lad? What say we take our reunion outside, so we don't disturb the others or interrupt the good captain's tale?"

Outraged, fuming, and humming with excitement, she shrugged off his arm and stalked out the door.

He followed right behind. "What do you think you're doing here, Catherine? How long has this been going on? When did you decide to sneak around behind my back? Why didn't you tell me?"

"I wasn't sneaking! If you were ever home you'd know I go out every day, and I've been doing so for weeks. I don't need your permission. I don't expect you to answer to me, Sinclair, so you'd best not expect me to answer to you!"

"I am a man, and you are a woman. It is *not* the same thing."

"I've been hearing that all my life, and I paid it no more attention than I do now."

"Do you realize how dangerous it is? What could happen to you? You could be robbed, raped, kidnapped, or killed! Well, it's over as of now. I forbid any more of these adventures!"

"You forbid me? You? My bought and paid for husband who gambles and drinks with my money while he trolls through alleys and ballrooms in search of his next whore?"

"I'm warmed by your fine opinion of me."

Her face reddened. "I'm sorry. That was uncalled for. I apologize." She sat down on a man-made stone outcrop overlooking the water, kicking her legs back and forth, shivering when he came to sit beside her. His anger surprised her. He seldom showed any strong emotion and he'd seemed all but indifferent to her comings and goings for the past several weeks. They watched in silence as the watermen ferried Londoners from landing to landing, heading toward Westminster.

"I really must bring you to see the ice skating next winter... if you're still here."

"What?" She turned and looked at him quizzically.

"Ahem, yes... what you said. It *was* uncalled for, though perhaps not unwarranted. That doesn't change the fact that London can be far more dangerous than you seem to think."

"You see? This is why I abhor the thought of a husband," she said, turning away. "You assume I'm an idiot child, without the understanding or ability to take care of myself."

"Let me finish, Catherine. You might at least allow that I know more about the place than you do. What kind of arrogant fool would you think me, if I flounced and huffed and then ignored you were you to warn me of the dangers in your Highlands?"

"I did not flounce and huff!" It was early summer and the sun was dappling the water, sparkling and dancing amongst a million tiny waves. She turned her face into it, enjoying the feel of it against her skin. Her heart was beating a quick and steady tattoo and it wasn't from anger. She'd been surprised to see him, but she'd felt a thrill of pleasure, too. Somehow, meeting like this, away from court, neither of them in their customary roles, they'd slipped back into the easy camaraderie she'd begun to think she'd imagined. In one instant, weeks of estrangement were gone as if they'd never been, and he was her Jamie again, annoyed perhaps, but no longer an elegant stranger.

"So… tell me then. I'm listening."

"I know you can defend yourself, love, but in the Highlands, in a battle, you know who your enemies are and you can see them coming. That's not so here. The streets aren't filled with warriors and soldiers. They're filled with cowards and thieves, rats and sneaks, those who haven't the skill or the strength to win an honest fight. You might pass for a man. You might hold your own one on one. You might even send some men running when they see how you handle a sword, but those aren't the men who'll kill you. It will be the grubby child who picks your pocket and leads you into an alley where his elders lie in wait, or the beggar so frail he can barely stand who rises up to club you from behind. People go missing and die in this city every day and night, Catherine, because they walk alone, or dress too fine, or wander just a little ways off of the path. Many of them are found in the morning, right there," he said, nodding in the direction of the river.

She looked down and her eyes caught something with an awkward shape, bobbing along towards them. Making a face, she pulled up her legs and turned to face him. "I *do* appreciate your lecture, Sinclair. You've taught me a great deal, your observations are generally sound, and I'll be sure to pay attention to everything you've said, but I can't live the way you expect me to. I need to *do*. I need to see. I…" Her voice trailed off.

"So I'm back to Sinclair now, am I? I can always tell when I've earned your disfavor. What say I come with you, then? At least until I've shown you more of the city and taught you some useful tricks?".

Her eyes sparked with excitement and her face lit with a huge grin. "What tricks? Oh, Jamie, I wish you would!"

"I'll show you. But not today. I've business to complete, yet. But if you'll ease my mind by going home, I promise I'll show you tomorrow."

She held out her hand as a man would. "It's a deal."

He took her hand and shook it, surprised at the strength of her grip. He realized it was the first time he'd touched her in weeks. He rose to his feet, pulling her up with him. Letting go reluctantly, he walked her to a hackney and deposited her inside.

"Be careful what you wish for, Will," he called, as the carriage rolled away.

He shook his head as he watched her leave. She was doing it to him again. Ten minutes alone with her and his good intentions had crumbled, just as they had when first they'd met. The wench had taken him completely by surprise. He'd been on his way to visit Alice Beaton. She'd been back in London for well over a month. She'd been good to him… good *for* him, at a time when he was filled with youthful hurt and rage. He wasn't inclined to renew their liaison, but he owed her the courtesy of a visit.

He'd stopped at Lloyd's on his way, to deliver a communiqué to John Churchill. It was the perfect place to meet, filled with sea captains and travelers just arriving or about to depart. It was assumed the coffee houses were rife with spies, and one more would hardly be noticed. Whig, Tory, Protestant, or Catholic, amongst the sort of men who noticed such things, no one knew which side he was on. Hell, he didn't know himself! He'd yet to decide, but with luck, any who watched would assume he did business for them.

It was a dangerous game he played. A watchful, waiting, deadly game. One false move, one wrong step, and his rotting head would be looking down at Catherine from atop Tower Bridge. The last thing he needed was any distractions. The last thing he wanted was her to be involved. But what was a man to do? The chit insisted on putting herself in danger. She insisted on doing whatever she bloody well pleased.

He'd been shocked to find her there. He'd known it was her the minute he'd entered. His eyes had been drawn immediately. His body quivered like that of a starving dog at the sight of her, and he'd felt himself stir at the sound of her voice. Even without perfume, he'd recognized her scent and... *Bloody hell!* The woman had a power over him that grew by the day. With those full lips and cat's eyes and soft creamy skin, how could the fools not have known she was a woman?

Well... she was stubborn and independent, and she'd have her adventures with or without him, she'd made that clear. Short of keeping her under lock and key, it seemed there was no way to prevent it. He might be a bought husband, he might sell his sword, and he might have a different set of values and scruples than more virtuous men, but the chit was his, and he took care of his own. If the only way to do that was to go with her, than so be it.

True to his word, the next day Jamie took Catherine to a part of London she'd never seen. Filled with shacks and dirty hovels, stinking of fish and guts, the pungent odor of unwashed clothes, and every kind of human waste, it was, in its own way, as vibrant, opinionated, and exciting as anywhere in the city. It existed in hidden enclaves amongst shabby canyons of tall narrow buildings and crabbed and twisting streets. It was often right next to more prosperous neighborhoods, just a sidestep, an alley, and a world away, but always to the east.

Dressed in scabrous rags, disguised with blackened teeth, pockmarked faces, and filthy hair, they passed unnoticed and unhindered, emerging into a busy street of shopkeepers and market stalls. Catherine was amazed how Jamie managed to twist and bend, hunching his back and shoulders to disguise his height. Some folk avoided them, looking away, crossing the street or stepping aside when they passed, while others knocked them away or would have stepped on them if they hadn't scrambled out of their path.

"Do you see, mouse? Now we're truly invisible. If you need to go somewhere dangerous, this is the way to travel, and, if you find yourself in need of a haven, back from whence we came is just the place to hide. We're not worth the effort to rob or murder, and no one wants to ravage a plaguey looking lad or a lass with a case of the pox. Always watch for gangs of rakehells though, out on a ramble. Their cruelty and courage grow with the drink and their numbers, and some think beating or setting fire to a beggar, or throwing one in the river, is fine sport.

"Remember that in these clothes, all men are your betters. Bow, scrape, doff your cap and avert your eyes, and if you hear a carriage coming jump out of the way or they'll run you down. For all that, this is the best and safest disguise for traveling the city at night, and if you get hungry, you can always do this."

Catherine watched in horrified delight as he approached a well-dressed passerby, tugging at the man's coat and holding out his hand to beg a coin in a singsong whining cant. The man tried his best to brush past him but he trailed after him, ducking his kicks and blows and refusing to let loose of his coat. He returned in triumph a moment later, proudly holding a coin between thumb and forefinger. "He proved to be a generous soul. I've earned us sixpence, my love. You've yet to realize what a lucky girl you are. You'll never want for bread whilst married to Jamie Sinclair. You mustn't try it yourself, of course. You don't know the language and it takes years of practice, though I suppose you might pretend to be a mute."

She shook her head in amazement, privately acknowledging she *was* a lucky girl. "I can't imagine I'd ever want to try it. Wherever did you learn these things, Jamie?"

"Ah, well now, therein lies the secrets of a misspent youth. But I think there's been enough lessons for today, don't you?" He threw the coin in the air and caught it, making it dance across his knuckles and disappear, before pulling it from her ear. "Would you care to join me for a bite and a pint at the tavern, Master William?" he asked, putting an arm around her shoulders.

He seemed to be doing that a lot lately, and she quite enjoyed it. "I should be delighted!"

Over the course of the next few weeks, they dressed as apprentices and churchmen, laborers and farmers, and tradesmen and servants, slipping in and out of the homes of acquaintances and strangers. Jamie taught Catherine the benefits and drawbacks of each disguise. Anything she wanted to try, anyone she wanted to be, it seemed he could make her, but he drew the line when she asked him to make her an orange girl. "You might as well ask me to be your pimp, love. They're the playthings of all the young blades and the theatre crowd. There'll be swords drawn and blood spilled and then a great deal of embarrassment and explaining to do, should I have to put some young sprig in his place."

Catherine was completely enthralled. She'd always felt an outsider and she'd never had a close friend, but now she was part of an exclusive club that consisted of only the two of them. They had secrets, went places, and did things no one else could possibly imagine, travelers and comrades in a fascinating alien world. She'd never imagined marriage could be so exciting, bring such freedom, or be so much fun. It also brought confusion. Though the closest of companions when on an adventure, at night she watched, teeth on edge, as the beauties of the court, Lady Beaton, Mrs. Russell, and several others, draped themselves around him fawning and flirting while he smiled back and treated her like a little sister rather than a wife.

She looked around for him now and saw him leading a willowy blonde out onto the floor for one of Mr. Playford's country dances, The Happy Bride. When it came to the part where the lovers exchanged a kiss that lasted four bars long, her hands clenched in tight fists and her fingernails dug deep in her palms. She turned away in disgust, only to see the king making his way in her direction. It was time to leave. An extremely elegant gentleman solicited his attention, pulling him to one side, and she took the opportunity to escape, hiding in the crowd surrounding the dancers and making her way down a corridor, through a side door, and out to a small garden. It was a chilly night, and she repented her decision immediately, but Whitehall, with its twisting corridors, hidden passages, and secret doors, was one maze she'd never learned to navigate.

She was hungry, cold, and tired, and her feet were sore. *Damn these stupid pointy shoes!* What kind of sadistic monster had set women to tottering about on tiny platforms whilst surrounded by yards of cumbersome material, trapped in a torturous device that gripped them cruelly round the midriff and wouldn't let them breathe?

Twenty minutes later, cursing and muttering under her breath, she tried yet another passage, climbed up more stairs, and stepped out onto… a large gallery overlooking the ballroom. "Holy mother of God! I'm trapped in the second circle of hell!" She heard a laugh behind her and turned around. Jamie was lounging on a settee that was recessed in the wall. Sitting slightly to one side, ankles crossed and his arm slung over the back, he had a commanding view of the ballroom below.

"Well… it's said to be home to Cleopatra and Helen of Troy, so you find yourself in good company."

"That's a matter of opinion," she said, somehow not surprised to find him there.

"Come, my dear, sit," He patted the space beside him, moving slightly to give her more room.

She sank down beside him, leaning into him as she made herself comfortable, relieved to be off her feet, and grateful for his warmth. Once she was settled, she stretched her legs, pointing her toes and moving her feet in little circles.

"Ouch! No wonder you've been skipping about like a hop toad in those ridiculous things. I wager you miss your boots, love."

"I do, Sinclair, most dreadfully."

"Oh dear! What have I done to annoy you now?" he asked, catching the attention of a footman who was passing with a tray of drinks and motioning him over.

"Why, nothing at all. Pray tell me, husband, what are you up to tonight?" she asked, reaching for some wine. "Countesses or cards?"

"Ah! I see. Neither, I think. I've promised to be discrete. Here, let me." He reached for an ankle and drew it into his lap, removing her shoe.

She could feel him stir under the arch of her foot, and when she started breathing again, her heart was hammering in her ears. She took a sip of her drink and closed her eyes so she didn't have to see him. His fingers encircled her ankle, stroking and caressing, while his thumbs worked the sole of her foot, kneading and squeezing from heel to toe.

"Scandalous!" someone hissed, but she didn't open her eyes, didn't care at all.

"And what of you, love? What have you been up to, besides saving yourself from the clutches of our lecherous king?"

"So you've noticed." She opened her eyes, but she didn't move her foot.

"That he's marked you as his prey? Yes. I've noticed. He's searching the room for you now. Look there. He sees us at last." Of course, he'd noticed. The man followed her every move with hungry eyes. His blatant ogling made Jamie's blood boil. He'd noticed Catherine's distaste as well, and thought to intervene, but she grew annoyed when he became protective and she'd seemed to handle it well enough on her own. Still, neither Stuart brother had ever caviled at poaching another man's wife, and if he thought to take his—

"It doesn't make you jealous?"

He shifted her foot, placing it firmly against his swollen cock. *Christ!* Looking up he caught the startled look in her eyes and answered with a slow smile. She was too much the innocent to be certain he did it on purpose, and far too green to return his massage with one of her own. "You're not the type of woman a man need get jealous over."

"I see," she said stiffly, pulling her foot away.

"Careful, love!" he said with a wince. "I didn't mean it that way. How can you not be aware of the effect you have on men? Unless it's true what they say, and your wooly Highland cousins have a preference for sheep. I assure you any normal man would—Ouch! Damn it, Catherine! That's enough!" He blocked her foot a moment before it reconnected with his crotch, wrestling with her a second or two longer, before she ceased her struggles and let it drop. "I was *referring*, to your quaint sense of loyalty and honor. It's been my experience such noble sentiments tend to preclude a taste for adultery."

"I'm glad you find it so entertaining."

"I find everything about you entertaining, hellcat. You are, in fact, by far the most entertaining woman I've ever met."

"But not the most interesting. Who is she? The woman you always dance with?"

"Don't be so sure about that, love. The one I always dance with is Alice, Lady Beaton."

"And she's your mistress?"

"She's a good friend. She has been for some time."

"I see."

"I'm not altogether sure you do."

Their conjugal *tête-à-tête* was drawing more than a few curious looks from passersby, some disapproving, some amused, and one that blazed with fury.

"I'm afraid I'm about to be reminded of one of my more ill-advised indiscretions. My apologies, love."

A bejeweled goddess was heading their way, surrounded by fawning courtiers, a footman struggling with several small spaniels on leashes, and two page boys, one carrying a muff and fan, and the other a diamond-encrusted patch box.

"Good evening, Sinclair," she said, her voice dripping ice. "I'm surprised to see you. I'd thought the duke of Buckingham was the only cheat and whoremonger welcomed at court." She turned to Catherine. "And this must be your Scottish camp follower."

"Lady Ware," he said, neglecting to rise, "might I present Catherine Drummond, Lady Sinclair, Countess of Carrick and Carlyle, and Countess of Moray in her own right. And I really must object, Caroline. I've never been caught cheating, and you're far too finely dressed to be publicly accounted a whore."

Their rapt audience was startled into shocked gasps and titters and Lady Ware's eyes sparked with hatred. "Enough! We are… *intimate* friends after all, aren't we, Jamie?" She looked directly at Catherine, favoring her with a cold smile.

"Were we, my dear? I confess I can scarce remember."

"Best you *do* remember to watch your back, my lord. The streets can be deadly at night."

"I *always* remember that, Caro."

Catherine watched her stately retreat, mesmerized, an icy, diamond-hard beauty surrounded by a constellation of hangers on and admirers. "Another mistress, Jamie? What in God's name did you ever see in her?" she asked, only half-joking.

"What strange questions you ask for a wife. Are you a spy? Are you a cheat? Is that one of your mistresses?"

"Is she?"

"She was. Very briefly. Not one of my wiser

choices. As I recall, I'd had a good deal to drink and it wasn't long after you had me bashed over the head and addled my brain."

"You called her Caro. Is she—?"

"Yes. My supposed victim and accuser."

"She's very beautiful."

"No, she's not. She's ugly as sin."

"What *did* you see in her then?"

"She's rich. She offered to pay my debts, was adequate in bed, and not overly tedious if one had drunk enough wine."

Catherine yawned and leaned back against him. "That's not a nice thing to say. You're a very bad man."

"*She's* not nice, and yes, my dear, I am."

"She looks like an angel, though. Is no one here what they seem?"

"Well, we're certainly not, are we?" He sat up straighter, warming to the topic. "Look down there, to the pillar to the left. That's the dour Sir Jeremy Felcher. A Puritan on a first name basis with the angels. He'd cast the lot of us into perdition if he could. He reminds me a little of my father, yet his was a cavalier, a charming, ruthless man, who died of apoplexy while laughing at a dirty joke. Sir Jeremy never misses Sunday service, and Sunday night he repents in private with his breeches about his ankles while a housemaid whips his arse."

"Your father was a religious man?"

"My father was a hypocrite."

"And what of your mother? You never speak of her," she said, changing the subject.

"That's right, mouse, I never do."

An awkward silence continued for several moments, and Catherine returned her gaze to the floor below. The elegant man who'd saved her from the attentions of the king was smiling up in her direction. "Who's that man, Jamie?" she asked, nudging him with an elbow, "and why is he always smiling at me?"

"That's *Monsieur* Barrillon, Marquis de Branges, the French ambassador and one of Louis' spies, up to his usual mischief. He smiles because the king wants you, you're a Catholic with ties to France, and he has a penchant for beautiful, witty women. He wonders what use you might be as he whispers sweet nothings into His Majesty's ear."

"What kind of sweet nothings?"

"He reminds him of his friends in France, urges him to stand strong in the Catholic faith, and reassures him of the divine rights of kings. He also counsels him to hide the excesses of the *dragonnades*. One would hardly know that eighty thousand Huguenots have sought refuge here from the persecutions in France. The English persecute Catholic Ireland and steal her lands, France persecutes her Protestants and steals theirs, and on it goes."

"My people kill each other over women and cows."

His bark of laughter caused heads to turn on the dance floor below. "Are you as weary of this place as I am, Cat Drummond?"

"I am indeed, Jamie Sinclair."

"Then might I escort you home?"

Twenty

It was so dim in the carriage Jamie could hardly see her. He didn't need to. She reached out to touch him from across a crowded room. Something molten smoldered between them, just waiting for an opening to burst into flame. Sometimes, when he watched his king undressing her with his eyes, he feared it was a conflagration that might consume him. The thought that James coveted what was his made him white with rage. *Perhaps I'm more like my father than I care to think.*

During their daylight rambles, the need to maintain a disguise put a damper on it, and in the evenings, he kept a safe distance, distracting himself with intrigue and light flirtations, but day by day, his attraction grew until he didn't know what he wanted anymore, except that he wanted her. Well… why not? The twisted logic that had stopped him before seemed less important every day. If he were careful to keep things light between them, careful not to hurt her or leave her with child, what harm was there in being lovers that hadn't already been done? His lips curled in anticipation. Perhaps it was time he taught his wife something new.

Catherine lay on her bed reading the same line over and over, not yet ready to sleep. There'd been something different about Jamie tonight. He'd seemed almost possessive, tracking her down and inviting her to share his refuge. He'd paid her more public attention than he had in months, claiming her as a man might claim his mistress. *Claiming me in front of the king!* How unexpectedly gallant! Now if only he would stop claiming dances and kisses from every female who batted her eyes at him.

She could hardly complain, though. He flirted and shared dances with many women, but his thoughts and opinions and his secret world he shared only with her. She tried to imagine the reaction of Lady Beaton or Mrs. Russell if he climbed through their window as Alverez the gypsy, Vagabond Tom, or Toothless Sam the beggar. She folded her hands behind her head, laying on her back with a wide grin, imagining their horrified screams.

"You find something amusing, wife?" He was leaning against the doorjamb, head cocked to one side, his arms folded across his chest.

"I was just... never mind. What are you doing here? We're still going to Newmarket for the races tomorrow, aren't we?"

"Perhaps I've come to seduce you."

"Can it wait until I've finished this chapter?"

His eyes sparked and he moved over to sit on the bed, tipping up the corner of her book. "*The Amours of Philander and Silvia*, by Mistress Behn? Tsk

tsk! Shouldn't you be reading a more edifying tome? Newton's *Principia Mathematica,* or Mrs. Woolley's *The Gentlewoman's Companion,* perhaps? Do you know that when asked her views on female education, she complained that most in this depraved age think a woman learned and wife enough if she can distinguish her husband's bed from another's?"

"How interesting. Can any of your lady-friends do so?"

He stretched out on his side, his head resting on his bent arm, and tugged lightly at the loose curls that tumbled down her back. "I'm far more interested in what you can do. How can you be accounted a learned lady if you've never shared a husband's bed?"

"I have. Have you forgotten? Why yes, of course you have." She twisted her head and pulled away, freeing her hair.

"Then let's create new memories," he teased. "Ones we'll both remember." His smile was seductive, his voice barely a whisper. "Finish your chapter, Catherine, and then I'll teach you things you'll never forget."

She lowered her book, looking at him through narrowed eyes. "It was a jest."

"We *are* married, love." He fingered the filmy cloth where her chemise gathered at her elbow, "and I'm beginning to think it decidedly unfair that I should suffer all of the duties and reap none of the pleasures." *The king might chase you girl. But you're mine.*

She shivered and pulled her arm away, remembering what a disaster his last visit to her bed had been. They hadn't talked for days. "Stop it, Jamie! I don't know what's got into you tonight but I don't appreciate being an object for your amusement. Nor do I accept being anyone's second, or third—or is it fourth?—choice. Go to one of your mistresses if you've the need to scratch an itch."

"I resent the implication, madam. I've been a faithful husband ever since we first made our bargain."

"Have you really?" *How very unexpected!* Her heart thudded with excitement.

"Indeed I have. I don't believe I've ever forgone the pleasures of the flesh for so long, but you bade me be discreet, and I'm ever mindful of your words." He'd returned to tugging at her ribbons.

"Hah! You probably had the pox and were waiting on a cure." She swallowed, breathless, as he drew the tip of his finger along the soft skin of the inside of her forearm, watching mesmerized as he drew it back and forth, wrist to elbow, elbow to wrist.

"I don't know why your opinion of me should be so poor," he coaxed. "You told me I might not bed you and I didn't. You asked me to forgo my pleasures and I did. I should think my efforts to please you merit a kiss. What's the harm?"

He plucked the book from her nerveless fingers and edged closer, pulling himself up and leaning against her as he nuzzled her neck. His voice was compelling and warm. "You're an honest girl, Catherine. You like it when I kiss you. I can tell. We're attracted to one another, we're married, and the deed's already been done. There's nothing to lose by it now. Why not enjoy one another while we can? You *asked* me to kiss you not so long ago."

He won't stop this time, and it will change everything. She closed her eyes and slowed her breath, tempted and afraid.

"Kiss me, Cat," he said in a husky whisper, as his fingertips skimmed the outer curve of her breast through her chemise. "You know you want to."

His knuckles grazed her cheekbone and then he cupped her chin, guiding her mouth to his, silencing her murmured protest with a lazy, teasing kiss. She turned into his arms with an incoherent cry. He eased her down onto the mattress, deepening the kiss, one hand entwined in a mass of curls as the other tugged at the clasps of her gown. He growled as he tasted her lips, enjoying the feel of her in his arms as she squirmed beneath him. *Christ!* It had been far too long, but well worth the wait. He was going to enjoy this. They both would.

The first clasp gave way and her breasts, freed from their bondage, spilled into his palm. He moaned low in his throat, gathering one and then the other in his hand, squeezing and tugging their rigid tips between the base of his fingers as he plundered her mouth, his tongue thrusting and prodding, urging her to open to him.

Caught up in sensations and feelings so new she had little defense, Catherine could do nothing but follow as he led her in a new dance. She shifted as he moved her, and pressed where he pulled her, her body pliant, eager, and warm, but all the while, a part of her brain was shouting in alarm. *He's placing me with all the others. Soon I'll be just one more.* Even as she thought it, he captured her hand, guiding it to the bulge that strained against his breeches and holding it there, thrusting his hips and groaning in a mixture of pleasure, frustration, and pain.

"Feel what you do to me, hellcat," he whispered, his voice rough with passion. "I'm at your mercy. I'm at your service. I'm going to show you things that—"

"Jamie, that's enough!" She pulled her hand away and pushed at his shoulders, shoving him back.

"Bloody hell, woman! What is wrong with you? One moment you want it and the next you don't. Perhaps you'll see fit to inform me, once you know your own mind," he snapped.

"I could say the same of you," she retorted, on the verge of tears. "I'm not as experienced in these things as you are, Jamie."

"I should hope not!"

"I'm not comfortable playing these games. I don't understand the rules. I can't separate my feelings the way you do."

That pulled him up short. He took a breath and calmed himself, moving to perch on the edge of the bed, caught in the distinctly uncomfortable throes of thwarted lust. It wasn't like him to have such strong reactions, to be so... emotional. He was always patient in his affairs, taking the rare rejection with easy grace. It was not as if a lover was hard to come by, but she had him acting like a child who'd been robbed of his candy. It was most unsettling. *The chit refused me! Jamie Sinclair! She's been begging for it for months and now she prattles on about her feelings!*

She was right, of course. She didn't know the rules, didn't understand them, and they must be clearly understood to avoid any unpleasantness down the road. It would be bad enough to make a mess of such things with a mistress; it would be completely unsupportable with one's wife. He should be grateful to her, really, for having had the sense to stop.

"Now you're angry with me and you'll avoid me and we won't talk for days."

"I'm not angry with you, Catherine," he said with a dry laugh, "though certain parts of my body remain... indignant. I think it best for both of us if I went to my room now. I apologize for any misunderstanding."

For all his efforts at cool nonchalance, he was trembling like a schoolboy with his first strumpet. That's what came from doing without, but what was a man to do? He'd lost interest in the women who used to amuse him the day Catherine arrived. He was a sensual man, not a lustful one, and he'd drained that cup to its dregs. Catherine was fresh, unique, a challenge, and other women seemed coarse and vulgar in comparison. When his only choices were cheap wine or a pale imitation, a connoisseur did without.

He stopped at the door and turned, favoring her with a tired smile. "First you try to seduce me and I refuse. Now I try and seduce you, and you refuse. We are a contrary couple, are we not?" He turned and left without waiting for an answer, calling back over his shoulder, "We'll talk in the morning if you like."

But of course, they didn't.

Catherine didn't know what to think over the next few days. He'd claimed not to be angry, but he appeared remote and distracted and their daytime jaunts had ceased. As an early fall turned leaves to shades of gold and the summer blooms were dying, it seemed their friendship was dying, too. She felt his absence keenly and told herself that a friendship so flimsy he'd toss it aside out of pique had been no true friendship at all. Yet he didn't deliberately avoid her as he'd done in the past, and though he paid her scant attention, the women she'd suspected of being his lovers he paid none at all.

That he'd been faithful since her arrival still surprised and shocked her. The unexpected courtesy and the memory of his kisses led to wild imaginings that left her feeling weak in the knees. Perhaps it was something else that left him looking harried and grim. All she could do was watch, wait, and wonder.

In October, a letter came from Jerrod, taking her completely by surprise. She'd hoped, by corresponding through third parties, to keep her business to herself. Jerrod acknowledged her success with trade matters and harangued her about her failure to conclude her business and return home. *You might at least have said you missed me, you crusty old scoundrel.*

She realized, with a start of surprise, that she'd been in London for close to a year and she'd been so caught up in her adventures she'd yet to do a single thing about a divorce. Where had the time gone? Jamie was well ensconced at court, their bargain had been kept, and it was well past time to see the thing done.

She went to the library and took pen to paper with a sigh. She wrote her solicitor, instructing him to investigate the options available for ending her marriage, indicating that money was no obstacle and her husband would not object. Halfway through she stopped, tapping her fingers, lost in thought. It was growing harder to remember why she'd ever wanted a divorce. The sight of Jamie quickened her pulse, the rest of her quickened to his touch, and she'd been freer in this marriage than she'd ever been without. When they were friends, there was no one's company she preferred.

I want him. I want to keep him. I'm going to make him mine. She wasn't sure in which exact moment she made that decision, but once she had, it seemed as natural to her as breathing. Refusing him her bed might have been a mistake, particularly if she didn't want him sharing someone else's, but at least now, she knew she had his interest, and besides, it was nothing that couldn't be undone.

He likes me. I know he does. He trusts me, too. He's capable of being faithful. Perhaps he can be friend... and lover, too. And maybe, if she let him teach her, he'd find she had something to teach him as well. Perhaps it was time to talk about their marriage, rather than their divorce. A broad smile lit her face. Now if only she could find him. She rose to go to dinner, leaving the letter unfinished and forgotten, lying on the desk.

Twenty-One

Jamie slipped into the stables dressed as a farrier and came out the other side as Lord Carlyle. Exhausted, he made his way to the library and poured himself a drink. Rumors were flying through back corridors that the royal couple would soon be making an announcement. In the past week, he'd been courted and pursued by people in high places and low. He'd met in taverns and coffee house with operatives from France and Ireland, as well as Harry, who was back again from Holland. He'd also been courted by the French ambassador, the Earl of Marlborough, and a cabal of Protestant lords. *Bloody hell! In the past few weeks, I've had more suitors than a Paris-trained whore.* He also hadn't forgotten Caroline Ware.

Everyone wanted to talk with him and find out what he knew. It was more than a little ironic that rumbles of rebellion, upheaval, plots, and treason should do more to make him popular than all of Catherine's efforts, but that was the way of it. Jamie Sinclair was a capable and pragmatic man. In times of trouble, such men were always prized.

There was no sign of Catherine. She was probably at some court function. Things hung on a delicate balance; one wrong move could be disastrous and he couldn't afford any distractions, but he couldn't seem to get her out of his mind. It still rankled that she'd played him for a fool, parading in tight breeches, begging for kisses, flaunting herself before the king, and then sitting prettily with her bare foot in his lap. He hadn't thought her the sort to play games, hot one moment and cool the next. Once the current round of deal making and espionage was over and things had settled down, he'd really take a mistress. An actress from the theatre. Some one easy and pretty who knew what she wanted and knew her way around a man.

He threw back the drink and poured another, leaning back in his chair and tapping his fingers on the desk. It was only then he noticed the letter. A note from Catherine? He'd have her hide if she'd taken to the streets of London at this hour on her own. She was no fool, though. Surely she knew better. He picked up the letter and began to read, and it all became clear. He'd been ambivalent about their divorce, but obviously she wasn't. She was a wealthy woman tied to an impecunious, barely respectable man with a questionable lineage, and he'd been an even bigger fool than he'd thought.

Twenty-Two

CATHERINE STOOD IN THE GLITTERING BANQUET hall, hoping for a glimpse of Jamie, but his continued absence from home or court wasn't the only thing catching her attention. The court was buzzing with gossip about Lady Ware. It seemed a letter she'd been writing to a friend had disappeared from her desk and then appeared as if by magic amongst the king's own correspondence. No one knew how it happened, but a copy was circulating the court, and *everyone* knew what it said.

It seemed she'd been entertaining His Majesty of late. Her missive bragged that he pined for her and was a slave to her every command. It complained that though his nose was as long as Charles Stuart's had been, his prick was but half his brother's size, and complained that the moniker Dismal Jimmy applied to his performance in bed. Needless to say, His Majesty wasn't amused. The lady's husband, obsequious and contrite, had banished her to the country before the mortified king banished them both from court. It was a delicious scandal and Whitehall rang with excited gossip as everyone delighted in trying to guess the author of the lady's misfortune.

When she arrived home, Catherine's heart leapt to see a light in the library. It meant Jamie was home. She hesitated just a moment—things had been awkward between them of late, but this was news she was certain he'd want to know. He was sitting on the settee by the fireplace, and the look he gave her was not encouraging. She plunged ahead anyway. One of them had to break this damned silence.

"Jamie, I'm so glad to find you home! I've some news I know you'll find of interest." She took the chair across from him and launched nervously into an account of the scandal, somewhat puzzled by his lack of response. The woman had been his mistress, for heaven's sake! She'd tried to ruin him, but he seemed cool and... bored. "It was a rather foolish error for a woman said to be so skilled in intrigue, don't you think?" she asked brightly when she was done.

He answered with a shrug. "It's a common failing of the overly proud. It's when they think themselves invulnerable that they begin to make mistakes. I'm glad to see you, too, Catherine. We've matters to discuss. It will be a year next month since you came to London. It's time our bargain be addressed. You've helped my situation immensely and I'm grateful, but I think now I can manage on my own. Buckingham had a niece, an heiress he offered me some months before he died. She's still available, and amenable I'm told, provided that I'm free. I do apologize for having neglected things. No doubt we should have been about it months ago, but I intend to remedy that now.

I've arranged for both our solicitors to meet with us next week so we can decide upon the ways and means. I hope that will be convenient?"

Her heart had dropped to the floor and tears threatened at the corners of her eyes, but she ruthlessly beat them back. "Why yes, of course," she replied in a voice as cool as his own. "How kind of you, Sinclair, to make the arrangements." They said a stiff and formal good night.

Two days later the royal couple joyfully announced that the queen was with child, and two days after that, James Sinclair, Earl of Carlyle and Carrick, was exiled from England.

Twenty-Three

"HE WAS SUMMONED TO COURT TO SEE THE LORD Chancellor, Baron Jeffreys, early this afternoon, my lady. He returned an hour ago seeming distracted. He's in the library now and I fear he's been drinking. He won't speak or listen to me. I fear something terrible has happened. Perhaps he'll talk to you."

Sullivan had assailed her as soon as she got in the door. She'd never seen him so agitated or upset. "You cannot have failed to notice that Jamie... Lord Carlyle... and I have not been on sympathetic terms for several days now. You know him far better than I do, Mr. Sullivan. I can't imagine there's anything he'd say to me that he wouldn't say to you. If he *asks* to see me, you'll find me in my room."

"Please, madam," Sullivan said, stopping her with a hand on her sleeve. "You're wrong. You're his friend, and there aren't many he's ever let so close as that. He's a good man, you know, much more than he lets on."

"I know," she said with a smile.

"He's far too proud to ask anyone for help, my lady, but I fear he needs us both right now."

"Is it that serious?"

"I don't know. I've never seen him this way before."

"Very well, Mr. Sullivan," she said with a worried sigh, "but if he bites my head off, I shall hold you personally responsible." She didn't want to see him. They were to meet to arrange their divorce in two day's time, and for the last several days, their interactions had been as cold and brittle as river ice. She knew her refusal had annoyed him, but his sudden rush to procure a quick divorce and replace her with someone else had left her hurt and shaken. She had no wish to submit herself to his chilling anger again.

The room was cold and dark and smelled of whiskey, and she couldn't see him at first. She found him slouched in shadow on the settee by a long-dead fire.

"Good evening, Catherine. Did Sullivan send you to beard the lion in his den? That was hardly chivalrous."

"What's wrong, Jamie?" Sullivan was right. She'd never seen him this way before. Whatever the situation, however grim the circumstance, there was always a glimmer of calculation and humor in his eyes. Now he just looked... bleak. She bent to light the fire, then went to light the candles, as he watched her in silence. "Well?" she asked again.

He stretched his arms, then folded them behind his head, regarding her with a sardonic smile. "It seems a certain *lady,* who claims an intimate connection, had information concerning my loyalty she felt she must present the king."

"Lady Ware has struck again?"

"Bloody Jeffreys, the Lord Chief Justice, is an old acquaintance, and the king is feeling generous after the news regarding his wife. I've been given a warning. I'm adjudged guilty without trial, but for past service to the crown, I may choose exile over arrest and execution. I'm to be gone from London by daybreak, my property confiscated, my title forfeit. Tomorrow I'll be declared traitor, and if I'm captured," he shrugged, "'twill be my turn to decorate Tower Bridge."

"What exactly are you said to have done?"

"Oh, some plot or other to overthrow the king and give William and Mary his throne. They're all variations on the same theme."

"Ah!"

"You don't seem surprised."

"Should I be?"

He took a sip of his drink and waved her away. "Go away. I've a deuced wicked megrim. Your chatter will only aggravate it."

"Why don't you try drinking like a sailor? I've heard that helps."

"And there speaks the voice of experience."

"There's no need to be snide."

"And there's no need for you to be here. You need to leave, Catherine. This evening. Divorce me any way you wish if I don't soon make you a widow. Forget about the money. It would only be stripped and forfeit to the crown."

"Do you think I'd take it at your expense? We're friends, are we not? We may be trying to rid ourselves of one another, but I'd hardly abandon you to these curs. Perhaps I can intercede. I'm on good terms with James. He's been courting the Highlanders along with the Irish, and I'm not without influence."

He gave a short bark of laughter. "Never put your trust in kings, my dear. I was told that you might stay and keep your dowry and one of your properties besides. When I replied that your lands and property had remained your own, I was told I might consent to a hasty divorce or a quick execution. You're to be married to a man of His Majesty's choosing so you might be well taken care of. If you wish to keep your fortune for yourself, you have to leave, mouse. I'm sorry."

"And where do you suggest I go?"

"Wherever you wish. Home?"

"No, I think not. It would just be more of the same. If I must be married to someone, I prefer you. I intend to accompany you, for I've a feeling if I lose sight of you, I might not find you again."

"Please don't argue. I know Sullivan thinks I'm the devil's own distillery, but I really do have a megrim. I'll be fine once it passes. The liquor and the darkness help."

"Oh dear! I'm sorry." Catherine jumped up and went around the room, snuffing out the candles so only the light of the fire remained.

"Bless you! Now could you get Sullivan for me, please?"

"I'm right here, milord."

"What? Ah, yes, so you are. Why are you always creeping up on me? You can stop calling me 'my lord.' It appears I'm not one anymore. The way things are going, I'll be your stable boy soon."

"That's not a bad idea," Catherine mused.

Jamie cocked his head to one side, giving her a quizzical look.

"Your pardon, milord, milady, but I feel I must point out that time is of the essence. We must pack what we can and leave. I'll make the necessary arrangements. Where will you be wanting to go?"

"France or Spain, I expect. I still have some skill with a sword. I can always find employment with Louis or Gervaise."

"I've just had a wonderful idea," Catherine ventured, trying again.

"What wonderful ideas are you having, love, as the world falls down about my ears?"

"Why not go to Ireland? You and Sullivan have land there, and you could take the horses with you. You of all people should know that things turn with the tide. We've only to sit things out. Wouldn't that suit? Would trouble follow you there?"

"Trouble follows me everywhere. I've only to look at the two of you to be reminded, but yes... perhaps," he said slowly, thinking it through. "I'm ordered gone from England but nothing was said of Ireland or the properties there, and they're not ones that anyone in England covets. With luck, they might be insignificant enough that they've been forgotten." His voice became more animated. "This might, in fact, prove a blessing. My sources suggest a move against the king sometime soon. This provides an excuse to quit the city and not become involved. If there's another civil war, we've a better chance of staying clear, at least until I've a better idea how it's all going to play out."

"Perhaps we might focus on more mundane issues as well as intrigue and politics," Catherine interjected.

"We can bring Charlie Turner and the grooms with us. They can accompany and care for your stallion and mares."

He caught her grin and couldn't help returning it.

"It's a good idea, don't you think, Jamie?"

"It's a wonderful idea and you're a very clever girl!"

She jumped up and clapped her hands. "Well, we best get to it. If we're to be gone by morning, there's no time to spare."

"Are you mad, woman? I'm about to be publicly accused of treason! *We* aren't going anywhere. You'll not be coming, Catherine. I forbid it. I release you from our bargain. Take your fortune, buy your divorce, and go home."

"Don't take that tone with me, my lord! You'll find it gets you nowhere that you really want to go."

"*Go… home.*"

"Doubtless I should, for all the appreciation I get, but you'll find I'm not the sort to abandon a comrade in times of trouble. We've no time to argue. Sullivan, get the carriage. There's not a moment to waste."

"Indeed, milady. Should I see if I can make arrangements for us to take ship from the city first, milord?"

"No Sullivan. There'll be nothing sailing before the tide, and I must be gone from London by then. I'll take the coach to Bristol and sail to Cork or Dublin from there."

Catherine hurried to her room and gathered her women, informing them she was making arrangements for them to return to Scotland. Maire McKenna insisted on staying in London to assist Sullivan with all his arrangements and then to follow behind.

"Who knows, milady. I might even find me an Irish husband, and you'll be in need of a maid."

"One never knows, Maire. You might even find yourself a rebel Irish lord."

When she found Sullivan returning from the stables, she asked him to arrange passage for her girls. "Maire will be staying behind to help with the packing and travel north with you when you're done. You'll see no harm befalls her, won't you, Mr. Sullivan?"

"Indeed, ma'am! I assure you… that is to say… " he blushed and stammered, turning red to the roots of his hair. "Milord has instructed me to make arrangements for you as well, milady."

"And have you?"

"No, madam, in times of trouble, a man should stay close to his friends. I… would like to thank you ma'am, for encouraging and standing by him. I knew it would do the trick."

"Why do *you* stay with him, Sullivan? It's been what, seven years now? He has no money, he seldom pays you. Why haven't you returned to your home?"

"Because he's kind to his women, his servants, and his pets, ma'am."

"Ah well, I may be his wife, but I assure you I'm not one of his women."

"No indeed, ma'am. You are one of his pets."

Twenty-Four

THE COACH SHUDDERED AND SWAYED OVER RUTTED roads. Catherine gritted her teeth and clung to the strap, sometimes bouncing so high she was airborne. She'd yet to decide what was worse, the sickening sideways slide as they wrenched clear of the sucking mud, or the bone-jarring jolt when she landed. She decided the worst was the sight of Jamie Sinclair's lanky frame, stretched across the opposite seat, his booted feet braced against the window as he slept.

A winter chill was in the air and snow was falling when they stopped to change the horses, and though it was full dark, they ate and were on their way again within the hour. They were traveling fast, they were traveling straight through, and they were traveling light. Mr. Sullivan and three grooms had gone to collect the horses before His Majesty's bailiffs might think to intervene. Jamie had taken several fine bottles of brandy, a case of wine, and a spare change of clothes. Catherine was dressed in boots and breeches.

"Is that your idea of the proper garb for a country wife, mouse?" he asked, collecting a bottle of brandy as they climbed back in the carriage."

"No, Sinclair. It's my idea of the appropriate garb for a traitorous fugitive wife."

"Ah, but loyal to her husband, at least. You look quite fetching, my dear. I'm almost grateful for our hasty departure. It's been a while since I've seen your magnificent *derrière* so cunningly displayed. The way your breeches hug your bottom, snug and rounded—"

"Jamie!" He was an incorrigible letch, as always. At least he was over his black mood and back to being himself. They started down the road again, and she twisted and turned, trying to get comfortable. "Damn it, Sinclair! Couldn't you have sprung for a decent coach?"

"No, my love. You've been miserly and have yet to give me an allowance. In any case, you're here of your own free will. I don't recall forcing you. I didn't ask you to come, in fact I warned you not to. Imagine my surprise when I leapt into my coach intent on my escape and poof! There you were."

"Do you know, Sinclair, your penchant for saying I told you so *is,* in my opinion, one of your least attractive qualities. And it discourages conversation."

"Really, my love? I hadn't noticed."

"Hmph!" Giving up any attempt at further conversation, she closed her eyes and pretended to sleep.

"One should never denigrate a man's carriage. It's representative of who he is."

"Then you are dilapidated, dangerous, unsteady, and unreliable."

"Hush, child!" he said with a chuckle. "If I'm all of those things, then you're being a very reckless girl."

She ignored him.

"It's not too late to change you mind, you know. It's damp and wild and cold in Ireland. Life is harsh and her people are poor."

"As opposed to the Highlands? I think I can manage."

"You don't think you'll miss London or your place at court?"

"I'm rather less attached to it than you are. It's a crowded, noisy, dirty town, and I grew weary of it months ago. I've made my choice."

"The more fool you," he said, tilting his head back and taking a swallow of brandy.

"Yes… quite." Catherine was annoyed with him. He could be a little more appreciative, after all, his past actions were affecting her now, too. She wondered why she hadn't done as he'd wished and abandoned him to his king, his creditors, and his fate. He could support himself as a mercenary. She could have her divorce and control of her money, and if the king sought to curb her, she'd be in Paris in a trice. A divorce was what she'd first come for, after all.

Jamie nudged her foot with his boot, and she accepted the bottle he proffered, raising it to him in a silent toast and managing a healthy swallow before handing it back. The last time she'd drunk brandy in a coach with him she'd been desperately hoping he'd kiss her. Her lips curved in a smile as she remembered. She leaned back, bracing her shoulders against the carriage wall, resting one ankle against her knee. When she closed her eyes, she could still taste the one he'd given her that first night in his tent, whiskey-soaked, firm, and heated. She could still feel how the bristle on his jaw and chin had rubbed her tender cheek. And then, a year later he'd come, luxuriant and predatory, dangerous and seductive, to her room, and she'd turned him away. *Fool, idiot, stupid girl!*

She'd been keenly aware of him ever since. Her skin pricked and she sensed his heat whenever he was near. Her nostrils flared, catching his scent before she saw him, and when he was close, like now, she could hear his heartbeat and the soothing rhythm of his breath. She was fascinated by the steady rise and fall of his chest, mesmerized by the strong lines of his collarbone and the shape of his throat with its—

"What are you thinking about, mouse?"

"Nothing that would interest you." Reaching for the bottle, she took it from him and managed another swallow, giving it back without spilling a drop. The pummeling she'd taken earlier in the evening had left her stiff and sore, but things were improving. Either the way was smoother now, or she'd learned to adjust her position to accommodate the rattling from the road. "Now if you don't mind, Jamie, I'd like to try and get some sleep." Folding her arms and tilting her head back, she closed her eyes.

"Mmmm." She squirmed and wiggled, smiling as she made herself more comfortable, imaging what it would be like if they made love. No doubt he'd be very good at it. She'd only to remember his kisses, the way he held and caressed her, and the effect he had on the ladies of the court. Her toes curled in her boots, and she stretched and sighed. When he'd taken her in the cave, she'd felt on the edge of a great discovery, but becoming a woman had been rather disappointing in the end. She didn't fault him, he'd been delirious and she ill-prepared, but instead of making her feel womanly and satisfied, it had left her feeling curious and aching for more.

Ever since the night she'd refused him, she'd wondered what she'd do if he tried once more. It was a game to him, but not to her. She knew he wouldn't purposely hurt her, but he could hurt her casually, in ways he'd never intended. So what to do? She had to learn to care less or make him care more. They'd escaped London and there were no solicitors to meet. She had him to herself, and now she had time. What could a girl do to make Jamie Sinclair fall in love with her? It was a pleasing notion. He was a sensual man. One would have to start with that. One would need to—

"Well at least *you're* enjoying yourself. Frankly, I'd hoped you'd be better company."

Why must he constantly interrupt! "I thought you didn't want any conversation?"

"Well, I've changed my mind, haven't I? You're an uninvited guest in my carriage. The least you might do is endeavor to provide some entertainment. Pray share your thoughts, my love. You were squirming and grinning so much I expected you to cackle with glee at any moment. What do you find so amusing?"

"Have you nothing better to do than watch me while I sleep?"

"Apparently not." In fact, watching her while she tried to sleep had been fascinating. His prick had sprung to full attention, straining and twitching with every blasted wiggle and sigh. If he hadn't vowed not to touch her again he'd have—

"Very well. If you must know, I was wondering how it is you've come to such a pass."

Liar!

"I married you," he said sourly.

She gave him a kick with her booted foot. "*I meant...* how did you came to have so many enemies and so few friends? How did you become so estranged from your family? Why do you resent and challenge authority, what did you do to warrant the king's anger, and how did you become a spy?"

"Good gracious, that's a great many questions! Why do you keep insisting I'm a spy?"

"I'm not a fool, Jamie. You do more than collect information. You also selectively pass it on. Lord knows what else you do. You can pass for a servant or a beggar. You have the skills of a soldier, a tinker, a gypsy, and a thief, and you've scars all over your body. My father used to say scars are the map to an adventurous man's life, if one knows how to read them."

"You've yet to see all my body, Cat."

"Actually, Jamie, I have. You made a point of flaunting yourself stark naked on our wedding night."

"Ah! You mean you peeked through your fingers as you trembled under the covers? What a naughty girl you are! Did you like what you saw?"

"I did not! That is... I mean... I didn't *peek*. You were also my patient, if you recall. I made a thorough examination of you in the cave."

"Well, my love, you're the only woman I know

who claims to drink whiskey and look at naked men for *medicinal* purposes."

"Pax, Sinclair," she said, blushing to her roots. "I've tied my fate to yours. I only wished to know you better. If you don't want to answer my questions, just say so and let me go back to sleep."

I've tied my fate to yours. Well, so she had. He'd lost his title and his lands and everything he'd worked for, but it seemed he'd gained a friend, and the wife who hadn't wanted him had decided now to stay. She had a right to know what kind of disaster she'd wed herself to, he supposed. He stood up, half crouching because of his height, with one hand on the doorframe and one hand holding the bottle, and moving with the rocking and lurching of the coach, dropped smoothly into the seat beside her. "Ah, that's better. I hope you don't mind my dear, but it's making me ill watching the countryside recede. I'd much rather watch it advance."

"As you wish," she said, scooting to the far side. He filled the space she left him with folded arms and stretched legs, pressing close against her every time the carriage swayed. She didn't object or attempt to dislodge him, as his body acted as ballast to stop her sliding to the floor. He nudged her and passed her the bottle, and as the fiery liquid warmed her belly, she relaxed against him. Despite their current troubles, she felt happier than she'd been in days.

"So… where to begin the sad tale of the traitor, Jamie Sinclair? It starts with—No… wait. A proper spy gets paid for giving information. If you want me to answer your questions, you'll have to forfeit a kiss."

She leaned over and gave him a quick peck on the cheek, her heart thrumming with excitement. "Tell me about your childhood and your family."

"That wasn't a kiss, Catherine."

"Yes, it was. You didn't say where. Now you must honor your part of the bargain."

"No, it wasn't. I'll claim my forfeit when I'm done. My story begins as all good dramas do. Betrayal, lust… revenge. My mother was a wanton who played my father for a fool. He was a Puritan: pious, hypocritical, and a vicious drunk. He hoarded enough money to buy a peerage while preaching humility and modesty and railing against pride. He beat my mother for infidelity while forcing himself on the maids, and he mouthed prayers, preached sermons, and consigned me to the devil as he worked vigorously and with great pleasure to beat the devil from my soul. There was a time I didn't know if hell-spawned bastard or whoreson was my name." *Christ! Why am I telling her this?* "He'd whip me at the slightest provocation, to make me obey, to instill humility, and to teach me respect for authority and religion, but by trying to beat it into me, he beat it out. Ironic, don't you think?"

"Is that where you got your scars?"

"Some are from childhood, a testament to my father's love. Many come from war and fighting, some are from my in-laws—I remember your uncle fondly—and a couple, of course, are from you." He saluted her with a cheerful grin.

"I don't understand. Why did he hate you so?" She moved closer, sliding her arm through his.

"I was a rebellious brat and often flogged for it, but

in truth I think it was because I resembled my mother and looked nothing like him. She had the good taste, but exceedingly poor judgment, to cuckold him regularly, and he was convinced that I was the product of her sin. Besides that, he was by nature domineering, brutal, and quite possibly insane."

"What did she look like? "

"I don't know, Cat. All I remember is her pushing and cursing me on the way out the door. I was very young when she left."

"My mother died giving birth to me."

"Did you miss not having her?"

"Every day. When I was little, I used to sit in the cave where I kept you, waiting for her to come back. I thought she was a selkie, you see. Did you miss yours?"

"You ask too many questions. Shall I finish the story or not?"

"Finish it, please. How did you learn to become other people?"

"That, my love, will cost you." He captured her jaw with his free hand, dragging his lips back and forth across hers, teasing and thrusting with his tongue, plundering her mouth in a rough, delicious kiss. "Now *that,* was a kiss, mouse," he whispered, before letting her go. "Where was I? Ah yes, disguises and such. I suppose I have my father to thank for that, too. If I couldn't be found, I couldn't be cursed at, whipped, or beaten. I lived with the servants much of the time, played with their children, and ate in the kitchen. It was rather an idyllic childhood in a way. I was a little wild, I suppose. I certainly ran free. It was then I first discovered the joys of invisibility and the virtues of disguise. I disguised myself as a linkboy once and lit my father's way home, and he never once suspected it was me. I was sorely tempted to lead him down a riverside alley and leave him there."

"I don't blame you," she said, still breathless and stunned by his kiss.

"You needn't feel sorry for me, love. I had the benefits of both worlds. I ran unfettered in the country on a large estate and free in the alleys of London. I had the benefits of good food, independence, and an adventurous youth, and an education that encompassed all I could learn on the street or in the university. I grew up strong and hardy. By the age of sixteen, when I first went to court, I was over six feet. Only King Charles and Rochester were taller. I liked it there and I wanted to stay. I liked Charles. He was an easygoing man, tolerant and good-natured, who knew how to enjoy living. I dedicated myself to embarrassing my father and pleasing my king, and my unique background made me a useful man.

"So you spied for him?"

"I did whatever he needed me to do, diplomat, soldier, courtier, and yes… spy. Are you happy now? He was so full of potential. He had such charisma and raw talent. I imagined him a great man. I wanted him to be. I thought at first he was. It wasn't until I was older that I understood what an opportunity he'd squandered. With a few noteworthy exceptions, however, he ruled with a benign indifference and spent his life and his greatness on pleasure and whores."

"Some might account that a good life."

He gave a short bark of laughter. "But think what he might have done, Cat."

"It sounds like you loved him."

"Pah! All men love the hand that feeds them, though he spent so much on my lady Castlemaine, he didn't feed me well. A shiny new title and an impoverished estate stolen from poor Sullivan. Proud but poor as a church-mouse I was, just before you met me, lass, but nothing an heiress wouldn't fix, eh? I'd hoped for one of those from Jimmy. I've been useful to him, too. A courtier, a tinker, a soldier, a spy, I've pulled his arse out of the fire more than once, and look how I'm repaid. Gervaise used to call us the whores of war. Protestant one day, Catholic the next, and one side as bloody and hypocritical as the other."

"What of the inheritance your father left you?"

"Mortgaged lands and a title I was never supposed to have. I'm a second son. My half brother was a saint. Saint George, slayer of dragons, a staunch and loyal supporter of crown and country and a model of filial duty. More importantly, *his* mother had the good grace to leave the plowing to my father and the good sense to die before he could find a reason to hate her." He leaned over, put an arm companionably round her shoulders and spoke, his lips next to her ear. "As it happens, Brother George was *so* saintly, he rode headfirst into glory and certain death, taking most of his men with him, poor sods. He brought great honor to the family name, and poverty and sorrow to the widows and orphans left trailing in his wake.

"Apparently, he was too saintly to mount a woman, or perhaps he never found the time. In any case, he died without issue, leaving my father little choice but to accept me as his heir if he wished the family name and his pretty new title to survive. It galled him no end. He mortgaged all the properties and left all his money to the church, leaving me nothing with which to maintain the properties or even pay the servants, some who'd served him loyally for over thirty years. I sold the plate and most of the furnishings and art works to pay the household, but I had to let most of them go."

"I'm so sorry! I didn't realize. If I'd known, I might have—"

"What? Refrained from clubbing me over the head and agreed to follow me home? Why? That was the only good bit of sense you've shown since we met."

Catherine snorted and reached for the bottle, realizing only then that she'd been holding his hand. Grunting and shifting position, she elbowed him in the side as she made herself more comfortable.

"Ladies shouldn't make such noises."

"No? What noises should they make?"

"Pretty sighs and whimperings, perhaps the occasional breathy moan or whisper, *please, Jamie, please*."

"Please, Jamie, please… remove your hand from my thigh."

"No, love. That's not it at all."

"You're very entertaining."

"Are you entertained, my dear? I have other skills if my wit fails to amuse you." He reached his fingers to tug at the buttons of her waistcoat and she slapped them away.

He sat back with a grin. "Ah! Entranced by my story, you refuse to be distracted. I shall finish, then. Where were we? Oh, yes! The heiress. It seems I needed one, and Jimmy was going to give me one, too. And then I married you. As you've noted, the rest is largely your fault. Annoyed at being spurned for a heathen savage, my titular sire, the king, banished me from his sight forthwith. With no heiress, no wife, no occupation or inheritance, I was forced to rely on my skill at cards and pleasing wealthy women to survive. And thus you find me, deprived of a father's love and guidance, robbed of my inheritance, a lost little lamb, a poor wayward soul."

"You were born for the stage, Sinclair."

"Thank you, my love. In any case, I'm grateful for my past. It's made me what I am today."

"And what is that?"

"A rational man, who uses reason, logic, and evidence to make his decisions, rather than superstition or the pronouncement of authorities. A man who thinks for himself... though on occasion I've been known to think with my prick."

"I believe that's true of all men," she said with a chuckle. "So you're an admirer of John Locke?"

"You know of him?" he asked with a look of astonishment.

"I've read several of his papers. He's a member of the Royal Society and we often discussed his theories at the Graecian."

"You constantly humble and amaze me."

"They say he was suspected in some plot and is in the Netherlands now."

"Mmmm."

"Do you think he was involved? It hardly seems rational for such a—"

"He wasn't. He held inconvenient beliefs and had inconvenient friends. Nothing more."

"It was hardly rational or logical for you to marry a woman you'd never met, knew nothing about, and suspected of being a camp follower or an enemy of your king."

"True enough. It was an impulse of virtue instantly regretted. You may credit me with some worthy, selfless, and otherwise noble reason, but in truth I was damnably bored and there was naught else to amuse or divert me in that godforsaken hole. I never expected to be saddled with you this long. React in haste, repent in leisure, a lesson you're about to learn, I fear."

"Can you not take anything seriously, Jamie? Is nothing important to you?"

"If I started taking things seriously, love, my disappointment would crush me. I must see it all as a great jest. My apologies if this annoys you."

They rode on a while in silence. Loose limbed and flexible, her feet braced against the far seat, Catherine was cradled between Jamie's lean form and the wall. She'd learned not to fight the lurch and sway of the vehicle, but to let her body move with it. Lulled by rumbling wheels, the dull thundering of hooves, and the rhythmic creaking of the coach, she closed her eyes and relaxed, picturing a handsome, bright-eyed, laughing boy with an endearing grin and a taste for adventure. His recitation had touched her deeply, though he'd made light of it all as he always did. She'd never known her mother, but she'd had her father and Martha and Jerrod. She'd never doubted she was loved. Who had loved Jamie? Who had marveled at his tales, listened to his hopes and dreams, or laughed at his jokes? Who had comforted him when he was afraid or lonely, taken him fishing, carried him on their shoulders or bragged of him to their friends? A wave of grief assailed her at a sudden image of her father.

"What's wrong, mouse? Are you crying?"

"No! It's nothing. Leave me alone. I was just thinking of my father." She wiped fiercely at her eyes with her sleeve and sat up straight, stifling little hiccups as she looked out the window into the dark.

He placed an arm around her shoulder and pulled her back, guiding her head to his shoulder. "Go to sleep, girl. Don't fight it. You're overtired. It will all seem better by morning."

Exhausted, saddened, yet feeling content, she did as he said; snuggling against his chest, listening to the steady beat of his heart, as his fingers stroked her hair. *I should be comforting him.* It was her last thought before sleep took her.

She woke hours later, damp, disoriented, and confused. The wind had picked up and a cold hard rain was drumming on the roof and coming in through the sides of the windows. She put a hand on Jamie's chest to steady herself and sat up to look out. It was dawn or dusk—she couldn't tell which. The roads were thick with mud and she was getting soaked.

"I'm famished. How much farther until we stop, Jamie?"

"An hour at most. I'm not surprised you're hungry. We've stopped twice to change the horses and you've slept all day. We can get some food in Bristol, but we'd best cross tonight if we can. It's not too late for you to change your mind, but it will be soon. Once we go to Ireland, there's no turning back. We can claim I kidnapped you, forcing you to come, but you'll be tainted."

"I like a man with a sordid past. I'm the type who frequents coffee houses and taverns, even the occasional brothel. You'll do well enough for the company I keep," she said with a yawn and a stretch. "Which reminds me, you still haven't told me what you did to precipitate our flight."

"Nothing, my love, other than make an enemy of Caroline Ware. I thought her neutralized, but apparently, I was wrong. The king can choose to listen to me, or he can choose to believe her, but though he's been mightily annoyed with the both of us, she's the only one who's warmed his bed."

"I'm relieved to hear it."

"Catherine! You're incorrigible," he said with a laugh. "You might pause to wonder if choosing to believe her didn't give him an excuse to be rid of me, so he could chase after you."

"Is he truly so venal?"

"I don't know, but I'll wager he won't be happy when he finds you're gone."

"So… no plot?"

"No plot. When one collects information and is paid for it one is spying. When one collects it for oneself, one is simply staying well informed. To plot one must first make a decision, and though I've been propositioned, courted, and cozened as assiduously as an accomplished whore new-come from France, I've played the coquette and have yet to decide."

An hour later, their mud-spattered coach stopped at the waterfront in Bristol. Jamie spoke with a tavern-keeper who directed them to a captain amenable to a quick departure if the price was right. Within short order, despite the foul weather, they were on their way to Ireland. Jamie had been generous, and the captain had given them his cabin. Catherine sprawled on the bunk in her damp clothes with a groan of pleasure. She didn't care if monstrous waves were gathering to dash the ship to pieces, or if giant leviathans lurked beneath. Her belly was full, nothing was jolting, and after two days in a cramped coach, she was stretched out her full length in blessed relief.

Jamie came to join her a few minutes later. Wrapped in a blanket, he settled in a chair by the bunk. "Well, as usual, it appears I'll be taking the long way home. The captain has debts in Waterford and will take us to Cork and no further. We'll have to journey inland from there. You know, Cat, you remind me of nothing so much as an infant. All you want to do is eat and sleep."

"You're just annoyed because I claimed the bed first."

"I'll have you know I'm a gentleman! I would hardly race a lady to a bunk so I might snatch it out from under her nose."

"Yes, you would, but there's room for us both. If you'll share your blanket I'll share the bed, provided you keep your hands to yourself."

"Well, that wouldn't be any fun, would it?"

"Suit yourself."

He joined her a moment later, settling close along her length, groaning as much as she had as stiff muscles started to stretch and relax. She snuggled tight against him. It was cold and he was warm, and she liked the way he smelled.

Twenty-Five

THEY CREPT INTO CORK ON A THICK BAND OF FOG. It hugged the coast and spilled inland, following the contours of the Lough Mahon and wending its way up the River Lee. As they approached the city, the sound of muffled cannon fire and ringing bells warned of the position of other ships, and an occasional gust of wind parted the mist, revealing a glimpse of docks and quays and the blue skies and brilliant sun that promised a fine day.

Before the fog had lifted, they'd acquired mounts and supplies and were ready to start the last leg of their journey to County Tipperary and Jamie's Irish home. Jamie had arranged for their baggage to follow with Sullivan, though he kept two flasks of wine and two of brandy to warm them on their trek.

"It's heartening to see that you never lose sight of your priorities," Catherine observed as he packed them carefully in the saddlebags.

"Would you care for a swig? It will take the morning chill from the air." She shook her head no, but held out her hand anyway. Crooking an eyebrow, he handed her the flask.

"What I'd really love is coffee," she said before handing it back.

Once the fog had burnt away, the weather was crisp and clear and they made good time, camping that night on the banks of the Blackwater River. The steep heights of the Knockmealdown Mountains lay to the east, and the Galties were visible farther to the north and west. They roasted a hare over the fire for supper and sat sharing whiskey and conversation in the circle of warmth and light cast by the fire. Under a glittering ceiling of stars, they argued over politics and debated philosophy and religion, their conversation punctuated by the hiss and pop of burning logs and the occasional sound of laughter.

"Sometimes, when the world is grand like this," Jamie said, making a sweeping gesture with his arm, "and other times, when I've been in danger, I've found myself almost believing in… something."

"My father used to say that all men are believers when they're staring down the barrel of a musket, yet sometimes, when I've been in danger, I've found myself fearing it's all a big hoax, and there's nothing to it at all."

There was a moment of silence, then Jamie guffawed and they both broke into helpless laughter.

"You're a bad girl, Cat Drummond! The kind who could lead a lonely soul all the way to perdition."

Catherine glanced at him quickly, then looked away.

Jamie rose, stretched, and threw another log on the fire. "Best sleep now, love. We've a long way to go tomorrow. I'd like to make it past the Galty Mountains and push on to the River Suir."

She curled up close to the fire, wrapping her blanket around her. He was singing quietly to himself as he checked their perimeter, his voice rich, warm, and mellow. A moment later, he dropped to the ground beside her. She could hear his even breathing just a heartbeat away. *Are you lonely, Jamie Sinclair?* she thought, aching to hold him. *I'm here, right beside you.* He didn't stir, and after a while, she slept.

Midway through the next morning, they approached the Galties, which seemed to rise out of nowhere from the middle of a fertile plain. Jamie pointed out the highest summit, Mount Galtymore, and told Catherine of the mysterious round lakes that were said to be found nearby.

"Can we climb up to see them?"

"Haven't you had enough of climbing your Highland mountains?"

"I miss them. It will give me a little taste of home."

It seemed a small thing to ask, even in late November, particularly from someone who'd stood by him as she had—and in truth, he was curious himself. Laughing and cursing, they scrambled up the slope, leaving their horses when the going got steep, passing gorse, wild sheep, and heather on the way.

"Just as I thought. It's as bad as Scotland," Catherine said, stopping to catch her breath as they finally approached the top.

"You've quite gone to seed from tripping about London in your pretty high-heeled shoes," he said, reaching down to grasp her hand and haul her up beside him.

"I'll have you know I... Oh, Jamie, it's magnificent!"

They sat side by side on a rock on the summit, hot and perspiring despite the coolness of the day. A pair of eagles soared overhead. To the south from whence they'd come, ridges of mountains folded into one another layer upon layer. In the far distance, they could see the ocean.

To the west, a little below the crest, they found a hollow with a perfectly circular lake about two acres in size.

"Well, I'll be damned, mouse! I swear this must be a volcanic crater."

"I suspect you're right. Look back at the summit. It's shaped like a perfect cone."

They took most of the afternoon to explore, finding two more lakes as they made their descent. Jamie was almost as hungry as Catherine was when they finally set up camp on the floor of the valley. The weather had been splendid for the time of year and, with luck, the next day they'd reach the River Suir. He watched, impressed, as she laid a fire, sitting back on her haunches and nursing it into a strong and steady burn. She was good company. Everything a man could want or hope for in a comrade or friend, but he should have dragged her from the coach and locked her in her room in London. He usually took good care of his own, but not this time. Caroline Ware's attack had dealt a serious blow and he'd been unwilling, unable, to turn Catherine's friendship away. It left him in a quandary. Despite her refusal of him in London, he couldn't miss her interest. She was an eager armful practically begging to be plucked. He smiled to think of her reaction if he told her so.

"Is something amusing you? Would you care to share the jest?"

"Nothing, love. Pull in your claws."

What to do? He'd come close to claiming her the night she'd been stalked by James, but despite their encounter in the cave, she was an innocent in the game of love. He had no wish to hurt, and innocents were too easily wounded. His lovers had all been women of the world. They took what they wanted and then they were done. But Catherine looked at him with searching eyes. She sought something he couldn't give, and to pretend otherwise would be cruel.

If only she'd stop parading in front of him with her shapely legs and tight breeches. If he didn't know better, he'd swear she did it on purpose. It was a deuced awkward position to be in, one's wife a starry-eyed innocent and loyal friend—and a hot and eager vixen just waiting to be fucked. He jumped up and went to stir the fire. A chill had followed them down the mountain and even standing by the flames, he could see his breath. "I'm going to sleep." He tossed her the horse blankets and his coat. "Your teeth are chattering. Go to bed."

Dissatisfied, disgruntled, sour, and now cold, he watched her sleep. She lay there, a warm, enticing bundle, a bastion against the cold. He moved closer to the fire and sat cross-legged with his sword across his lap, and hugged himself against the chill. She was just feet away. If he reached out, he could share her heat. He sighed and leaned back against the tree trunk and tried to get some sleep.

A loud shriek wrenched him from his dreams and he leapt to his feet looking wildly about. It was just past dawn and her sleeping pile was empty. He whirled to look behind him at the sound of splashing, and relaxed when he saw her scrambling up the riverbank, dripping wet.

"I'm sorry to wake you. I slipped on the rocks and the water's bloody cold. Look!" she said proudly, hefting two fine brown trout.

"Now how did you manage that?"

"I'm a very resourceful woman."

"I've never doubted it."

"I had fishing line and hooks in my pack."

"You did? How did you know we'd be camping along the way?"

"I didn't. Ever since I was a girl, I've always carried hook and line. My father taught me how to fish. He said one should always carry it—we were surrounded by water, and that way I'd never go hungry."

"We certainly wouldn't want that! Most of the ladies I know carry brushes and combs, fans and powders and whatnot. You are by far the most singular woman of my acquaintance."

"Thank you," she said uncertainly, wondering if he mocked her.

"Well, we'd best get you dried out." But November had caught up with them. Heavy clouds were racing in and stacking up against the mountains. "Never mind. We need to find some shelter. Here, take that off and take my shirt." He gave her his coat, warm from his body, and watched with amusement as she hid behind the tree to put it on. "Better hurry, love. It'll be upon us soon." Even as he said it there was the plink, plink, plink of rain.

The temperature was dropping and by noon, they were buffeted by gusts of gale-force winds mixed with sleet, stinging pellets, and flakes of snow. Catherine wished she'd listened to Jamie earlier and removed her wet breeches. She'd never dried out, she'd never warmed up, her skin was almost blue, and her teeth chattered from the cold.

"There's an abandoned cottage just ahead. It'll see us though this storm," Jamie shouted back over his shoulder.

A few minutes later, she saw it; a solid looking stone and timber-framed cottage almost swallowed by bushes and ivy, half-hidden by a copse of trees and the driving rain. It was too hard to hear over the howl of the wind, and as Jamie reached for her reins, he motioned her inside. Bending her head into the gale, Catherine fought her way to the cottage door while Jamie took care of the horses, leading them to a sturdy lean-to and settling them nose to tail. Catherine forced the door to the cottage with a heave of her shoulder, and as it sprung open, she almost fell inside. The interior was quiet as a churchyard compared to the wailing din outside.

She looked around, straining to see in the dim light. As her eyes adjusted, shadows took on form and she saw sacks of grain and potatoes, and stacks of wood and coal. The cottage was well stocked, if sparsely furnished, and she blew on her fingers, rubbing to warm them, then knelt by the grate and began building a fire. A moment later the door blew open with an icy blast, and Jamie followed it inside. She leapt up to close it, struggling to hold back the tempest, as he set their packs and her fish on a table inside. A moment later, he was at her shoulder, and with a shove and a kick, the storm was shut outside.

"Why are you still wet, mouse? Do you want to catch your death? Get out of those clothes and get warmed up, and I'll take care of dinner and a fire." He tossed her some blankets from a chest in the corner and turned his back as she hurried to remove her boots and sodden clothes. "In," he said pointing to a cot set in the corner directly across from the hearth.

Wrapped in her blankets, Catherine crawled under the covers and turned onto her side, watching him as he went about his work. He set her clothes and boots in front of the fire. His hair was wet and tangled, plastered against his neck and chest, and his wet shirt clung to his torso like a second skin. She watched the play of muscle as his back flexed and tensed and he busied himself, humming, reaching for this thing and that.

"Aren't you going to dry your shirt, too?"

"Mmmm? Oh, yes, once the fire's going strong and it's warmed up a bit."

"How did you know where to find this place, and why is it so well stocked?"

"It's a little off the beaten path, isn't it? I passed this way before on campaign and stumbled upon it by accident. I don't know why it was abandoned, but it had been for some time. It belonged to someone killed or displaced during Cromwell's day, I expect. A man like me needs a bolt-hole or three. I try to keep it stocked and check on it whenever I'm in Ireland. You must pretend you've never seen it, mouse. Even Sullivan doesn't know it's here." He poured her a healthy tumbler of whiskey, and came over to sit by the bed. "Here. It will help to warm your belly."

"My lips are sealed," she said, trying to keep her eyes from roaming the ridges banding his stomach. "Are you going to do anything with my fish?"

The storm continued unabated throughout the afternoon and into the evening. The cottage was well built. It was snug, and with a fire, it was soon cozy. They dined on fish and potatoes, and Jamie's shirt now hung alongside Catherine's clothes. He lounged on the floor beside her, bare-chested, one knee bent, an arm resting against the bunk. They joked and chatted, passing the whiskey back and forth, their voices a quiet counterpoint to the wind that wailed and moaned outside.

"How long do you think this rain will last?" she ventured.

"I don't know, love. Perhaps it's a flood of biblical proportions, sent to wash away a saucy-bottomed strumpet in breeches and boots and a traitorous, womanizing rogue."

Catherine had lost track of how much whiskey she'd had. At first, it was to warm herself and stop the shivering, and then it was to muster her courage. If she wanted to keep him, she had to catch him first, and after she'd rebuffed him, he wasn't going to make a move to claim her. He'd told her in London to tell him when she knew her mind. Well, she knew it now. *It will be tonight.*

He continued talking: about the lakes they'd found on Galtymore, and his frustration over recent political events. His voice was as rich and melodious

as when he sang. His scars were revealed in the
flickering light from the fire, and she tried to read
them as she would a map. Those that were thin and
white were from his childhood. Her heart clenched
at the thought. There her uncle, and there a sword
wound, and there... she winced at the angry scar
on his chest. That one Donald's man had given him
with a hot iron. Her fingers reached out of their own
volition to touch and soothe, but, uncertain, they
hovered and withdrew.

"Catherine, have you been listening to a word
I've said?"

"Jeffreys is a monster, Churchill can't be trusted, all
William cares about is Holland, and James is a fool."

"Am I that predictable? No more talk of politics.
Tell me about you. Tell me about your father, and
how you came to be so fierce."

She blinked and sat up, frustrated and flustered,
turning to face him with the blanket wrapped around
her legs and her back against the wall. *I've absolutely
no idea how to seduce a man.* She was a Drummond,
though, and if strumpets and witches and empty-
headed courtiers could do it, then she could too.

"I will if you come up here and sit beside me.
I'm cold."

"You should get back under the covers."

"The room moves around me and my head gets
dizzy whenever I lie down."

"Ah!" He plucked the bottle from her and set it on
the floor before settling down beside her.

"What do you want to know?" She wondered if
she should go back to wearing dresses.

"From everything you've told me, your father was a good man, yet you seem so unhappy whenever you speak about him."

"Of course I do. He died the year before we met."

"I'd swear there's more to it than that."

She sighed, giving up any pretense of seduction. She was what she was and that was that. She told him of her father and how he'd raised her as a son, grooming her as his successor, but refusing to name her chief. "I did all that I could to be worthy of it, and of him, but in the end he tried to sell me off like chattel, just like any other girl."

"Not like any other girl, Cat. Women like you are expected to marry, but few are allowed any choice. If he'd been a crofter he might have had the luxury of putting you first, and then you could have married the sheepherder of your choice instead of a debauched, black-hearted cur, but you'd never have been allowed to parade about as gloriously as you do. You'd have had a babe slung over your back and a scythe in one hand before you were fourteen. That's no fit life for you."

"I know. I don't blame him for it anymore. That's not what saddens me. I was childish, selfish, and stupid. I... I told him I hated him, Jamie. I cursed him and told him I'd never forgive him. That's how things stood between us when he died, and now he'll never know how much I loved him, how much I appreciated... how much he meant. He used to carry me on his shoulders, you know, when I was a child, and I thought I was the queen of the world. We'd go fishing, just him and me. He made the most beautiful flies from peacock feathers while he told me stories, and he'd lift me up and put me on the saddle in front of him and we'd go galloping…"

"He knew, Cat. Of course, he knew! You were only doing what any worthy young heir should do, what he taught you to—standing up for yourself and fighting for what you thought was yours. He was probably pleased and proud behind his bluster." He gave her a hug and the tears spilled down her cheeks.

"You see! This is why I don't like to talk about it. Now look what you've made me do!" She dabbed at her eyes with her blanket, and pulled away from his arms. "It wasn't supposed to be like this. I was trying to seduce you. And look at me now. My eyes are red and puffy and no doubt so is—"

He growled low in his throat, spread his fingers though her hair, and pulled her mouth to his in a kiss that devoured her. She whimpered as he pushed her back into the mattress, covering her body with his own. His hands roamed her surface, rough and demanding, tugging at her blanket, bunching the material and rasping it across her belly and her breasts as he worked to set her free. She gasped and arched into him as it brushed across her nipples, sending an exquisite throbbing thrilling to her core. His tongue plunged in and out of her mouth in urgent rhythm, matched by the movement of his hips, and she sought eagerly to meet him, opening herself to him and following where he led. Nudging her legs open, he spread them wider with his knee. Wrapping one arm around her, he encircled her waist, jerking her hard against him and grinding his straining erection in the valley between her legs. Groaning his satisfaction when he found her naked skin through her blankets, he caught a nipple between his fingers and thumb. She moaned and rose against him, begging him for more, and he complied, his lips joining his fingers to tease and play.

She began to rock against him, clutching at his back, whispering into his hair, "Please, Jamie, please."

He returned his lips to hers as his fingers tugged and tweaked, silencing her pleading with his kiss. She smelled like the Highlands, tasted as sweet as her whiskey and he—

"Damnation! Bloody hell! Ah good Christ, mouse, I can't." He let her go and sat up, dragging his fingers through his hair in frustration.

"I swear it's true, Sinclair! You're just like Lord Summerset—capable with every species of woman but your lawful wife!" she snapped, perilously close to tears again.

"I assure you I'm more than capable in your presence, love," he said, clasping her hand and pressing it against his swollen penis, "but I'm reminded that you've drunk more than a few tots of whiskey. The last time we did this I don't remember, and you won't remember if we do it now. I've been an errant fumbler with politics and with women, and the only things I've excelled at are drinking, cards, and war, but I promise you this, when next I make love to you, it will be something you'll remember the rest of your life."

Though it almost killed him, he adjusted her blankets, and pulled the covers up to her chin, then gave her a kiss on the top of her head. "Now be a good girl and go to sleep." He settled on the floor beside her. *What in hell is wrong with me?*

"It's cold. There's room for you here if you like."

"I'm fine, thank you."

They lay in silence, but for the sound of the slates vibrating on the roof, and the sleet and hail battering the windows.

"Jamie?"

"Yes?"

"How much have *you* had to drink?"

"Too much."

"You won't remember any of this in the morning, will you?"

"No, love. I won't remember a thing."

Twenty-Six

THE NEXT DAY'S JOURNEY BEGAN IN AWKWARD silence, progressing over time to nods, clipped questions, and one-word replies. Remembering how he'd made her beg and whimper, only to leave her pleading like a child, Catherine followed Jamie in stony silence. Recalling his mocking words in the coach and her own pleading ones last night, *"Please, Jamie, please,"* she clenched her fists and gritted her teeth, looking straight ahead. *He plays with me! I'm a toy for his amusement. I hate him! I wish we were back on the mountain so I could push him off!*

The storm had blown itself out overnight, but the ground was still wet and boggy, and as they left the mountains behind them, they squelched and sloshed over scrubby hills that soon gave way to squares of wood and fields. The weather remained undecided. The sky would darken suddenly, gushing rain, and a moment later the sun would return, changing it back to a brilliant cerulean blue. *Just like him. Shining down on you in all his glory one minute, then pfft, gone, the next. I will never kiss him again. I will never touch him again. I will never drink whiskey again.* She repeated the mantra over and over, using it to fuel her march.

Jamie made several attempts to engage her in conversation, pointing out interesting features they passed on the way, but she studiously ignored him. Heading east, they entered a fertile stretch of land he insisted on telling her was the Golden Vale, part of the basin of the River Suir, which crossed the county from north to south. Here, lush expanses of farmland were separated from each other by ranges of gentle hills, kissed by the heavy mists that rolled inland along the river. They passed through it on roads lined with ancient, twisted trees clothed in vine and moss, and bordered by stone-walled pastures.

By nightfall, the country was level and they'd reached the banks of the Suir. Jamie told her of a legend that the river began to flow on the night King Conn of the hundred battles was born. Curiosity piqued, she spoke at last, asking for the story, but he only shrugged. Sullivan had told him. He didn't know the rest. *Yet another disappointment,* she thought sourly.

The property was on the north bank of the Suir. Comprised of five hundred acres of farmland and lush pasturage, it was crowned by a large, tower-house castle, surrounded by walls and defensive turrets, perched on top of a small rise. They approached through a park-like setting, down an avenue of ancient oak and yew, and entered the courtyard through a medieval arched gateway. Inside were several stone-faced buildings that included a stable for twenty horses. The house stood five stories tall and had numerous gun loops and four towers with a timber guard walk between them. Catherine was impressed. Though not as large or imposing as Castle Drummond, it did a more than adequate job of combining the virtues of a comfortable manor house with a formidable defense.

"This is a good deal grander than I was led to expect, Sinclair."

"Just so. I apologize if I've disappointed some romantic notion about living in a hovel, but it doesn't do to flaunt one's good fortune, lest some fool get jealous and attempt to take it away. Most gentlemen of my acquaintance lust after lands in England, not Ireland, and many who've been given land here have never been to see it. They rent it back to the original owners at exorbitant prices or sell it for development. Charles would never have given me this had he known its worth, but there's been a tradition since Cromwell's day to reward with lands the soldiers you can't pay, and now they're mine."

"Will James strip them from you, as he has your property in London?"

"If he thinks of it he might, but I'm hoping if I stay out of sight and mind, my Irish properties and I will be considered too insignificant to warrant much attention. If not, I think I can persuade Dick Talbot to argue they be returned to Sullivan. It was an excellent idea you had… coming here. I was so… If you hadn't talked some sense the other night, I'd be on my way to some meaningless campaign somewhere in Europe. I consider you a good friend, Catherine. I hope you know that."

Catherine stopped in her tracks, astonished. Sometimes he said the most unexpected things. Just when she thought she had him figured out, she found she didn't know him at all.

He continued on through a grilled door without her, and she had to hurry to catch up. They entered a large hall, paneled in Irish oak, that stretched over one hundred feet in length. It was hung with beautiful tapestries and boasted mullioned windows and a handsome limestone mantel. A spiral staircase led to the upper floors.

"I thought you said you were poor."

"I am. Selling this would pay off most of my debts, but I've not wanted to take anything away from the place to use in England. I've kept my hands off for the most part, though God knows, mouse, there's times I've been tempted. Sullivan manages the property and he's got a good head for business, and Mrs. O'Sullivan, his mother, manages the people. Come, let's find her."

"Why do you call Sullivan and his mother by different names?"

"Because I don't want my ears boxed. Sullivan is the English version of the name and Granny O gets piqued if one uses it in her vicinity."

They walked through the hall and down toward the kitchen, a swell of excitement building in their wake. Servants came to greet them with curtseys, smiles, and handshakes, messengers left on the run, and dogs and children crowded around. The hubbub reached the kitchen before they did.

"Well, God bless and protect us all, 'tis the devil himself come to call." A stout, motherly-looking woman, with piercing blue eyes framed by wire spectacles, stepped forward and enfolded Jamie in a warm embrace. "You might have sent word you were coming, Jamie lad, so we could have prepared a feast."

"I do apologize, Mrs. O, but my wicked past overtook me, leaving deuced little time to write." The children were clamoring around him, laughing with excitement, pulling at his pockets and jumping up and down. "Mrs. O'Sullivan, there's a child attached to my leg. Kindly detach it."

"Off you go now, the lot of you, before I find you work to do." Mrs. O'Sullivan clapped her hands and shooed them toward the door. Calling them back, Jamie reached into his pocket and pulled out a handkerchief. Passing it through a circle formed by his thumb and forefinger with a dramatic flourish, he opened his hand to reveal several pieces of hard boiled sugar candy. They shrieked in delight as he tossed it to them one by one, and then they and the dogs tumbled out the door and into the kitchen garden.

"I feed them all candy so they won't revolt and murder me in my bed—except for Granny O, who's sweet on me anyway and likes to watch her figure," he confided to Catherine with a cheeky grin.

"So you were chased out of England for some kind of mischief, then. Did my boy come with you?" Mrs. O'Sullivan peered over his shoulder into the now empty corridor.

"Alas no, Mrs. O. I left him cavorting with strumpets and hussies. He's yet to produce a son and I thought it best. Your boy is forty-two years old. A bit of practice won't hurt him. He'll be along directly once he's done."

"You're not too old to have your ears boxed, Jamie Sinclair. Who's the girl then? Will she be staying, or should I be sending to the village? If you plan to keep her, be sure to tell her the way things are."

The old woman gave Catherine a challenging look that would have made a lesser being quaver. All of a sudden, Catherine was acutely aware of her scuffed boots, torn shirt, and stained breeches, and she had to restrain an urge to fix her tangled hair.

"Now, now, Mrs. O. I admit she resembles a ragamuffin more than a lady, but I do intend to keep her. I'll grant she's a wanton bent on seduction, who clubbed me and beat me and won't let me go, but that kind of thing appeals to me, you see, and I can't seem to resist her wiles. She's Lady Catherine Drummond, Countess of Moray, Carrick, and once Carlyle, and she's my wife, and *that's* the way things are."

He turned to Catherine. "Darling? May I introduce Granny O'Sullivan, matriarch and queen of the O'Sullivan clan? I don't know why they call her granny, as her lump of a son has yet to produce any children and she herself is eternally youthful, like an Irish spring."

Catherine brushed by Jamie and offered her hand. "I am pleased to meet you, Mrs. O'Sullivan. Your son has been kind to me, and Ja... my husband, speaks of you with great fondness." *I don't need to push him off a mountain. A battlement will do just fine.*

Mrs. O'Sullivan returned the gesture, her face warming to a smile. "Welcome, my dear. So the lad's finally done something right, has he? You must be his Highland lass, and every bit as fierce and lovely as he described. Come with me and I'll show you the castle while the servants prepare your rooms."

Jamie nudged Catherine, as they trailed behind her. "You're shameless! It took me gifts and bribes and months of trying, and you've tamed the dragon with a few honeyed words. You must have stopped and kissed the Blarney Stone near Cork when I wasn't looking."

"*I'm* shameless? Where in heaven's name did you get candy?"

"Like you, I'm very resourceful. You carry supplies to catch fish wherever you go, I, to lure small children."

"You play so many games, Sinclair, I swear you remind me of a child yourself."

"It's not children's games I play, love," he whispered before stepping away.

Mrs. O'Sullivan was also resourceful, and that night the great hall rang with song and laughter as the castle inhabitants and local farmers and villagers came to celebrate and welcome Jamie and his lady. They sat around the edge of the room with their backs to the wall and feasted on salmon cooked over an applewood fire and mutton and pork spitted and basted in honey. Mead, sloe wine, and cold sweet ale added to the festive mood as they listened to singers and storytellers, harpers, fiddlers, and drummers.

"I swear I'm feeding every displaced farmer in County Tipperary. I wonder how I'm paying for it all," Jamie said to Catherine under his breath, but his voice was amused, his posture relaxed, and his smile appeared to be genuine.

Singing and music led to dancing, which led to competitions. Catherine watched in amazed delight as Jamie accepted a challenge, removing his coat and leaping onto the table, arms outstretched and hair flying, matching his opponent step for step in an intricate eight-bar dance as they battered their feet on the thick wood in a percussive rhythm like drummers. They went faster and faster and the hall erupted in whoops, cheers, and applause, until both of them jumped laughing to the floor. Triumphant, Jamie strutted over to her through a backslapping, shouting throng, and pulled her into a wild reeling dance. She forgot her anger, she forgot her embarrassment, and she forgot all her good intentions. *God help me, I'm falling in love with him. I'm well and truly lost.* She threw back her head, laughing, and joined him in the dance.

Six days later, Sullivan arrived in the first of three large carts, all overflowing with towering piles of furnishings and baggage. He informed them gloomily that the London house had been confiscated by the crown, but it was nothing they hadn't expected, and looking at the mounds of rugs, tapestries, and furniture in the wagons, Catherine had difficulty imagining he'd left anything worth taking. He was accompanied by a beaming Maire McKenna, a grumpy Charlie Turner, two grooms, a frothing and fretting stallion, and six high-stepping mares. There was another feast that evening as the O'Sullivan scion was joyfully welcomed home.

It was a bustling, cheerful home, prosperous and well run. Catherine fell in love with it and its inhabitants and enjoyed the feeling of being surrounded by friends and family, something she'd been missing for a while. Taking her cue from Jamie, she participated where she was invited, which was often enough to feel welcome, and otherwise stepped aside. She watched with interest the subtle shift between Jamie and Sullivan. Though she'd noted in London that they were far more familiar than master and servant, in Ireland they met as friends, with Jamie and Kieran replacing Sullivan and milord.

If she'd not understood at first why Jamie had been so protective, leaving the place and its people untouched, she did now. *He loves them. This is as close as he's ever had to family, brothers and sisters and a mother of his own.* She loved them for it, though sometimes at night it made her weep.

The constant buzz of activity reached a high point as the Yule approached. An army of workers and servants scrubbed, polished, beat carpets, and whitewashed walls, while the children scoured the countryside for crimson-splashed holly and fresh ivy boughs. Mrs. O'Sullivan oversaw the placement of candles and kept a watchful eye on the whiskey cakes, as Kieran, Mr. Turner, and Jamie settled the horses and prepared for the St. Stephen's day races the day after Christmas.

Catherine found it easy to settle into the life and rhythms of the castle—which were not that different from the ones back home—and harder to maintain her reserve around Jamie. By day, she was captivated by his teasing grin, easy humor, and ready smile. At night, asleep in her tower room, she tossed and moaned, caught in fevered dreams that left her soul and body aching. He was happy here in a way he hadn't been in London, except when on an adventure. His eyes

sparked with enthusiasm, his wit was warm and
playful, and he charmed without calculation or guile.
*The London courtier is the mask. This is who he really is. I
wonder if he knows?*

They were friends again, back to the easy camaraderie they'd shared on their adventures and on
the road, but things were different, too. As they sat
together deep in conversation, or with heads bent
playing chess, she was intensely aware of him. She
watched him when he wasn't looking, fascinated by
the curve of his mouth, the sweep of his lashes, and
a small tear-shaped scar high on his cheekbone just
below his eye. His voice stirred her as surely as a caress,
and her body thrilled to every inadvertent touch. A tap
on her wrist to draw her attention, a hand on her back
or waist to guide her through a door, his arm brushing
hers as they leaned side by side at the paddock fence—
they stole her breath and raised the hair on her arms in
a crackle of anticipation.

The night after Christmas, with the St. Steven's Day
racing, mummery, and traditional feast over, Catherine
relaxed in the sitting room adjoining her bedroom and
Jamie's. With its fanciful carved fireplace, painted sky
ceilings, and a recessed alcove that abutted the river, it
was one of her favorite places. The day had been full,
and Kieran—how strange that sounded—had stolen
the show on Jamie's stallion, winning race after race.
People had come from miles around to marvel at the
son of Old Rawley. Catherine hadn't missed Maire's
interest. She'd have to speak to Sullivan… Kieran…

soon, about his intentions. She'd have to speak to Jamie soon about his, too. He was somewhere he belonged now, and it was time to make a decision to stay or go.

It was full dark and the feast was long over, but the singing and dancing in the Great Hall would continue for most of the night. She'd stayed a while, enjoying the merriment and celebration, but two days of festivities had made her miss her own family and left her feeling isolated and alone. *I'd rather be alone by myself than alone in company, making others uncomfortable or pretending that I'm not.* She poured a tumbler of her own Scotch whiskey and raised it high.

"'Here's to the heath, the hill and the heather,
The bonnet, the plaid, the kilt and the feather!
Here's to the heroes that Scotland can boast,
May their names never die—
To the Highlands, I toast.'

"Here's to you, Dad. You were always my hero. I love you and miss you and I hope I make you proud." She tilted back her head and downed the fiery liquid in one swallow, then slammed the glass on the table, her eyes watering. A slight cough startled her. Jamie lounged against the fireplace, one arm resting on the mantle.

"'Here's to them that like us
Them that think us swell
And here's to them that hate us
Let's pray for them as well.'

"To Caroline Ware and your cousin Donald. *Slàinte, agus Nollaig Chridheil*, Cat Drummond," Jamie said, raising his glass to her.

"And good health and Merry Christmas to you, too, Jamie Sinclair," she said with a grin, returning his salute. "How do you come to speak Gaelic so well?"

"I was robbed of my birthright, rescued by gypsies, and enchanted by a fairy queen who forced me to travel the Highlands peddling my wares. I've learned a great many things."

"So… your father's servants taught you?"

"Some. I like my story better. You're lucky, mouse, to have someone to miss."

"I know. I wonder what he'd think if he could see me now?"

"Let's pray he can't. Fathers of daughters don't approve of men like me."

"You never met my father. I suspect he would have liked you very much. Do you miss your mother?"

"I told you I don't remember her, Cat."

"Surely you must remember something. Is she still alive? Where is she?"

"I've no idea if she's alive or dead. I've had no contact with her since she left."

"But surely you must be curious. Have you ever tried to—"

"No! I… no… I've not tried to find her." He finished his drink and placed his glass on the mantle. "Nor has she ever come in search of me. As to what I remember… If you must know, I remember finding her in a hallway with her skirts hiked above her waist with a man who wasn't my father, and I remember begging her not to go. I remember she told me I was a mistake and she wished I'd never been born. She hated me, mouse, even more than he did."

Shocked, Catherine could find no response.

"Well! It's always nice to reminisce. The night's still young and we're not fit company for anyone else. Would you care to join me in a game of chess?"

"What? Oh, yes. Yes, of course!" Grateful for the change of subject and promising herself never to bring it up again, she busied herself searching for the chess set, but it wasn't in any of the usual places. "The board appears to have absconded from the room."

"Ah! Of course. I'd forgotten. I enjoyed a game with Kieran in my chamber last week and neglected to put it back. Would you care to join me there?"

Her heart leapt at his words, even as her head urged caution. He'd already rejected her attempts at seduction twice. She was likely the only woman in Ireland invited to a renowned rake's bedchamber for a game of strategy instead of games of love. Still, it had to be now, or she feared it would be never.

She took another healthy swallow of whiskey and followed him into a spacious room, paneled in wood and leather. Brightly colored rugs lay strewn across the floor, a chest, an armoire, and a wardrobe stood along the far wall, and the south wall boasted mullioned windows that overlooked the river. Brussels tapestries hugged the walls, depicting battle scenes and hunts, but though the room was comfortable, there was nothing in it to reflect his personality. It reminded her of the façade he adopted in London, elegant and impersonal, with no hint of the man beneath. Her eyes were drawn to a carved and gilded four-poster bed with rich green hangings and a magnificent bedspread embroidered in shades of forest, leaf, and gold. *Ah! Now that looks like him,* she thought with a grin.

They sat across from one another in comfortable armchairs in front of a blazing fire, a rosewood-veneered chessboard, its pieces made from brass and silver, on the table between them.

"Jamie?"

"Mmm?"

"Have you ever considered that we share a great deal in common?"

"Of course I have. We both enjoy gambling, brothels, alcohol, and adventure. We're rogues of the first order. Speaking of which, would you care to lay a wager on this game?"

"I meant," she said with great patience, "have you considered that it might work well for us to stay together?"

"You mean forget about a divorce? Why would you want to keep me now, at a time when our association can only hurt and hinder you? I noted you wrote your solicitor before we left London, and you were wise to do so."

She remembered her surprise at his coldness the night she'd found him in the library. *The night I wrote my solicitor about a divorce. Is that what made him angry?* No. That was nonsense. "You're right, of course. It was just a thought. Foolish, really. I could never be what you want, and you would never do for me."

"Check." He took one of her pawns with his knight, and then sat back, nursing his drink. "I'm curious now. What exactly *do* you want, Catherine?"

Her eyes caught his, then darted away. "I'm fairly certain you know."

"And what is it you think I want?"

His voice made her shiver.

"You want a buxom beauty who'll warm your bed, do as she's told, ask no questions, and cause no trouble. Blonde, preferably." She took his knight with her bishop.

"And yet I married you. You'll grant you're neither blonde nor biddable, though you are a buxom beauty."

"Don't mock me, Jamie. I'm well aware I'm not the sort of womanly creature most men want. I'm far from delicate and far too bold."

"Your experience of men is somewhat limited. I like you well enough and you've never pretended to be less than who you are. Find yourself a real man, one who'll appreciate you, not some swaggering bully."

"Yes, thank you for the advice. I'll bear that in mind when I'm shopping for my next husband." She stood up, her question answered before it was asked.

"I mean it, Catherine." He rose to his feet, the game forgotten. "Any man worthy of the name would think himself lucky to have you. Any man would want you. Surely you know that."

"You don't."

"Oh no, my love. You're very wrong about that." Reaching out a long finger, he wrapped it in a tendril of her hair, winding it gently, and tugging her toward him. Breathless, she came. He rubbed it between his fingers, and raised it to his lips, kissing it softly as he inhaled her scent. "I think about it all the time." His knuckles brushed the nape of her neck just below her ear and she whimpered, stepping closer and putting a hand on his chest. He trailed his fingers along her cheek and jaw, leaving delicate thrills of sensation, then caressed her throat, his eyes holding hers. Curling his fingers around the back of her neck, he drew her lips to his.

Please don't stop. Please don't stop. "Please don't stop," she murmured, wrapping her arms around his neck and raising on her toes, pressing eagerly against him.

Grabbing her hips, he jerked her tight against him, grinding into her soft belly. "Be careful what you wish for, mouse," he rasped. Splaying his fingers through her hair, he took her mouth in a searing kiss, his tongue plunging in and out as he walked her backwards to the bed. Hefting her in his arms, he dropped her on the mattress, pinning her beneath him with a groan of pleasure and pain. He'd been so long without a woman his cock was nigh exploding, and he hiked up her skirts with one hand as the other scrabbled at the fastening of his breeches, trying to free himself, seeking relief. *Christ, I'm going to spend before I can take her. Oh, bloody hell! I can't take her as if she's a common whore.* Cursing, he rolled off her and sat up, panting, aching, and shaking with need.

Catherine sat up on her elbows. "What is wrong with you? What's wrong with me? Why won't you make love to me?" Her voice was trembling. She was almost in tears.

"You're just a bit the worse for drink again, love," he said, running his fingers through his hair. "It seems in order to partake of love's lusty pleasures one of us must be drunk or unconscious."

"You were not unconscious!"

"Well, I was certainly incapacitated. You took terrible advantage of me. I'm not inclined to do the same to you."

"I didn't—"

"Shhh! I'm teasing, love. I enjoy the way you puff and hiss like an angry kitten."

Catherine sat up, straightening her skirts and gathering her composure. "You're a jade, sir. You make pretty promises and when the time comes and the thing is upon us you are suddenly coy. Do you find it amusing?"

"Dear girl, when you speak like that I find it intimidating. You're making me feel like a timorous maid."

"This game you play is cruel! You lead me along and then abandon me, always with some sorry excuse. I am *not* drunk, and I wasn't at the cottage. I was nervous and cold and I drank to give me courage and relax, but I knew what I wanted. I remember it clearly, and I know what I want now. The problem isn't me, Sinclair. It's you. I've offered you something you haven't the ability to appreciate. I apologize. You can rest assured I shan't trouble you this way again."

"You trouble me this way with every breath you take, love, but I know what you want and I know your worth, and it's more than I can give you."

"And what is it you think I want, Jamie?"

"This." He trapped her face between his palms, capturing her lips in a sweet slow kiss, then murmured low against her ear. "I love you, hellcat. I want you and need you and can think of nothing else. You're my heart and soul. Every time I see you the world is fresh and new. I'm yours… now and always." His voice was warm and tender, and he smelled of citrus and spice. Even though she knew he feigned it, her knees turned to water and her heart thudded in her chest.

"That, love," he said, letting her go, "is what you want. And that I can't give you."

"You're wrong," she lied. "If you told me that, I'd wonder what ailed you. I lived a full life before I met you, and I'll continue to do so after you're gone. I expect you to treat me with honesty and respect, nothing more, but I'm a grown woman and right now, you're the only husband I have. What I *want* is to know what all the fuss is about. I want to know what happens between a man and a woman that makes poets write about it, men duel over it, and women risk their reputations. I want you to show me. I want you to teach me, but if you can't or won't, I'll find someone who can."

Jaw thrust forward, back rigid, she stood to leave, but he caught at her elbow and with a skillful tug and a nudge from his knee, he toppled her backwards and into his arms. Rolling over, he positioned himself above her, trapping her beneath him at wrist, chest, and thigh. Despite a heroic effort, his attempts to protect her—and himself—had failed miserably. If anyone would be teaching her lessons it was he, but he owed her honesty, and one last chance to repent.

"I like you, Catherine… as much as I've ever liked anyone… more, in fact. I've had many lovers, but very few friends. You've been a good one. One I can trust. God knows I want you, but if I disappoint you—when I do—I'm afraid I'll lose your friendship and I don't want that. The biggest mistakes I've made have all involved you, and each time I've known I was making one, yet I've done it nonetheless. I'm decidedly uncomfortable that things have come this far, but I can't seem to stop. I need you to understand I offer friendship and pleasure, nothing more."

"That's all I ask." She relaxed beneath him, unclenching her fists and parting her lips in unwitting invitation. His admission was more than she'd expected, and more than she'd dared hope. *Oh my God! It's really going to happen!* She felt a thrill of fear and anticipation, knowing this was a moment she'd been waiting for all her life.

He lowered his head and touched his lips to hers, nibbling and caressing, breathing the rich sweet taste of brandy into her mouth. His skillful tongue cajoled and teased, coaxing her to open, and when she did, he moaned and thrust deep inside her mouth. His tongue joined hers in a voluptuous dance as his hand roamed her body, squeezing and kneading and claiming all the places he'd been longing to touch.

"You wore this gown to breakfast once," he murmured between lazy kisses, trailing his fingers across her silk-clad breasts. He tugged at the jeweled clasps that joined her bodice. "I was jealous of the way these held you... here." His whispered words sent a tickling sensation along her back and arms that raised the hair on the nape of her neck.

"You were angry with me, and I wished you weren't, because I longed to kiss and hold you... here." He caressed the luscious curves that strained against her clothing, his fingers itching to feel her naked skin. "And here... " He trailed hot kisses across the mounds that swelled above her lace and ribbons. "And... here." His finger flicked a pebble-hard nipple that begged attention through the sheer fabric of her dress.

She gasped and arched against him.

"Easy, love, we're only just beginning. I'm going to touch you and taste you all over," he promised, warm against her ear.

He nipped at an earlobe and a thrill of sensation traveled down her spine, pulsing and rippling between her legs and curling her toes. She tossed and moaned as his wet tongue teased and tickled, and his hot breath played against her ear. He trailed kisses along her jaw, the edge of her mouth, and along her throat, and then returned his attention to the fastenings of her gown, loosing them with expert fingers, freeing her eager breasts from their confinement, groaning with pleasure as they bobbed and bounced beneath the loose fabric of her chemise. "Good Christ, sweetheart, I could devour you."

He caught one breast in his hand, squeezing it like ripe fruit, brushing its tip with his thumb. Catherine whimpered, straining against him, begging for she knew not what. He bent his head and bit her gently through the fabric, and a wild jolt of pleasure coursed through her, making her cry out. He busied himself with tongue and mouth until the silk was soaked and plastered to her skin, then blowing softly upon it, he slowly peeled it back. When his mouth fastened on her bared nipple and his hot tongue stroked her naked flesh, he took her well past doubt or caution, banishing modesty or restraint.

Gripping his shoulders, she begged and pleaded, bucked and writhed, moaning, "Please... please... please," between ragged breaths.

He sucked and nibbled, nipped and teased, one peak and then the other, while his hands roamed her body, playing her like a virtuoso, each touch, each kiss, striking a new chord as he used teeth and tongue, palm and fingers to weave delicious thrills, guiding and shaping her, but denying her release.

Her body responded, aching and tender, and unable to separate feeling and sensation, body and soul; her heart did, too, swelling with emotion as her flesh ripened with pleasure. *Kiss me, touch me, love me, Jamie, as I love you.*

Unable to say it, afraid to break his rules, she tried to show him with her touch what she couldn't say with words. She tugged at his shirt, pulling it up and sliding her hand underneath to feel his naked flesh. His skin was smooth and hot and he shuddered at her touch. "Show me what to do," she whispered against his throat.

"God bless you, lass." Catching her wrist, he guided her to the bulge in his breeches, pressing her hand against his engorged penis as he worked to set it free. It fell into her hand with a soft thump, and he moaned and shivered as she hefted it curiously, testing its weight. "It's smooth as silk and hot and rather heavy," she whispered, running her fingers along its length. She tapped it curiously with her finger, smiling slightly as it bounced and twitched. "It's moving by itself!" Continuing her exploration, she squeezed experimentally, stopping at his groan. "Am I doing it wrong? Am I hurting you?" she asked, pulling her hand away.

"It's an exquisite torture, love. Don't stop."

He gripped her hand and pulled it back, wrapping her fingers around him and moving her hand up and down his shaft. He let go and she continued on her own, fascinated as he arched and bucked as she'd done earlier, realizing for the first time that in the games he played, she had power, too.

"What else shall I do?"

Christ! She was going to unman him. "You could kiss it… if you like," he gasped.

"Really? You'd like that?" She continued to stroke him.

"It's very pleasurable to a man," he said through gritted teeth. "You don't have to if it makes you uncomfortable."

"If it gives you pleasure, it will make me happy, too." She lifted his penis in the palm of her hand and pressed an awkward kiss on the underside, then wrapped her fingers around him and kissed its tip. His hips jerked under her inexpert ministrations as if she was a houri come from paradise itself.

Taking her by the waist, Jamie hauled her up against him, then took her face between his palms for a searing kiss. "I thank you, Catherine, for *all* your gifts, but it's been months since I've had a woman and I need to have you now." He eased her onto her back and straddled her, then bent to plunder her mouth once more. His roving hand caressed a breast, fondled her waist and brushed across her belly, leaving a trail of heat and shivers in its wake. He found the hem of her gown and, in one swift move, he hiked her skirts above her hips.

She murmured a protest, feeling embarrassed and exposed, but when she tried to pull them down he stopped her, and as his long fingers deftly spread her open and caressed wet curls, he shushed her with a kiss.

"Trust me, Catherine."

She relaxed and followed where he led her, a shameless wanton, knowing she was his. She lost all sense of space and time or any world beyond the moment, and all that mattered was centered on his touch. As his fingers flicked and played, his teeth grazed her nipples and delicious waves of sensation pulsed and gathered, building at her center. When he brought his mouth, hot and seeking, to her private places, the dam shattered and she cried out as something inside her clenched and released, over and over, and waves of exquisite pleasure rocked her to her core.

He rose along her length, capturing her mouth and entering her in one fluid move. She was hot and wet and aching and he lifted her legs over his shoulders, thrusting harder and faster and deeper, moaning her name. Her fingers scored his back and she made animal sounds low in her throat as her muscles clenched around him and another wave of pleasure shook her, and then it came again. She floated in an ecstasy beyond her wildest imaginings. It was everything she'd dreamt of and a thousand-fold more. It was perfect—all that was missing were three small words.

Jamie got up, stretched, and poured himself a brandy before stirring up the fire. An unruly gust of wind rattled at the windows and stinging pellets of ice skittered against the pane. It had been a harsh winter so far, but it was warm and comfortable in his room, with a fire blazing in the hearth and Cat Drummond asleep in his bed.

She still wore her gown, despite his best efforts to relieve her of it, and, passion spent, she'd turned shy and demure. *I'll have to work on that.* He'd spent a long time after, kissing and petting her, hugging and holding her in his arms. But when he'd tried to speak, to praise and reassure her, she'd ducked her head, blushing and suddenly shy, as bashful and embarrassed as she'd earlier been wanton and bold. It was utterly charming. She'd been well worth the wait. He couldn't remember ever being so satisfied or so deeply moved.

He watched her now with possessive pride. She lay across the creased and crumpled coverlet, her hair tousled and disordered, spread about her in sleepy chestnut waves. Her skin, illuminated by the glow from the fire, was without blemish, except where his lovemaking had left its mark: a rosy flush still staining her cheeks, the rasp where whisker had brushed tender skin, here and there the imprint of impassioned fingers, and a slight mark where his teeth had grazed her throat. She looked achingly beautiful, vulnerable, and lovely, and he felt the urge to protect her against any who might harm her, including himself.

He moved to stand by the bed, and drew his knuckles gently across her cheek. She'd been trusting and responsive, curious and eager, and breathtaking in her innocence. "You disarm me, Cat Drummond. You've laid siege and you'll conquer if I leave any chink." He shivered, gripped by the same certainty that had seized him when he'd set out to follow her after she'd escaped him on the banks of the River Clyde, that he'd taken a turn, stepped onto a path, begun a new journey, and there was no going back.

Well then, that was that. No point fighting it. Best enjoy what couldn't be changed. She wanted to learn, and he was the man to teach her. In return, throughout the cold and dreary months of winter, she'd be warming his bed. Tomorrow he'd have her girl Maire move her things. The thought of having her naked beside him, warm and willing, every night, made his palms itch to touch her again. His cock twitched, heavy against his leg, and he shifted, easing it. If he'd hoped a taste would lessen his thirst he'd been mistaken; it had only left him craving more.

Twenty-Seven

IN THE WEEKS IMMEDIATELY FOLLOWING HER initiation to Jamie's bed, Catherine could be found singing, humming, or whistling everywhere she went. Her heart raced whenever she saw him, and her breath quickened at the sound of his voice. She felt beautiful, desired, deliriously happy, and very much in love. Their days overflowed with talk and laughter and at night he was a magician, turning her into a carefree wanton as he wove spells of sensual delight. Awakened to passion and her own earthy sensuality, she'd never been as comfortable in her womanhood or herself. Their new intimacy only added to what was between them, dissolving the tension and burnishing their friendship with a lustrous glow. Though he'd claimed friendship was all he had to offer, his look and his touch said otherwise, and for now she was content.

Nevertheless, there were storm clouds on the horizon and as a new season approached, they grew harder to ignore. They talked of many things—king and country, family and religion, their childhoods and their philosophies—but anytime she mentioned their relationship or the future, he changed the subject or walked away. Things were always pleasant between them—provided she didn't mention the topics he wished to avoid. He used a sheath to prevent her getting pregnant, a thing she hadn't questioned as she wasn't eager for a child, but as time wore on she couldn't help but wonder if he did it to keep their hopes for an annulment alive. The spring brought visitors and news from London. The king had concluded a naval treaty with France. Jamie appeared distracted, and though their lovemaking grew ever more wild and torrid, as the world outside intruded, she could feel him withdraw.

In June, Captain Carrot Top, the man who'd tried to interest Jamie in French harlots at Peg's, came brimming with secrets and information. He greeted Catherine with polite disinterest and no sign of recognition, clearly eager to be rid of her so he could tell Jamie his news. She wished him gone and wondered why he and his London companions couldn't leave them alone. She refused to ask questions, but the answers found her anyway. The king's wife, Mary of Modena, had given birth to a son, James Francis Edward, in June—a male heir who would supplant his Protestant sister's right to the throne.

"We won't be able to stay out of it now, Catherine. It's the Catholic heir they've all feared."

"Not the Irish and my own folk back home."

"They'd be wise to fear it, too. There'll be trouble soon. Here, in England, and in Scotland. Trouble all ways round."

"What do you intend to do?"

"Anything I can to avoid it, I suppose."

"That shouldn't be too difficult. We're at a good distance and largely forgotten except by some few of your friends. We can be circumspect and neutral if only they'd stay away and mind their business. Tell them not to come. Tell them we want no more news from London. If we stock supplies and fortify, this place can weather any storm."

"I meant there are ways to avoid a civil war, love. There are men with cooler heads than most, who see a way clear. William of Orange—"

She held up her hand to silence him. "And they've come to you for help, have they? Where were they when you needed help? Why would you risk Sullivan and his people? Why involve yourself? Need I remind you of your own precious rules? Watch and wait and don't act unless it's to your advantage. Or is there some grand reward? Something that glitters so bright it's worth risking this place and these people? Your lands back, perhaps? A shiny new title? What's the going rate to betray one's king?"

"Perhaps I would do it for the good of my country," he said quietly.

"That doesn't sound like you at all." She could see the hurt in his eyes, though it was quickly hidden. She told herself she didn't care, he was about to embark on an adventure that might ruin them all. "Don't tell me things I don't want to know, Jamie."

"And what would you have me do, Catherine? What would you do?"

"Honor forbids me from acting against the king. I concluded a treaty with him on behalf of clan

Drummond. He's honored his part. Our whiskey flows through London, and Drummond coffers overflow with gold. We've promised him our allegiance. My father would have stayed to one side if he could. He'd have found himself terribly busy elsewhere, but he'd not have acted against the king. I'd do the same were it my decision, but it's not. If there's war, the Highlands will rise to support him, and Donald and Jerrod will be among the first to join. I intend to stay out of it if I can, and I hope for all our sakes you do the same."

Things were strained between them after that in a way they hadn't been since leaving London, and though they shared a bed that night, they barely spoke. Catherine regretted having hurt him. She hadn't known she could until she'd seen it in his eyes. She looked at him now, asleep beside her, and reached out her fingers to caress his brow. She knew he'd been grappling with a difficult decision, trying to find his way to what was right. *I owe him an apology. I ought to have listened. I'll tell him so when he wakes.* But the next day, respecting her wishes, he left for Dublin without telling her why he was going, what he was doing, or when he'd be back.

The journey took him four days. The place he sought was a favorite haunt from simpler times. Down by the docks, nestled on the south bank of the mouth of the River Liffey, it was a private little corner in a thriving city that had been Ireland's main port for hundreds of years. Variously held by the Irish, the Danes, and more recently, the English, Dublin was the commercial, industrial, and social center for the

Anglo-Irish aristocracy, who'd displaced and replaced their native Roman Catholic foes.

Such matters were inconsequential to Moll. If a man wished to drink in her tavern, he left religion at the door. They came for privacy and discrete conversation, and the creamy dark stout that tasted better than anywhere else in the world.

Jamie stepped into the hall on a loud burst of laughter, tugging down the brim of his hat to hide his face. It was force of habit more than anything else. Only the regulars would recognize him here, and they didn't concern him. Spies and assassins, smugglers and pirates, men of the sea and dogs of war, they were a loose brotherhood, and men of business first. Alliances changed—loyalties, too. A man fought who he was paid to fight, and did what he was paid to do. The fellow whose throat joined yours in drink and song today might be one whose throat you cut tomorrow. It was never personal, and you never betrayed a friend. It was a different circle than he frequented in London: rougher, dirtier, and altogether more trustworthy.

He eased into a seat and a moment later Molly herself sidled up next to him, pressing one heavy breast against his cheek and a tankard of stout into his hand. A good country lass with a sharp northern wit, she had a plump body that cushioned a man when he needed comfort, and comfort was something she offered proudly: good food, good beer, good company, and if a man wanted it, a very good time.

She motioned over a sallow-looking fellow with a lanky frame, coal dark hair, and cold black eyes. "Johnnie Mercer! Look over here! See what's just returned from the dead and walked right through my door. Ain't you been asking after him the past few days?"

The tall man spoke in a cultured voice, with a trace of an accent. "Molly, my dear, you're the soul of discretion as always. Fetch us some bread and oysters, *ma belle*." He rose and came to join them. "James! What a shock it is to see you looking so well! I heard you'd died a traitor's death and been spread in four pieces about the land."

"So sorry to disappoint, Johnnie. It's just my restless ghost, you see."

"Can an apparition share a pint?"

"Let's try it and see." They raised their mugs in a toast, and Jamie moved over to accommodate Moll and her oysters.

"And how fares your widow?"

"Blast it, man! How do you know about that?"

"I know everything. It's why you come to see me."

"Widow? Did you finally get your heiress?" Molly asked, bouncing and shoving her way onto his lap.

"Aye, Molly, I did," he said, giving her a warm hug.

She sighed and leaned against him, biting his ear as one hand reached for the front of his breeches. "It's nice to have you back."

"You're a naughty wench, Moll." He trapped her hand in his and fended her off with a grin. "I've just told you I'm dead and married. Illicit congress under either circumstance would send you straight to hell. I must protect you from yourself." He kissed her hand, and maneuvered her off his lap.

"Even married and dead you're still functioning in all your parts. I've just felt the proof of it!"

"I assure you I wouldn't be if my lady found out. She's a quick-tempered Highland savage. Now off you go, love. Johnny and I don't want to bore you with our talk." He gave her a charming grin and she couldn't help but smile back.

"Next time I see you I'll ride you to a lather, Jamie Sinclair. Just see if I don't."

His cadaverous-looking friend stirred and stretched. "Dear me! I hope you didn't stop on my account. I've never known you to be shy. Our business could have waited a few minutes more."

"When I have business with a woman it takes hours, not minutes, my friend. Christ, Jean! I mean *Johnnie,* you look more like a corpse than I do. What happened to you?"

The man called Johnnie Mercer gave a Gallic shrug. "Louis is no kinder to Huguenots than your king is to those who sign the covenant. I was a guest on one of his galleys."

"Louis made *you* a galley slave? I can't believe he would dare!"

"It's of no matter. I escaped. I have a new master now, and a new country."

"You were a patriot, Jean. You fought for—"

"Please, it's not what we're here to discuss. Are you willing to meet the gentlemen I wrote you about? One of them waits upstairs."

I wish I'd been able to tell you, hellcat. I pray you'll understand. He followed Jean upstairs, meeting his London gentlemen and their Dutch friends, and then, with his business concluded, he started for home, still thinking about Catherine and hungry to hold her in his arms. He should have told her he was going, if not why. He should have said goodbye. She'd be angry, but he wasn't unskilled when it came to women. He'd make it up to her. He'd make her purr and make her forget, and once he had her properly contented, he'd make her understand.

Twenty-Eight

CATHERINE SENSED JAMIE'S PRESENCE THE MOMENT he arrived. It was no surprise. She'd been worried and waiting from the moment she'd discovered him gone. She knew better than most that he was well able to care for himself, but Dublin would have been seething with rumors, rife with treason, and crawling with every species of revolutionary, fanatic, patriot, king's man, and spy. She'd no doubt he would have enjoyed himself immensely, but somehow, in his absence, she'd become the creature she'd always despised, the forgotten wife stowed safely in her tower while her man lived his life and she waited and prayed for his safe return. *Well, bollocks to that!*

He was a deeply sensual man, and she'd come to understand the power she wielded. She'd wait for him to come to her. When he was hungry enough she'd insist on knowing what he was up to, where he placed her in his life, and what he expected from the future, and if he couldn't tell her or he didn't know, she'd know it was time to move on.

She poured a drink, preparing for battle. Leaning back in the chair, she tilted her head, eyes closed as she held the glass to her nose, savoring the scent captured in its depths: honey, barley, and the rich and musky Highland peat unique to her home. It transported her back to the innocent days of her youth, when her father was all-loving and all-powerful, the horizon stretched before her limitless and beckoning, and everything seemed possible. Fleeting days, gone as quickly and surely as any pretty dream. A painful yearning gripped her and a lone tear escaped her tightly closed eyes.

"Missed me that much, did you?"

She opened her eyes and regarded him in silence. He looked rough and dangerous. He was clad in leather jerkin, boots, and breeches, and his hair hung loose in unruly tangles. He hadn't shaved or changed, but had come to her straight from the road. Her heart, thumping slow and steady, was so loud to her ears it was a wonder he couldn't hear. He took another step into the room, and she imagined for a moment that he was as uncertain as she was.

"No? Do you cry for some other lover, then? I wouldn't blame you. You told me not to tell you, mouse, but I ought to have said goodbye."

He could see the hurt and anger in her eyes. Why had he left her that way? It had been thoughtless and cruel, things he seldom was with women. She sprawled in a plush leather chair, one magnificent leg hooked over the arm. A glass dangled from her fingers and she was naked beneath a silk chemise that was sliding off her body despite a desperate attempt to cling to every luscious curve. Everything within him stirred to life. *Christ, she's superb!*

Riveted, he stalked her, hunger blazing in his eyes. In one quick move he knelt by her chair, gripping the legs and pulling it closer, making both her and the chair squeal in protest. Resting his head in her lap, he drank in her scent, musk and spice, heather and pine.

Unable to resist, she trailed her fingers through his hair, curling round the back of his neck.

"I missed you, Catherine. I missed you on the road, I missed you by my side, and I missed you in my bed. I thought of you every moment." His voice was rich, deep, and slightly hoarse, and he used it as a caress. He brushed the inside of her thighs with cool fingers, lifting the thin chemise and opening her to his view. Embarrassed to be so exposed, she moved her hands to readjust it, but he muttered an incoherent protest and used both his hands to anchor her by the thighs. She was about to protest when he lowered his mouth to nuzzle her. She would have jumped from the chair if he hadn't been holding her firmly in place. As it was, she let out a startled gasp. "Jamie, what are you doing?"

Ignoring the question, he continued to nuzzle her, rubbing his chin against the warm juncture between her thighs, feather-light, then harder, whispering tender words and apologies. "You're so beautiful... so soft and lovely. I'm sorry if I upset you. I should have talked to you before I left. Don't be angry with me, love. Let me make it up to you."

A delicious lassitude possessed her, and she couldn't have summoned her anger, or even the reason for it, if she'd tried. She was unwilling to stop him, and then unable, as his wicked tongue, hot and wet and agile, reached out to caress her with firm, even strokes, his lips nibbling and sucking, his teeth tugging, until she thought she'd go mad with the aching, delirious pleasure coiling and building inside.

She watched him as he knelt before her, fully clothed, his head and mouth and tongue bent over her as his hands gripped her thighs. She felt sinful. It felt heavenly. *But he controls it. As he does all our interactions.* She blushed when he suddenly raised his gaze to hers as his clever tongue swirled intricate patterns over the center of all her pleasure, now the center of her world. His eyes held hers like a predator, intense and knowing. He continued, nipping and sucking and licking as he raised his hands to her breasts, cupping them, kneading them, flicking and tugging at her nipples, and she left all coherent thought behind.

Waves of pleasure coursed through her. "Please, please, please," she begged him, whimpering and squirming and wriggling, the leather rubbing her bottom as she desperately lifted her hips toward his hot, seeking mouth. He moved his hands then, one flicking and tickling and stroking, working with his tongue, as the other cupped her buttocks, pulling her closer, tighter against his mouth. His thumb pressed between her cheeks as he continued to sip and drink from her until she was in a frenzy. She cried his name as she exploded into rapturous waves that shook her body one after the other, and still he continued, groaning in satisfaction.

She grasped his shoulders and slid off the chair, landing astride his lap.

"Please, Jamie," she moaned.

He hugged her close against him, flipping her onto her back, kissing her wildly as they both scrambled frantically to loosen his breeches, fingers brushing, entwining, and working together until he sprang free. Painfully engorged, rock hard, he sought her opening and plunged inside her slick tight heat. Stroking her with hands and tongue and pulsing organ, he slammed against her, pumping and writhing, harder and harder, until she exploded again, bursting from within in a starburst of incredible sensation, gripping him tight inside her as she felt the pulsing and tremors of his own release.

"Oh my God, Jamie, that was incredible!" she said when she could breathe again.

He grinned and gathered her in his arms. Picking her up easily, he deposited her into the bed, jumping in after her, and pulling her close. "This is where I always want to be, mouse. Next time I go somewhere, I'll tell you first, or I'll bring you with me. Am I forgiven?" he whispered into her hair.

He'd not even allowed her the time to be angry. With a look and a touch he'd melted her resentment, overcome all her defenses, and laid waste to all her plans. She snuggled closer and kissed his shoulder. "I shouldn't let you off so easily. It will only encourage bad habits, but I fear I love you far too much to stay angry with you for long."

She regretted it the instant she said it, and even more an instant later as he stiffened beside her and then sat up.

"Catherine… I thought we'd discussed this," he

said wearily. "It's important we both understand this is a friendship, nothing more."

"Nothing more? It's a marriage, for God's sake!"

"Quite so. And how many of our married acquaintances do you know who are as good friends as you and I? Do you want to jeopardize that? We'll both be happier if you'll just accept things as they are."

"You mean if we follow your rules? Friends care about each other, Jamie!"

"So they do, and I don't deny that you've wormed your way into my affections, but I have trouble enough making my way in the world, Catherine. Can't you see I'm trying my best to keep everything under control? Things are complicated right now. I'm dealing with a difficult situation. I have to look out for Sullivan and his scold of a mother, all the people here, horses, cats, dogs, children, and now you. I have my hands full already without adding unnecessary complications."

"I've wormed my way in, have I? With your servants and horses and all the other poor creatures you've rescued? And we're terrible distractions, are we? So bad that you have to run away? We distract you from what, my lord? Your busy social calendar? Your successful enterprises? Oh, no! I do beg your pardon! From your plotting and drinking and gambling and whores! Well, let me tell you something, Sinclair. You might have rescued me once, but I have rescued you *three* times, and I do a damn good job of taking care of myself! Get off my chemise!" She tugged franticly, reclaiming her chemise and wrapping it furiously around her body. "Now get out!" She pointed at the door.

"Catherine… I didn't mean to—"

"Out! Out! Get out!"

"It's my room, love," he said calmly.

"I'm not your love! Don't ever call me that again. You haven't the right! Now step aside please, so I may leave, and rest assured I'll endeavor to be gone from here as quick as I can so your life can return to what it was before I came along and *complicated* it."

"Catherine! Damn it! I'm trying to be honest with you."

"And I should be grateful for it, I suppose, but I find myself wishing that sometimes you'd lie." She'd managed to keep her dignity this far, but she was desperate to leave before she burst into tears, embarrassing them both.

"You see? This is exactly what I feared. You said you understood. I'm very fond of you, Catherine. More so than anyone in my life. You're my best friend. Someone I can talk to and count on and be myself with. I don't *want* to lie to you. I don't want to have to. Once you start talking about love and such nonsense, everything gets ruined. There's anger and jealousy and lies, and you spend all your time worrying about the other person's feelings. I'm not good at that. Only look! I've made you shout and cry. I witnessed enough of this with my parents. I know where it leads. You'll end up hating me and I'll end up hurting you. I don't need that. I don't want it. I won't have it."

"Damn it, Jamie! People argue. It doesn't mean… It's normal! And don't you dare walk out on me while I'm talking to you! Your father was a bully and a tyrant, and your mother was shallow and disloyal.

We are not them! You'd never hurt me. I broke your nose. I hit and kicked you. I bit you and all you did was laugh. You don't want to lie to me? Well, I don't want to lie to you either. I want to love you. I *do* love you, but I love myself, too. If you don't want what I have to offer, if you can't give it back in return, then you're right, and this is wrong, and I should go."

Her hair was disheveled, her lovely face stained with tears and he felt a gut-wrenching ache that spread to his chest and squeezed his throat. "There are things that hurt worse than blows. Trust me on this. You have my friendship and I need yours. You said it would be enough." He took a step toward her and stopped. "Please don't go, Catherine. I don't want you to leave. Promise me you won't do anything foolish."

"Like what? Jump in the river because you don't love me?" she snapped. "Go away, you conceited man!"

He wanted to take her in his arms and comfort her, but short of telling her what she wanted to hear, he had no idea what to do or say. He took the escape she offered and retreated from the room.

His attempt at making things right between them had ended in dismal failure, and he was expected back in Dublin within a week. He walked along the river's edge, deep in thought. He'd met with agents of William while in Dublin, and those of Henry Sydney, who represented a cabal of seven influential English lords. They intended to issue a formal invitation to William and his wife, James's eldest daughter Mary, to land with a small force and defend Mary's rights as heir to the throne. They claimed the new prince was a changeling, and the king's true son had died being born. Preposterous, yes, but a convenient excuse. They offered to rise in support, promising that William would be greeted as a liberator. It wasn't farfetched. Until the birth of James's son, Mary had been second in line to the throne, and William, third. Both were Stuarts, Protestant, and grandchildren of Charles I.

Jamie had met William while performing duties for King Charles. He was a good soldier, but though he'd acquired the reputation of being a champion of the Protestant cause, he'd never seemed particularly interested in England. Still, this new Catholic heir, coming on the heels of a naval agreement between England and France, had doubtless caused him concern. A Catholic Britain would be a natural ally of France against the Netherlands, something he'd want to avoid, and Jean, who was in a position to know, had made it clear he was not averse to accepting a formal invitation from his English friends.

Jamie had been asked to deliver one to The Hague, using his talents to see that it wasn't intercepted. He would go as a common seaman. It was a delicate business, with the future of England, Scotland, and Ireland balanced on the edge of bloody revolution, and Europe on the brink of yet another war. It was an opportunity to help his country avert another rebellion. He would earn the gratitude of his countrymen and his new monarch, and would be amply rewarded in return.

There was no doubt in his mind that James II was bad for England. He was incapable of nuance, blind to circumstance, and committed to a course that would destroy him and all those who gave him their support, but although Jamie changed masters as it suited him, he'd always done so in a forthright way, completing his commission, collecting his pay, and keeping his own counsel. He'd never stooped to betrayal. Now he had to decide between his own honor and the good of his country.

His lips quirked in a smile as recalled one of Buckingham's quips from Charles's day. *"Charles could see things if he would, and the duke would see things if he could."* He missed that man, rogue and scoundrel though he was. He could use someone to talk with. Catherine had cured him of the habit of solitude, and then cruelly banished him back to it again. He'd come home in part to seek her opinion, whether she wanted to hear about it or not. She was his wife, damn it! He could bloody well use some advice!

"Don't tell me things I don't want to know." What kind of help was that? *"I find myself wishing you'd lie to me sometimes."* She was as perverse and contradictory as any woman, probably worse. Right now, they should be together, snug in his bed. He'd fumbled things with her like a green lad. His palm itched as he imagined the feel of a rounded breast and pert nipple, and he swelled and twitched as he imagined the feel of her lush bottom pressed firmly against him.

Why not tell her what she wanted to hear? He wasn't even sure it *would* be a lie. God knew he'd only made a mess of things the way he'd managed her up until now. He wasn't welcome in her bed and she wouldn't even talk with him. He sighed and folded his arms. He was running out of time and there seemed little point in trying to sort things out right now. He'd leave her a letter; attend to his business, and when he returned, he'd settle the discord between them for good or ill. Relieved to have a plan in which he didn't have to face her, he scribbled a hasty note, and slid it under her door.

Twenty-Nine

CATHERINE KICKED AT HER BLANKETS, FRUSTRATED and angry. It was clear she was no seductress. Rather than bending to her will and acknowledging what was between them, Jamie had managed her expertly, playing her body like an instrument, diverting her anger and her questions, silencing her with skilled caresses, and withdrawing when she'd broken his rules. She hadn't meant to. It was something she'd blurted out in the heat of passion—but it should have delighted him, not made him recoil. *I should leave. I'm looking for something that exists only in my imagination, and he's surely embarked on an adventure that could bring us all down.*

Maire brought her breakfast on a tray, and with it, a note.

> *Dearest Catherine,*
>   *I'm sorry to leave you this way again. I fear as you read this you're mightily annoyed. I meant to discuss it with you last night, but things got out of hand. I'm throwing my support behind William,*

and the time to act is now. I know you think my
motives mercenary and selfish, and I know you'll
not approve, but I've been to war too often, and if
any action of mine might help avert another, I feel
duty bound to try. I think of you, and Sullivan and
his family, even as I make my decision, and I'll do
all I can to keep you safe. I pray you understand. I
shall return within the month.

I do have feelings for you, Catherine. It's not
something to which I'm accustomed. I don't know
what to call them. I don't know if I want them,
though they assail me whether I wish them to or
not. I promise to make every effort to resolve them
upon my return.

If things don't go as planned, I wish you
to return to London immediately. Tell them I
abducted you so I might keep your inheritance, and
you took your first opportunity to escape. You're
young, wealthy, and beautiful, and no one will
question you too harshly. You'll know what to do
for the O'Sullivans. I've made arrangements so
my Irish lands and properties will pass to Kieran's
heir, if only he can get one. Enlist Granny O and
marry your girl to him. They seem fond of one
another. Besides you, he and his kin are the closest
thing to family that I have. I count on you for this,
Catherine, and I know my trust is well-placed. I
appreciate your friendship and all your kindnesses
to me more than you can imagine. Wait for me,
please. I'll return as soon as I'm able.

                                        Your husband,
                                        James Sinclair

"Damn him to hell and back again!" She crumpled the note and hurled it against the wall, then scrambled from her bed to retrieve it, and threw it into the fire. *Fool! Imbecile! Putting his treason on paper!* They were isolated and forgotten, fortified and well stocked. Why couldn't he leave well enough alone? Why not wait for events to transpire and align himself after? What Jamie needed to do was take care of his own. She was done with waiting and wringing her hands as events overtook her. She needed to know exactly what he planned so she'd be in a position to deal with it. Like it or not, they were going to have a serious talk.

She was on the road early the next morning, accompanied by two well-armed retainers. They said clothes made the man. She wasn't entirely sure it was true, but back in the saddle, back in her breeches and boots, with her sword on her hip, a carbine slung over her back, and two pistols holstered on her saddle, she felt confident, capable, and in control of her world in a way she hadn't for weeks.

Thirty

JAMIE ARRIVED AT MOLL'S TWO DAYS BEFORE HIS ship was to sail. He might have stayed an extra day with Catherine, but there'd seemed little point. He would have had to lie to her or tell her things that would only make her more upset. He was confident she'd be waiting for him on his return. She was angry now, but he knew women well enough to tell when one was besotted. She'd even admitted it. He couldn't help a slight grin. She'd said she loved him. No one had said the words to him before and actually meant them, but he knew Catherine did. It was awkward, to be sure, but he was already growing accustomed to the thought. It had proven easier than he'd expected, and not at all unpleasant. It was another burden, though, one that bound and tangled, demanding acknowledgement and some kind of reciprocal response.

Molly came up behind him, as if sensing his thoughts, wrapping both arms around him. "Remember what I told you I'd do to you the next time I caught you?" she murmured, nibbling his ear and reaching a hand to tug at the fastening of his breeches.

"Remember I told you I was married?" Removing her hand, he encircled her waist and hauled her down, settling her comfortably on his knee.

"That's never stopped a lusty lad who's far from home." She pouted and rubbed against him, then reached across the table for a tankard of stout. "We've known each other a long time, Jamie. Have you no kiss for your old friend Moll after all the joy she's given you?"

"I'm hard-pressed to refuse you, lass, when you put it like that." He took a healthy swig of beer, placed his tankard deliberately on the table, and bussed her on the cheek.

"Not like that!" Molly protested, shifting around to straddle him and lowering her mouth to his.

"Here now, lass! You've claimed your kiss already." Jamie wrestled her back onto the bench beside him. Their exertions were having a salutary effect on his anatomy, and his eager prick strained against the material of his breeches, much to Molly's delight.

"She must be old and ugly to leave you walking around all swollen like that. Let Molly kiss it better, poor boy."

"No, Moll," he said patiently. "She's young and pretty—a beauty, in fact."

"But this is where you are tonight, Jamie, and this is what you're wanting. Your prick can't lie." She tried to guide his hands to where her nipples thrust hard against her bodice.

"My prick doesn't know its own mind, love, but I do. Whatever I've got to give belongs to her. Leave off, sweetling."

"Well, I've never known you to pass up a tumble. God's blood! Are you fallen in love, Sinclair?"

"Do you mean am I subject to melancholy, tears, and terrible fits of jealousy? Does my heart tremble when she passes? So it appears, my dear, but I've yet to decide. Next, I'll be subject to vapors and trembling, fits of megrim, and sleepless nights. She's quite unmanned me."

"You've bedded her?"

"Of course I have. It hasn't helped. It's only made things worse."

"Those are the symptoms. I'd say you've tumbled hard."

"Will it pass, Moll?"

"That's hard to say, Jamie. For some it's said to be a lifelong affliction."

"Good evening, friends!" The door burst open and the sound of penny whistle, fiddle, and clinking glasses drifted into the street as Jean, a Dutch sea captain named Van Kroeger, and a nondescript bookish man named Fredrick, wearing a black frock coat, crowded through the door. "Are we interrupting?" Jean asked, pushing through the crowd with his entourage and planting himself at the table.

"How could you be, my dears, when you're all so unobtrusive, padding about on little cat's feet," Jamie said, reaching out to shake their hands.

"We're soldiers and sailors. A brawling, noisome lot. It's for others to move out of our way. What are we discussing—trade, high seas adventure, a woman?'

"Not *a* woman, *the* woman," Molly said, taking advantage of the moment to reach under Jamie's coat

and search for his purse, running her hand appreciatively across his chest as she did.

"You'll not find it there, Moll, try a little lower,"
Jean encouraged. Leaning in toward Jamie he crooked
a finger, and pointed to the corner, whispering in his
ear. "Look over there, *mon ami*. A veritable goddess.
That, my friend, is the devil's playground. I wonder
who she is?"

Jamie's gaze followed where Jean pointed and
stopped, transfixed. Freezing amber eyes watched
his, unblinking and stony. His breath caught in his
throat. *Merde! Her eyes look like hell frozen over.* She was
dressed in boots and breeches, but it was clearly for
her own comfort. She'd made no attempt at disguise.
Honey-colored hair tumbled past her shoulders, and
proud breasts were outlined clearly beneath the linen
of her shirt. Two of Sullivan's men were with her, and
all three were well armed.

"*That,* my friend, is my wife." He lifted his
arm and carefully removed it from around Moll's
shoulders, wondering how long Catherine had been
watching. *Too fucking long, Jamie boy. How will you
explain this, and what the hell is she doing here?* He
extracted Moll's arm from beneath his coat and tossed
her several coins, his eyes never leaving Catherine's.
"My company's arrived, Moll. Prepare us a meal and
a room upstairs, if you please, there's a good girl."
He should go and talk to her, try to explain, but
her eyes cut through him like daggers, there were
king's men in the room, and tonight he was a lowly
merchant seaman, with no excuse to approach such
an exquisite creature.

Molly coughed, beckoning from the stairway for him to follow. Looking back at Catherine, he raised his mug in a toast.

"I have known many,
and liked not a few,
but loved only one
this toast is to you."

Downing his drink in one swallow, he slammed the mug on the table and went up the stairs without looking back.

Catherine rose and threw some coins on the table. "Come, gentlemen. There's nothing for us here." *Wait for me.* She snorted, recalling his words, then tossed down her drink, reached for her hat, and elbowed her way out the door, letting the wind slam it shut behind her.

Thirty-One

THE NETHERLANDS, A FLAT, LOW-LYING COUNTRY interlaced with waterways and canals, huddled against the North Sea, defended from the encroaching waters by a network of dikes and dunes. At a time when most of Europe was ruled by monarchies, it was a republic of semi-autonomous cities and provinces. The Hague housed Holland's royal court and government. It was a vibrant center of art and culture, one of the chief diplomatic and intellectual centers of Europe, and home to the Princes of Orange. It was here Jamie came, disguised as a simple seaman, inviting a coup d'état against his king.

Identified by secret code, he delivered the letter on the last day of June. There was little fanfare and no surprise. William had invited the invitation in April, when he'd first heard of James's naval agreement with France, and he'd been making preparations to accept it ever since. Greeted warmly, if discreetly, Jamie was much surprised when William deigned to thank him in person for his efforts, acknowledging the risk involved and promising his service to his country and to William would be remembered. Jamie didn't put any more faith in that than any other Stuart promise, but it was a courteous gesture, the kind Charles might have made.

Anxious to return to Ireland and explain things to Catherine, he fretted impatiently, spending his days waiting at the docks while William and his advisors crafted a reply. *His answer is right in front of me, crowding the harbor for any fool to see.* Watching the buildup of ships and men, there were moments he felt sick at heart. *The people who mean the most to me won't understand. Catherine already suspects me false and unfaithful, and Kieran is full of dreams for a free Ireland. If James is replaced, it will break his heart.*

Nevertheless, he was sure of his decision. The Netherlands were tolerant in matters of religion, and their leaders were used to sharing power and control. William would be far more amenable than his Stuart cousin to working with Parliament, and he was the best hope for bringing an end to political turmoil and the constant threat of civil war. Kieran had best accept he'd never get his family's lands back through revolt or insurrection, and he'd have a thing or two to say to Catherine about her behavior—traipsing about Ireland when he'd bade her wait at home.

A stab of yearning gripped his vitals and he remembered the hurt and anger in her eyes when she'd found him with Moll. *Bloody hell! Months on end of virtuous behavior and she has to find me with a strumpet on my lap with her tits in my face. What else did she see? It's going to be Christly difficult to explain.*

He needed to hold her in his arms again, to apologize and tell her how he felt. *Why is it I can tell a whore how I feel about my wife, but I can't tell the woman herself? What in God's name am I doing here? I belong with her. I tell myself I'm charmed, diverted, hungry, when the truth is I love her. When I get home, I'll make certain she knows.*

He took ship for Dublin early the next morning, without awaiting word from William and without saying goodbye.

Thirty-Two

"I DON'T WANT YOU TO LEAVE. WAIT FOR ME."
Wait for what? Wait for him to finish his dalliance
with barmaids and treason? Wait for him to come to
his senses? Catherine was tired of waiting. She'd been
tirèd of it when she'd followed him to Dublin and
found him with his doxy. Most wives would consider
themselves lucky if their man confined himself to the
occasional tavern whore whilst far from home, but
since they'd been intimate she'd thought... hoped...
well, she'd been as foolishly romantic as any moonstruck girl.

At first, she'd hoped he'd come chasing after her
with some earnest explanation, but that had been six
weeks ago. She'd nearly completed her arrangements,
honoring their agreement and doing what he'd asked
for Kieran. It was time to admit she wasn't good at the
type of games he played. She cared too much, and he
too little, for her not to be hurt.

She was startled from her reverie by the sound of
thundering hooves and shouting men. *He's back! What
shall I say to him?* Her heart beat a rapid tattoo and her

breath caught in her throat. She hastily arranged her clothing and her hair before leaning back in her chair in a pose of studied nonchalance. *Let him come to me.* It was a moment more before she realized the shouts were cries of warning and challenge, not welcome. She leapt to her feet as a booming voice rose above the din.

"Cat Drummond! We're looking for Catherine Drummond! We've no quarrel with the Irish. Hand her over and no harm will befall you."

Catherine raced to the window and looked down in astonishment. A score of brawny Highlanders wearing tartans of crimson, blue, and green milled about the courtyard, held at bay by Granny O'Sullivan, in all her fearsome glory.

"There be no Drummonds here, you bloody big lummox! You're on the wrong side of the pond! Now get you gone before I set the hounds on you."

"There are now, ya scolding harpy! Jerrod Drummond at your service, and we're not leaving till we have the girl. Now step aside." He had a scowl that could make grown men quaver, but Mrs. O'Sullivan was made of sterner stuff, and firmly stood her ground. Jerrod tried maneuvering his horse around her as men came streaming from the village and fields. "Cat!" he bellowed again. "We know you're here. Get your arse out here, girl. We've come to fetch you home."

"He is indeed a bloody big lummox, Mrs. O'Sullivan, but he's also my uncle," Catherine called from the casement above them. "Kindly bid him enter and make him welcome. I'll be right down."

"You're a poor liar, old woman. I'd have sworn you claimed the girl wasn't here," Jerrod said, dismounting.

"And you're a fine big bully. If my boy weren't down to Cork, you'd not be so brave. I may be old, but at least *I'm* not deaf and senile. I said there were no Drummonds here. The girl is Lady Sinclair, Countess of Carrick, and her husband might have a thing or two to say about you taking her away."

"Would he now? So she really is married!"

"Of course she is, you stupid man! Well… come in. It seems she's bid you welcome."

"Aye, she has, and very gracious you are about it, too. Perhaps you can make yerself useful and find some food for me and my men, and maybe some of that watered-down tea you Irish like to call whiskey."

"You're about to get your ears boxed, Uncle Jerrod," Catherine said, stepping into the great hall.

"Cat!" Jerrod sprang to his feet, enveloping her in a crushing embrace that lifted her toes off the ground. "You're a sight for sore eyes, girl! What in God's name are you doing here? Don't tell me you got lost on the way home."

"I've missed you too, Uncle," she grunted, extracting herself from his embrace.

"So where's your man?" he asked, looking curiously about the hall. "Heard we were coming and ran away?"

"He had affairs to tend to up in Dublin."

"The cocks are all gone? Down to Cork, up to Dublin, and the place left in the charge of the hens? You must be missing real men, lass. I thought you came to be shed of him. Why haven't you done so and come back home?"

Servants had begun to arrive with platters of cold meat and flagons of beer. "We've a quaint custom in these parts. It's called hospitality. Sit yourself down. I'll greet the men, we'll share a tankard, and you'll tell me of home. *Then* we'll speak of business."

"Well, pardon me, Lady Carrick. You're a fine one to lecture on hospitality when your people refuse me whiskey and serve me beer."

"No doubt Mrs. O'Sullivan felt you undeserving."

"So the servants run the place do they?"

"Aye, Uncle. The servants and the women, just like back home. Mrs. O'Sullivan is no servant, though, and you'll do well to remember or you'll be sleeping in the fields tonight. I'll be back in a moment." Catherine made her way down the table, greeting the men with hugs and smiles, noting with disappointment that Rory wasn't among them. She'd known them all since childhood: cousins, neighbors, comrades, and friends. She sent for Maire to come and join them, and returned to sit by her uncle near the head of the long table. "Tell me of home. How are Martha and Donald and Alistair? Why didn't Rory come with you?"

"There's trouble to home, Cat. You're needed. Bloody Donald's gone and got himself killed, yer brother has hied himself off to France, and there's talk throughout the Highlands that there's going to be war."

"Donald was killed? When? How? Why did no one tell me?"

"You haven't exactly been easy to find, lass. He was killed six months ago, feuding with the Murrays."

A hollow ache took her breath away, and she had to blink back tears. How could someone you'd known all your life just slip away without your even knowing?

"I… I'm very sorry to hear that, Uncle. We had our differences, but… "

"I know, lass. He was fond of you, too. He just didnae know what to make of you." He reached across the table and patted her hand. "You've been missed, Cat. It's time for you to come home."

She pulled her hand away. "I'm deeply sorry to hear about Donald, Uncle Jerrod, but that makes you laird and chief now, and I'll not stand in your way. Why come seeking me?"

"I'm a simple man, Cat. Show me an enemy and tell me whether you want him baked, boiled, or fried, and I'll see it done, but I'm not one for politics and strategy. I've not the patience. The council's met. They want the old fox's daughter. They're asking for you."

"You're as canny as any man yet born in the Highlands! There's more to it than that."

"James is King of Scotland too, and a Catholic prince. If the English try to give his throne to William, the Highlands will rise to defend him, and the Irish will as well, no doubt."

"No doubt. Just what we need. Another bloody war."

"We've no choice, lass. We gave our oath. *You* gave our oath. He knows you. That could be a great help."

"I was careful with my words, Jerrod. We pledged to support him as we may and not bear arms against him. It left a good deal of room for interpretation."

"Aye, of course it did. You're yer father's daughter. That's why we need you. These are dangerous times. It's brains we need as much as brawn."

"And what of my husband?"

"The Sassenach? Sinclair's his name? I wasn't certain he was real before today. You signed all your correspondence Catherine Drummond, and your bloody lawyers wouldn't tell us where you were."

"How *did* you find me, then?"

Jerrod winked and tapped his nose with a finger. "Follow the money, Cat. So what does your man do when he's not killing Scots or lording it over the Irish? Do you want me to kill him for you?"

"That's kind of you, Uncle, but no. You've tried and failed before. When he's not killing Scots or lording it over the Irish, he plays at being a Highlander, hiking about the mountains stealing heiresses and fixing broken pots."

"The devil you say! That was him? The cheeky bastard! And you never said a word!"

"You'd have killed him outright if I had. I owed him my life. Leave him out of it. He's not my man or anyone else's, and he has troubles of his own.

"And what about you, lass? Will you do your duty by your clan?"

"As they did theirs by me?"

"I know I failed you and I'm sorry for it, but I'm asking you to be bigger than that. Your people need you now."

"Things are complicated here, Uncle Jerrod, and my connection to the king is not what it once was. There's nothing I can do for them that you can't do as well."

"I'm tired, lass. I haven't the heart for it anymore."

She noticed it then, the haggard lines etched on his face, the slight stoop to his broad shoulders. *When did he grow old?* "Nonsense! You've the heart of a lion and Rory to help you besides."

"Rory's dead, Catherine."

"*What?*" It hit her like a blow.

"He died guarding Donald's back, as was his duty." Jerrod's voice was steady but his hands shook.

"Oh no!" *Not Rory too!* Eyes hot with tears, she reached out her hand, wanting to comfort, seeing the grief and pain in her uncle's eyes. *How could I have missed it?* All this fighting, all this killing, all this wasteful snuffing of precious lives. Her mother gone, her father gone, and now Rory and Donald, too. Sobs tore at her throat and she struggled to contain them. Moving around the table, she gave her uncle a fierce hug.

"I'm so sorry, Uncle Jerrod! I know how much you loved him. I loved him, too. He was the best of us all."

"Aye, lass. He was. And he loved you, too. Now stop your tears. We're making a spectacle of ourselves. Will you come home, Cat? I can nae do it on my own."

She thought of Jamie. He was doing what he could to stop a conflagration that threatened his country. *I have to do what I can to stop the one that threatens my clan.* She winced, remembering how she'd accused him of betrayal and greed, wishing she could talk to him, wishing she could take it back. *I told him not to tell me things I didn't want to know. I'm as responsible for the distance between us as he is, and wishing doesn't make things so.*

"I'll come with you, Uncle, but only on my terms."

"You're going to set conditions?"

"Aye, I am. There'll be no attempt to harm my husband, and no attempts to find me another one. What I decide in that regard shall be no one's business but my own. I'll expect to be acknowledged and treated as chief. That means when I consult with you and the council, your purpose must be to help, not hinder. When I give orders, they'll be followed. There's no point in my coming if all we're to do is sit and bicker like bored old women. I also tell you this. I'll not waste my—or anyone else's—life in useless battles and stubborn pride. If war comes, as you fear, I intend to do all I can to keep us clear of it."

"Your father would have done the same. I can speak for the council. They'll accept your conditions."

The decision made, Catherine was almost as eager as Jerrod to be on her way. She wanted to see Martha, her people, the Highlands, and home. She loved Jamie, but she loved them, too. She had a duty toward them. They needed her and he didn't. It was as simple as that. Speaking with a noticeably unhappy Mrs. O'Sullivan, she made arrangements to leave the next day.

"He'll not be pleased, child. Shouldn't you wait for his return?"

"We've no idea when that will be. He's been gone over six weeks, with no word or any indication if, or when, he'll be back, and I've pressing business to attend to."

"Where shall I tell him you've gone, lass?"

"Tell him my family had need of me."

"And when shall I say you'll be back?"

Catherine looked at the older woman, but made no reply.

"So you think he's good enough for loving, but not for keeping? I know him well. He's a better man than you think, and he cares for you deeply. If you go, you'll break his heart."

"If I stay, he'll break mine. I know he's a good man and I know you love him. So do I. But no one can keep him. He stays where he wants to and goes where he will, and so must I."

"Just a few more days, child. What can it hurt?"

"I have the same duty to my people as you do to yours, Mrs. O'Sullivan. I didn't come here to argue with you. I want to make sure you've adequate funds, and there are arrangements that need the attention of my solicitors and bankers regarding Ja—my husband. I need you to witness the papers. That's all."

Catherine dealt with what she had to, wrote Jamie a letter and gave it to Mrs. O'Sullivan, and set out the next morning in a cold rain, just past dawn. *How strange we come to such cross-purposes, Jamie. Catholic against Protestant, king against king, though we both know better and want the same thing—an end to these infernal wars.*

Granted what she'd always thought she wanted—the trust of her people and a chance to lead them—she had no choice but to leave the man she loved behind. Her father had always put duty before what he wanted, and now she understood the sacrifices he'd made. Jamie had never tried to rule or direct her. Like her father, he'd let her be, giving her respect and freedom, and accepting her as she was. Wasn't that love? Why did she need more? Why couldn't she accept them both as they'd accepted her? Like her father, Jamie was a good man, doing his best, and she could do no less. Hunching her shoulders against the wind, she turned her pony south.

Thirty-Three

IT WAS A CRISP, CLEAR, MID-AUGUST NIGHT, AND Jamie had stopped to camp on the banks of the Suir. Tomorrow he'd be back at Castle Carrick. Tomorrow he'd see Catherine again. She'd turned his world upside down from the first moment he saw her, and since then he'd made one inconvenient decision after another—rescuing her, following her home, giving up his pleasures and his women, sharing his adventures, and letting her in on secrets no one else knew. It had annoyed him terribly at first. He failed to see the reason for it and couldn't understand, but once he'd stopped struggling and accepted the obvious, it all made sense. *The sky is blue, when it rains you get wet, and I love Cat Drummond.*

Tomorrow he'd tell her. She'd be difficult and sullen at first, upset at his abrupt departure and angry about Moll, but she was a reasonable girl, and she'd let him explain. He was done with intrigue and he'd tell her so. *Charles, James, William, Mary, and sister Anne as well, every fucking Stuart on God's green earth can go to hell!* Tomorrow he'd cozen and cajole, explain and promise, and by the next moon's rising, he'd be warm in bed with his woman, making sure she knew how much he loved her. He raised his wineskin to the stars. "To Catherine Sinclair, mysterious and lovely as the evening sky and seductive as a summer's night. Her radiance puts the stars to shame and guides me through the dark. *Tá grá agam duit.* I love you, Catherine."

Early the next day he arrived at Castle Carrick and knew at once that something was wrong. He tore through the castle room by room, calling her name, a sickening feeling building inside. "Where is she, Mrs. O'Sullivan?" he demanded, when she came running to see what was wrong.

"She's left, Jamie. Her family came and took her. You've missed her by no more than a week."

"They took her? You did nothing to stop them?" *Hell and damnation!* He should never have left her unprotected and alone.

"No, lad. She went willingly enough. She's left you a letter."

Gut twisting, he took the letter from Mrs. O'Sullivan, holding it carefully between his fingers as if it might contain some virulent poison. A part of him wasn't surprised, had always expected that, sooner or later, he'd make one mistake too many and she'd leave him. Once again, he'd ignored hard lessons sternly taught, and once again, he'd been a fool.

"I'll read this in my rooms. Kindly send along some whiskey and see to it I'm not disturbed." He brushed past the eager children who'd come to greet him, sparing them not so much as a glance. He was chilled, though the day was warm, and when he sat at his desk, he felt weightless and hollow inside. A stiff shot of whiskey did nothing to warm him, so he followed it with another, and when he opened her letter there was only a slight tremor to his hands.

"So, Catherine, what exactly is there left to say?"

> *Dearest Jamie,*
>
> *Our adventures in London and our idyll over the past few months will live with me forever, and warm me when I'm a woman grown old. You've been good for me and to me, but I've matters to attend to that are no concern of yours and can only cause you trouble.*
>
> *You've given me my freedom, and in return I give you yours. I've written my solicitor agreeing to a divorce, and leaving him instructions to proceed. My previous contract with Cormac O'Connor and a healthy stipend to the powers that be should suffice to see the thing done. The solicitor should be able to find me when and if my signature is required, but I expect my written statement will be enough. I've sent a missive to my bankers instructing they release half my personal funds. I have, of course, retained all assets that properly belong to clan Drummond, but I'm sure the sum I've left you will more than suffice. As you've grown idealistic of late, I'll make bold to insist you accept it, and to remind you that it's safer to put your faith in the guinea than in kings.*
>
> *I've no wish to be an inconvenience. It would ill become us both. Love shouldn't be a burden and I regret if mine was one for you. You've given me*

*many gifts—laughter, joy, pleasure, and my life
not the least among them. I'll be sad for a while,
but in time, when I think of you, it will make me
smile. Good luck, Jamie! I shall always think of
you fondly. I thank you for your care of me, and
wish you long life and happiness, and though you
may not credit it, I wish you love. You deserve it,
I wish you joy of it, and I hope someday it finds
you. Farewell.*

> *Your friend,*
> *Catherine Drummond*

"She wishes love to find me? She wishes me joy
of it? She offers it, then takes it away! I asked her to
wait. I trusted her. Bitch!" He crumpled the letter and
threw it into the fireplace, and a moment later, he
hurled his glass against the wall.

The Prince of Orange landed in November and Jamie,
who wasn't suited to farming and had lost interest
in his horses and most everything else, was there to
greet him. Within two weeks, most of the cities and
bishoprics in England had declared for William, and a
mass defection of officers had begun. John Churchill,
King James's commander in chief, was one of the
first to abandon his Catholic king. The king's second
daughter, Anne, was not far behind.

Near the end of December, William allowed King
James to flee to France, and took over the provisional
government. In February, Parliament resolved that
James's flight amounted to abdication and jointly

offered William and Mary the throne. It was hailed as a bloodless revolution, and claimed that not a shot had been fired. The whole affair could not have ended better—for England, at least.

William wasn't a man to neglect those who'd served him well. Jamie was warmly received at court. His Irish estate was confirmed and his English lands and title returned, and more lands were given him besides. The bloodshed he'd feared had been prevented, and with the new king's gifts and favor, he was a man of influence, someone to respect. As for his wife, nobody asked. Unlike his royal cousins, the new king seemed to take little interest in anyone's wife, including his own. Jamie should have been happy, at least content, but he took no pleasure in his holdings, no notice of the women who pursued him, and no interest in the affairs of the court.

Catherine was the only thing on his mind. He'd read her letter through an incendiary fog of hurt and anger, but he'd had time to reflect since, and his fury at her abandonment had long since lost its edge. He thought about her by day, and dreamed of her at night, and every time he looked to the north, he felt sick with worry. James Stuart might have vacated the throne of England, but he was already making mischief in Ireland and the Highlands, with the help of the French. His supporters, the Jacobites, were a growing threat, and William was a fighting man. If they rebelled, William and his Orangemen would crush them, and Catherine and her family would be caught in their midst.

Although he'd thrown her letter in the fire, the

contents were burned in his heart, and words he'd first regarded with dismissive contempt played increasingly on his mind. *"I've matters to attend to that can only cause you trouble. Love shouldn't be a burden and I regret if mine was one for you."*

It was always easier to see some things from a distance. She wanted to help her people as he'd tried to help his, and she sought to protect him. She'd not awaited his return because she didn't want him involved, and she'd not abandoned him, he'd abandoned her. *I was gone six weeks without a word, and the last she saw of me I had a strumpet in my lap.* Well... she'd also wished that love would find him and it had. *She* had, but they were on opposite sides of the Isle of Britain, and might soon be on opposite sides of another bloody war.

Thirty-Four

CATHERINE SAT IN THE GREAT HALL, ENSCONCED in the ancient seat she still thought of as her father's. It had been in her family, a part of the chamber, for generations, and as her hands gripped its ornately carved arms she could almost feel the history coursing through it. *May it lend me patience and wisdom.* With Jerrod's backing, Donald dead, and Alistair gone to France, her status as head of the clan had not been contested, but her people were a loud, opinionated lot who equated discussion with shouting and negotiation with shouting louder. They'd been known to argue over petty disputes for days, and this one had been raging for hours.

Greeted with joy by Martha, and cautious acceptance by the rest of the clan, she'd set to work avoiding an escalation of the feud with the Murrays, pointing out that Donald and his men had been in Murray territory, and too many men had been killed on both sides, leaving them weaker when they needed to be strong. "There's a threat on the horizon much larger than our petty feuds and border disputes, gentlemen. We must look to what's coming. We must sue for peace so we can prepare for war."

She'd managed to cajole and coerce them into a grudging truce, but it seemed all of Europe was rolling the dice, and events were happening faster than she could contain them. Over the winter months, Ewen Cameron of Lochiel had undertaken to write or meet every chief of note in the Highlands, hoping to form a confederation of clans loyal to James to defend his Scottish throne. She'd responded, pledging loyalty, but had avoided offering aid. In March, King James had sailed from France to Ireland with an army of twelve hundred men. He'd landed in Kinsale, marched to Dublin, and was greeted as king of Ireland by cheering crowds.

She wondered what the O'Sullivans… what Jamie… thought of that. She'd been so busy she'd hardly had time to think of him by day, and though she ached for him at night, it was a dull, familiar pain now, no longer jagged and sharp. A good thing, too—he'd made no attempt to contact her, and though she might be disappointed, she wasn't surprised. *He'll be alert to the danger, and the O'Sullivans, just like my folk, will be filled with patriotism, hope, and pride. How can we possibly keep them all safe?*

Avoiding the maelstrom grew harder by the day. At the beginning of April, a convention in Edinburgh declared William the king of Scotland, but a number of people, most of them Highlanders, remained loyal to James. One of them, John Graham of Claverhouse, Viscount Dundee, known as Bonnie Dundee to his friends and Bloody Clavers to his foes, had decided to raise an army of liberation in concert with Lochiel, and was touring the Highlands with the royal standard, gathering clansmen for war. It was this they were discussing now. She rubbed her temples to clear her head, and returned her attention to Jerrod.

"There's no staying out of it, Cat. It's coming whether you will it or no. 'Tis said of us there are no better allies in all the Highlands. If we don't stand with them, we'll be shamed and dishonored. Our friends will turn against us and we'll stand alone."

She knew he was right. What Jamie had hoped to avoid for England was coming to her homeland instead, another religious and civil war. Highlander against Lowlander, Catholic and Episcopalian against Presbyterian and Covenanter, Williamite against Jacobite, Scot against English, and Scot against Scot. There was no avoiding it. *Bloody hell!*

Thirty-Five

IT'S GOING TO BE A LOVELY SUNSET. CLAD IN HELMET and leather cuirass and armed with her father's sword and shield, Catherine watched from a hilltop overlooking the Killiecrankie Pass. The key communications route into the Highlands from Perth to Inverness, the six-feet-wide riverside track threaded through a steep, dangerous, densely wooded gorge, carved by the rushing waters of the Gary River. They'd been waiting, ducking potshots and sporadic cannon fire, since marching from Blair Castle and claiming the high ground in the mid-afternoon.

The ancient seat of the Dukes and Earls of Atholl, Blair Castle was the gateway to the Grampian Mountains. Whoever controlled it, controlled access between the Highlands and the Lowlands. The Marquis, its current owner, had prudently left to take the waters in Bath, and Dundee had taken steps to secure it for the Royalist cause. The moment he heard a government force under Hugh Mackay was on its way to reclaim it, he'd sprung into action. He'd held a brief war council with those clan leaders who'd arrived, and set out immediately to cut them off. They'd marched without halting, arriving before the Orangemen, and set up position on a ridge above the pass.

They'd been waiting nearly two hours for the sun to set so it wouldn't blind them. Three hundred Irish under the command of Major-General Cannon had joined them, but from what Catherine could see, they were still outnumbered two to one. *Outmanned, outgunned, but not outgeneraled.* Her father had taught her that speed won battles, conferring the advantage of flexibility, choice of terrain, and element of surprise, but Bonnie Dundee was the first man she'd seen put it so adeptly into practice. *A valuable lesson, if I survive to remember it.*

A cloud passed overhead and she shivered, though it was late July and hot. It wouldn't be long now, a few minutes at most. She looked toward the horizon. The sun hung low and the sky had taken an orange cast against a background of magenta and purplish-blue. *This will be my last sunset. I'll never grow old. I'll never have a child. At least I had the chance to know a man. I've had a lover. I've loved Jamie.*

Jerrod sidled over next to her, and their horses bumped noses. "You've led us here, Cat. Time now for you to go."

She snorted and made a rude gesture. "I'll go when the other chiefs do, Uncle, be it up or down the hill."

"Your father'd be bursting with pride, could he see you now, lass."

"My father would have counselled me to do like the Marquise of Atholl and take the waters in Bath."

But he wouldn't have. The first battle in the Jacobite cause, a daring gambit against desperate odds—despite all his words of caution and prudence, he'd shared the Highland thirst for wild adventure, and he'd not have missed it for the world. And here *she* was, after all her efforts to avoid it, about to embark on a piece of foolishness and destructive waste her people had romanticised and gloried in for centuries, and the part of her that had listened with childish wonder to the tales of storytellers and poets, trembled in anticipation. She was about to lead her clan into battle. She was about to take part in the kind of heroic deeds men wrote songs about. Swept by a fierce hunger, all her senses heightened; afraid, exhilarated, and never more ferociously alive, she looked down the hill, her heart pounding with excitement, and then looked to Jerrod and grinned.

Thirty-Six

JAMIE PEERED THROUGH THE BRANCHES, SCANNING for movement along the ridge, but heavy foliage obstructed his view. Behind him, the walls of the canyon rose perpendicular to the angry waters that clawed at its jagged base, blocking most of what remained of the sunlight. Cavernous and deep, the narrow defile was cool despite the heat of summer. It had a dank, metallic taste and a claustrophobic air that reminded him of the inside of a cave. Despite their marked numeric advantage, their cavalry, and their guns, he didn't like their situation or their odds.

This wasn't the way to fight a campaign in the Highlands. Dragoons and cannon were little use against surefooted mountaineers in this terrain. If anything, they were a disadvantage, slowing them down and lending a false sense of strength. He knew Hugh Mackay had been a mercenary in Dutch service for many years and was no fool, but he'd been outmaneuvered *and* outflanked, and he'd led them straight into what was obviously a highly vulnerable position. Hubris or folly, the results were the same. When they'd stopped at the far end of the pass, Dundee was waiting for them on the high promontory to their right. Everyone was surprised but Jamie.

So now, they waited, with cavalry, a baggage train, and four thousand English, Scottish, and Dutch foot soldiers, most of them raw recruits. They'd been firing anxiously into the hills with muskets and cannon on and off all afternoon. They'd yet to flush the enemy out, though they'd caught a glimpse of Bloody Clavers. *He's waiting for sundown, and when he comes, half this lot will piss their breeks, while the other half will piss their breeks and run away.* Jamie had been in more than enough engagements to know when a mission was in trouble, but that wasn't what worried him now. He looked to the hills again, eyes straining to see in the gathering dusk, and still couldn't find what he was seeking.

At seven o'clock, with the sun behind them, the Jacobites rose to their feet as one, dropped their packs and plaids, and came screaming down the hill. Firing, then dropping their muskets, they advanced relentlessly through three rounds of fire before tearing into Mackay's forces, swinging their huge two-handed claymores without mercy as his panicked men struggled to reload. The onslaught was so ferocious that even seasoned soldiers had no time to fix their bayonets. Gunfire silenced, an eerie hush descended, and the only sound was that of grunting, the shriek and clang of battered metal, and the groans and truncated cries of dying men. Jamie thought he heard a familiar battle cry but didn't have time to place it as, a moment later, Dundee and his cavalry charged Mackay's center and swept it away.

Cutting his way through the throng, Jamie watched incredulously as the English cavalry fled into the pass without firing a shot. Locked toe-to-toe in combat with a grinning, blood-drenched Highlander, he had to disengage and jump aside to avoid being knocked into the river. Evenly matched in skill, size, and strength, Jamie had a mission, while his opponent fought for glory. In no mood for gallantry, he took the opportunity to deliver a vicious kick to the man's kneecap, watching as he toppled over the rocks and slid into the torrent. His cry of alarm was lost in the rumble of the river as the swiftly moving water carried him away.

Around him, the scene was one of massacre and panic. There were hundreds, if not thousands, dead on both sides now. Mackay's forces had broken ranks and, pursued by the Highlanders, were running through the pass in terror. The ground was slick with blood, the dead strewn everywhere, and bits and pieces of severed limbs and broken weapons littered the path. He heard the cry again, slightly louder now, and moved toward it, careful not to slip and plunge down the bank, stepping aside when he could and knocking men down when he had to. He didn't care which side they were on; if they wouldn't move from his path, he killed them.

A cry of excitement went up from behind. *Good. They've found the baggage train.* It was the only thing that might save Mackay and his men from complete annihilation. It sparked a sudden change in interest and direction. The lure of plunder was a hard one for the Highlanders to resist, and the thirst for spoils rapidly replaced the thirst for blood. Though there was still sporadic fighting, many broke off the pursuit. Mackay seized the opportunity to muster the few survivors who hadn't fled, and called a hasty retreat. Jamie ignored him, bent on his task.

He strode purposefully, his gore-covered sword at the ready, checking bodies and the faces running by him as he went. He wore no uniform, and covered in blood he might have been friend or foe. He was neither, and most men he encountered, eager for this new diversion, paid him no attention or stepped aside. *Where in Christ's name is she?* A cold dread was taking hold, almost choking him, and the first seeds of panic had begun to spread. He heard the cry again, "A Drummond! A Drummond!" and looked to his left. He recognized the plaid and Bucephalus, his bald-headed torturer, but there was no sign of Catherine, and they seemed upset.

Fear clutched his vitals, stopping him in his tracks, and then he saw it: a limp shape resembling a broken doll, long hair trailing behind. She bobbed and tumbled, borne by the frothing current, passing within inches of serrated rock that could slice her open or smash her skull. Tossing his sword, he dove in after her. She'd been heading toward him, but when he surfaced, she was already a few feet beyond. He struck out after her, jolted by fear, and in three quick strokes, he had hold of her cuirass. Using all of his strength, he managed to shift around so his back was to the current and his legs extended forward, facing downstream. Hauling her against him, he wrapped his arms beneath her breasts, hugging her tight to his chest and bracing her with his body and his legs. In this position, knees slightly bent, his booted feet took the brunt of most collisions and allowed him some small means to maneuver and steer a course.

He was taking a pounding nonetheless, but though his hips and shoulders were torn and battered, his breathing was steady and his grip was sure. She'd yet to show any signs of life, and he prayed frantically she was unconscious and not dead. He moved one hand, bracing her with his forearm as his fingers pressed against her neck, just below her jaw. Her blood pulsed, slow and steady, and he almost wept with relief. Exhausted, he relaxed into an almost dreamlike state, letting the river pull them along, his only focus the rocks and his woman.

He was startled from his reverie by a dark shape hurtling overhead. It was one of William's soldiers. He blinked in astonishment. *Good Christ!* The man had cleared the pass, leaping over the cataract from one immense boulder to another in a jump that must have been close to twenty feet! "God see you safely home, lad! It must be a night for miracles," he called after him with a laugh.

Catherine stirred in his arms. "I didn't know you could swim." It was said as if nothing unusual was happening, as if his being there was the most natural thing in the world.

She was bleeding a little from a cut just below her hairline, and he hugged her tighter. He needed to get her out of the water soon, and get her warm. "I told you before, I'm full of surprises, love," he whispered against her ear. Her head slumped back against his shoulder, and she didn't answer.

There were stars overhead now. The battle was far behind them and the only sounds were the dull rumble of the river and the steady rhythms of heart and lung. The moon was rising and it was getting hard to see, but the pummeling he'd taken from the river lessened as it widened, and when gentler waters deposited them in a quiet pool, he started pulling her to shore. It had been the most savage battle he'd ever taken part in, and that was saying a lot. Fought under a blood-red sky, the whole thing had been over in ten minutes, leaving thousands of dead, but he had his prize, he'd found what he came for, and he was content.

He crawled out onto a rocky shoal of gravel, slate, and shale, and sat a few moments, too tired to move. He was bruised and torn, blood dripped from gashes on his arm and the back of his thigh, and he suspected he'd cracked a rib, but otherwise, miraculously, he was unharmed. Catherine's lip and cheek were cut and she had a fearsome bump on her head, but the wound on her scalp had stopped bleeding. She felt cold in his arms, though. He thought they'd been a good forty minutes in the river, and though the day had been warm, it was cool in the mountains at night. He had no heat of his own to give her, and nothing with which to make a fire. He had a sudden image of the highflying soldier. *What did he do with his weapon and pack?*

He was anxious about leaving her alone. What if somebody found her? What if she woke, not knowing where she was? But she'd shown no sign of awareness since noting he could swim, and they wouldn't get far in the mountains without supplies. He hid her in a dry hollow, covering her with branches and leaves. Moving as quickly as his aching body and the treacherous terrain would allow, it took him thirty minutes to reach the place where the soldier had made his spectacular leap. Luck was still with him. The lad's rifle and pack were in the bushes where he'd tossed them. "God bless you, boy."

He pushed his luck a little further, climbing to the ridge above. There he found several packs and breacans, dropped at the start of the charge and never reclaimed, their owners dead or moved on to something better from the spoils of the baggage train. He snatched another pack and two woolen plaids. Catching the glint of moonlight on metal, he explored a bit further, finding swords and a bow, souvenirs of men who'd died on the hill. He gathered them, too. It was close to midnight and the moon was directly overhead when he finally crawled in beside Catherine, wrapping them both in the thick woven plaids of her homeland.

From the moment he'd entered Will's and heard that an army was being raised to quell an insurrection in the Highlands, he'd known what he had to do. Nothing else mattered—not lands or titles, or any of the other baubles William had thrown his way. All that mattered was she be safe, and now she was.

Thirty-Seven

BLOOD WAS EVERYWHERE, AND EVERYONE AROUND her was killing or dying. Some fought with businesslike detachment, severing heads and limbs and calmly moving on. Others dealt death with teeth bared wide and eyes alight with glee. Then there were those like her and her opponent, grim and wary, locked in a desperate struggle to survive. *He's just a boy. I've just become a woman. Why does one of us have to die?* But he was as frightened as she was, and just as determined to survive. She wielded a saber rather than one of the two-handed swords used by her comrades, but she was exhausted now and barely able to lift it.

The young lieutenant caught her with a glancing blow, knocking off her helmet. His eyes widened and he paused a moment as her hair spilled about her shoulders. As if of its own volition, her sword thrust out and took him though the throat. She watched in shock and horror as he dropped his weapon and clutched at his neck, his eyes white with fear. He took a faltering step toward her, his hand thrust out, choking as blood gurgled from the wound. Something struck her from behind and she was flying though air, falling... falling... as *the bruised sky wheeled above her. She seemed to fall for a very long time, and then something caught her... and then he was there.*

Catherine groaned and clutched her blankets. Her head was pounding and every movement was agony. The acrid smell of smoke assailed her nostrils and tickled at the back of her throat, and the sound of busy water burbled close by. She opened her eyes, wincing as she slowly turned her head. "Sinclair?" she croaked, disoriented and confused.

"Ah! My delicious enemy! My lovely wife."

Hitching herself onto her elbows, she looked around. They were on a gravel outcrop by the side of the river, sheltered by an overhanging tree. Jamie had a fire going and was busy cooking something. The delicious smells of field bread and frying salt pork wafted toward her, and her stomach grumbled.

"Hungry, are you? I'm glad to hear you're almost back to your old self."

How did he... what is he doing here? "I thought I dreamt you."

"Women say that all the time."

She nodded toward the neat little camp as she struggled to remove the wet leather that was chafing her neck and under her arms. "You did all this?"

"I'm more than a pretty face, love," he said, reaching to help her.

She raised a hand defensively and pushed him away, seeing to the task herself, then glared at him suspiciously as he handed her meat and bread. "What are you doing here? Shouldn't you be in London with William and your whores?"

"What do you remember?" he asked, ignoring her ingratitude.

"I remember the charge. I remember fighting by the river, and then everything went dark."

"Be glad you didn't see it all."

"I saw enough."

Her tone gave him pause, and he looked at her carefully. "Are you alright?"

"I'm alive. I need to go back and find my family. I need to make sure *they're* alright."

"They're fine. I saw them hale and hearty after the battle was won."

"We won?"

"You did. A complete victory, your enemies destroyed, though I saw your leader fall and fear him numbered among the dead. Congratulations."

"Please, don't mock me. I really can't bear it right now." She saw him again, the young lieutenant, hands scrabbling at his throat, and ran into the bushes, stomach heaving.

"Are you sure you're alright?"

"Everything hurts, other than that I'm fine. You're dripping more blood than I am. Why didn't you say something?"

"I'm not a bawling baby like you."

She flung a handful of gravel at him, pulling up short as the muscles in her neck and shoulders screamed in agony. "Be quiet, stupid man! Why are you here?"

"I've come to take you home."

She looked at him, moved suddenly from anger to the edge of tears. "I have to go see it first."

"I know. It's on the way."

She'd slept through all of one day and most of a second, and by the time they made the pass again, a full three days had passed. The Highlanders had already gathered their dead and moved on, but government troops and locals were picking their way through what remained. Catherine sat on a hill above the river, watching through a steady drizzling rain.

Jamie came and sat beside her, placing his arm around her shoulders. She didn't protest.

"All these men had families. What have I done?"

He gave her a hug. "Your duty as a chieftain and what you needed to survive."

"It was senseless, stupid! It's not what I wanted. I tried my best to keep us out of it, but it happened anyway, and when it did I was in the thick of it. I ran screaming down the hill with all the rest. Look at them, poor bastards. Most of them were only boys."

She was shaking. He kissed the top of her head. "Some things you just can't make sense of and this is one of them. It will only make you crazy if you try. You have to take them in, accept them, and then move on. It gets better once you do."

"Is it always like this... after?"

"I can't really say, love. I usually drink myself unconscious and find a willing whor—Here now, look what I've found!" He pulled out a hip flask. "What say we have a spot of this? Just the thing for a rainy day." They passed the flask back and forth between them, the liquid warming them on the inside as the rain stopped and the early morning sunshine inched up the hill.

"Shall we go now, Cat?" he asked after a while. "They'll be able to see us soon."

She nodded and stood. They walked on in silence throughout the afternoon and into the early evening.

"Why are you really here?" she asked after several hours, tired of hearing only birdcalls, snapping branches, labored breathing, and gravel crunching underfoot. "Are you on a mission for William?"

"I told you, I came to find you."

"Is there some trouble with the papers? Why didn't you write me instead?"

"I haven't looked at the damned papers. They're still sitting on a desk somewhere. I came because I was worried about you. I missed you. I came because I love you, mouse. You've melted my cold heart."

"Spare me, please!" she snorted. "What game are you playing now?"

"The rest of it's the game. You're the prize, the only thing that makes this bloody farce worthwhile. I just wanted to keep you safe. It's become a habit."

She'd been shocked to see him, and though she was relieved and grateful he'd come, it distressed her that the unruly longings she thought she'd tamed had returned, as raw as they'd ever been. She wanted to believe him, but she remembered his abandonment, and she remembered Moll. "I thank you for your help, but I know the way from here. I can get home safely on my own."

"Maybe so. But I'm here now, so you won't have to."

They bedded down that night in the lee of a granite boulder, still miles apart, despite being close enough to touch.

Catherine continued waspish and sullen throughout the next day, and Jamie decided to try a different approach.

"I didn't sleep with her, you know."

"Are you never quiet, English?"

He refused to respond, proving her wrong. It was another twenty minutes and almost dark before either of them spoke again.

"That's not what it looked like."

They clambered over a rocky ledge and slid and scrambled down a barren hill. It would be full dark soon, and they'd yet to find a place to make camp.

Jamie pointed to a shallow overhang. "I've no taste for mountaineering in the dark. Let's set up camp over there." They went about the business of getting comfortable for the night in a strained silence.

"I'm sorry if I hurt you, Catherine. God knows I never meant to."

"For an avowed atheist, you call on God as witness rather a lot, English."

"My beliefs have changed. I've become an agnostic. Open-minded, willing to believe, prepared to be convinced."

"And what's brought on this sudden conversion?"

"It's not sudden. It started in the Highlands, shortly after I met you, and it's been growing ever since."

"Goodness gracious me! Next thing I know you'll be off to the monastery!"

"Heaven forbid." He threw another branch on the fire and came to flop down beside her. "I'm not talking about religion, Catherine. I'm talking about you and me."

"Are you now?" She felt a start of pleasure, but his withdrawal had hurt her badly, and she was tired of playing his games and following his rules. "Has it occurred to you, Jamie, that it's not my life's goal to convince you of anything? I've no intention of convincing any man I'm worthy of his love. I'm something special, English. A man should get down on his knees and weep tears of gratitude if he's lucky enough to have me. He should thank whatever god he believes in every day and... and if he's just too stupid to realize how lucky he is to have me, then I don't want him!"

"I know that, love." His voice was husky, pleading, and she could feel the heat from his body, just inches from her own. She tried to move away but he leaned on top of her, using his weight to pin her under her blanket. She struggled to free herself, though not very hard.

"It's for me to convince you. I may not say the things you want me to, and I can't claim to have been faithful to you through the full course of our marriage, but you did bash me on the head and toss me away. I never expected to see you again and a man has to amuse himself somehow, but I swear I've never looked elsewhere since you walked back into my life. I told you I'd been faithful since you came to London, love. That certainly didn't change after we made love. I didn't sleep with Moll and I wouldn't have, even had you never seen me there. What you saw... well... she's just an old friend. I've known her many years."

Catherine snorted.

"*She* was pursuing *me*, Catherine. Would you have had me drop her on the floor?"

"Oh, heavens no. It must have been very distressing. No wonder you struggled so. In any case, it's no business of mine."

"Yes it is. I had no wish to embarrass her or be cruel, but when you saw us I was telling her goodbye."

"Why?"

"I… because I wasn't interested anymore. Because when I took you to my bed, I felt I'd made you some kind of promise. I don't know. You're not like the other women I know. You're not the type of woman a fellow plays with." Even as he said it, he was playing with the collar of her shirt.

She slapped his hand away. "No, of course not, hulking, mannish—"

"Hush!" He lifted the blanket and slipped underneath, ignoring her kicking and squirming. "Enough, lass. There's a chill in the air tonight. Don't be so sullen as to keep us both cold. I love how you're made. You're a glorious woman, muscled and sleek, yet soft and rounded in all the right places." His hand cupped her breast and squeezed. "It stirred my blood that first night in my tent. I wondered what it would be like to have you willing."

"Well, you're not likely to find out tonight." She elbowed him sharply in the side, and he grunted in pain.

"Jesus, hellcat, watch out! I think I cracked a rib in the river."

"I'm sorry!" She was instantly contrite. "I didn't know. You never said anything. I didn't mean to hurt you. Let me see."

He pulled up his shirt, revealing a chain of scrapes and cuts and ugly bruises running from shoulder to hip.

"Oh, Jamie! I had no idea. The river did this to you? And you came in there after me!"

He nodded solemnly. Doubtless, they looked worse in the firelight, and some were a result of the battle, but her smile was tender, her touch was gentle, and her voice was warm for the first time since he'd found her. He held his breath and held his tongue as cool fingers carefully explored his chest, his waist, his hip, gingerly probing and lightly caressing before moving on.

"Are you enjoying this?"

"Go just a little further and you'll see."

"You're badly bruised. It must be painful for you to breathe, but I don't feel anything broken. You're in far worse shape than I am. It seems you took the brunt of it in my stead. Once again I owe you my thanks."

She tugged at his shirt to pull it back down but he caught her wrist and stopped her, pulling her up against him so that she covered his length. "You owe me nothing, Catherine, but I owe you the truth. I didn't sleep with Moll because I knew it would hurt you. I knew you'd forgive me William, but you'd not forgive me that. I've caused you pain in other ways, I know, but you've given me many gifts and I'd not repay you like that. I swear there are no other women, only you."

She believed him. He'd never lied before, why would he start now? Why come all this way for that? She felt a warm rush of relief. She relaxed against him and let her head drop to his shoulder, careful of his left side. He wrapped his arms around her, one hand gently feathering the hair on the nape of her neck.

"I don't doubt your word, Jamie. If you say you didn't, then it's true."

"But you doubt my affections."

"You've warned me to, often enough." *Make me believe you, Jamie… Please.*

His hands were wandering again, trailing up and down her back, and brushing the outsides of her breasts.

"Are you trying to seduce me?"

"I am. I'm hopeful that it's working. I've got you in my arms and you aren't hurting me anymore."

She sighed and lifted her fingers to trace his lips. "It's so hard to stay angry with you when you exert yourself to charm. You feel some obligation after sharing a bed. Is that to be enough?"

"For an intelligent woman, you're very muddle-headed about some things, love. I've broken every rule I've lived my life by, starting the moment I found you at the River Clyde. Trust no one, depend only on yourself, always act in your own self-interest, and when you accept a commission, always see it through. All of them," he snapped his fingers, "out the window, just like that. William offered lands and titles, things I once held dear. I've abandoned it all, ignored a lifetime of hard-earned lessons, all because of you. I'd do it again, too, did you but crook your little finger. Why would I do such things if I didn't care for you deeply?"

"Sullivan says I'm one of your pets." She shifted slightly. Her knee rested against his groin and she slid her hand under the blanket, her fingers trailing patterns across his chest.

"Sullivan knows I love my pets." *Christ! It's been so long!*

"So you hold me in as much esteem as you do your horses and the dogs?"

"I swear that I do," he said solemnly. "OW!"

She smoothed the hair she'd just yanked and kissed him on the temple. "Do you know what I was thinking when I waited on the hilltop, expecting I was going to die?" She drew her thumb along his collarbone, and spoke warm and close, her words tickling his ear.

A delicious shiver traveled along his spine, and his arousal stirred, swelling and straining against its restraints. *Oh God! She turns me into a schoolboy and she hasn't even kissed me yet.* "What?" he asked, breathless.

"I thought… it's not the things I've done I regret, but those I didn't do." She drew her fingernail down his torso, hard enough to quicken his breath, but not enough to hurt, and her lips nibbled the sensitive arc of ear, throat, and jaw. "I thought… I never regretted you." Her fingers played over his abdomen now, and her lips were close to his. "I thought of all the things I'd do to you if I ever had the chance again." *Oh Jamie! You came!*

"And did you think that you still loved me?" he asked, taking her face between his hands and drawing her into a kiss.

"No," she murmured against his lips. "I didn't think of that at all."

He groaned as her hand moved lower, tugging at the fastening of his breeches. She gave a final pull and he sprang free, leaping into her hand. His hips thrust forward and she gripped him tighter, stroking, and squeezing, making him gasp. He deepened his kiss, his tongue thrusting and dancing with hers in a fierce tempo that matched the rhythm of his hips. He traced the contours of her neck with a delicate touch, then slid his hands beneath her shirt and smoothed them over her shoulders, enjoying the feel of her skin, hot against his palms. "Your flesh is soft and yielding, but your heart is hard as iron."

"I might say the reverse of you."

"Naughty girl. Come closer if you dare." He reached for her knee, pulling it forward until she was on top of him. "Like that," he whispered as he brushed the hair from her face. As she wiggled and squirmed, making herself comfortable, the fabric of her clothing rubbed his naked flesh. His breath caught in his throat and he released it in a groan. His fingers lifted, brushed, and tugged, and her shirt slid off her shoulders and down her back, pooling at her waist. "Oh, sweet Jesus!"

As Catherine learned forward to kiss him, the movement pushed her tight against his straining erection. The muscles between her legs flexed and quivered, and a moist heat fluttered and ached inside. She squeezed his hips between her thighs and ground against him, delighted by the power to make him moan. *I could make him do anything right now. I could make him say whatever I wanted,* but she was too proud to ask.

Strong hands gripped her waist and suddenly she was beneath him. "You're so beautiful, Catherine. I've dreamt of this, night after night, every night since you left me."

"You left me. You knew where to find me. You never wrote. You never came."

"And I'm sorry for it. I was angry you were gone, Catherine, and hurt you didn't want me, and given my last reception I could hardly walk straight into your home. When I heard about the Jacobite uprising, I attached myself to Mackay's army. I thought you'd be in the thick of it and you were. I came, love. Surely you knew I would."

"I didn't. I thought I was a burden to you. How could you ever think I didn't want you?"

"This is my dream, Catherine. The best one I've had in a very long time. I don't want to argue in it. If you're still in my arms when I wake, we can talk about anything and everything you like."

The swell of joy and hope she'd tried to contain escaped her and she murmured her assent through an onslaught of hungry kisses. When he bent his head to nuzzle her eager nipples she let go of all that weighed between them, losing herself in the moment and the man. *You came... I love you Jamie... you came.* Her body blushed and prickled, pulsing, aching, each time his knowing lips brushed her tender flesh. Strong fingers plumped each breast in turn as his hot mouth moved from swollen tip to swollen tip, nibbling and sucking, teasing and tugging, leaving a trail of hot kisses in between.

"I love you, Catherine. You claimed my heart soon after we met, a beautiful Highland selkie who kept me safe within her cave. No one ever came to my rescue before. I laughed and I teased you, but I'd never been so deeply moved. While I was waiting at The Hague, I promised myself I'd tell you as soon as I saw you again." He wet a taut nipple with his tongue and blew on it gently. "It made me very happy to admit it. You're the only one I've ever truly loved." He turned his attention to the other tip, one hand plumping her as the other tickled its peak. She whimpered and he soothed her with a wet kiss. She moaned, gripping his shoulders as her heels dug in the ground.

He lifted his head and looked straight into her eyes. "I feared I'd lost you when I saw you in that river. You're the only thing that gives my life meaning, Catherine. I love you." His lips brushed the corner of her mouth. "I love you," he breathed against her lips. "I love you!" He enfolded her in his arms and thrust his tongue deep in her mouth, claiming her in a voluptuous kiss.

Catherine pushed against him, working frantically to remove her breeches, kicking in annoyance when they tangled in her boots. Jamie chuckled, wriggling his hips as he shrugged off his own, but before either could finish, their bodies joined together in a tangled bundle of bedding, limbs, and clothes. He entered her with one deep thrust. She was slick and hot and ready, and as he drove into her again and again, she rose to meet him, her hunger as fierce as his own. Their cries echoed off the walls of the nearby mountains and rose into the night. They found their release together, shuddering and shaking, raw with pleasure and shouting their joy.

They sank back into each other, contented and at peace. The stream trickled in the distance and there was the hiss and pop of the fire, but otherwise all was quiet. Catherine's heart was singing and she couldn't stop touching him, petting and squeezing, stroking and caressing, as if making certain he was really there. Her head rested on his chest and he absently stroked her hair. They lay like that for several minutes before

Jamie set her gently aside and jumped to his feet.

"HELLO!" he shouted. *Helloooo...* the mountain answered back. "JAMIE SINCLAIR LOVES CATHERINE DRUMMOND!" *Loves Catherine Drummond... Catherine Drummond,* it repeated in kind.

"Get back down here, you bloody fool! They'll hear you all the way to Inverness!"

He dropped down beside her, snuggling close. "Make room, love. Your man is cold." She lifted the blanket so he could slide in beside her, and then wrapped an arm around his back. They lay together nose to nose, toes entwined. "You never said it to me."

"Said what?"

"You know... the words."

"I believe it was your turn."

"I don't deny it, but there's something of a protocol isn't there? When one person says it, the other says it back."

She raised an eyebrow.

"Ah."

"I'm teasing you, Jamie," she said, relenting immediately. "You know I love you. I've learnt that I can live my life without you, but it's being with you that makes each day a joy."

"Say it."

"I love you. I love you madly!"

"When did you know?"

"I believe I recognized the danger in the selkie cave, just like you did."

"But you bashed me on the head!"

"No... I had someone do that for me. I was a sensible girl in those days, and when you kissed me, you called me Molly."

She shifted onto her back, clutching his hand tight in hers. She felt giddy. *He said it! He shouted it! He'd never have done that if he didn't mean it. He'd not have come if it weren't true. One moment you think you're about to die, and the next your life's starting over again, wonderful and new.* Despite being nighttime, the world was alive with color. The stars glittered with icy fire, embers danced and fluttered like brilliant crimson leaves, and the crescent moon glowed gold and yellow, hanging halfway up an inky sky.

"The world is perfect!"

"Yes it is," Jamie said with an indulgent smile. "At least it is when I'm with you."

"At moments like this… do you ever wonder if there's some higher force at work?"

"I'm an adult, love. I don't believe in fairy tales."

"You don't believe in anything?"

"I believe in you, Catherine. That's all I need."

"What if I disappoint you some day?"

"You wouldn't."

"How do you know? You were gone for several months. I thought you had a lover. Perhaps I found some husky barelegged lad and… mmppphhhh."

He stopped her with a forceful kiss. "No, mouse. Not you. Not that. You're a jewel of many facets, love. Beautiful as a summer's day and tempestuous as the sea, but without her fickle disposition. Betrayal's not in your nature. Why all these questions? Lay back and enjoy the sky. Or if you wish… "

"Stop!" She pulled his hand back from its wanderings, and held it tight to her chest. "You promised you'd answer my questions. I didn't understand why you couldn't love me, and why you kept pulling away. I don't want unanswered questions between us. If you answer me now, I promise I'll never ask you again."

He lay back with a sigh. "I said I couldn't give you what you wanted. I never said I didn't love you. I think I loved you from the start. That was the problem. I've always tried to avoid strong feelings, Catherine. They say bad blood runs deep, a man takes after his parents. I'm the offspring of a vicious bully and a slut. I wanted a wife who... didn't excite strong emotions. One of whom I wouldn't be jealous, and who wouldn't be hurt when I strayed. Then you landed in my lap and I had no idea what to do with you. I grew muddleheaded. I started making mistakes. I... had difficulty maintaining my detachment. Christ, Catherine! I took you brawling and whoring with me in London. What kind of husband does that? I let you see what—

"What lies behind the mask?" She kissed his shoulder and then wrapped an arm around his chest. "Perhaps you were rebelling against the idea of a loveless marriage."

He turned his head, trying to see her in the dark. "Perhaps. It would make sense in an odd sort of way. You did the same. I suppose we're both rebels, Cat. Perhaps that's why we suit. But you left me with so few defenses. It unnerved me."

"So... let me see if I understand. You love me, but it's against your will and better judgment, lest I betray you, which you scoff at, as I'm as trustworthy and loyal as an old hound. You fear you're as inconstant, lustful, and fickle as your mother, yet for well over a year you've been faithful to a wife you've only been able to fu... *mph.*

He held his hand clamped firmly over her mouth. "I've fucked hundreds of women, Catherine. I make love to you."

"Well, I hope it's to your liking, as it's all that you're allowed. You're not like your parents, you know. You're not like anyone I've ever met. You make me laugh and you've taken me wonderful places and shown me marvelous things. As you said, what kind of husband does that? No one but you. You're good natured and kind-hearted, gallant and loyal, and I find you vastly entertaining when you pretend to be otherwise."

"I know a king or two who might argue with my loyalty."

"Perhaps. I put friends and family first, and I'm content if you do, too. How could you possibly think I didn't want you, or wouldn't want you back?"

"I... no one who knows me has ever wanted to keep me, mouse."

"Oh, Jamie! No one knows you as I do. You're my dearest friend and my greatest love and I'll keep you gladly. I know I said some cruel things to you when I was angry. I'm sorry. I didn't mean them and I knew they weren't true. And don't ever think I didn't want to keep you. It made me furious and broke my heart to see you with that woman, but I waited six weeks after for you to return. I'd not have left if my family hadn't needed me, and if I'd known you wanted me, I'd have promised to return. Nothing could make me stop loving you. I promise you, Jamie, your heart is safe with me."

He kissed her hungrily, his hands roaming her body, possessive and sure, and when he entered her his movements were deliberate, exquisitely careful, and deliciously slow. *If there's anyone who listens, I thank you for this gift.* They moved as one, in a rhythm as old as the mountains, using words they'd been afraid to say for months, with every new caress. When Jamie finally sank against her in grateful release, he knew that he'd come home.

Thirty-Eight

"YOU'RE NOT PAYING ATTENTION TO ME, ARE YOU?"

"Eh? What's that? Sorry, love, I didn't hear you. Wasn't paying attention. I had my eyes on your perfectly formed arse."

Catherine fixed him with a glare worthy of a Scottish schoolmaster. "This is serious business, Jamie. If you're to pass for a Highlander, you've got to get the kilt just so."

"Bah! You're a hoydenish vixen. You just want to ogle my knees."

"Nonsense. I'm sure you'll find the ah... freedom and... utility very appealing once you try it on."

"You mean you think I'll like the feel of the family jewels waving free?"

Blushing, she spread both great kilts on the ground. "One lays down on it like so. Oh stop grinning, Jamie, and do try."

She was so earnest and eager in her lesson that he hadn't the heart to tell her he'd worn a kilt a time or two before. He watched with solemn attention as she showed him how to roll it around his hips and then drape the upper half across his shoulder.

She surveyed him critically, nodding her approval, and he seized her by her hips and pulled her up against him hard. "Ah yes, my love. I see now exactly what you mean."

His new kilt bulged in an unseemly manner and Catherine had no trouble imagining what lurked beneath. She felt a stab of excitement and didn't object when he grasped her bottom with one hand, and the back of her head with the other, and pulled her mouth to his. Blushing crimson, eyes tightly shut, she ran a hand down his hips to his thighs, flipping aside his kilt and reaching underneath to take him in her hand.

It was another hour at least before they left.

They continued on like happy children, laughing and merry under sunny skies and brilliant star-filled nights, until they came to the edge of the Great Glen. There they perched, side by side, regarding the valley below. Beyond it lay the ocean and her home.

"Well, my dear, the world descends upon us. Here we are, rebels both. You can no longer come home with me, and I can't go home with you. What are we to do?"

She couldn't believe it had never crossed her mind. She'd been lost inside a blissful dream, but they were back to the real world now, a world in which he was a Sassenach who'd marched with William's army, and she was a Jacobite rebel. Her heart stuttered and a chill ran down her back.

"I want you to stay with me." *It's not supposed to be this way. It isn't fair!*

"I'm not sure how we do that, my love. I don't see your people welcoming me. I still bear the scars from my last visit with your family, and it leaves little room for hope. I think your uncle might have seen me at Killiecrankie. I doubt his feelings will be warmer to me now."

"*Can* you go back, Jamie? Won't they think you a traitor and deserter?"

"I *am* a traitor and deserter, but they were all so busy running they might just think me dead."

"Do you want to go back?"

"No. There's nothing that interests me in London anymore. There never really was."

"Then stay. I'll speak with my uncle. I'll talk to the council. I'll make them listen. You can wait in the hills and I'll come for you once it's safe. It was different before. Donald was chief and he wanted me married to Cormac O'Conner. I know I can convince them now."

He looked at her doubtfully. "Even if you could, now you're safe I need to see what I can do for Sullivan and his people. They're my responsibility, and the closest thing I had to family before I met you."

"Of course you do. I understand that, but you don't have to do it right this minute. Come with me first. Meet my family. I want to be certain you feel it's your home."

He touched a finger lightly to the tip of her nose. "You're my home, mouse. If I must suffer your ill-natured, ill-mannered, ill-favored family in order to have you, then I'll try. The question is, will they suffer me?"

Two day's later, and just a few miles from home, Catherine set a small fire in a clearing on top of a hill. When it burned down to the coals, she smothered it in a thin layer of wet leaves, then used a breacan as a blanket to catch the rising smoke. She released two puffs, followed by a pause, and then three more. After twenty minutes, she did it again, then put the fire out. "Jerrod knows this signal. He'll see it and come or he won't. There's no point making others curious."

"And will he bring a host of raging Scotsmen with him?"

"No. He'll recognize it as a private message from me and come alone. We're the only ones that use it, now my father and my cousin Rory are gone."

Jerrod burst upon them two hours later. "Lord love you, Cat! You live up to your name! I swear you were born with nine lives though you can nae have more than one or two left." He enveloped her in a crushing hug. "I saw your signal and my heart almost stopped. I feared it was your ghost sending me a message. When you tumbled in the river, I was certain you were gone. We held a lovely service for you." He put her down and turned to look at Jamie. "And what have we here? Who's this fine-looking fellow? You caught yourself a braw fish in the river, it seems. Step forward, lad, don't be shy."

Jamie spoke in a slightly bored British drawl. "I'm with the lady, sir. If you're looking for braw laddies you'd best look elsewhere. Perhaps you can find a pretty sheep that—

"Jamie, stop it!"

"Aha! Sinclair is it? I thought you looked familiar."

"Good evening, Bucephalus. I'd rather hoped you'd fallen in the river and drowned."

"So you're her husband? You've a nerve showing your face here, Sassenach. You should be dead with your friends at Killiecrankie. What happened to you? Got mixed up and ran the wrong way?"

"He was there to find me, Uncle. It was he who pulled me from the river and now he's brought me home. He saved my life. *Again.* It's *our* name you shame by your insults."

Jamie, standing behind her, gave Jerrod a mocking smile.

"You think it's funny, Sassenach? I saw you there. Wondered who you were. Didn't recognize you without a bloody back. You're big for an Englishman, and you were bashing heads like a Highlander. How many of our lads did you kill?"

"The other day? Or since I first took up the sport?"

They'd been testing each other, both of them bristling like angry wolves, and the instant Jerrod reached for his claymore, Jamie drew his.

"Stop it! This instant! Jamie! You promised to behave. You said you'd try to make things work. Jerrod… he can drop you in a heartbeat, I promise you. I didn't come here to watch the man I love kill my favorite uncle. Put down your swords!"

Jamie was the first to lower his weapon.

Jerrod followed a moment later. "Well, you did fish her out of the river and bring her back. I'm grateful to you for that," he said grudgingly. "I'll see to her now, though, so you can scamper off home."

"No, Uncle. I want to bring him home with me. That's why I wanted to speak with you first."

"Are you barmy, lass? He might pass as a Highlander for a stretch, but he was cutting through men and tossing them in the river at Killiecrankie, his own as well as ours. People take notice of such things. We lost over six hundred men there, Bonnie Dundee as well. As soon as someone recognizes him, the lads will kill him."

"I've no intention of pretending to be someone I'm not."

Jerrod looked him slowly up and down, noting his kilt and claymore. "No... I can see that, Sassenach. It's clear as day. What would you do amongst us, then? Do you think to claim our lands through her?" He nodded toward Catherine. "Will you murder your own kind for a bit of land and join us in our rebellion?"

"Twelve Highlanders and a bagpipe make a rebellion, *Uncle*. I doubt you'll be needing me."

"Ha! He's a funny one, your man, Cat. Lucky you. What you ask is impossible. To accept him as your husband is to give a Sassenach our lands. He'd best return to his own if they'll still have him. He'll find no welcome here."

"I fear he's right, love."

Catherine turned to face him. "Nonsense! I'll speak to the council as their chief. You *are* my husband. They'll have no choice but to accept it."

Jamie and Jerrod exchanged a look, but they both knew her well enough not to argue.

❦

Catherine departed with her uncle early the next morning, anxious to be home again, and anxious to have Jamie safe. She left him waiting on the banks of the Spey, promising to return the next day. Things hadn't gone as well as she'd hoped between him and her uncle. *Well, Jerrod tortured him. There's bound to be tension between them. But they didn't kill each other. Surely, that's a promising start.*

Her meeting with the council didn't go any better, despite their joy at her miraculous return. These are dangerous times, they said. How can he be trusted? He could be William's agent sent to spy. He'd fought with Mackay, who'd killed hundreds of their men, and among them were a dozen of their own. And never forget, Catherine was their chief, but also a young woman. Perhaps he sought ships and lands that couldn't be had through conquest by using rogue's tricks: pretty looks, charm, and guile. They were grateful he'd returned her and would gladly see him safely through the Highlands, but they'd give him nothing more.

"Well, what did you expect, lass?" Jerrod asked, when she came to him seeking advice. "It's war now, and we've only just got started. No one will rest until the king is returned to his throne. Your man threw his lot in with William. We can't be worried about enemies within when we're preparing to fight enemies without."

"What do you mean, preparing to fight enemies without? We've done our part. We lost several men. None can say the Drummonds didn't defend their honor and their king. That should be the end of it."

"But we had a glorious victory, Cat! The momentum's ours now. We're going to take Dunkeld next. Alexander Cannon will lead us. We leave to join him in two day's time. We'll crush them as we did at Killiecrankie."

"No, you won't. Cannon is not Dundee, and Dunkeld is a town with a walled compound and good defenses. You'll not be fighting raw recruits, but Camerons and Covenanters, men fanatic enough to be ferocious but not ungovernable like our own. It's a mistake, just as Killiecrankie was, and it will only waste more men."

"Killiecrankie a waste? It was one of the most splendid victories the Highlands have ever known! You were there. You were a part of it. Men will tell stories of it, sing songs about it, for years to come."

"And will that feed us over the winter now our trade with England and the lowlands is gone? Will it bring back any of the fathers, sons, and husbands we lost? I've no doubt it'll fuel that mad taste for glory that seems to run through our race, but it cost us a brilliant commander and a third of our men, and woke a sleeping giant as well. William can't ignore us anymore."

"I'd expected more from you, Cat. Your heart's not in it. Your heart is with your man."

"That's so, Jerrod, but it's never stopped me from seeing my duty. Perhaps your pride is stopping you from seeing yours. We've done our part. Now we should take care of our own."

"You're right. It is pride, the only thing an old man who's lost his son has left, but you'll find it shining bright in all your people, too. It's a glorious time for the Highlands, lass, and our people want to be a part of it. They need you to lead them where they have to go."

They'd thought her dead and Jerrod had taken over, and what they wanted was at odds with what lay in her heart. *I can't lead them down a path I know to be wrong, but they won't follow me anywhere else. There's nothing more I can do for them. I'm free to follow my heart.* She felt a sudden rush of relief, followed by a thrill of excitement.

"No, Uncle Jerrod. For this... they need you."

Catherine hopped over boulders, skipped through streams, and ran up and down hills on her way back to Jamie. The relief she'd felt when she'd made her decision had turned to elation as soon as she'd set out. Decisions that had once seemed agonizing and momentous now seemed obvious and hardly worth a fuss. It was a beautiful day! She bounded from a copse of trees into the clearing and her face fell flat. The fire was cold, the camp abandoned, and he was gone. Her legs wobbled and she dropped to the ground by the river, her heart pinched and aching, blinking back tears. The sun was setting over her shoulder when she finally left for home.

Thirty-Nine

THE THING SHE HOPED FOR COULDN'T BE. JAMIE HAD seen it in her uncle's eyes and the slight shake of his head, no. He'd never really expected it. He'd made his bed. He'd known what he was doing when he'd ruined his chances with James. There was no future left for him in Ireland or Scotland, and now, by going after Catherine, he'd destroyed any future in England as well. He'd taken everything William had given him and thrown it in his face. If he showed himself in London, he'd be branded a coward and deserter, or a traitor to the crown. The best he might hope for was to be taken for dead, one of the first casualties of a Jacobite war. At least then, his lands might pass to Kieran—if the fool could mind his business and get himself a son.

That's all that remained now. He'd make sure of the arrangements, send the O'Sullivans on to London, and after that… France? Portugal? The East Indies? Spain? There were mercenary companies who weren't too particular about a man's past, so long as he knew how to handle a sword.

Catherine had a home, people who cared for her, and a place where she belonged. She was safe. It broke his heart to leave her behind, but the only places left to him were dark and dangerous—the battlefields of Europe, or those places between the cracks where hunted men hide. He had no intention of taking her there with him. He'd never expected anyone to love him, never guessed he'd had so much to give. He'd always survived by taking care of himself. He'd never apologized to anyone, never said a prayer, never asked for help, and never truly cared until he'd met Catherine. He'd warmed to her attention like an eager puppy, making what lay before him that much harder to bear. It seemed ironic that her love, the very thing that gave him faith and hope, was what forced him into exile. *If you do exist, you twisted bastard, I bet you're having a hearty laugh at my expense right now.*

He left before she could return. He left knowing that if he saw her he'd beg her to come. He left thinking that maybe, if he'd asked her to, she would have, but a man put what was best for those he loved ahead of what he wanted for himself.

Jamie arrived at Castle Carrick in the midst of noisy celebration. It seemed that Catherine's girl Maire had finally made Kieran a man. He could expect to be a father soon. At least something was going well. The happy news had led to hurried nuptials, and Jamie arrived in time to kiss the bride and congratulate the groom.

Three nights later, the festivities over and guests long gone, Jamie sat by the fire with Kieran. "Dismal

Jimmy's holding court in Dublin, backed by Talbot's army. There's been a Jacobite victory in Scotland, and the French king stirs the pot. William can't afford to ignore them anymore. There's going to be fighting, Kieran. You've got the girl with child. I want you to stay out of trouble. I want you to take your people and go to London."

"Abandon my family's lands? Turn my back on my king? You're right, milord. Dick Talbot *has* raised an army and King James sits atop the Irish throne, and any man who loves Ireland knows it's time to stand tall. For the first time in years, we've the chance to reclaim what's been stolen and make our ancestors and our children proud. There *is* going to be a war, for Irish independence, and the O'Sullivans won't be hiding behind an Englishman's fancy coat. Join us, Jamie. You may be English but you've an Irish soul. The king will forgive your betrayal if you return when he needs you. He's a better man than you think. He's passed an act that grants religious freedom to all Catholics and Protestants in Ireland. Isn't that the kind of toleration you've always advocated?"

"I won't join you in the killing of my fellow countrymen, Kieran. The idea doesn't sit well. As for James, he has his moments. I don't deny it. But I know him and you don't. He's politically inept and he'll botch the job. He's cruel when he should be forgiving, weak when he should be resolute, and he puts his pride before his people. I can't forgive him that. William will crush this rebellion. He'll land an army the likes of which you haven't seen since Cromwell, and sweep away anything that stands in his path."

"He crushes us now! The English turn us into slaves, take our lands, and strip and sell our forests and our fields."

"It needn't happen to you. I've made arrangements. Go to London and keep clear of this mess. You can keep your bloody lands, Kieran. Christ! You're executer of my estate, You can have mine as well, if they take me for dead! Think of your mother, think of the girl and your unborn child."

"I *am* thinking of them! I want to give them a past and a future that makes them proud. One that belongs to them and hasn't been lent them by somebody else. How can I do that? How can I face them with pride and honor if I don't fight for my freedom, if I don't protect my religion and my king?"

"Maybe you should be more concerned with protecting your family."

Sullivan jumped to his feet. "And what do you know about family? You don't even have one. Your own father disowned you! What do you know about having your rights and your dignity abused? You're one of them. An English occupier! A conqueror! How can you understand honor when you betray your king and country and sell your loyalty for a price? My honor means everything to me, milord, even if yours means nothing to you."

Jamie felt it like a blow. *He's right. They're not my family. They never were. That's just something I made up to keep me warm when I was cold.* It took him a moment, but when he stood, his movements were steady, and when he replied his voice was cool. "Aye, Kieran, you may be right. Perhaps I know nothing of loyalty or honor, but you can't deny I've shown both to you and yours. I'm sick of honorable men with their honorable intentions, honorably killing as they lead their innocent families to grief and ruin. May your precious honor comfort you when your village burns and soldiers lay waste to your fields." He bowed, and left without a backward glance.

Kieran ran after him. "Wait! Milord! Jamie! I didn't mean it as it sounded!" But Jamie was deaf to him. He kept on walking, and in a moment he was swallowed by the dark.

Two nights later he sat perched on a rock, high in the Galty Mountains. He'd finished his supply of whiskey, and the heavens were dull and sullen, shrouded in cloud. No stars, no moon, no family, no friends, no country, no mouse… nowhere to go. *Shit!* He hurled the empty flask over the side, leaning over curiously to watch its fall. It bounced and slid, breaking branches and dislodging pebbles before sliding to a halt. He knew he indulged in self-pity, but he felt entitled, and there was no one to see or know. The years stretched in front of him, bleak and lonely, though probably not too long. Men who lived by their swords didn't tend to die from old age. *Where do I go now?*

A fat drop of rain spattered against his cheek, followed by another and another, and then several more. He wagged a finger at the sky. "You really don't like me much, do you?" The wind picked up suddenly, as if in answer, and he had to slide off his perch or risk being dashed against the rocks below. It battered and pushed in powerful gusts, as if trying to propel him forward, but he squared his shoulders, jammed his hands in his pockets, and refused to be cowed.

By the time he reached the valley floor, his hair was plastered against his face and neck and water streamed down his back. The wind shivered through the trees with enough force to break branches and set his sodden coat flapping. It was almost September, and the rain fell hard and cold. He missed his flask with its honey-sweet whiskey, but he knew where there was more.

He was weary and distracted, and he'd had his share of drink, but years of experience drew him up short, several yards from the cottage. A wisp of smoke trailed from the chimney, so thin it was barely visible, swallowed almost immediately by the harrying wind. The windows were shuttered tight, but a small sliver of light escaped from the crack beneath the door. He drew his sword and advanced, silent through the storm.

The door wasn't latched and he eased it open, his eyes scanning intently through the half-lit gloom. A low fire flickered in the grate, illuminating a figure slumped in a chair. It looked to be an English soldier. It was hard to see in the dim light. He looked to be little more than a boy, but a musket lay within easy reach on the floor beside him. Jamie entered noiselessly, creeping forward, coming to a stop with the tip of his sword resting against the base of the intruder's throat. The lad yawned and stretched, turning his face toward the firelight.

Jamie's sword clattered to the floor. "Sweet Christ! Catherine?"

Catherine gasped and jumped to her feet, leveling the musket at his chest. "Jesus, Sinclair! You scared the devil out of me! Where have you been? I've been waiting here almost a week."

"I took the long way home, mouse. Are you going to shoot me?"

"I'm very tempted," she said, putting down the weapon.

They stood, awkward and silent, two feet apart, neither of them sure what to say next. Then Jamie reached out to tuck a stray lock of hair behind her ear, and she was in his arms. He moaned and pulled her tight against his length, his grip so fierce she winced in pain, but she made no protest, and her hold was just as tight as his.

"Catherine, Catherine, Catherine," he whispered against her hair. "What are you doing here? I might have killed you." He was the closest to tears he'd been since childhood.

"I feared if I let you go you'd wander too far and never come back."

"You were right, love! Don't ever let go of me. If you do, I'll soon be lost."

They managed to stumble to the cot, peeling off boots and breeches and wet clothes before falling in a tangled heap. Jamie was cold from the inside out, but Catherine wrapped him in a blanket of warmth, rubbing his limbs and covering his body with frantic kisses. He tasted like he had the first night she'd met him—heat and life, whiskey and rain—and her heart swelled. *Thank God I found him before he slipped away.* She was full of questions but she didn't ask them now. They spoke without words, through heated caress and tender embrace, using the ancient language of lovers, gasps and murmurs and sighs at first, then low moans, animal sounds, and wild cries.

Spent, they lay in each other's arms, hearts still pounding, slick with sweat, finally capable of speech.

"I could never love you enough, Catherine."

"You're doing just fine," she said, giving him a tight hug.

"How did you know where to find me?"

"You showed me. Don't you remember? You said it was where you came when you needed a place to hide. When I found you gone, I decided if you were here, then you wanted me to find you. You did, didn't you?"

"God yes! With all my heart. You can't imagine... your love, it's the only thing that means anything, Catherine. You're all that matters to me.

"Why didn't you wait for me?"

"I knew what your council would say. I could see it clearly in your uncle's eyes." His fingers trailed absently through her hair as he talked, and one hand stroked her back. "I've betrayed or abandoned two kings and their causes. I'm done. Finished. I can't go back to the life I knew, and I can't live here anymore. You still have a home you can return to. I couldn't ask you to come with me, but I knew if I waited and saw you, I would. You should never have come, love. I don't know what's right or wrong anymore. I'm not sure of anything except what I feel for you. I don't think I can let you go a second time."

Her hands had begun to wander and her lips fastened on his nipple.

His hips jerked and his chest expanded on an indrawn breath. "Catherine, are you listening?"

She folded her arms on his chest and rested her chin on her hands. "Yes, Jamie. You have my full attention. You're saying you have to leave. What about the O'Sullivans? Have you settled matters with them?"

"No. Kieran's married to Maire, and they're expecting a child."

"I saw that coming a while ago. That's good news, isn't it?"

"He's being stubborn. He intends to stay and fight for James. His thoughts are much like your uncle's and he's set upon his course. I've done what I could and now it's beyond my control. We... had words."

"I'm sorry to hear it. That must have hurt."

"It did, but I'm feeling a good deal better now." He grinned and tapped the end of her nose.

"So what now, Jamie?"

"I wish I knew, love. The best I can hope is that William has taken me for dead. I can't afford to be seen by the English or they'll know I'm not. Talbot's men will recognize me as no friend of James, and I can't stay with the O'Sullivans anymore. Your Highlanders will kill me if they can, and I'll be seen as a traitor by the lowland Scots. I'm like to be harassed and chased no matter how I approach it. I'll affect a disguise, I suppose, and make my way to the continent. Perhaps... if you wish it... once I'm settled you might join me there."

"Why is it that we fit so well when it's just you

and I? When we're together like this, or in disguise, it seems we're in our own world and no two souls were ever closer. It's only when we have to deal with other people that things go wrong."

He ruffled her hair. "I know, mouse. We're rebels, you and I. We refuse to accept the life others have chosen for us and when they press too hard, instead of breaking or bending, we slip through the cracks and disappear."

Catherine's heart stuttered as she realized how close he'd come to doing just that. She grasped his hair and turned his head so he looked her straight in the eye. "You'll not disappear on me again, Jamie, will you? I won't forgive you if you do."

"No, love, I promise. Not without telling you first. Sometimes I think it's too bad we can't both just don a costume and disappear, like we did in London."

"Why can't we?"

"What?"

"Why can't we?" Catherine was growing more excited by the second. "It's the perfect solution!"

"No, it's not. You've been with me that way before. You've seen what it's like. It's dangerous and uncertain, and if you come with me, you leave all you hold dear behind."

"Pah!" Catherine scoffed. "Are you dense, man? *You* are what I hold dear! If I let you go, I lose everything that matters, so you'd best believe that if you head off adventuring, I'll be coming, too. I'm no stranger to danger. Didn't you once tell me I had the soul of a traveler? So it doesn't matter where I am, if I'm with you, I'll be at home." She straddled his waist and grabbed his wrists, holding his hands above his head as he'd once held her. "You're mine now, Jamie Sinclair. And I'm not letting you get away from me again." She lowered her head and stole a kiss from his parted lips, and then she kissed the bridge of his nose. "I did that to you."

"Aye, lass, you've left your mark on me, inside and out." He freed his wrists and gathered her in his arms, giving her a tender kiss that churned her insides. They fell asleep with their lips touching, their breath intermingling, and their bodies wrapped in a warm embrace.

They woke in time to watch the dawn light the valley from the east. After a breakfast of black pudding, oatcakes, and tea, Catherine straightened her uniform, slung her musket and haversack over her back, and gave Jamie a jaunty salute. His heart ached to look at her, and for the second time in less then a day he found himself blinking back tears. He offered her his hand. "Tinker, tailor... soldier, sailor... gentleman, apothecary... plough-boy, thief," he said, quoting an old rhyme. "Will you take to the road with me, Catherine?" Catherine's face lit with a brilliant smile. "Aye, Jamie, I will." Hand in hand, they started down the road.

Historical Note

THE FIFTY-YEAR PERIOD BETWEEN 1640 AND 1690 was a time of religious and political upheaval in Britain. There was conflict between different forms of Protestantism, and between Protestantism and the older Catholic faith still practiced in much of the Highlands, Ireland, and parts of England. An ongoing struggle between parliamentary rule and the divine rights of kings led to civil war and the execution of King Charles I, followed by a commonwealth republic and eventual dictatorship under Cromwell. The monarchy was restored under Charles II, whose hedonistic court rebelled against ten years of Puritan rule. Dissolving Parliament when it attempted to exclude his Catholic brother from the succession, Charles was arguably the last British king to hold absolute power. A bloodless coup d'état against his brother, King James II, the last Catholic monarch, ushered in a constitutional monarchy under William and Mary, that has been uninterrupted since.

During this time, two political parties were born. The Tories (Irish slang for a "popish" outlaw) descended from the Cavaliers and landed aristocracy, and upheld the divine right of kings and the Anglican Church. The Whigs (a term of contempt in Scotland for a fanatic Presbyterian), descended from the Roundheads, represented the commercial classes of the cities and championed Parliament against the king.

James II's attempts to establish a base in Ireland after his expulsion from England were defeated at the battle of the Boyne in 1690, a year after the events described in this story, and despite the Jacobite victory at the Battle of Killiecrankie (which according to historical accounts really was over within ten minutes), the uprising in the Scottish Highlands was effectively quelled by the loss of Bonnie Dundee and the subsequent Williamite victories at Dunkeld and Cromdale. White-water rafting is popular today at Killiecrankie, and visitors can see the soldier's leap where Willie MacBean is said to have dropped his gear and made the eighteen-foot leap with claymore swinging Highlanders in hot pursuit. James II died of a brain hemorrhage in 1701 in France, but efforts on behalf of his son James and his grandson, known to history as Bonnie Prince Charlie, fueled Jacobite rebels for years to come, culminating in a Battle at Culloden in 1746.

Highland Rebel is a work of fiction, and of necessity, greatly simplifies these complex times. There were Covenanting Highlanders and Catholic Lowlanders and Protestants who supported the Catholic king. There were also, not surprisingly, men like Jamie, who tried their best to balance competing loyalties, and when faced with shifting circumstances often shifted for their families and themselves. Lady Castlemaine's erstwhile lover, John Churchill, Earl of Marlborough, a prominent example, abandoned his patron and sponsor King James for William and Mary, and later became a Duke. There's an interesting discussion on the growth of Restoration era apathy and indifference in religious matters, and the loosening of ties to the church after a generation of religious turmoil, in David Cressy's *Birth Marriage & Death: Ritual, Religion, and the Life-cycle in Tudor and Stuart England*.

It should be noted that another invitation to William was delivered at the same time as Jamie's was, by a similar character under similar circumstances, Arthur Herbert, Earl of Torrington.

Women like Catherine were not unheard-of, either. During the civil war, some donned armor and led their people in defense of their homes. There were women who went to war as soldiers, women who inherited, and women who ran businesses or wrote plays and books. Restoration-era ladies were comfortable traveling the city, shopping, and going to the theatre accompanied only by a maid, and in seventeenth-century Holland, England, and Germany, some women chose to dress and live as men. These freedoms gradually disappeared through the Georgian and Regency periods, and to all intents and purposes were gone by Victorian times. Readers who are interested in learning more about the lives of seventeenth-century woman might enjoy Antonia Frazer's *The Weaker Vessel: Woman's Lot in 17th Century England*, or *The Tradition of Female Transvestism in Early Modern Europe* by Rudolf M. Dekker and Lotte C. Van De Pol.

Catherine, Jamie, their families and retainers, are fictional characters, as are Jamie's mistresses. Characters such as the Duke of Buckingham, Lady Castlemaine, and John Churchill, as well as other court personages, are historical figures. I claim some literary license in their interactions with Jamie and Catherine, but the quotes or comments attributed to them or about them are readily available in the historical record. Readers who are interested in reading more might start with Antonia Fraser's *King Charles II;* Christopher Sykes's *Black Sheep;* Stephen Coote's *Royal Survivor,* or Graham Hopkin's *Constant Delights.*

There were Earls of Carrick in County Tipperary, but the title became extinct in 1652. Peerages could be bought in seventeenth-century England if one could afford them, and many English soldiers of higher and lower degree were paid for their services with Irish lands and titles, much as Jamie was. The Drummond clan were supporters of the Jacobite cause and fought at Killiecrankie, but for story purposes, I've moved my Drummonds farther north, to the lands of Moray. *Kinsmen and Clansmen,* by R.W. Munroe, gives a history of many of the major Scottish clans, including some who passed lairdship on through the female line.

Several variations of the fortune-telling rhyme, "Tinker Tailor," were in common usage going back to at least 1695, and it seems safe to assume it was around long before that. A Tom Otter was a term used to describe a henpecked husband, and referred to a character in Ben Johnson's *The Silent Woman,* and the first recorded usage of the term tomboy in the sense we know it today was in 1592.

The English coffee houses, called by Charles II seminaries of sedition, played a key role in the dissemination of political, social, and scientific ideas, and were the forerunners of the gentlemen's clubs of later years. Brooke's began as a coffee house and White's as a chocolate house. The interested reader is referred to *The Penny Universities: A History of Coffee-Houses* by Aytoun Ellis, and *London Coffeehouses: A Reference Book of Coffee Houses of the 17th, 18th and 19th Centuries* by Bryant Lyllwhite.

Readers who are interested in learning more about day-to-day life in Stuart England from firsthand accounts might enjoy any of the following highly entertaining, readable, and informative firsthand accounts: *The Diary of Samuel Pepys* tells all, even the naughty bits; *Memoirs of the Courts of Europe: Court of Charles II* is a highly entertaining, gossipy account of court life by the handsome French courtier and diplomat, le Compte de Gramont; and *The Diary and Correspondence of John Evelyn,* esteemed member of the Royal Society, a man of science and philosophy who was familiar with the highest levels of society, covers a span of fifty years.

Acknowledgments

Writing a story is a solitary process, but taking a story and turning it into a book involves a great many people. I would like to thank my agent Bob Diforio, editor Deb Werksman, Susie Benton, Sarah Ryan, Danielle Jackson, and all the other fine folks at Sourcebooks who made this possible. I would also like to thank my good friends Cheryl and Nick for reminding me there's a life outside whatever story I'm writing, and my family for their constant encouragement and support. Special thanks goes to Sandra, who spent hours at a very busy time, reading and making comments that were always insightful and often invaluable. Thanks also to Anne, for her support, help and friendship, and to those wonderful diarists, Pepys, Evelyn, and Gramont, whose words bring the seventeenth century alive in vigorous, colorful, informative, and delightfully entertaining detail, making research not a burden, but a joy.

About the Author

Judith James has worked as a legal assistant, a trail guide, and a counselor. Living in Nova Scotia, her personal journey has taken her to many different places, including the Arctic and the West Coast. Her writing combines her love of history and adventure with her keen interest in the complexities of human nature and the heart's capacity to heal.

THE
PRINCE
OF
MIDNIGHT

BY LAURA KINSALE
New York Times bestselling author

"Readers should be enchanted."
—*Publishers Weekly*

INTENT ON REVENGE, ALL SHE WANTS FROM
HIM IS TO LEARN HOW TO KILL

Lady Leigh Strachan has crossed all of France in search
of S.T. Maitland, nobleman, highwayman, and legendary
swordsman, once known as the Prince of Midnight. Now
he's hiding out in a crumbling castle with a tame wolf as his
only companion, trying to conceal his deafness and despera-
tion. Leigh is terribly disappointed to find the man behind
the legend doesn't meet her expectations. But when they're
forced on a quest together, she discovers the dangerous and
vital man behind the mask, and he finds a way to touch her
ice cold heart.

"No one—repeat, no one—writes historical
romance better." —Mary Jo Putney

978-1-4022-1397-7 • $7.99 U.S./$8.99 CAN

MIDSUMMER MOON

BY LAURA KINSALE

New York Times bestselling author

"The acknowledged master."
—*Albany Times-Union*

IF HE REALLY LOVED HER,
WOULDN'T HE HELP HER REALIZE HER DREAM?

When inventor Merlin Lambourne is endangered by Napoleon's advancing forces, Lord Ransom Falconer, in service of his government, comes to her rescue and falls under the spell of her beauty and absent-minded brilliance. But he is horrified by her dream of building a flying machine—and not only because he is determined to keep her safe.

"Laura Kinsale writes the kind of works that live in your heart." —Elizabeth Grayson

"A true storyteller, Laura Kinsale has managed to break all the rules of standard romance writing and come away shining."
—*San Diego Union-Tribune*

978-1-4022-1398-4 • $7.99 U.S./$8.99 CAN

SEIZE THE FIRE

BY LAURA KINSALE
bestselling author

"Magic and beauty flow from
Laura Kinsale's pen." —*Romantic Times*

AN UNLIKELY PRINCESS SHIPWRECKED
WITH A WAR HERO WHO'S GOT HELL TO PAY

Her Serene Highness Olympia of Oriens—plump, demure,
and idealistic—longs to return to her tiny, embattled land
and lead her people to justice and freedom. Famous hero
Captain Sheridan Drake, destitute and tormented by nightmares of the carnage he's seen, means only to rob and abandon her. What is Olympia to do with the tortured man
behind the hero's façade? And how will they cope when
their very survival depends on each other?

"One of the best writers in the history of the
romance genre." —*All About Romance*

978-1-4022-1396-0 • $7.99 U.S./$8.99 CAN

A *Duke* TO *Die For*

BY AMELIA GREY

THE RAKISH FIFTH DUKE OF BLAKEWELL'S UNEXPECTED AND shockingly lovely new ward has just arrived, claiming to carry a curse that has brought each of her previous guardians to an untimely end…

Praise for Amelia Grey's Regency romances:

"This beguiling romance steals your heart, lifts your spirits and lights up the pages with humor and passion." —Romantic Times

"Each new Amelia Grey tale is a diamond. Ms. Grey…is a master storyteller." —Affaire de Coeur

"Readers will be quickly drawn in by the lively pace, the appealing protagonists, and the sexual chemistry that almost visibly shimmers between."
—Library Journal

978-1-4022-1767-8 • $6.99 U.S./$7.99 CAN

Lady Anne
AND THE
HOWL
IN THE
DARK

by Donna Lea Simpson

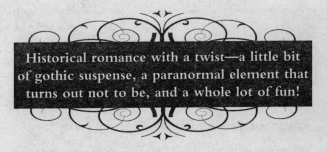

Historical romance with a twist—a little bit of gothic suspense, a paranormal element that turns out not to be, and a whole lot of fun!

LADY ANNE ADDISON IS A RATIONAL AND COURAGEOUS woman. So when she's summoned by a frightened friend to Yorkshire to prove or disprove the presence in their woods of a menacing wolf—or werewolf—she takes up the challenge.

Lady Anne finds the Marquess of Darkefell to be an infuriatingly unyielding man. Rumors swirl and suspects abound. The Marquess is indeed at the middle of it all, but not in the way that Lady Anne had suspected…and now he's firmly determined to win her in spite of everything.

978-1-4022-1791-3 • $6.99 U.S. / $7.99 CAN

No
Regrets

BY MICHÈLE ANN YOUNG

"A remarkable talent that taps your emotions
with each and every page." —Gerry Russel,
award winning author of *The Warrior Trainer*

A MOST UNUSUAL HEROINE

Voluptuous and bespectacled, Caroline Torrington feels dowdy
and unattractive beside the slim beauties of her day. Little does
she know that Lord Lucas Foxhaven thinks her curves are
breathtaking, and can barely keep his hands off her.

"The suspense and sexual tension accelerate
throughout." —*Romance Reviews Today*

978-1-4022-1016-7 • $6.99 U.S./$8.99 CAN

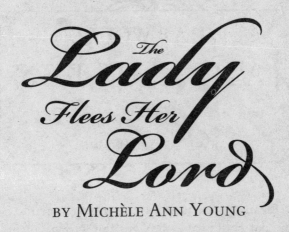

The Lady Flees Her Lord

BY MICHÈLE ANN YOUNG

DESPERATE FOR PEACE AND SAFETY...

Lucinda, Lady Denbigh, is running from a husband who physically and emotionally abused her. Posing as a widow, she seeks refuge in the quiet countryside, where she meets Lord Hugo Wanstead. Returning from the wars with a wound that won't heal, he finds his estate impoverished, his sleep torn by nightmares, and brandy the only solace. When he meets Lucinda, he thinks she just might give him something to live for...

Praise for Michèle Ann Young's *No Regrets*

"Dark heroes, courageous heroines, intrigue, heartbreak, and heaps of sexual tension. Do not miss this fabulous new author." —Molly O'Keefe, *Harlequin Superromance*

"Readers will never want to put her book down!" —Bronwyn Scott, author of *Pickpocket Countess*

978-1-4022-1399-1 • $6.99 U.S. / $7.99 CAN

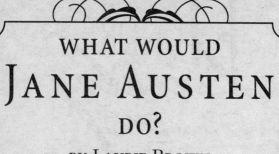

WHAT WOULD

JANE AUSTEN

DO?

BY LAURIE BROWN

Eleanor goes back in time to save a man's life, but could it be she's got the wrong villain?

Lord Shermont, renowned rake, feels an inexplicable bond to the mysterious woman with radical ideas who seems to know so much…but could she be a Napoleonic spy?

Thankfully, Jane Austen's sage advice prevents a fatal mistake…

At a country house party, Eleanor makes the acquaintance of Jane Austen, whose sharp wit can untangle the most complicated problem. With an international intrigue going on before her eyes, Eleanor must figure out which of two dueling gentlemen is the spy, and which is the man of wher dreams.

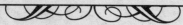

978-1-4022-1831-6 • $6.99 U.S. / $7.99 CAN

HUNDREDS OF YEARS TO REFORM A RAKE

BY LAURIE BROWN

HIS TOUCH PULLED HER IRRESISTIBLY
ACROSS THE MISTS OF TIME

Deverell Thornton, the ninth Earl of Waite, needs Josie Drummond to come back to his time and foil the plot that would destroy him. Josie is a modern career woman, thrust back in time to the sparkling Regency period, where she must contend with the complex manners and mores of the day, unmask a dangerous charlatan, and in the end, choose between the ghost who captivated her or the man himself—but can she give her heart to a notorious rake?

978-1-4022-1013-6 • $6.99 U.S./$8.99 CAN

call of the highland moon

BY KENDRA LEIGH CASTLE

A Highlands werewolf fleeing his destiny, and the warm-hearted woman who takes him in…

Not ready for the responsibilities of an alpha wolf, Gideon MacInnes leaves Scotland and seeks the quiet hills of upstate New York. When he is attacked by rogue wolves and collapses on Carly Silver's doorstep, she thinks she's rescuing a wounded animal. But she awakens to find that the beast has turned into a devastatingly handsome, naked man.

With a supernatural enemy stalking them, their only hope is to get back to Scotland, where Carly has to risk becoming a werewolf herself, or give up the one man she's ever truly loved.

"*Call of the Highland Moon* thrills with seductive romance and breathtaking suspense." —Alyssa Day, *USA Today* bestselling author of *Atlantis Awakening*

978-1-4022-1158-4 • $6.99 U.S. / $8.99 CAN

DARK
HIGHLAND
FIRE

BY KENDRA LEIGH CASTLE

A werewolf from the Scottish Highlands and a fiery
demi-goddess fleeing for her life...

Desired by women, kissed by luck, Gabriel MacInnes has
always been able to put pleasure ahead of duty. But with
the MacInnes wolves now squarely in the sights of an
ancient enemy, everything is about to change...

Rowan *an* Morgaine, on the run from a dragon prince who
will stop at nothing to have her as his own, must accept
the protection of Gabriel and his clan. By force or by
guile, Rowan and Gabriel must uncover the secrets of their
intertwining fate and stop their common enemy.

**"This fresh and exciting take on the werewolf
legend held me captive."**

—NINA BANGS, AUTHOR OF *ONE BITE STAND*

978-1-4022-1159-1 • $6.99 U.S. / $8.99 CAN

WILD HIGHLAND MAGIC

BY KENDRA LEIGH CASTLE

She's a Scottish Highlands werewolf

Growing up in America, Catrionna MacInnes always tried desperately to control her powers and pretend to be normal…

He's a wizard prince with a devastating secret

The minute Cat lays eyes on Bastian, she knows she's met her destiny. In their first encounter, she unwittingly binds him to her for life, and now they're both targets for the evil enemies out to destroy their very souls.

Praise for Kendra Leigh Castle:

"Fans of straight up romance looking for a little extra something will be bitten." —*Publishers Weekly*

978-1-4022-1856-9 • $7.99 U.S. / $8.99 CAN

Georgette Heyer
Regency Romance

Frederica

The Marquis of Alverstoke is too bored and cynical to concern himself with his own sisters, let alone some distant cousins. But the irrepressible Frederica Merrivale has a few surprises in store for him. Frederica brings her younger siblings to London determined to secure a brilliant marriage for her beautiful sister, with or without Alverstoke's help. And with his country cousins getting into one scrape after another right on his doorstep, before he knows it the Marquis finds himself dangerously embroiled.

The Reluctant Widow

When Eleanor Rochdale boards the wrong coach, she ends up not at her prospective employer's home, but at the estate of Eustace Cheviot, a dissipated young man on the verge of death. His cousin, Mr. Ned Carlyon, persuades Eleanor to marry Eustace as a simple business arrangement. By morning, Eleanor is a rich widow, but finds herself embroiled with an international spy ring, housebreakers, uninvited guests, and murder. And Mr. Carlyon won't let her leave…

Charity Girl

Miss Charity Steane is running away from the drudgery of her aunt's household and trying to find her grandfather. When Viscount Desford encounters the lovely waif, he feels honor bound to assist her, but dashing about the countryside alone with an unknown young lady is sure to bring ruin upon her—and him, if he's not careful.

Regency Buck

Miss Judith Taverner and her brother Peregrine are none too pleased when they find that their new guardian, Julian St. John Audley, Earl of Worth, is an insufferably arrogant dandy not much older than themselves. Lord Worth doesn't want the office of guardian any more than they want him. But when someone tries to kill Peregrine, Lord Worth cannot help but entangle himself with his adventuresome wards, leading to witty repartee, surprises, and an unexpected and delightful ending.

Faro's Daughter

When Max Ravenscar offers her a fortune to *refuse* his young nephew's proposal of marriage, the beautiful Deborah Grantham is outraged. She may be the mistress of her aunt's elegant gaming house, but Miss Grantham will show the insufferable Mr. Ravenscar that she can't be bribed, even if she has to marry his puppyish nephew to prove it.

Black Sheep

Abigail Wendover, "on the shelf" at 28, is determined to prevent her high-spirited young niece from falling prey to a handsome fortune hunter. The only man who can help her is scandalous Miles Calverleigh, enormously rich from a long sojourn in India, but the black sheep of his family. Miles turns out to be a most provoking creature—with a disconcerting ability to throw Abby into giggles at quite the wrong moment.

Lady of Quality

The spirited and independent Miss Annis Wychwood is twenty-nine and well past the age for falling in love. When Annis embroils herself in the affairs of a pretty runaway heiress, she has no choice but to engage with the wayward girl's uncivil and high-handed guardian, Mr. Oliver Carleton, who is quite the rudest man Annis has ever met.

Friday's Child

When the impetuous Lord Sherington is spurned by the incomparable Miss Milbourne, he vows to marry the next female he encounters. That just happens to be the young, penniless Miss Hero Wantage, who has adored him all her life. Whisking her off to London and the excitement of the *ton*, Sherry soon discovers there is no end to the scrapes his young bride can get into.

False Colours

Kit Fancot returns to London from the diplomatic service only to find that his twin brother Evelyn has disappeared, and his extravagant mother's debts have mounted alarmingly. The Fancot family's fortunes are riding on Evelyn's marriage to self-possessed Cressy Stavely, but if Evelyn doesn't turn up to meet Cressy's grandmother, the betrothal could be off. Thus begins a romantic masquerade with unexpected twists and a hilariously satisfactory conclusion.

Cotillion

Young Kitty Charing stands to inherit a vast fortune from her eccentric guardian—provided she marries one of his great nephews. Freddy Standen is immensely rich, of course, and not bad-looking, but he's mild-mannered, a bit hapless—not anything like his handsome, rakish cousin Jack. Resolving to decide her own fate, Kitty engineers a sham betrothal to Freddy and an escape into London high society. But no one is more surprised than Freddy when he finds himself in the role of a most unlikely hero.

Simon the Coldheart

In the early 15th century, the time of real knights in armor, Simon rose from obscurity to become friend to Prince Henry and a bold warrior against France. Known for his silence and uncompromising principles, Simon "the Coldheart" nonetheless had a complex personality and earned the fierce loyalty and admiration of soldiers, kings, and children alike. When Simon was sent to lay siege to Belremy, he engaged the Lady Margaret in a battle of wits and words until she not only surrendered to the English but became his bride. Brilliant period language and Heyer's perfect grasp of the details of daily life make for a fascinating and blood-stirring read.

The Conqueror

The Conqueror tells the story of William the Conqueror and his queen Matilda—who at first spurned his base blood but was eventually won over by his strength and resolve. The stirring tale begins with William's ignoble birth, then follows his ascension to and continual defense of the Dukedom of Normandy, his wooing of the woman he was determined to win, and culminates in the Battle of Hastings in 1066, where William's fortitude, courage and innovation won him his kingdom.

Royal Escape

After Cromwell's forces defeated King Charles II at the Battle of Worcester in 1651, the young king embarked on a daring flight to France. For six weeks, Charles hid in the English countryside disguised as a servant, unable to find a way across heavily guarded borders, until two young women finally helped him escape. His courtiers were in constant fear for his life as he defied their warnings and flirted with disaster at every stage of his journey.

The Spanish Bride

The Spanish Bride follows hot-headed Brigade-Major Harry Smith and the spirited young Spanish noblewoman he met and instantly married during the Peninsular Wars, when the Duke of Wellington's forces fought Napoleon's army in Spain and Portugal. Heyer illuminates in fascinating detail the wearying marches, hand-to-hand battles, wildly varying camp conditions and stolen moments of leisure, in a stirring account of the life of a military wife who "followed the drum" during the Regency period.

An Infamous Army

In the summer of 1815, Brussels is a whirlwind of parties, balls and soirees, as Napoleon Bonaparte marches down from the north and the Duke of Wellington struggles to cobble together an army to meet the threat. At the center of the glittering social scene is the beautiful, outrageous young widow Lady Barbara Childe. Even her betrothal to the dashing Colonel Charles Audley fails to curb her wild behavior—but as the Battle of Waterloo begins to rage, Lady Barbara discovers where her heart truly lies.